I0775752

A Heart Worth Finding

AMANDA CHAPERON

A Heart Worth Finding is a steamy college hockey romance full of explicit language and sexual content. To avoid—or locate—the open door chapters, please flip to the Dicktionary I've provided in the back. For the complete list of *A Heart Worth Finding* content warnings, please visit my website at <u>www.ach aperonauthor.com</u>.

*To the women who refuse to put
their dreams on hold to let a man chase his.*

Jack

NOW: October 7, 2023

THE STENCH OF BURNING meat hit his nostrils a moment before smoke enveloped his head.

Whirling toward the grill and finding it unattended, he turned again and surveyed the patio in search of Aiden.

Unfortunately, his friend was nowhere to be found.

Which meant whoever Aiden had tapped to take over for him was shirking their duties.

"Who the fuck is supposed to be watching the food?" Jack shouted over the crowd as he stepped to the grill and removed the ruined food from its surface, tipping it directly into a nearby trash can.

Several heads turned in his direction, the bulk of his teammates murmuring that it wasn't them, the friends and family gathered watching him curiously.

"I think Pascoe was supposed to," one of the freshmen said.

"Pascoe?" Jack yelled. "Where are you?"

From the back corner of the patio, Pascoe's dark head appeared over the shoulder of the tiny blonde girl perched on his lap.

"Get your ass over here," Jack said through gritted teeth, and with a few whispered words and sheepish grin to the girl, Pascoe stood and dragged his feet all the way over to Jack.

"What's up, DeLuca?" Pascoe asked, stuffing his hands deep into his pockets.

Jack crossed his arms over his chest, widening his stance and giving the kid a stare down.

"What do you see when you look at the grill, Pascoe?"

"Nothing."

"And you know why?"

"No."

"That's because you burnt the burgers and dogs, dipshit, and I had to toss everything," Jack said, reaching out to smack his teammate upside the head. "Didn't Fuller ask you to man the grill while he went to get his girl?"

"Yes."

"Then how did this happen?" Jack waved at the mess.

"I got distracted."

"You got distracted," Jack said, incredulous.

Pascoe stepped closer and whispered, "Yeah, *distracted*. Did you *see* her?"

Jack craned his neck and studied the blonde over Pascoe's shoulders.

And, okay, he could see the kid's point. Jack was incredulous, but also amused. He had also been led astray by a pretty face before; he was, after all, a red-blooded male.

With a sigh, Jack said, "Clean this up and get a new batch going."

"Aye, aye, captain," Pascoe said with a mock salute.

"Did someone say captain?" Luke Hayes, the Spartans' actual captain, asked as he strode up to Jack's side.

"Pascoe was just being a smartass."

"I thought Fuller was grilling?"

"He was. But he disappeared. I'm assuming he went to meet Kenzie."

Luke smirked. "He's so gone for that girl, it's disgusting."

"I—" Jack cut himself off. "Yeah."

In truth, Jack thought it was sweet. He had once been that sprung over a girl—still was most days—and it made him happy to see his teammate happy.

Secretly, Jack could admit he was also a little jealous. Every time he looked at Kenzie and Aiden, he saw what he'd had once. And no matter how brief that time had been, he'd spent the last three and a half years searching for that same magic.

Luke's attention was dragged away by one of the freshmen wanting to talk shop, and Jack's phone buzzed in his pocket, so he stepped into the quiet hall off the patio to answer.

"Hey, sweets," he said to Sofia in greeting.

"Hey you!" she hollered in his ear.

"Where are you?" he asked. "I thought you were coming by Munn with Kenzie?"

"Something came up!"

Surely *something* was an "issue" with one of her sorority sisters, but he wasn't about to say that. They'd been here before in the few months they'd been...doing whatever it was they were doing, and he wasn't in the mood for a fight.

"Will I see you tonight?"

"Possibly! Depends on how this goes, and how we're feeling after the game. We might go to the bar with the Theta boys."

Jack bit back a groan. Theta Chi, or The Lodge, was the bane of his existence.

Scratch that. It wasn't the entire fraternity, only a brother in particular—Silas Jeffers.

Jack and Sofia hadn't been together long, but Jack could admit he really liked her. Unfortunately, so did Silas. And thanks to the proximity with which her sorority and his fraternity operated, they spent a lot of time together—away from Jack's watchful gaze.

Jack wasn't a jealous guy, but he also wasn't a fan of Silas's attempts to insert himself into Sofia's life and shove Jack out of it.

Sofia always claimed that Silas had a girlfriend, and it wasn't like that between them, but Jack had never seen this mysterious girlfriend, nor did Silas act like he was in a relationship.

He didn't know where his own relationship with Sofia was headed, but he at least wanted the chance to find out.

"Well," Jack said finally, "you let me know when you figure it out."

"Are you mad?" she asked. "You're mad. I can tell."

"I'm not mad," he said automatically, and truthfully, he wasn't. He was more...annoyed. "I just haven't seen you in a few days."

"But we're going to the cider mill tomorrow."

"With your sorority sisters and their dates," he reminded her. "What if I wanted some alone time?"

"Alone time, huh?" Sofia asked, and the background noise on her end cut off abruptly, as though she'd stepped behind a door. "What exactly would this alone time entail?"

"Me and you," he said slowly, the corners of his lips tipping up. "My bed—"

"I like where this is going."

"—a big bowl of popcorn, the latest season of *The Bachelor*..."

Sofia faked a moan, and Jack laughed. "I love it when you talk dirty to me," she said.

"Soon?" he asked.

"Soon, babe. I promise." All at once, the noise level on her end picked up again, and Sofia said, "Gotta go. I'll see you tomorrow!"

"Bye," Jack replied, but she'd already gone.

He scrubbed a hand down his face, his rough stubble scratching at his palms.

As a college athlete, Jack had less time than most to conduct any sort of social life that didn't heavily involve his teammates, but when he could barely get his own—girl? friend? girlfriend?—whatever to spend time with him, something was definitely wrong.

Was she pulling away from him? Was there someone else? Was she simply no longer interested in him anymore? Had she ever been? These were the thoughts that endlessly plagued him.

Next weekend, Jack would be commencing his fourth season with the Spartans, and he'd started all but three of the sixty-eight games he'd spent in the green and white over the course of the first three. Hockey wasn't as big of a deal at Michigan State as football or basketball, but it was still one of the big three sports, and that meant he and his teammates were considered celebrities on campus. They routinely showed up on The Green, Michigan State's online version of a gossip rag, and always had people clamoring for their attention when they went to the bar. And Jack, as the Spartans' starting goalie, tended to garner more attention than most.

Sofia had introduced herself to Jack at Dublin during Welcome Weekend. Typically, he and his roommates preferred Rick's. It was less pretentious, more relaxed. That particular night, however, Luke had suggested Dublin, claiming he wanted a "change of scenery." Since Luke never asked for anything, and was usually content to go with the flow, Jack and their other roommates—Aiden and Asher Rhodes—decided to humor him.

Jack had been standing at the counter off the dance floor, waiting for the bartender to return with his tequila soda, when a warm body pressed into his arm. He'd glanced down to find an ebony-skinned girl, her peculiar caramel eyes glinting in the lowlights of the bar.

"Buy me a drink," she said.

Jack raised an eyebrow, then extended his hand. "Hi, nice to meet you. I'm Jack. And you are?"

The girl tipped her head back and laughed, then gripped his hand in her own. "Sofia. Now buy me a drink."

Jack opened his mouth to protest, then thought better of it. Sofia was beautiful, with her deep skin, those compelling eyes, and legs that went on for days, which were showcased in a pair of pale denim shorts with frayed hems. A slice of her taut stomach was visible between the waistband and hem of her bright pink tank.

The bartender delivered his drink, sliding it over to him with a wink, but Jack withdrew his credit card from his pocket and passed it over to her. "I'll get hers, too"—he pointed at Sofia—"and you can keep it open."

Bewilderment warred with something that looked a lot like jealousy on the bartender's face, and Jack bit back a laugh.

The problem with being a division one college athlete was a lot of people thought Jack owed them something simply for existing, but he'd never felt compelled to hook up simply for the sake of doing so. This bartender had no right to be jealous, because Jack had given her zero signs that he was interested.

"What can I get you?" the bartender asked Sofia, her tone clipped.

"I'll have a vodka cranberry, please."

With a nod, the bartender was gone again, and Jack turned fully to Sofia, taking a long sip of his drink as he further studied her.

"You're awfully bold," he said.

She shrugged. "I saw something I liked. I went for it."

"The drink or me?"

A mischievous grin bloomed across her face. "Both."

Jack returned the smile, and the bartender dropped Sofia's drink unceremoniously in front of her. Sofia reached for it, and Jack extended his.

"To going after what we want," he said, and she nodded, clinking her glass against his.

And that was that. They'd been hanging out—and hooking

up—for the past few months. But there were times when Jack wondered if Sofia only stuck around because of his status on campus. On top of being in a sorority and planning to get her master's in marketing research after graduating in the spring, she was also the social chair at her sorority and an Instagram influencer.

All that to say, she didn't need Jack to get noticed, but he wryly admitted his presence in her life certainly hadn't hurt matters. Her social media following had grown exponentially in the two months since he became a regular feature on her profile, and he knew her followers were begging for more content featuring Sofia's "hot goalie."

To be fair, he *was* hot, and he *was* a goalie, but he didn't enjoy being viewed as a cash cow.

Chances were high he was reading too much into it. This season would pass, and things would go back to normal before he knew it.

With a sigh, Jack shoved his phone into his pocket and stepped out onto the patio once more.

"Where'd you go?" Asher asked.

"Sofia called."

"Where is she, anyway?" Luke asked.

"Some issue with one of her sisters," Jack told them, waving a dismissive hand.

He was pleased to find that, in his absence, Pascoe had once again fired up the grill, and a platter next to the heated flat top was piled high with perfectly cooked brats, hot dogs, and burgers. Starving, Jack pushed past his roommates and grabbed a paper plate, fixed both a hamburger and hot dog the way he liked them—ketchup, mustard, pickles on the burger, relish on the dog—added spoonfuls of sides, then moved to one of the long folding tables and pulled out a chair.

Moments later, Asher and Luke joined him.

"You okay?" Luke asked quietly.

Swallowing a mouthful of hamburger, he nodded and said, "Yeah."

"You don't look like it."

"I'm fine," Jack said, a little harsher than he intended.

"Okay, bud. Just know I'm here if you want to talk."

This was both a good and bad thing about Luke. Where Jack would consider Aiden his best friend, Luke had always been the best at reading people. It's what made him such a phenomenal captain—that innate ability to gauge the mood of a person or an entire hockey team with a single, sweeping glance, and act accordingly based on what he gleaned.

Jack, who wore his heart on his sleeve, wasn't all that difficult to read to begin with, and usually he appreciated Luke's intuition. Unfortunately, this was one moment where he wasn't interested in talking about what currently ate at his stomach.

"He's probably got his panties all twisted about Sofia," Asher said to Luke as though Jack wasn't sitting right there.

"Shut up, Ash," Jack said.

"I'm just saying," Asher said with a shrug. "I've noticed your bedroom has been especially quiet lately. Did Little Miss Sorority Sister get sick of looking at your ugly mug and move on?"

When Jack was in high school, he had three best friends. They'd grown up together, gone to all the same schools in their Philadelphia suburb of Ardmore, played hockey together from the time the four of them were barely able to walk, let alone skate. And within that friend group, each of them had their own distinct personalities, their own set of specific strengths and weaknesses they brought to the table.

Asher reminded Jack of his friend Chad, who would open his mouth and spew bullshit, only to make himself look like more of an asshole than whoever he was trying to insult.

"Why have you been paying such close attention to what's going on behind my bedroom door, Ash?" Jack asked before shoveling a heaping spoonful of potato salad into his mouth.

"Since we share a wall."

"It's none of your business."

"I'm just saying you always do this."

"What's that supposed to mean?"

"It means," Asher said, swallowing his food and setting his silverware down, "that you always go all in on a girl at first, then you wonder *why* when it fizzles out. It's because you come on too strong. You have to let her come to you, man. Leave her wanting more."

Jack and Luke stared at Asher in stunned silence. As much as Jack wanted to disagree with him, he had to admit he was right. Jack always went full send at the beginning of relationships. He'd never learned how to hold himself back, and when he was experiencing that high of a new crush, he wanted to be with that person all the time, or remind her that he thought about her when they weren't together.

Maybe it wasn't the smartest tact, but he was searching for something that would stick, and he'd never been very good at beating around the bush.

"You know what, Ash?" Jack began, looking his teammate in the eye.

Only...his gaze snagged on something over Asher's shoulder, beyond the glass that served as the exterior wall of this side of Munn.

Walking toward them down the hall inside was Aiden, trailed closely by Kenzie and a blonde girl.

A blonde girl that looked incredibly familiar.

It was impossible.

She couldn't be here. That was simply...too much to hope for.

But when Aiden stepped onto the patio, and Kenzie and the blonde followed him out, Jack rose slowly from his seat, all the blood leaving his face. All thoughts of Sofia, or any other girl he'd been with—hell, even his own name—flew from his head.

"Jessica?"

Aiden and Kenzie stilled, and out of the corner of his eye, Jack clocked Asher and Luke staring up at him, sharing a glance, then looking behind them.

"Jack?" Jessica responded, so quiet he was surprised he heard her from this far away.

"Holy shit," he breathed. "It is you."

Their gazes held, the moment lengthening, stretching out across every single second of the years he'd spent missing her.

Jack stepped toward her, but with a small shake of her head, Jessica spun on her heel and disappeared inside. After a brief, whispered conversation with Aiden, Kenzie followed her.

"What the fuck just happened?" Asher asked.

Dazed, Jack lowered himself onto the bench, eyes still fixed on the door inside, willing Jessica to reappear.

"That," he said, surprising himself by the steadiness of his tone, "is the one who got away."

THEN: April 5, 2020

JESSICA DANIELS WOKE WITH a start, the shock of cool water splashing her sunbaked skin instantly forcing her upright.

"What the fresh..." she began, but the curse she'd been about to utter was cut off by the sight of the boy in front of her.

As he pulled himself from the pool, using nothing but the flexing of his arms and the clenching of his abdominals, water sluiced over the ridges of his muscles, setting his bronzed skin sparkling in the midday Mexican sun. He settled a green-blue gaze on her, mouth stretching into a smile, revealing two rows of straight, pearly white teeth.

That smile blinded her nearly as much as the sun, and she blinked rapidly under its glare.

"Come play volleyball with us," he said when he reached her side, blotting out the sun and dripping water onto her thigh.

"What?" she asked dumbly.

The boy laughed, a low, husky sound that, despite the balmy air, sent goosebumps skittering across her skin.

"Come play volleyball with us," he repeated, slower this time.

"I...why?"

Smooth, Daniels.

"I'll play!" Bethani said, hopping up from the lounge chair next to Jessica's. "C'mon, J. It'll be fun!"

The boy turned to Jessica. "J?" he asked.

She rose and extended her hand, suddenly wishing she was covered by more than three flimsy triangles of fabric so she could wipe her clammy palms. "Jessica," she said.

The boy gripped her proffered hand in his and pumped her arm once, twice, sending a jolt shooting up her arm.

What is happening to me? she thought. *Is the sun short circuiting my brain?*

No, it wasn't the sun. It was simply that she'd never laid eyes on a more beautiful boy in her life.

"Jack."

Jessica had to admit, the name suited him perfectly. With floppy blond hair, turquoise eyes, and a tall, well-proportioned frame, he definitely looked like a Jack.

When she met his stare again, she found him smirking at her, obviously not having missed the way she'd dragged her gaze along the length of his body.

"Shall we?" he asked, gesturing to the pool behind him, the water the exact shade of his eyes.

Jessica nodded and padded across the sun-heated concrete until she reached the ladder. The instant she dipped her toes in, she nearly backed out, the temperature a shock after basking in the sunshine for hours. Instead, she gritted her teeth and lowered further until the water reached her chest. Then she fully submerged, goosebumps breaking out on her skin.

"You guys here on spring break?" she heard Jack ask Bethani when she resurfaced.

"Yep!" Bethani grinned. "You, too?"

Jack nodded. "College? High school?"

"We're high school seniors," Jessica said, and Jack turned toward her voice, as though he'd forgotten she was there. Then he and Bethani followed her into the water, and Jack waded toward a group of guys gathered around the net strung up across the shallower end.

Over his shoulder, he said to Jessica, "You can be on my team. But you should know, I'm very competitive. So don't screw up."

Jessica nearly volleyed back an insult, and got as far as opening her mouth, but Bethani cut her off. "I think we can keep up."

Jessica smirked. Both she and her friend were four-year varsity volleyball players at their high school, and their senior season in the fall had culminated with a state championship victory.

"You better," Jack said, then swam away.

"Asshole," Bethani breathed.

Jessica laughed, her eyes glued to the muscles of Jack's back as they bunched and jumped with each stroke through the water. "Hot, though."

Bethani shot her a look. "What're you thinking?"

Jessica smirked. "Nothing at all. Just pointing out that he's extremely attractive."

Bethani's lips twisted into a knowing smile. "For what it's worth, I say go for it."

"Chop chop, ladies!" Jack yelled.

"Damn, he really is an asshole," Jessica muttered, and Bethani laughed.

"The upside is you don't have to talk to him, if you know what I mean," she said with a wink and an eyebrow wiggle.

Giggling, they waded through the water and joined the group formed by Jack and his three friends.

"Boys, this is Jessica and her friend..."

"Bethani," Jessica's friend supplied.

Jack nodded sharply. "These are the boys. Tyler, Zach, and Chad," he said, pointing at each in turn. "We'll play three-on-three. Me, Zach, and Jessica against Tyler, Chad, and Bethani."

The group dispersed, Jessica following after Jack and his curly-haired brunette friend. Jack positioned her in the middle about ten feet from the net. Across from them, Bethani's black hair barely bobbed above the surface of the water as Jack's other friends directed her about twenty feet off the net as they lined up on either side near the antennas.

Jessica was prepared to show these boys her skills. She'd been a defensive specialist on her high school teams, which meant Jack had unintentionally placed her exactly where she would've lined up normally.

The thing was...water volleyball was *nothing* like normal volleyball, and she made an absolute ass of herself.

Jessica stood halfway between five and six feet tall, and the five-foot deep pool water sloshed around her shoulders and chest as she dove for balls. More often than not, she wound up missing entirely and going under. By the time the game ended, her nose and throat stung from all the water she'd unintentionally inhaled.

Jack hadn't been lying about his competitive spirit. He took every opportunity to point out her mistakes, and Jessica found herself wondering what about him she'd found attractive in the first place.

Yeah, he was hot, and he was clearly some sort of athlete based on the way he instinctively knew where the ball would be the second one of his friends made contact, rising from the water like Poseidon to block shots and slam the ball back into his friends' faces. But this was supposed to be a friendly game on vacation, not the Olympics. Unfortunately, Jack didn't see it that way.

"Move faster!"

"How did you miss that?"

"Have you ever even seen a volleyball match before?"

Thankfully they held on to win by two points, but Jessica's jaw ached from clenching her teeth together.

"Nice game," one of Jack's losing friends said to her and Bethani when they all gathered at the net.

"Bro, were you watching the same shit I was?" Jack asked. "She"—he pointed at Jessica—"was terrible."

"Oh fuck off," Jessica said, then swam away in the direction of the bar at the far end of the pool.

Bethani caught up with her and waited until they'd ordered drinks before saying, "So...still think he's hot?"

Jessica rolled her eyes. "You know he is, but I have zero desire to spend any more time with him. Let's hope we don't see him again this week."

That night, after washing the chlorine, sunscreen, and sweat from their bodies—and sneaking in a quick nap—Jessica and Bethani found themselves at the bar in the lobby of their resort.

It was barely past nine p.m., the sun having long since disappeared below the horizon, but the bar was packed with spring breakers like herself. Jessica pressed through the crush of bodies and slid up to the counter to order drinks while Bethani grabbed them a seat at a nearby table.

"Can I buy you a drink?" a voice next to her asked, and Jessica turned to face him.

He was probably in his mid-twenties, with close-cropped hair an indeterminate shade between brown and blond, and nondescript brown eyes. Some sort of military tattoo was visible on his right deltoid below the short sleeve of his white button down. Jessica squinted in the dim lights and made out the words *Semper Fi.*

Marine, then. That explained the buzz cut.

He stared at her expectantly, and Jessica realized she hadn't answered his question.

"They're free," she said finally.

Buzz Cut shrugged. "So?"

Jessica snorted. "Alright then, sure. I'll take a marg. But get one for my friend, too," she said, hooking a thumb over her shoulder in Bethani's direction.

Buzz Cut nodded and signaled the bartender, who efficiently moved around, splashing tequila, mix, and ice into an industrial blender.

Over the whirring of the machine, the guy asked, "What's your name?"

"Jessica!" she said.

"Joe," he replied, holding out a hand.

Joe's palm was sweaty against hers, his callouses scraping her skin, but somehow she didn't mind. Briefly, she questioned why someone so much older than her was even giving her the time of day. Maybe he didn't realize she was still in high school. Either way, she had to admit the attention was nice.

The bartender set their drinks on the sticky bar top in front of them, and Jessica grabbed hers and Bethani's, turning away from Joe with a, "thanks!" before heading to their table.

Joe followed. "You're not getting rid of me that easily," he said, voice low, mouth close to her ear.

Jessica fought a shiver, and Bethani's surprise was evident when Joe trailed her to the table like a lost puppy.

"Bethani, this is Joe. Joe, this is my friend Bethani."

"Nice to meet you," Joe said, then abruptly yelled, "RICK!"

Joe hurried away from their table, and Jessica whipped her head around as he pulled a similarly dressed man into one of those single-arm, back-pounding hugging rituals only true bros participated in.

"Two hot guys drooling over you in one day?" Bethani said next to her. "I'd be annoyed if I didn't love you so much."

Jessica gave her a playful shove. "Jack was hardly drooling over me," she said, then nodded in Joe's direction. "And *he's* not that hot."

"I don't know," Bethani said, tilting her head this way and

that, studying Joe. "The whole military thing is really doing it for me."

"That's because you spent the first twelve years of your life on Army bases," Jessica reminded her. "You were conditioned from a young age. You basically have a Pavlovian response to buzz cuts."

Bethani burst out laughing but knocked her plastic cup against Jessica's. "Touché, my friend. Touché."

Joe returned to the table and said, "Ladies, this is my buddy, Rick. Rick, this is Jessica and…"

"Bethani," Jessica supplied, even though they'd done this less than five minutes ago.

"Right. Bethani."

"Hello, Bethani," Rick said, lips unfurling into a smirk, his eyes taking on that *this-one-is-mine* twinkle.

Bethani slid her palm into Rick's. "Hello, Rick."

Jessica sighed and sipped her marg.

"Are you guys going out tonight?" Joe asked her.

"We were planning on it," Jessica said. "Though we're not quite sure where yet."

"We're going to The City," he said, flashing a neon orange wristband. "You should come! They're selling these in the lobby."

"Yeah!" Rick said, hooking an arm around Bethani's shoulders. "Come out with us!"

The resort they were staying at also happened to be spring break headquarters for this travel company called StudentCity, which offered full service travel packages to students to give them the best bang for their buck. Jessica and Bethani had walked past the little booth on their way to the bar earlier, but hadn't thought anything of it until now.

"Wait, you don't have to be here with them to get a wristband?" Bethani asked.

"No!" Rick said proudly. "They sell these for twenty bucks to anyone staying at the resort. And they provide a shuttle to and from the club. There's a different one every night, and the wristbands get you bottle service and free cover."

Jessica blinked in surprise. That sounded like a dream come true, and a relatively safe way to go out and experience Cancún's nightlife.

Joe pressed closer to Jessica, and she fought the urge to back away. "Stay close to me, Jessie," he said, his beer-laden breath fanning uncomfortably across her cheek. "I'll take good care of you."

She opened her mouth to remind him her name was Jessica, but snapped it shut.

"So what's The City like?" Bethani asked.

"It's the largest nightclub in Latin America," Rick informed her. "It's *insane*. Wall-to-wall bodies, a massive dance floor, multiple levels, club music, the works. Stick with us, and we'll make sure you have a good time."

Bethani stared at Rick as though she'd never heard a more enticing proposal, and Jessica fought a groan. At first, the attention from Joe had been nice, but now she didn't like the familiar way he put his hands on her body, as though he now possessed something she hadn't given him.

Honestly, what was with these guys? And why was Bethani falling for it?

Buzz cuts, Jessica reminded herself.

But she had to admit, The City sounded like a blast, and their moms would be far more amenable to letting them venture out on their own if they had two strong, capable guys like Joe and Rick looking after them. Even if Jessica would rather not spend the entire night pretending to be attracted to Joe.

Jessica pulled Bethani away from the table with a mumbled, "Excuse us," to the guys.

"Where are we going?" Bethani asked, struggling to keep up.

"To make sure the moms are okay with us going out," Jessica replied with a grin. "And we need money to get those wristbands."

"But you don't even like that guy," Bethani protested.

"No, but you like his friend, so I'm willing to take one for the team."

Bethani smiled widely. "What did I do to deserve you?"

"You were probably a nun in a past life," Jessica said. "Stored up all that good karma."

Bethani pinched her arm playfully, the girls giggling as they entered their hotel room.

"I thought you were getting a drink?" Jessica's mom asked when they walked in, flicking her wrist to check her watch. "You were only gone for ten minutes!"

"We met a couple boys," Jessica said, purposely referring to them as *boys* instead of *men* to prevent her mom from asking too many questions. "They want us to go out to this club with them tonight. Before you say no, it's the club those spring break people are sponsoring, so we can get wristbands and take the shuttle there and back with the group. It'll be totally safe."

"Totally," Bethani quipped.

Their moms—Jessica's petite like her sister Berkley, though all three Daniels women had the same honey blonde hair; Bethani's average height with the same curtain of straight black hair as her daughter—stood shoulder to shoulder, arms identically folded over their chests, gazes narrowed.

Jessica sucked in a breath, ready to launch into an argument about why they should let them go—her brother, Logan, was an attorney and Berkley was studying to be one; she'd picked up a few things—but her mom held up a hand.

"Don't drink anything you didn't order yourself and watch the bartender make," she said. "Don't go anywhere without each other. When you're ready to come back, take the hotel shuttle or one of the buses. Under no circumstances are you to get into one of those cabs. Am I clear?"

Jessica nodded solemnly, Bethani's hair swishing against her arm as she did the same.

"Do we..." Bethani trailed off. "Do we have a curfew?"

Jessica elbowed her hard, but Bethani's mom shook her head. "We're on vacation, and you're adults. Just don't do anything stupid."

"We won't!" the girls said in unison, then rushed forward to hug their moms.

"Thank you," Jessica said to hers.

"Be smart," her mom said when she pulled away.

"One more thing," Jessica said sheepishly before she and Bethani turned to leave.

Her mother heaved a sigh. "Yes?"

"Can I borrow twenty bucks?"

Twenty minutes later, Jessica and Bethani were armed with their very own neon-orange wristbands and walked hand-in-hand with Joe and Rick to the shuttle that would take them to the club.

Much to Jessica's chagrin, Jack and his buddies were in the queue right ahead of them.

"Ugh," Jessica groaned. Bethani turned a quizzical gaze in her direction, and Jessica nodded toward that sandy blond head bobbing several people in front of them. Jack was so tall that he stood head and shoulders above anyone else in line, save his friends. The four of them were like towering oaks in the middle of a dandelion field.

Bethani grinned wickedly. "This is going to be interesting."

Rick and Joe remained oblivious to their conversation, talking over the girls' heads about guns or something.

They climbed the steps onto the shuttle, and Jessica and Jack immediately locked eyes. Joe placed a hand on her shoulder to steer her forward, and Jessica swore Jack's gaze darkened.

Jack

THEN: April 5, 2020

THE INSTANT JESSICA SET foot on the bus, Jack's mood brightened, then soured almost as quickly when a guy boarded after her, his hand settling with unnerving familiarity on the smooth, naked skin of her shoulder.

"That could be you right now," Chad whispered. "Who knew Jack DeLuca could get rejected?"

"Fuck off," Jack growled.

But Chad wasn't wrong, and for the millionth time that day, Jack asked himself why he'd been such a prick to her at the pool.

Wasn't there a saying about catching more flies with honey than vinegar?

You're a fucking idiot.

It wasn't even that he'd been a prick so much as he wasn't great with girls. Despite the fact that, both at their high school and anywhere they traveled for away games, girls threw themselves at him, Jack's friends and teammates would be shocked to learn he'd never actually gone all the way with anyone.

It was his deepest, darkest secret, and his greatest shame.

Jack DeLuca, star high school goaltender and Michigan State University hockey commit, was a virgin.

It really wasn't that big of a deal in the grand scheme of things; after all, he *was* only eighteen. But his friends—especially his teammates—had all given up their v-cards years ago. Jack remained the lone wolf.

And it wasn't that he didn't *want* to have sex. Obviously, he didn't plan on being a virgin for the rest of his life. But he wanted it to *mean* something. He wasn't interested in a one-time thing with no emotional connection. He was holding out for something...*more*. These days, waiting was a foreign concept, a lost art to people who had everything they could possibly want or need at the tips of their fingers.

All that to say, despite the way he'd treated her, Jack had seen the way Jessica looked at him: with a fire in her eyes, like she wanted to get to know him better.

The feeling was mutual.

But he'd fucked it up, so now he had to sit and watch while she and some douchey guy who was clearly way too old for her passed a bottle of vodka back and forth.

He wanted that to be him. He wanted to press his mouth to her lips, the same way she pressed the bottle there and let it linger for every sip.

His attention was pulled away from Jessica, who giggled as the guy leaned close and whispered something in her ear, by a head appearing between his and Chad's seats.

"Are you boys ready for this insanity?"

"What insanity?" Jack asked.

"The City. It's the biggest night club in Latin America, and things have been known to get crazy."

Clearly intrigued, Chad twisted in his seat to face the talking head. "How crazy?"

"The last time I was here, I saw people doing lines in the bathrooms, an incredible number of tits and body shots, and more than one same-sex couple absolutely going at it right out in the open."

Chad's eyebrows rose nearly to his forehead, and Jack was sure his expression matched.

With a shit-eating grin, Chad turned to Jack and said, "This is gonna be fun."

Further conversation on the short ride to the club yielded the following information: the talking head's name was actually Rick, and he was a Marine. He was here in Cancún with his buddy, Joe, who turned out to be the guy draped across Jessica's lap while she poured vodka into his open mouth. They were from Mississippi and about to deploy overseas, so they wanted to blow off some steam before they left.

Jack had been right on two counts:

One, the guy with Jessica was a douche.

Two, at twenty-six, he was way too old for her.

When they arrived at the club, Jack quickly realized Rick hadn't been exaggerating earlier when he'd used the word *insan-*

ity to describe The City.

The darkness inside was illuminated at regular intervals by flashes of strobe lights, and strips of LED lights lined the bars and pathways on the floors, which were completely obliterated by the sheer mass of people packed inside.

Within the first five minutes, Jack witnessed body shots, two girls making out, and a guy with some sort of canister blowing air at the crotch of a couple girls, the already too short skirts of their dresses riding higher from the force of it, revealing skimpy panties—or none at all.

The second they'd walked through the doors, Jessica disappeared, whisked away by Joe, who unsurprisingly knew his way around. Jack shook his head, then rolled his neck and cracked his knuckles, preparing to forget about Jessica and actually enjoy himself.

Chad led Jack and the rest of their friends through the crowd, pausing every so often to compliment girls, or accept a shot from one walking around with a tray laden with tubes filled to the brim with glowing green liquid.

"Are you sure you should be accepting random drinks like that?" Tyler asked skeptically.

Jack was inclined to agree with him but, not wanting to be a wet blanket, kept his mouth shut. He and each of his three friends had a role to play on this trip, exactly as they did on the ice during hockey games, and Jack was comfortable in his.

Tyler was the captain, and a forward, which meant he was responsible for keeping them in line. He was the level head, the voice of reason, the one to get them home safe at the end of the night.

Chad was a defenseman, more of an enforcer than a finesse player, who would inevitably be the one caught in the middle of a fight, or encouraging the boys to get into some sort of trouble.

Zach was also a forward, and the team's leading goal-scorer. He was charismatic, funny, and what could only be described as a pretty boy. On vacation, that meant Zach would be the reason girls approached them, and Jack wouldn't be surprised if Zach hooked up with more than one on this trip.

Jack, meanwhile, was their starting goaltender, and had been his entire four years of high school, even starting over a senior during his freshman season. Despite his floppy blond hair and blue eyes, which gave off more of a laid back, California surfer vibe than a guy who wanted to take pucks to the face for a living, Jack was often described by his friends as the shy, strong, silent type. Girls he'd had relationships with—more like situation-ships, meaning they made out a few times, maybe participated in some over the clothes groping, and several blow jobs for Jack before parting ways—liked to call him standoffish and emotion-ally unavailable.

Truthfully, he didn't think he was either. One thing people failed to realize about goalies is that their brains were wired dif-ferently, and Jack was no exception. He had his quirks, and a lot of them revolved around his game. Even off the ice, he had a habit of constantly tracking his surroundings. He wasn't quiet, or "standoffish," because he was shy or emotionally unavailable. He was quiet because he overanalyzed every interaction, oftentimes preferring to observe than engage, his goalie mind refusing to rest even outside of game play.

Come to think of it, that's probably why he was still a card carrying member of the virgins' club.

True to form, Chad sidled up to the bar, demanding the bartender give them a round of shots and a round of beers. Tyler, for his part, smiled apologetically at the girl working and in flawless Spanish, politely repeated what Chad had asked for.

Jack didn't dare ask what they were shooting, simply tipped his head and threw the liquid back, the liquor burning a path down his esophagus before hitting his stomach, the warmth spreading.

Once they'd all downed their shots, Chad turned to survey the crowd and let out a cry of victory before grabbing Zach by the forearm and hauling him into the melee that was the dance floor.

Tyler stayed at Jack's side, tipping the neck of his beer bottle into Jack's.

"Let's have a good night, yeah?"

Jack smiled. "Yeah."

"You know…we're on vacation," Tyler said.

"Yes?" Jack responded, unsure where he was going with the comment.

"We don't have to be who we are at home. In fact, I think this is a good opportunity for both of us to be completely different than we are in Philly."

"How so?" Jack asked, equal parts intrigued and confused.

"Like…maybe I don't have to be the straight-laced captain. Maybe I can take a page out of Chad's book and let loose."

Tyler tipped his head and lifted his beer bottle, indicating where Chad and Zach were in the middle of the dance floor, surrounded by girls.

"Okay," Jack said slowly. "So get out there and dance."

"Only if you come with."

"Dancing isn't really my thing."

"And that's the whole point," Tyler said, giving Jack a meaningful look.

Jack sighed and said, "Get to the point, Ty."

"You don't have to be top-Pennsylvania high school goalie, Michigan State hockey commit, strong, silent, and broody Jack DeLuca here. If you want to go out there and dance with hot girls, do it. If you want to walk over to that group"—Tyler nodded over Jack's left shoulder to a girl laid out on the bar, guys lining up, the bartender holding a bottle of liquor over her navel—"and offer to take the next shot out of that girl's belly button, do it. Or, if you want to spend your night making out with that girl we met at the pool today, I don't think she'd complain if you walked up to her and said that to her. In fact, she seems the type to appreciate a guy who goes after what he wants."

Jack studied his friend, who flashed him a toothy grin. Maybe Tyler was right. Maybe this was his chance to try on a different Jack DeLuca for size. Afterall, he was going to college in the fall, and if there's one thing he knew about college, it's that the female population loved athletes. And if he was going to start—and he *would* start; he would accept nothing less—he'd quickly become easily recognizable, and forced to socialize with not only an entirely new set of teammates, but classmates, coaches, staff, and other university officials. In college, he didn't think he'd be able to get away with simply standing on the sidelines and watching the world pass by. No, he'd have to actively participate.

What better place for a trial run than Mexico?

"It really could be that simple, couldn't it?" Jack said finally.

"It really could," Tyler said with a knowing smirk. "So what do you say? Shall we?" He swept his arm out at the mass of bodies gathered in front of them, and Jack grinned.

"We shall."

As they made their way to Chad and Zach, Jack rolled his shoulders back and set his face in one of those bored expressions he'd seen Zach adapt on more than one occasion. For whatever reason, girls were drawn to men who appeared uninterested, and he'd witnessed Zach secure hookups that way more times than he could count.

And when he reached the outer circle of girls gathered around Zach and Chad, Jack did something truly bold. He settled his hands on the hips of the nearest girl and pulled her back against his body.

He felt more than heard her gasp when she bumped into him, and when she tilted her head back to check him out, her look of indignation quickly became one of excitement and, dare he say...want? She looked at him like a snack she wanted to consume.

Jack didn't understand a single word of the song that blasted from the massive speakers hanging from the ceiling, but instinctively, his body knew how to sway side to side to the beat. The girl backed her ass into his crotch and took control, and Jack could do nothing but settle his hands tighter on her hips and grind with her

One song melted into the next, and the next, until Jack was so parched he had to disentangle himself from the girl—whose arms were wrapped around his neck, her fingers scraping at his nape—and head back to the bar for a drink.

As he weaved through the crowd, it was impossible not to bump into bodies as he carved his path in search of hydration, but when he collided—hard—with someone, it was enough that he staggered a step and threw his arms out to steady them both.

"I'm so sorry—" the girl started, then cut off when her gaze collided with Jack's.

Jessica.

Even in the dim lights, he didn't miss the angry set to her mouth or the sheen in her eyes he somehow knew had nothing to do with alcohol.

"What happened?" he asked.

"How do you know something happened?"

"You just ran into me with enough force to knock a college linebacker on his ass, and your whole face says *pissed off.*"

Jessica choked on a laugh, then fell into Jack when someone bumped into her from behind. He gripped her gently by the elbow and steered her to the bar, ordering two shots of tequila.

"I shouldn't even be mad," she said while they waited for their drinks. "And I'm actually mostly mad at myself for even being bothered by it."

"What happened?" he asked again.

"Joe," she said with a sigh and a wave of her hand. "Some girl threw herself at him, and he started making out with her right in front of me."

She glanced back over her shoulder, and even through the crowd, Jack's gaze zeroed in on the man in question. Joe sat in a plush armchair in one of the roped off VIP sections, a girl in a silver-sequined dress perched on his lap, his hands grabbing fistfuls of her ass as they consumed each other with their mouths.

Without making the conscious decision to do so, Jack stepped in their direction, but was halted by Jessica's hand on his forearm.

"He's not worth it," she said quietly, and Jack nodded.

When the bartender arrived with their shots, Jessica wasted no time in licking the backside of her hand and sprinkling it with salt, then picking up a lime wedge in one hand and the glass in the other.

She looked at Jack expectantly.

He hurriedly followed suit, and before downing their shots, Jessica clinked hers against his and said, "To Mexico."

Jack echoed her sentiment, but before he could tip the liquor back, Jessica gripped his hand and licked the salt from his skin, then downed her own. Not wanting to be upstaged, he mimicked her, sweeping the salt from her skin with one quick pass of his tongue before throwing the shot back. It scorched a path to his stomach, a sensation he was quickly growing accustomed to after only two days in Cancun.

Jessica shoved her lime between his teeth, and he returned the favor. Once she withdrew enough juice, she dropped it into her shot glass and set it on the bar, then turned a wide, self-satisfied grin on Jack, leisurely licking the lingering juice from her lips.

Jack's eyes grew to the size of golf balls, and Jessica chuckled softly.

"I'm sorry about earlier," he said.

"Huh?" Jessica asked, and Jack laughed.

"I'm sorry I was such a dick during the volleyball game. I'm an athlete, you know? It's not an excuse, but I'm really competitive.

I hate to lose."

Jessica waved her hand. "It's fine," she said. "You can't spell 'jackass' without 'Jack,' right?"

Okay, he deserved that, and he told her so.

Conversation halted while they ordered fresh drinks—Jack another beer, Jessica some fruity concoction she'd already consumed a few of if the unnatural red stain on her lips was any indication.

The bartender returned, and Jessica quickly sucked up some of her drink. Jack's gaze focused on the way her lips wrapped around those flimsy straws. When she let them go, a bead of liquor clung to her full bottom lip, and Jack fought the urge to bring her mouth to his and kiss it away, to suck that lip into his mouth.

"You know how little boys are only mean to the girls they like on the playground?" he blurted.

Jessica cocked an eyebrow. "You're saying you were an asshole because you like me?"

Jack gave her a sheepish grin and nodded. "That's exactly what I'm saying."

"You don't even know me."

"I'd like to."

She stepped closer until they were toe to toe, until each inhale had their chests brushing together. Their gazes locked, and Jack held his breath, waiting for any sort of sign from Jessica. Had he been studying her any less intently, he would've missed the subtle, near-imperceptible nod she gave him.

But he didn't, and he wasted no time in claiming her.

Jessica

THEN: April 5, 2020

Jessica hadn't been aware that her small, almost subconscious nod was her giving Jack approval to kiss her but, well...she wasn't exactly mad at the turn of events.

Outside of his ridiculous body, with his broad chest and torso that tapered into a vee of muscle like an arrow pointing straight to the ultimate prize, Jack's mouth had been the first thing Jessica had noticed about him. Soft, sensual, just this side of too wide for his face; she'd be lying if she said she hadn't wondered what it would feel like on hers.

Truthfully, her imagination hadn't done him justice.

He was tentative at first, giving her one slow kiss, then two quick pecks, mouth closed. He pulled away far enough to study her, as if confirming this was okay.

Once again, Jessica nodded.

When he came to her again, there was nothing hesitant about

it. Jack settled his hand on the column of her throat and used soft but insistent pressure of his thumb to tilt her head back, giving him a better angle to deepen the kiss.

When he sucked her bottom lip into his mouth and nibbled softly, she opened for him on a gasp, and he swept his tongue along hers. He tasted of the sharp, tangy bite of tequila and the more crisp and refreshing flavor of beer.

With a sigh, she bunched the material of his shirt in her fists and tugged him closer, losing herself in the feel of his hard body against hers.

Somehow, this *boy* felt like more of a man than the Marine who'd ditched her ever had.

Jessica didn't know how long they kissed for, and she immediately mourned the loss of him when he pulled away and settled his forehead against hers, his labored breaths fanning across her face.

"I've been wanting to do that since I first saw you at the pool today," he said.

She drew back to study him, surprised when she found no hint of deception in his eyes. Boys weren't supposed to be this...open, at least not in her experience.

"Why didn't you?"

"Do you have any idea how intimidating you were in that bikini?" he said. "They don't make girls like you back home."

Jessica's cheeks flushed with the compliment, but she scoffed. "Please," she said. "Have you seen yourself? You're basically Adonis."

Jack chuckled. "I'm not sure many would agree with you."

"I find that hard to believe," she said, "unless the girls back home are blind."

"They're not," he said. "I'm just not exactly what's considered a lady's man."

"I think you're doing pretty good for yourself." She rose onto her tiptoes to give him a lingering kiss. "Where is home, anyway?" she added when she pulled back again.

"Pennsylvania," he said. "A suburb outside of Philly to be exact."

"And how did you get to look like...this?" she asked, waving a hand at his body. "You mentioned you're an athlete."

"I play hockey," he said. "I'm a goalie, actually."

"I'm not really a hockey fan," she admitted. "Which is crazy because I'm from Michigan. If you ask my sister, something in my brain is broken."

Jack's eyes widened, a hand flying to his chest. "I'm sorry, what?"

"I don't like hockey," she shrugged. "Not my thing."

"Not your thing? But...next to Minnesota, Michigan is like the epicenter of hockey in the States."

She shrugged again. "It's more my sister's thing," she said. "And my brother's."

Jack rose to his full height and craned his neck, dramatically looking around the dance floor. "Where is this sister? She seems more like my kinda girl."

Jessica playfully shoved his chest, though the boy was built like a brick wall and didn't sway so much as a centimeter.

"Rude," she said, adopting an expression of mock hurt.

Jack settled a hand on her hip and tugged her close. "I'm kidding," he said, and kissed her again.

When she pulled back, she said, "If you must know, I'm here with my mom, my best friend, and her mom. Berkley is back in Michigan, finishing up her second year of law school."

"A lawyer in the family?" Jack's eyebrows shot up. "That's impressive."

"Oh, not just one," she said, holding up a peace sign. "Two. My older brother, Logan, is also an attorney."

Jack whistled low. "And you?"

Jessica sighed. "I want to be a teacher."

She waited for the furrowed brow, the pursed lips, the "why would you want to do that?" to leave his mouth, but none of those things happened. He studied her thoughtfully, and Jessica tried not to squirm under his gaze.

Her older siblings had always been close. With only thirteen months separating them, they were glued at the hip growing up. Unfortunately for Jessica, that didn't change much with her arrival when Logan was seven and Berkley was six. They had already started school when Jessica was still in diapers, and graduated and started college before she ever made it to high school.

She loved her siblings dearly, and she lucked out having two ridiculously smart, talented, and driven people serving as role models as she grew up. But...a lot of the time, she felt like she was letting them down by not following in their lawyerly footsteps.

For as long as she could remember, she'd wanted to be a teacher. When she was younger, she was often helping her classmates understand homework assignments when their teacher's explanations went right over their heads. In high school, she worked with a few different tutoring programs in her hometown of Traverse City and its surrounding areas. Logan and Berkley might not understand it, but she knew without a shadow of a doubt this was what she was meant to do.

Jessica had a plan for herself.

She'd be attending Michigan State University in the fall, where she'd get her teaching degree in secondary education, probably with a focus on English because she loved books and writing and languages, though that was subject to change. She would student-teach in her senior year, hopefully both semesters, before graduating and getting a job doing what she loved.

Finally, Jack said, "I think you'll be amazing at that."

"You don't even know me," she said, for the second time that night.

"You've got that look about you," he said, narrowing his gaze, the corner of his mouth tipping up in a half smile. "Like you're fully capable of handling rowdy children and shaping young minds."

"I don't know exactly what age I want to teach yet. Or even what I want my specialty to be."

That was a lie, actually. She knew exactly what she wanted to do, but she wasn't about to lay all of her fragile hopes and dreams at Jack's feet so he could step all over them.

"Well I'm confident you'll be amazing whatever you decide to do."

She grinned at him then, and he returned it.

The urge to do something spontaneous gripped her, and she said, "Let's get out of here."

Jack raised an eyebrow. "And do what, exactly?"

"Not *that*, you perv," she said, swatting at his chest. "I'm starving."

"So you want to wander out onto the streets of Cancún in the middle of the night in search of food?"

"Yep!" she said brightly, then turned from him and rose onto her tippy toes, searching the crowd for Bethani. "Can you use all this"—she gestured at his over-six-foot body—"and find my friend?"

Within seconds, Jack was leaning into her and pointing. She followed the direction of his finger to the center of the dance floor, finding Bethani tangled with a guy who looked vaguely familiar.

"That's my buddy, Zach," Jack told her. "You want to go tell them we're leaving? See if they want to come with?"

"No!" she said quickly, and he turned a quizzical gaze on her. "I mean, yes, I want to tell Bethani where I'm going, but no, I don't want them coming with."

"You trying to get me alone, Jess? Trying to take advantage of me?"

"Absolutely not," she said, but her mind spun with the possibilities of what would happen if she *did* want to get him alone. Would he be into that? They were at that awkward age where virgins weren't uncommon but becoming less so. Jessica herself was still a virgin, but Bethani wasn't. If she had to guess, Jack wasn't either. Although, something about him, despite that face, that *body*, seemed innocent.

And why was she even thinking about this? She had only met this guy this morning, and was on vacation in a foreign country with her *mother*. Michelle Daniels was a lot of things—an incredible cook, fiercely protective of her children, easy to talk to—but she would not be okay with Jessica asking to have the room so she could lose her virginity to some guy she barely knew and would never see again.

Still, something about Jack had Jessica thinking if she were to go there with him, he would take care of her. Despite his size, when he'd kissed her, he hadn't been demanding or insistent. He'd been gentle, never taking anything she didn't give right back, never asking for anything she wasn't willing to offer him. Distantly, she wondered how that would translate to the bedroom.

She'd been wondering that a lot lately, when she'd be ready to yield her v-card—and with whom.

"Jess?" Jack asked, settling a hand on her shoulder and jolting her from her reverie.

"Right, food. I'll be right back!"

Without waiting for a response, she shoved her way through the crush of bodies until she reached the center of the dance floor and stood in front of Bethani.

Tugging on her best friend's wrist, she pulled her away from Zach and leaned in to shout in her ear over the music.

"I'm going to get some food!"

"With Joe?" Bethani asked. She'd disappeared almost as soon as they walked in, presumably with Joe's friend, Rick, so Jessica had been surprised to find her with her ass backed into Zach's lap.

But that was a conversation for another time.

"No, Joe ditched me like an hour ago," Jessica told her. "I'm going with Jack."

"Jack as in..." She flicked her eyes over her shoulder at Zach, then back to Jessica, and Jessica nodded.

"You go girl," Bethani said with a grin. She flicked her wrist to check the time on her watch. "It's nearly one now. Do you want to rendezvous outside the doors in an hour and catch a ride back to the hotel together?"

Jessica nodded vehemently. "You know our moms will kill us if we come back separately."

"Exactly." Bethani squeezed Jessica to her, let go, and said, "Have fun!" with a mischievous twinkle in her eyes before returning to Zach's waiting arms.

When Jessica once again reached Jack's side, she slid her hand into his and said, "Let's go."

He didn't argue, didn't ask questions, didn't utter a word; he simply let her tow him from the club.

Stepping outside was like stepping into a vacuum where all sound had been sucked from the world. The sudden plummet in noise level had Jessica's ears ringing. She felt like she'd been plunged underwater, and she paused for a moment, closing her eyes and taking a deep breath.

"You good?" Jack asked, louder than was probably necessary.

"Yes," she said, quieter. "That's just...weird."

Jack nodded, sticking a finger in his left ear and wiggling it around. "I felt like my head was a balloon about to pop."

She laughed and reached for his hand again, surprised by how easy it was to touch this boy, and how quickly she'd let him into her personal space.

They wandered away from the club and onto the sidewalk. Across the street, the lights of a Hooters blinked out, so they kept walking in companionable silence until coming to a crossroads.

Down the way, a lighted sign read PEPPERS TACOS. Warm light spilled onto the street, and a small group of people milled around, either waiting for their food or already armed with Styrofoam takeout containers.

"When in Mexico!" Jessica sang, and pulled free of Jack to skip to the stand.

Above the counter, a black dry erase board detailed the menu in neon markers lit by a blacklight. Jessica perused the options, leaning into her partial fluency in Spanish to decipher the words.

A warm presence appeared at her back, and Jessica peeked over her shoulder at Jack.

"Can you understand any of that?" he asked, leaning close to whisper in her ear.

Despite the balmy night air, she shivered at his proximity. "Of course I can."

"Of course?" he asked, dubious.

"I've taken three years of Spanish," she said proudly. "I know enough to get us by."

"Then by all means," he said. "But I'm allergic to shrimp, so keep that in mind."

"Noted," she said, then turned to the man working the register, his wide smile glowing in his dark face under the blacklight.

"*¿Pido dos tacos de pollo y dos de carne, una quesadilla con solo queso, dos platos de arroz y dos margaritas clásicas?*" *Can I get two chicken tacos, two beef, a cheese quesadilla, two orders of rice, and two of your classic margs?*

"*Si, subiendo enseguida.*" *Yes, coming right up.*

"*Gracias. ¿Cuánto cuesta?*"

The man quickly tapped keys on his register, and Jessica

turned to Jack, who stared at her, clearly impressed. "You continue to surprise me," he said.

She settled her hand on his bicep and squeezed. "We're just getting started."

"Ahh...twenty dollars," the man said in heavily-accented English.

Wordlessly, Jack handed Jessica a bill, and she passed it to the worker, then stepped off to the side with Jack to wait for their food. When it was finished, they spread out at one of the red-and-white-checkered picnic tables.

"So what'd we get?" Jack asked, surveying the feast.

"Two chicken tacos, two beef tacos, a cheese quesadilla, two sides of rice, and margs!" she said, noisily sipping her drink, loving the way the smooth tequila mingled with the tart bite of the margarita mix on her tongue.

As they tucked into their meal, Jessica studied Jack. She quickly came to realize everything Jack did, he did with intention. The boy didn't believe in unnecessary words, movements, or emotions. He ate with the same efficiency he'd used to kiss her: straight to the point, but savoring nonetheless. In minutes, his half of their order had been demolished, leaving only stray pieces of tomato, a glob of sour cream, and a smear of hot sauce on his chin.

"You've got something," she said, tapping the center of her own chin.

Jack stuck out his tongue and stretched it down his face, trying to lick it up, but couldn't reach. Before he could lift his hand to swipe it away, Jessica reached out with her own, mopping it up with her pointer finger then shoving her finger in her mouth to lick it clean.

All the while, Jack watched her, the intensity of his stare never wavering. It should've freaked her out, the way he hardly blinked—and when he did, it was slow like an owl. Then she remembered he was a goalie, and that single-minded focus probably made him very good at his position.

"How long are you here for?" he asked suddenly, breaking the moment like a child sticking their finger into a bubble and popping it.

"We head back Friday morning."

Jack groaned. "That's only four days. Not even."

Jessica frowned. "Only?"

"I..." Jack trailed off and broke her gaze for the first time in minutes. His eyes darted around as his shoulders rose and fell, and he slumped forward slightly then straightened his spine again. Finally, he returned those sea green eyes to her, which in the low light strayed more green, almost emerald, than blue. "I guess we have a lot to pack into four days, then."

Jessica's eyebrows shot up in surprise, though secretly, she was pleased. "You think I'm spending my entire vacation with you?"

Jack leaned forward onto his elbows, and Jessica mirrored him. "Honey," he said lowly, "if I have anything to say about it, you're not leaving my sight until you have to get on that plane to go home."

The feminist in her, the girl Berkley had taught her to be, wanted to argue with that, wanted to tell Jack in no uncertain terms that he didn't get to make those kinds of decisions for her.

But a shiver worked its way down her spine, and she couldn't deny how drawn to Jack and his steady confidence she was. So she said, "You've got yourself a deal."

Jessica

NOW: October 7, 2023

"WHERE THE FUCK HAVE you been?" Silas hissed as he clapped along to the chant the band and cheerleaders were leading. Jessica had just reached his side in the sea of the student section, and she'd known even before she was within his reach that he was *pissed*.

Which, quite frankly, was bullshit. He'd known where she was going, and had been content to tailgate with his brothers instead of coming with her.

"With Kenzie," Jessica said with a forced smile.

She felt more than heard his exasperated sigh. "She's a bad influence."

"How, exactly? I'm here, aren't I?"

"Yes, but you stink of beer. What were you doing, keg stands?"

"No, I was playing beer pong at the hockey tailgate."

In one smooth move, Silas turned and pulled Jessica to his

chest, settling his hands low on her hips, pressing his mouth to her ear. To those around them, it would appear as nothing more than a lover's embrace, but the ferocity with which his fingers dug into her skin and his scathing words told a different story.

"Why were you at the hockey tailgate and not with me?"

"Because Kenzie is dating one of them, and she invited me. And need I remind you, *I* invited *you*."

"Yet another check in the con column of Mackenzie Jean," Silas said. "And I would rather chew my arm off than tailgate with the hockey players."

Jessica shifted so she could look up at him.

Silas wasn't overly tall. He was what those in the bookish community would consider a "short king"—five-foot-nine and...lean.

Jessica and Silas had met freshman year at the basketball campout, where students literally camped outside on the field in front of Munn. Student section basketball tickets were hard to come by, especially lower bowl ones, and events such as the campout were a way to earn students points in the hopes that they'd get enough to secure one of those coveted spots. It was the unofficial kickoff to basketball season, and one of Jessica's favorite events of the year.

Silas was a journalism major, and his dream job was to become an athletic director at a Power Five school. He'd attended the campout his first year at MSU not to get tickets, but to network.

They'd officially met when he'd interrupted her conversation with one of the student assistants—he was a high school classmate of hers—saying, "Sorry miss, but I just have to pick this kid's brain about the season. You understand," and shooting her a flirty wink.

She hadn't understood, not really, but her friend had given her a tight, apologetic smile, and Jessica trudged off in search of her roommate.

A few hours later, Silas had approached her, once again butting into a discussion with her friends.

"Hey," he said.

"Hi..."

"Look, I'm sorry about earlier. I'm just trying to make the most of my time here, and that guy can get me in with the basketball team. It's nothing personal."

"Okay," she said simply, then turned back to her friends.

Silas had not liked that blatant brush off, and he'd lightly wrapped his hand around her upper arm and towed her away from the group.

"What are you doing?" she asked.

"I'm trying to apologize."

"You're not doing a great job."

"I know." He ran his hands through the thick waves of his hair, seeming a little exasperated. *"Look...how about you let me make it up to you."*

Jessica scoffed. "It's really not that big of a deal."

"Please."

She studied him for a moment—his golden brown hair, hazel eyes, olive-toned skin, and angular but somewhat soft features. The boy was...pretty, if shorter than guys she normally went for.

Then again, she'd only truly been with one guy since spring break, and it's not like anyone would ever measure up to a six-foot-three hockey player who was built like a Mack truck.

"What exactly did you have in mind?"

"Go on a date with me."

Stunned, Jessica sputtered, "I don't know..."

"Please," he said again, pouting and giving her puppy dog eyes.

She'd had half a mind to turn him down. At first glance, Silas wasn't her type, and it seemed too early in her college career to be going on dates. Then again, just because Silas didn't seem like her type on the surface didn't mean things between them couldn't evolve into everything she'd ever dreamed of.

Even if she'd already had that...and lost it.

So she'd agreed, and they'd been together for the last three years. It hadn't always been sunshine and rainbows—and there had been more than a few "breaks" in that time—but they always found their way back to each other.

But on days like today, when he got all pissed off and indignant because she was spending time with Kenzie—who was family thanks to the fact that her brother was married to Jessica's sister—she wondered why she kept coming back.

"What is your problem?" she asked, returning to the conversation at hand.

"My problem is that hockey players are pricks, and you shouldn't be going anywhere near them."

Oh, if Silas only knew how close she'd been to one hockey player in particular, and how her vacationship with Jack DeLuca had shaped the way she would forever view relationships.

Jack DeLuca, here at Michigan State. And not only *here*, but the starting goalie for the hockey team.

What were the odds?

It showed how little Jessica paid attention to the sport that she hadn't heard his name mentioned once in the last three years. Plus, they'd never exchanged last names in Mexico. It had been one of her stipulations. Their time together had been magical, a once-in-a-lifetime experience, and Jessica hadn't wanted to sully it by bringing it home and letting the real world poke holes in their bubble.

But now, he was *here*, and Jessica wasn't sure what to do with that information. She had Silas, but...did she really? Things between them had been strained for a long time, and she knew they weren't going to last after graduation. Not with him staying here and her hopefully...not.

Then again, she wasn't about to leave Silas for Jack, for some pipe dream. She was not the same girl she'd been in Mexico, and she'd bet good money Jack had changed as well.

After all, he was the starting goaltender for one of the most storied college hockey programs in the country.

"I'm not going to argue with you about this in the middle of a football game," she gritted out, clenching her teeth so hard her jaw ached. "We'll discuss this later."

"Fine," he said, turning his back to her in favor of conducting a conversation with his frat brother at his side.

Internally, Jessica scoffed. Silas calling hockey players pricks was rich considering she had yet to meet a single one of his brothers she could stand.

The football game was nail-biting, the Spartans eking out a victory in overtime, and Jessica was thankful for the adrenaline rush distracting her from the showdown she knew she and Silas would have the moment they were away from prying eyes.

They moved with the throng from the stadium, his hot palm

wrapped possessively around her upper arm, as though he was afraid she'd bolt at the first opportunity.

And Jessica couldn't lie—she'd considered it.

When they finally broke free from the mass exodus, rivulets of people dispersed in all directions across campus. Silas directed Jessica toward Munn, where the crowd was the thinnest. They reached Munn Field, and Silas reached down to lace his fingers through hers, giving her an insistent tug onto the cool grass.

Without preamble, Silas spun on her. "I want you to stay away from Kenzie and Aiden and his teammates."

"No."

"No?" Silas parroted, a dark eyebrow arching toward his hairline.

"No," she confirmed. "Kenzie is my family, and one of my best friends. I'm not going to stop hanging out with her just because you don't like her boyfriend."

"Her boyfriend is a pompous asshole," Silas said through clenched teeth. "All hockey players are."

"Don't talk about Aiden like that. In fact, don't talk about hockey players in general. Are you forgetting that my brother-in-law is one of the most talented and decorated professional players of our generation?"

"I know exactly what kind of man your brother-in-law is," Silas said.

"What's *that* supposed to mean?" Jessica asked, not missing the sharpness of his tone.

"It means that your brother-in-law is a fuckboy."

"Take that back!" she yelled, sounding like a petulant child but unable to care.

Jessica was many things, but the one she took most seriously was how loyal she was to her friends and family. Silas was skating on very, *very* thin ice. One more wrong word and she'd shatter it beneath them both.

"Keep your voice down!" he hissed, reaching out to clasp her biceps again.

She yanked free and crossed her arms over her chest, staring him down.

They'd played this little battle of wills game many times before and, at this point, Jessica was unsure of the tally. But she wasn't backing down this time, and Silas knew it.

He blew out a breath through his nose, his tensed shoulders dropping away from his ears. "I'm sorry," he said finally, though she could tell he didn't really mean it.

Stepping closer, she leveled her finger in his face and said, "Never insult my family again."

"I get the point, Jess. Let it go."

"Fine," she said, the fight leaving her. All she wanted to do was go home and crawl into the bath with a bottle of Rosé, but for the sake of moving past this, she asked, "Do you want to come over?"

"Can't, babe," he said as he turned them off the lawn and toward the path that wound around Munn. "Frat thing tonight."

"Just the frat?"

"Nah," he said casually. "We're going out with the DG girls."

"Of course you are," she mumbled under her breath.

"What?"

"Nothing!" she said brightly, looking up at him with a feigned smile. "I'll see you tomorrow then? You're still coming with me to brunch, right?"

"Sure, babe," he said, and she never knew four letters could grate on her so much. She *hated* being called "babe," but he'd so far ignored every attempt to get him to stop.

After a quick, passionless kiss, Silas loped off toward the stadium, presumably to meet his brothers before heading toward Grand River and the bars.

With a sigh, Jessica turned in the direction of the Breslin Center, where she'd loop around to Michigan Avenue and her house a few blocks down.

She chuckled softly to herself at the memory of eighteen-year-old Jessica setting foot on this campus for the first time. Traverse City wasn't a small town by any means, but Michigan State's student population tripled that of her hometown and then some. In her freshman year, Jessica barely liked to use the community restroom in her dorm by herself let alone walk across campus and the city in the dark. She'd heard horror stories of girls who didn't travel in packs, and the last thing she wanted was to become another headline.

Now, she felt more safe in East Lansing than just about anywhere else in the world. This city, these buildings and walkways, the people—it was all home to her now.

The further she walked, the more irritated with Silas she became. There were nights like tonight when she wondered why she stayed, why she continued to put herself through these arguments when it was clear what they had wasn't working anymore. But she loved him...or, she thought she did, and it wasn't so simple to walk away from something she'd devoted the better part of the last three years to.

Although, seeing Jack today had shaken her, and she'd be lying if she said she hadn't considered what her college experience would've been like if she and Jack decided to have that conversation about the future in Mexico, if she'd given them the chance to make a go of things in the real world.

With a rough shake of her head, she tossed that thought aside. There was no sense in playing the what-if game, because she couldn't go back and change it now. All she could do was move forward and, for the moment, *forward* included Silas.

But damn...*Jack*. She still couldn't quite wrap her head around the fact that he was here. That he had been here this whole time.

Ahead, a figure approached, and Jessica swerved to the right, intent on taking another path toward the main road. But then the figure said, "Jess?" and she froze.

That voice and the way it said her name had graced her fantasies for months after Mexico—and well beyond that.

"Jack," she breathed, unable to contain the grin that stretched her mouth wide.

For a moment, they remained rooted in place, ten feet apart, simply drinking in the sight of one another.

The years since Mexico had been great to Jack. Back then, he'd been buff, but his muscles then were mere ghosts of his current physique. What she could see now of his arms and legs indicated he'd trained hard and had been rewarded. His biceps stretched the cuffs of his t-shirt sleeves indecently, his forearms thick. The sharp edges of his quads were visible below the hems of his shorts, tapering into calves and shin muscles—what were those even called?—that flexed when he shifted slightly on his feet. And she knew if he turned around, she'd find his already glorious eighteen year old ass had only gotten more impressive in the time since.

She bit her lip, the pain sobering, and Jack said, "You're staring."

"So are you."

Even in her perusal of him, she hadn't missed the way his eyes had raked her body from head to toe. The path those blue eyes had taken scorched her skin like a brand, reminding her of all the times he'd done it before.

Reminding her of him following those same paths with his hands.

A little head shake brought her back to reality before she could lose herself completely in that entirely unhelpful daydream, and Jack chuckled.

"I can't believe you're here," he said.

"This is truly unbelievable," she agreed.

"You came right after high school?" he asked. "You didn't transfer recently or something?"

"Nope," she said. "I've been here since that fall."

"Me, too," he whispered thickly, his words carried to her on the light breeze.

"Jack..." she said, unsure what she'd been planning to say after.

But something within Jack seemed to snap, and in three long strides, he ate up the distance between them and wrapped her in his arms.

It was second nature to sink into his embrace, to open the floodgates where she stored her most precious memories and allow everything they'd experienced that week to return in a deluge that would've swept her off her feet had he not been holding her. A sob tore free from her throat, unbidden, and she inhaled deeply, trying to regain her composure.

Only...he still smelled exactly the same, and that hit of pure *Jack* had her sobbing harder into his chest.

Jack didn't pull back in revulsion or scold her to pull herself together. He simply tightened his grip, those strong arms holding her together as she fell apart.

"I know, sunshine," he said reverently, resurrecting the long-buried nickname. "I missed you, too."

Jack

THEN: April 6, 2020

"Where's your girl?" Zach asked as they descended the worn wooden stairs to the beach.

"Where's yours?" Jack shot back with a smirk.

"It's not like that and you know it," Zach said. They reached the hot sand then, and both boys slipped off their Adidas slides and picked them up.

"Does she know that?" Jack asked. "You two looked awfully cozy last night when Jess and I came back to meet you."

"Oh, so she's *Jess* now?" Zach asked.

"Don't change the subject, dumbass." Jack spun and placed a hand in the center of Zach's tanned, naked chest, halting his trek across the beach. "I really like her, man, and if you fuck with her friend, that ruins my chances."

"Dude, you just met her!" Zach said incredulously.

Jack simply shrugged. "Doesn't matter. I like her, and if you fuck with her friends, you fuck with me. Got it?"

Zach raised his hands in mock surrender. "Aye, aye, captain."

"Did someone say captain?" Tyler asked as he raced up to join them.

"No," Jack and Zach said in unison.

"Okaaaay then," Tyler said, moving past them and further down the beach, Chad rushing to follow.

"For real, though, man," Zach said, dropping a hand on Jack's shoulder and looking him dead in the eye. "If this girl helps you loosen up, then I'm all for it. Just...don't lose sight of the fact that this is Mexico, and the chances of it becoming more than a vacation fling are slim."

"Yeah, yeah," Jack said, shoving Zach away and starting down the beach after their friends.

He'd only taken two steps when someone yelled his name. "Jack!"

He turned toward the sound, a wide grin splitting his face in half when he found Jessica running down the stairs, blonde braids bouncing against her tanned shoulders, her lean arms and legs on full display in a bright pink bikini, which beautifully offset her tan. He barely spared a glance for Bethani coming down behind her.

The second Jessica's feet hit the sand, her flip flops flew off, and Jack moved toward her.

He'd never been one for PDA—actually, he'd never had someone to participate in PDA with—but all reservations about being open about his feelings went out the door with Jessica. When they reached each other, he scooped her up into his arms and planted a lingering kiss on her mouth.

They pulled apart, and he licked his lips. "Drinking already?" he asked, the taste of orange juice and what he guessed was champagne lingering on his tongue.

"It's vacation," she said with a shrug. "And it's all free. I have to take advantage."

Jack gave her a small head shake. "Crazy girl," he said quietly.

"You have no idea," she grinned.

"Well how about we take advantage of something that won't get us arrested in the States?"

"What did you have in mind?"

He turned and pointed down the beach, where his friends had reached the small hut set up near the water. "You ever been boogie boarding?"

"No, but I'll try anything once," she said, throwing him a flirty wink and taking off down the sand.

This girl, Jack thought.

The beautiful thing about staying at an all-inclusive resort was that, in the same way all food and drinks were free, so were the activities. Only resort guests were granted access to this stretch of beach, so the man working the stand asked no questions as he passed out foam boards to each of them.

"Don't go out too far," the guy said. "Once you get out past the sandbar, the current is gnarly. Wouldn't want anyone to get pulled away never to be seen again."

A shiver raced down Jack's spine as he considered that. He'd never expected this to be dangerous, but he liked to think he wasn't scared of anything. After all, he willingly took pucks to the face and found it enjoyable.

Jessica was already shin-deep in the water, his friends out far enough that the waves broke over their heads. Their shouts latently reached the beach, cheering Chad on as he flopped down on his board and let the wave carry him to shore.

He smiled as he watched them, then waded out to meet Jessica.

"You ready?" she asked.

"Lead the way, sunshine," he said.

Her nose wrinkled at the nickname. "Sunshine?"

Jack laughed. "Just trying it on for size, but I kind of like it." He reached out to weave one of her bright blonde braids through his fingers, then trailed them across the smooth, tanned skin of her shoulder. "I think it suits you."

A slow smile unfurled on her face, revealing those pearly teeth, lighting her bright-blue eyes.

Yeah, she was definitely sunshine.

"Well come on then, big guy," she said, grabbing his hand. "Let's get out there and enjoy my namesake."

"Big guy?" he asked dubiously.

Jessica turned to him fully and gave him a slow perusal from head to toe. "Yeah, *big guy*. I'm just trying it on for size." She smirked as she parroted his words back to him. "But tell me, Jack...does it suit you?"

Those words were a caress on his cock, and he shifted uncomfortably on his feet, willing himself not to pop a boner on a public beach. He stepped closer to Jessica, both to hide the evidence of his desire and to whisper his next words. "Why don't I show you?"

"You're playing with fire, Jack."

"Don't worry, sunshine. I can handle the heat."

Jessica heaved a deep breath and stepped away, and Jack

chuckled.

His toned physique was a relatively new development, brought on by puberty the previous summer. The height had come at the start of high school, when he was fourteen, and it had taken him an entire season to settle into his new, longer limbs. But he'd been gangly, a string bean. Somehow, he'd still been the best goaltender in their league, but that was only because the talent in front of him was far better than any other team they'd faced. After that year, he'd done everything he could to fill out, to bulk up—lifting constantly, increasing his food intake, even going so far as to dabble in some questionable supplements—but nothing worked. It wasn't until last summer, during off-season training, when he'd finally started to pack on the muscle he'd worked so desperately for.

That was when he'd finally gone from an awkward teenage boy to something closer resembling a man.

"Jack?" Jessica asked, breaking him from his reverie. "Where'd you go?"

He gave his head a little shake and met her eyes. "Just wondering if a girl like you would've given me the time of day a year ago." Her forehead scrunched in confusion, and he continued. "I didn't have all this," he added, gesturing to his ample pecs and bulging biceps.

Jessica stepped closer, the foamy water eddying around their ankles. She stretched up to place a kiss on the underside of his jaw, then reached up to tap his temple. "But you had this," she said. "The rest is just window dressing."

His smile was wide as he tipped his head to give her a kiss, what he meant to be a quick peck heating up in an instant.

"Stop sucking face and get your asses out here!" someone yelled, and Jack broke free from Jessica to find Chad twenty feet away, waving his arms like a mad man.

"He's got a point," Jessica said, grinning before taking off into the surf.

Jack had assumed boogie boarding would be easy thanks to his athleticism.

That had been a mistake.

Getting on the board wasn't the problem so much as staying on when wave after wave pounded his back, threatening to pull him under.

The six of them tried and failed more often than not to ride waves back onto the beach. Zach, the showoff, was the only one who ever actually accomplished it, and only once.

After an hour of fighting against the swells, Jack was ready to head back in. He opened his mouth to yell for Jessica when a shout at his back had him spinning away from her.

"Help!" someone screamed, and Jack scanned the water, frantically searching for the commotion. "Help!"

There.

About fifteen feet away, a blond head bobbed on the surface of the water, there one moment and gone the next.

Tyler.

Without thinking, Jack sliced through the water, reaching the spot where he'd last seen his friend at the same moment Chad sputtered to the surface.

"That way!" Chad pointed, then took off in that direction, Jack following closely behind.

He chose his steps carefully, the current tugging at his ankles and threatening to pull him off his feet. Tyler was already in trouble; the last thing they needed was him going under, too.

They reached the spot where they'd last seen Tyler, and Chad dove under, presumably searching through the murky salt water for any sign of their friend. As soon as Chad disappeared, Tyler's head popped up another ten feet away, gasping out, "Help!" before submerging once again.

Jack moved quickly, his heart pounding so hard he swore it was bruising his sternum. When he reached the approximate spot he'd last seen Tyler, he went under, the salt water stinging his eyes as he opened them and groped around for his friend.

At the point when his lungs burned so bad he knew he'd have to go up for air, his hand grazed something—an arm—and Jack latched on, pulling them both to the surface and swimming hard for shore, glancing over his shoulder only once to confirm he had Tyler firmly in his grasp.

The moment they flopped onto the beach, they were swarmed.

Immediately, Tyler flipped onto all fours, coughing and spitting a concerning amount of water onto the sand. Jack, meanwhile, fell onto his back and closed his eyes, attempting to calm the rapid rise and fall of his chest.

The cacophony of voices around them grew until they became a roar, and Jack retreated into his mind the same way he did during a game, where the only sounds that reached him were his deep breaths and beating heart.

Sometime later, when a shadow fell over his face, Jack opened his eyes to find Tyler hovering over him.

"Bro," Tyler said, giving Jack a shaky smile. "You fucking saved my life."

Jack sat up and settled his hands on Tyler's shoulders. "Do me a favor, Ty?"

"Anything."

"Stay out of the ocean for the rest of this trip."

Tyler boomed out a laugh that turned into a coughing fit. When he finally collected himself, he said, "Deal."

A hand settled on Jack's left shoulder, and he turned to find Jessica's face a hand's width from his own.

"You okay?" she asked quietly, eyes shining with concern.

"I'm not sure," he said. "A kiss might help."

Jessica rolled her eyes but couldn't completely fight off her smile.

"Only because you just saved someone's life," she said, then leaned forward to press her mouth to his.

An hour later, after a resort medic came down to examine both Tyler and Jack—and given both clean bills of health—the group returned to its standard spring break shenanigans.

Amidst the commotion, they'd managed to overlook the DJ booth being erected in the center of the beach, and when the opening notes of "Get Low" blasted from the speakers on the plywood stage, Jessica grabbed his hand and towed him across the sand, bobbing her head to the beat.

"What are you doing?" he yelled.

"Dancing!" she yelled back, shimmying her hips and dropping to the ground.

Like an absolute dumbass, Jack stood still while Jessica writhed against him. The space around them quickly filled as vacationers joined them, and soon they were completely surrounded.

Jessica spun toward him and rested her hands on his shoulders, looking up at him as she moved side to side.

"You have to move!"

"I don't...I wasn't sober!"

"C'mon, big guy," she said. "Put your hands on my hips and move with me." Then she turned and backed into him, reaching for his hands and settling them on her hips, using her ass and grip on his wrists to force him to move with her.

"I need a drink," he muttered.

Once more she faced him, and said, "If that's what you need to stop acting like a robot, then go get one. And bring me back a tequila sunrise while you're at it!" she added with a playful shove.

Jack grinned at her then snaked through the crowd, looking over his shoulder once to find she'd already been swallowed by the mass of bodies on the makeshift dance floor.

When he'd secured their drinks—a beer for him, the requested tequila sunrise for Jessica—he paused halfway down the stairs and took a moment to survey the scene in front of him. There had to be at least fifty people gathered on the sand, but Jack easily picked out Jessica's vibrant hair smack dab in the middle of it all.

By the time he made it back to her side, about a quarter of each of their drinks had sloshed out to cover his hands and wrists thanks to people jostling him. A thin trail of grenadine ran down his wrist, and when Jack handed her drink over, Jessica took the opportunity to lick it clean.

Her tongue on his skin had his dick instantly hard, and when she pulled away, he quickly adjusted himself in his swim trunks. The peal of her laughter was quickly lost in the crowd, and Jack tugged her close and pressed his mouth to hers, silencing her.

He sucked her bottom lip into his mouth, then swept his tongue in when she opened on a gasp. She tasted like tequila and sunlight, and he wanted to bask in it forever.

Before he could get too carried away—though one of her legs was wrapped suggestively around his waist and he had two handfuls of her practically bare ass—someone slammed into him, breaking their kiss. Breathing hard, he rested his forehead against hers, inhaling the scent of sunscreen and alcohol—intoxicating, but only because there wasn't a single thing about Jessica that didn't turn him on.

Gripping her hips, he pulled her flush against him, groaning when the hard length of his cock pressed into her stomach. He dropped his head to her neck, growling against her skin.

"Jack," she said breathlessly.

"Yeah, sunshine?"

She leaned away from him, and he met her gaze, her normally bright-blue irises turned darker. "Don't start something you can't finish."

He choked on a laugh and looked between them, examining the way his cock tented his trunks, straining against the material.

"Later?" he asked, choosing to ignore the fact that he'd never experienced what he was offering.

"Really?" she asked. "We don't even know each other."

"Really," he confirmed, surprised by the confidence in his tone. "I..."

He didn't know what he'd been about to say, but she shushed him with a hand over his mouth. "Let's just...play it by ear, okay?"

The corners of Jack's mouth pulled down. "Do you...not want me?"

Great, now I sound whiny and insecure, he thought.

Jessica barked out a disbelieving laugh. "Of course I want you," she said. "I haven't thought about anything but you since we met yesterday."

"To be fair, we haven't exactly spent a ton of time apart since then," he reminded her.

"Not the point, Jack."

"Then what is the point, Jess?"

"I've never...done that," she said, gesturing to the situation in his shorts.

"Never done *what,* exactly?"

Hope bloomed in his chest, but he didn't dare entertain it, didn't allow himself to believe that this stunning girl was as inexperienced as he was.

"Sex, Jack," she said quickly. "I've never had sex."

"You're fucking joking."

Jessica huffed out a sigh, her warm breath fanning across his collarbones. "I'm dead serious."

"*How?*" he blurted.

Smooth, DeLuca.

"I just haven't found anyone I wanted to do it with..." she said, trailing off. "I've done other stuff, just never...that."

"Other stuff like what?" he asked, unable to stop his voice from dropping several octaves as he considered the possibilities—namely Jessica's pretty pink lips wrapped around his dick.

"Lots of oral," she said with a smirk. "Though never receiving."

"Me, too," he said. "Mostly receiving."

He loved the way her eyes widened in surprise. "You've never either?"

"Nope," he said proudly.

Jessica simply stared at him for several beats on his heart until *she* surprised *him* by bursting into excited laughter.

"How is that even possible?" she said. "How did we end up here?"

"I don't know," he said, tipping his chin to press a kiss to her smiling mouth. "But I'm glad we did."

THEN: April 6, 2020

Despite the dry tiredness clinging to the edges of her eyes, and the loose exhaustion clinging to her bones after spending all day on the beach under the hot Mexican sun, Jessica wasn't about to let a single second of time she could be spending with Jack pass without him near.

So once the DJ packed up, and Jessica was sufficiently intoxicated on the tequila coursing through her veins, the paradise sunshine, and Jack's kisses, they reluctantly parted ways to get ready for the evening. The plan was to rendezvous in the lobby in a few hours and get dinner somewhere in the resort together before going out again.

"What are you wearing tonight?" Bethani asked as she exited the bathroom in their suite, steam billowing out around her. Their moms were out on the grounds somewhere, enjoying some "kid free time," as Jessica's mom had said before they'd taken off.

With Bethani's question, Jessica rifled through her suitcase, which was wide open, its contents spilling out on the bed she and her mom shared. Grabbing two fistfuls of clothes, she whirled on her friend and said, "I don't know!"

Bethani laughed. "Okay, since when do you get all worked up about what to wear?"

"Since..." Jessica stopped herself from finishing the thought, though Bethani knew her well enough to do so for her.

"Since Jack," her best friend said with a knowing smirk.

Jessica threw herself dramatically onto Bethani's bed. "Do you think I'm insane?"

The mattress sank next to her as Bethani sat. "No," Bethani said firmly. "I think you're a teenager, on vacation, and infatuated with an admittedly super hot guy."

"I think it's more than infatuation," Jessica said quietly.

"Do you...want more than a vacation fling?"

Jessica shot upright, gaze locking with her friend's. Bethani didn't appear judgemental in the slightest, only genuinely curious. "Am I crazy to say that maybe I do? I don't even know him!"

"Look, we're young," Bethani said. "But I also firmly believe that soulmates exist, and when you know, you know. Maybe this is that moment for you."

Jessica wanted to argue with her, to tell her it was absolutely unfathomable that she, Jessica Daniels, could come to Mexico only to meet the guy she was supposed to spend the rest of her life with.

But...something had drawn her and Jack together. Some invisible force had nudged them both to this moment, their paths converging in an instant that was years in the making.

So maybe she wasn't sure what life after this week would look like for them, but she knew one thing for certain: she wanted to savor the time they did have.

"It makes absolutely no sense to me," Jessica said at last. "But I really like him."

"So focus on that," Bethani said simply. "Worry about everything else later."

And it really was that simple, wasn't it?

***

"My god," Jack said when he laid eyes on Jessica an hour later, and she blushed. "You are..."

"You like?" she asked, twirling in a circle. The skirt of the pale pink dress she'd chosen ballooned around her, the spaghetti straps balancing delicately on her shoulders. Despite the humidity she knew would wreak havoc on it later, she'd chosen to curl her hair, letting it fall in loose waves down the mostly-bare skin of her back. Her only makeup was a swipe of mascara and lip gloss, and she'd laced strappy sandals onto her feet.

In two long strides, Jack was sliding his hands around her waist. "Like? *Like?* That doesn't even begin to describe what I'm feeling right now."

He pressed his hips flush against hers, and Jessica giggled when he thickened against her stomach. The ease with which she turned this guy on made Jessica feel infinitely powerful, and experimentally, she wiggled against him, grinning when he dropped his head to her shoulder and groaned.

"Jessica," he gasped.

"Yes?" she asked sweetly.

"We're in public," he reminded her.

She craned her neck to look at him, then darted her eyes around the lobby, remembering they weren't alone.

"Kiss me," she whispered, and he obliged.

"Jack!" someone shouted the instant their lips met. "I know she's really hot and everything, but I'm starving so let's get moving."

Jack groaned again—albeit different from the one moments ago—and pulled away, sliding his hand between them to adjust himself before grabbing her hand and turning to face his friends.

Jessica was surprised to find Bethani tucked into the crook of Zach's arm, and her friend shot her a smirk.

"Since you're soooooo hungry," Jack said to Chad, who had been the one that shouted at them, "you can pick where we eat."

"I want steak," Chad said.

Their resort consisted of a central tower with guest rooms, the main level of which was dominated by a massive indoor green space full of trees and flowers, bushes and other plants. Branching off to each side from there were two low slung buildings housing several hundred more rooms. The front of the complex was the lobby, sports bar, lounge and meeting spaces. The grounds extended far beyond the buildings, though, and included the three pools, beach access, and various dining establishments.

The restaurant Chad wanted to go to was about a five minute walk from the lobby, so they set off in its direction. Now that the sun had sunk below the horizon, the air had cooled to a more comfortable temperature. For no reason other than because she wanted to, Jessica looped her arm through Jack's and clung to his side.

"Can we consider this our first date?" Jack asked quietly as they strolled behind their friends.

"No," she said quickly, and laughed when she saw Jack's frown in the low exterior lights of the resort paths. "No offense, but I didn't imagine our friends on our first date."

"In that case, remind me to take you on a proper one before this week is over."

A thrill raced through her at the promise in those words.

When they arrived at the restaurant, it was early enough that there were plenty of tables available, and the hostess sat them on the patio beneath a canopy of palm fronds and twinkling lights.

"This is magical," Jessica breathed once she was settled in her chair.

"You're magical," Jack said, scooting close to her.

"You guys are disgusting," Chad groaned.

Jessica stuck her tongue out at him, and Jack said, "You're just jealous."

Chad's gaze swept over her like a brand—across the delicate lines of her exposed collarbones, around the slopes of her shoulders, and down the length of her arms, pausing on where her hand was clasped in Jack's on the table.

"I mean...you are pretty hot," Chad said finally.

Jack made a noise of warning in the back of his throat, and Jessica giggled, squeezing his fingers.

"I'm with you," she reminded him. "I *chose* you."

He rewarded her admission with a small smile. "I still don't understand why. I was kind of an asshole to you."

"There's no *kind of* about it," she teased, prodding him in the side before leaning closer and dropping her voice. "But let's just say I like your mouth better when you're kissing me instead of cussing me out."

Jack tipped his head back and laughed, and Jessica grinned in response. His eyes sparkled when he met hers again. "Trust me, sunshine, there's a lot more where that came from."

The shiver that shot down her spine had nothing to do with the breeze rolling in off the ocean.

Soon, the drinks were flowing and the table in front of them was laden with dishes of meats, appetizers, veggies, and various carbs. Before they dug into their feast, Chad insisted on a celebratory shot.

"To the Admirals!" Chad shouted, raising his shot glass over the table and aggressively clinking it against everyone else's before downing what little liquor remained.

"The...Admirals?" Jessica asked, shooting Jack a quizzical glance.

"It's our high school's mascot," Jack explained.

"What even is an Admiral?"

"An army guy. Like a general, but not."

"What a strange mascot," she said with a giggle.

"It's alliterative. Our town name starts with an A."

Jessica turned her wide-eyed gaze on him. "*Alliterative?*"

"What?" Jack asked, eyebrows raised. "I know words."

"Color me impressed," she said, slapping a palm to his chest, the warmth of his skin creeping into her hand. "You're not just a pretty boy dumb jock after all."

"Rude," Jack said, absently downing another shot—handed to him by Zach this time—without tearing his eyes off Jessica.

"You can punish me later."

Jack choked, half the liquor he'd consumed dribbling out of his mouth and onto the lengths of his thighs bared below the hems of his shorts.

"Jessica!" he hissed. "You can't say stuff like that to me. Definitely not in public."

She gave him a serene smile and turned to her food. She'd been on a healthy diet of rum and tequila all day, and she needed something of substance in her stomach before going out that night.

As if reading her mind from across the table, Bethani said, "What's the plan for tonight?"

"We were thinking about Señor Frogs," Tyler said. "Seems a little more lowkey than The City, but they've got this waterslide I'm dying to check out."

"Waterslide?" Jessica heard Jack murmur to his friend.

"Different people, remember?"

Jack only nodded.

"What's he talking about?" Jessica asked him.

"I'll tell you later."

Later never came, at least not from Jack. By the time they left the resort restaurant in favor of heading into the city and Señor Frogs, Jack was already so drunk Jessica was practically carrying him. He'd started dinner off with a margarita, then proceeded to challenge Zach to see which of them could take more tequila shots before they vomited.

Jack won—after five shots.

The night really went downhill from there, especially when the boys started ordering shots to congratulate Jack on saving someone's life—and Tyler for surviving such a harrowing experience. Jessica found herself wondering if that's why Jack was drinking so much, if this was his way of coping with nearly losing one of his best friends.

"Different people, huh?" Jessica hissed at Tyler when they hauled Jack's giant ass off the bus and onto a bench in front of Señor Frogs, presided over by a massive fiberglass rendition of the amphibian.

"This is *not* what I meant," he said through gritted teeth.

"We shouldn't have even come," Jessica said, studying Jack with her hands on her hips. He listed dangerously sideways, held upright by some incredible feat surely aided by the muscles of his abdominals.

Tyler took a beat then burst out laughing, and Jessica whirled on him, glaring daggers.

"I'm sorry!" he said, raising his hands defensively. "It's just...look at him."

Jessica blinked and turned back to Jack.

And...okay, the way he hung over the arm of the bench, his knuckles grazing the ground, the dopey smile on his face and the fact that, for some unknown reason, he kept humming to the tune of "Wonderwall" by Oasis had Jessica cracking up alongside Tyler.

"He's not fit to go inside," Jessica said once their moods sobered. "They'll never let him in the door like this."

Tyler heaved a sigh, his shoulders rising and falling dramatically. "I'll go back with him."

"You'll do no such thing!" Jessica protested. "What happened to being different people? What about the waterslide?"

Tyler narrowed his gaze. "Did he tell you what that was about?"

Jessica shook her head. "He got too...this"—she gestured to Jack's inebriated form—"before he could explain."

Tyler sighed and sat beside Jack, patting the spot beside him, and Jessica dropped down next to him.

"Jack is a good guy, you know?"

Jessica nodded. "I do." That much was obvious, despite their brief time together.

"He's our goalie, the glue that holds us all together. And because of that, he carries a lot on his shoulders. He's shy. Despite his stupid good looking face," Tyler said, turning to look at his friend then back to Jessica with an expression of disgust, "and the fact that he's got girls clamoring for his attention all the time, he's not really like Chad or Zach where he goes after what he wants."

"What are you trying to say?"

"I'm saying that, last night when he saw you with that other guy, he was pissed."

Jessica shuddered at the memory of Joe, of letting him put his hands all over her...before he found someone better.

"Yeah," Tyler said, catching her reaction to the mention of last night. "That's pretty much how he felt. And I told him that here, on vacation where no one knows us, we have the opportunity to be different people than we are at home. To let loose."

"And that's what this is?" Jessica asked, dubious, gesturing at

Jack.

Tyler snorted. "Not exactly what I had in mind, but yeah."

"You stay here," Jessica said firmly, rising and moving to stand in front of Jack. "I'll get this one home."

"Are you sure?" Tyler asked. "He's...heavy."

"I'm sure," she said. "You go inside, have a good night. Go down that waterslide. Be a different guy."

"Let me at least get you a cab," he said, not waiting for a response before he moved toward the road and flagged down a speeding taxi. Then he helped Jessica load Jack into the car, and as he hurried inside, Jessica called after him.

He screeched to a halt and turned to her again, expectant.

"Don't be too different," she said. "Don't become someone completely new."

"I won't, Jess," he said, then nodded. "Take good care of my boy."

"I will."

As the cab driver pulled away from the curb, talking in rapid-fire Spanish that even Jessica's passable fluence in the language couldn't decipher, Jack leaned away from the door and fell across her lap.

She brushed his hair away from his forehead, and he gave her a soft smile, like a little boy being comforted by his mother when he's half asleep.

"Hey Jess?" he said, words hushed and slow.

"Yeah?"

"I'm sorry I ruined your night."

The corners of her lips tipped up. "You didn't."

"I did!" he whined, heaving himself upright, then gripping his head. "Oh fuck," he said. "The room is spinning. Why are we moving?"

"We're in a car," she reminded him gently.

"Right," he said, throwing himself back against the seat hard enough that the tiny car actually shook with the force of it.

"Are you gonna make it?" she asked. The last thing they needed was Jack hurling all over the inside of this cab and having to pay cleaning fees.

"This is our song," he said, ignoring her question.

"This is...what?" she asked, confused by the abrupt shift in conversation.

Jack didn't respond; he simply hummed along to the faint notes filtering through the speakers. And she realized...

"'Wonderwall.'"

Jack reached up and clumsily booped her nose. "Because you're gonna be the one who saves me."

"From yourself?"

"Yes," Jack said, smile unfurling slowly.

"Well, you certainly needed it tonight."

"Different person," he said, as if that explained everything.

Jessica sighed heavily through her nose. "I never want to hear that phrase again as long as I live."

"Whatever you want, sunshine," Jack said sleepily, and she pinched his arm to force him awake. "Whatever you want, I'll give it to you."

Throat thick with emotion, she whispered, "We don't even know each other."

"Doesn't matter," he mumbled. "My life changed the moment I laid eyes on you."

"How can you know that?"

One of his shoulders lifted in a half-hearted shrug. "Just do."

With that, his eyes closed and stayed that way, his breath evening out, and Jessica could do nothing but sift her fingers through his silky hair, thinking that, maybe, he was right.

The cab driver pulled up to the end of the long drive leading to the resort and, in broken English, said, "I leave you here."

"Right," Jessica groaned, then turned to her companion. "Jack."

"Yeah, sunshine?" he asked, voice a breathy whisper.

She smiled, reaching out to brush some of his floppy hair out of his eyes. "We have to get out and go inside now."

"Mmmmno," he said, lips curving down as he burrowed deeper into the seat.

"Jack," she said, pulling on his arm, but yanking on him was like trying to move an impossibly heavy statue.

"No!" he said, more forcefully this time.

She leaned closer, until her lips were a hair's breadth away from his ear. "I'll give you a blow job upstairs," she whispered.

He shot upright and reached for the door handle, his alcohol-addled brain fumbling his movements.

With a smirk, she reached past him and pushed the door open, unceremoniously pushing him out. Jack landed in a heap on the concrete, Jessica scrambled after him, and the cabbie took off before she'd even fully closed the door behind them.

"C'mon, big guy," she said, kneeling and hauling one of his arms across her shoulders. "Let's get you upstairs."

Unsteadily, Jack got his feet under him and rose, using Jessica as a crutch.

This wasn't how she'd imagined her night—or vacation—going, but she figured there were worse ways to spend her time than with a ridiculously good looking guy draped over her, even if he was drunk as hell.

The trip up to Jack's room was slow and laborious, and they received more than a few questioning, dirty, and openly judgemental looks as they trudged through the lobby. The stairs were the trickiest part to navigate, but Jack seemed to regain some control of his motor skills, and he used the railing as well as Jessica to aid his ascent.

"What's your room number?" Jessica asked. Past knowing it was on the third floor, she was walking blind here.

"Uhh..." Jack's eyes and forehead crinkled as he screwed up his face in concentration. "Three-four-seven," he said finally.

Room 347 happened to be at the opposite end of the long hall, about a hundred feet from where they'd entered. With a world-weary sigh, Jessica started walking, Jack's weight growing heavier and heavier by the second.

When they finally reached his room—and he shuffled in his pockets for his key so long that Jessica was certain he didn't have it—they let themselves in.

Unsurprisingly, the room was a disaster. Clothes were strewn haphazardly across the entirety of the floor, and Jessica gave zero fucks about whether they were clean or not as she trudged over them.

"Which bed is yours?"

"Window," Jack said.

Of course.

Thankfully, the room wasn't all that big, and she made quick work of the distance between them and the bed. Jack dumped himself on it without fanfare, flipping onto his back and peering at her through heavily lidded eyes.

"So how about that blow job," he said with a lazy smirk, his hands moving to his fly.

"In your dreams."

"But you said..." He tried to sit up several times, failing miserably with each new attempt until he finally gave up, throwing his arm over his face.

"That was just to get you out of that cab," she said. "My work here is done."

She turned to go, wondering if she should go to bed, or try to head back out and meet Bethani and the rest of Jack's friends, but Jack mumbling "sunshine" stalled her.

"Yeah?" she asked, moving to his bedside.

"Thank you."

She softened, bending to plant a lingering kiss on his forehead. "Good night, Jack."

"Good night," he said, then turned onto his side and promptly passed out.

Again, she moved to leave, but stilled once more.

She wasn't going back out, and she wasn't going back to her room without Bethani. That would invite too many questions from their moms. So she shot Bethani a text—thankful they'd splurged on the international data plan for this trip—telling her where she'd be when they returned to the resort.

Then, she crawled onto the bed and curled up next to Jack, once again draping his big, heavy arm over her body, its comforting weight and the way he nuzzled her hair before settling again lulling her to sleep.

lulling her to sleep.

Jessica

NOW: October 13, 2023

"ARE YOU SURE YOU need me to go with you?" Jessica asked.

Seeing as they were already halfway to Munn, the ship for getting out of this little excursion had already sailed, but still...she tried.

"Yes!" Kenzie said, clearly exasperated by Jessica's reluctance. "Now stop asking. I promise, you're going to have a blast. Hockey games are the best."

Jessica didn't share her siblings' obsession with the sport, and found it difficult to get excited about sitting in a freezing arena watching grown men chase after a tiny piece of rubber.

And the fact that Jack would be playing did little to lighten her dark mood.

Unbidden, her cheeks heated at the memory of last weekend after the football game, when she'd destroyed his t-shirt with her snot and tears. But Jack had seemed unbothered; he simply held her until she calmed. She'd apologized profusely, but he'd waved it off, telling her it really wasn't a big deal.

"Even when you're a crying mess, you look amazing," Jack had said, reaching up to tuck an errant lock of blonde hair behind her ear.

"I have a boyfriend," she blurted, stepping away from him.

Jack cocked his head to the side, brows drawing together. "Okay?"

"I'm just telling you. The deal...it's not happening, Jack."

"I didn't say a word about the deal, Jessica."

Her name on his lips lacked all the warmth he'd used minutes ago for her nickname, and Jessica felt that chill settle on her bones. Good, *she thought.* The sooner we draw boundaries, the better.

"I'm just letting you know."

"Well, good. Thanks for that." He shoved his hands into his pockets and nodded his head in the direction he'd been walking. "I'm just...gonna go."

"Right, sure," she said, moving to the right side of the path so he could pass her.

She walked away without looking back, gripping the hair at her temples in her hands and pulling. What the fuck, Daniels?

"Hey, Jess?"

Fuck.

Slowly, she turned toward Jack again, and each time she looked at him, even though this was only the third time since he'd walked back into her life, it became harder and harder to tear her gaze away. He'd always been beautiful, but these past three years had turned him into the kind of man dreams were made of.

"Yeah?" she croaked.

"It's good to see you." One corner of his mouth tipped up in a

half-smile, then he turned and walked away.

"Do you want my number?" she blurted at his retreating form.

Jack stopped so quickly his shoes scuffed along the path, and he threw his arms out for balance.

And...what the fuck, Jessica? What in the fresh hell possessed you to ask him that?

This was a mistake, and she couldn't take it back.

She'd never thought clearly with him around. The combination of Jack's reappearance in her life and her fight with Silas had her mind spinning in a million directions but...

Kenzie and Aiden were completely gone for each other. She'd just texted Jessica and some Sofia girl a bit ago, freaking out because Aiden finally asked her out on a real date. Those two were finally going to stop dancing around each other, and Jessica couldn't be happier for her. Kenzie was one of Jessica's best friends, and Jack was one of Aiden's. The way Jessica saw it, the chances that she and Jack would be spending some time together were high, whether she liked it or not.

Level-Headed Jessica decidedly did not, but Hopeless Romantic Jessica was jumping for joy.

Jack started toward her, stopping in front of her.

"Are you sure?" he asked. "You kinda just made a big deal out of telling me you have a boyfriend..."

"I..." She trailed off. She knew she should rescind the offer, but...she didn't want to. Maybe that made her a bad person, but fuck it. It was only a phone number, right? That didn't mean he'd use it, or that she had to respond if he did. "Yes, I'm sure," she said finally.

Jack's grin was tentative as he turned back to Jessica and, with shaky fingers, she punched her number in, fighting the urge to text herself from his phone.

Jack had no such compunction, and a moment later, her phone dinged in her pocket.

"Now you have mine, too," he said, then winked and took off into the night.

Now, walking the same path she'd taken that night—only in reverse—Jessica groaned.

"What is your damage?" Kenzie asked. "Does this have anything to do with a certain big, sexy goalie?"

"Can you even call him sexy?" Jessica asked. "Isn't that against some sort of bro code?"

Kenzie gave Jessica a criminally offensive side-eye and said, "I suppose it would be if I were a *bro*. But I'm not, so it's not really an issue. Plus," she added, craning her neck to glance around the groups of people making their way to Munn's various entrances, "it's not like Aiden is around to hear me. And I don't hear you denying that Jack DeLuca is sexy."

"He's not," she said, the lie weak to her own ears.

Kenzie leveled her with a blue-eyed glare, reminding Jessica so much of Kenzie's brother in that moment that she nearly burst out laughing. "Get real."

"Okay, fiiiiiiine," Jessica conceded. "He's...arguably the best looking guy I've ever laid eyes on."

"HA!" Kenzie shouted, and several heads swiveled their way. "I knew you had a thing for him."

"I don't have a *thing*," Jessica protested. Although...nope. Not going there.

"You totally do," Kenzie said, grinning widely. "There's clearly something there. The way you guys looked at each other at that tailgate..."

Jessica winced then quickly schooled her features into indifference, but Kenzie caught her regardless.

"Fess up, Daniels."

"Okay, fine! Jack and I know each other."

"How?"

"We met in Mexico on spring break our senior year of high school."

"Oooooooh," Kenzie crooned. "A vacationship. I love it. What happened?"

"We had fun for a week, then the vacation bubble burst, we didn't stay in touch, the end."

"*Fun*, huh?" Kenzie asked with a suggestive eyebrow wiggle. "What kind?"

"Not *that* kind of fun, you perv," Jessica said with a laugh, shoving Kenzie away.

This time, Kenzie didn't catch the untruth.

"I'm missing something here," Kenzie said, turning to face Jessica in the queue to enter Munn, eyes narrowed and searching Jessica's face.

"You're not missing anything."

Kenzie's gaze narrowed further, but then the arena attendant was scanning their tickets and they were breezing through the door, and Kenzie's attention turned to the atrium above them, seeking out her brother's name.

Over the years, Jessica had gotten very good at lying about how much Jack DeLuca really meant to her, and it would take a lot more than Mackenzie Jean's prying to break her.

"Aiden is such a shit," Kenzie said, though the smile on her face belied her words.

"What'd he do this time?"

"He's up in the press box," Kenzie said, nodding to the boxes hanging over the rows of seats opposite the arena from them.

When they looked up, Aiden waved happily.

"What the hell is he doing up there?"

"I guess he's about to join the radio broadcast," Kenzie said, blowing out a puff of air. "He better hope Coach doesn't find out. He's already in hot water with this suspension. It would kill him if it got extended."

Truthfully, Jessica didn't see why such a big deal had been made about a very attractive and well-built college athlete running around naked, but it wasn't her call to make.

"I'm sure it'll be fine," Jessica told her honestly. Aiden was hardly getting himself in trouble by hanging out in the press box.

"Right, yeah," Kenzie said, though she didn't sound convinced.

There were still several minutes until the game started, so Jessica took the opportunity to inspect the arena. From the outside, Munn looked like a spaceship—low slung and grey—but inside, it was surprisingly spacious. The rafters were laden with banners, the walls carefully detailing the history of the program and every coach and player who had come through here. It wasn't the most modern, although the addition they'd made last year to the south entrance of the arena certainly updated it. Jessica could feel the history, and she understood why her brother-in-law, and now Jack and Aiden, had wanted to play here.

All at once, the arena darkened, and the sound system blasted to life as a hype video started playing on the jumbotron. The student section went wild with cheers, the band striking up a low but heavy bass beat as the soundtrack to player introductions. There was much fanfare, and when Jack's name was announced as the Spartans' starting goaltender, she'll admit—she cheered with the rest of them.

This was Jessica's first opportunity to watch Jack play and, at least in the first period, she wasn't disappointed. Despite his big body, he moved fluidly, faster than anyone his size had a right to, and seemed to have a radar for where the puck would be at any given moment. The Spartans were playing Princeton, and while the Tigers managed a couple of good looks, there wasn't a single instance during the first twenty minutes where Jack was truly tested.

And now Jessica wondered why she'd never taken to hockey like Berkley and Logan had.

It was fast and brutal, lethal and graceful, poetry on ice that could bloom into an all-out war at any moment.

At the end of the first period, Jessica turned to Kenzie, dazed. "That was…"

Kenzie smirked. "I know. Bet you're glad you came."

She really was.

By the time the final seconds ticked off the game clock—in a four to nothing victory for MSU—Jessica had found herself a new obsession. She was actually looking forward to getting home and telling Berkley all about it, demanding her sister teach her everything she needed to know immediately.

Or maybe she'd call Logan. Berkley was, after all, pregnant and had recently gone back to school; she had a lot on her plate. Her big brother, on the other hand, was free as a bird, and Jessica hadn't talked to him in a while, anyway.

In the end, she texted them both.

Attached to Logan's last text was a photo of him posing shirtless in front of a mirrored gym wall. Jessica squeezed her eyes shut and typed her response, giggling when she saw Berkley's text come through right before hers.

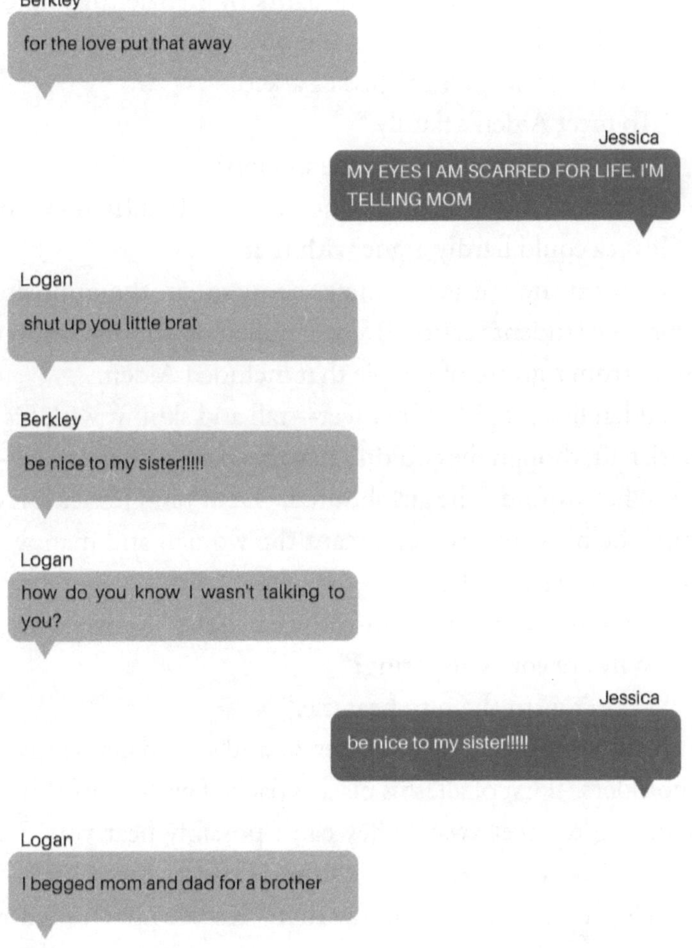

Jessica chuckled at her phone. Despite being so much younger than Logan and Berkley, Jessica loved how close the three of them were.

And, okay...Logan wasn't lying. Her big brother worked out

almost as much as Brent, and it showed. They just loved to tease him.

She was jarred from her thoughts by Kenzie tugging on her arm, pulling her up the stairs and onto the concourse.

"Where are we going?" Jessica asked.

"To meet Aiden's family."

"Why exactly is this a two person job?"

"Because I'm a little bitch who needs my best friend with me."

Jessica could hardly argue with that.

Around the corner of the concourse, on the opposite side from the student section, Kenzie pulled up short about ten feet away from a group of people that included Aiden.

Aiden lifted a girl off her feet—tall and skinny, with his same dark hair, though she couldn't have been more than twelve—and spun her around. The girl shouted, "Den!" and Jessica knew this must be his sister. Which meant the woman and man were his mother and stepfather.

"Do I just walk up and introduce myself?" Kenzie whispered.

"Why are you whispering?"

"I don't want them to hear me."

Jessica stepped in front of Kenzie and settled her hands on her shoulders. "First of all, this place is packed with people and we're standing ten feet away. They can't possibly hear you. Second, you're Mackenzie Jean. Little sister of badass Brent Jean—"

"Don't let him hear you say that," Kenzie interrupted with a snort.

"—and business owner. You are a boss bitch. You're smart, funny, unfailingly loyal, incredibly kind, and one of the most beautiful people I know, inside and out. His family is going to adore you."

"Okay," Kenzie said, taking a step in Aiden's direction, then immediately whirling on her heel. "No, nope, can't do it, let's go."

Kenzie's hand was a vise grip on Jessica's arm, and Jessica tried to pull her to a stop, trying to make her see reason, but Jessica could see it in her eyes: this was a flight or fight response, and *flight* was winning.

Until Aiden yelled, "Bunny!" and rushed up to them. "Where do you think you're going?" he asked.

"You were busy with your family," Kenzie said quietly, and Jessica wanted to slap her. "I didn't want to intrude. Jess and I were going to say hi and go get dinner."

They hadn't been about to do either of those things, but Jessica wasn't about to throw her under the bus.

"Trust me, you were not intruding. I was hoping you'd come to dinner with us, actually."

Kenzie turned a pleading gaze on Jessica, and Jessica gave her a subtle shake of the head in return. She wasn't saving Kenzie from this one.

"Are you sure that's a good idea?" Kenzie asked, and again...Jessica wanted to slap her.

Jessica tuned out the rest of their hushed conversation, of Aiden's placations and Kenzie's counter-arguments. She was in limbo, unsure if she should feed her friend to the wolves and take off, or hang out in case Kenzie needed her.

But Jessica drew the line at standing by like a pervert while Aiden and Kenzie made out a foot away from her, so she said, "And this is where I take my leave," and booked it.

In order to get home, the best place to exit was the west entrance, which was on the opposite side of the arena, so Jessica started in that direction. Halfway there, she was stalled by the video screen at the south entrance that featured a running slideshow of the current roster. It sorted through the players numerically, and Jessica knew Jack's number was in the thirties, so she stood and waited, watching as a few faces she recognized—including Aiden—came and went before Jack finally appeared.

The team had worn their white jerseys for picture day, and Jack stood in front of the net in a white sweater, all-white pads with slashes of dark green across them, a matching green goalie mask with the Gruff Sparty logo tucked under his arm. His face was void of the usual warmth Jessica had come to expect from him, and he looked every bit the brick wall she'd seen him be in net tonight.

"Good looking dude."

Jessica jumped, her hand flying to her throat where her heart currently lodged when she spun to find Jack standing behind her.

She swallowed thickly and said, "Yeah, he's alright."

Jack smirked. "Did you enjoy the game?"

"Yes," she breathed, unable to contain her excitement over this new thing she'd discovered. "It was...beautiful."

"It's the best thing in the world," Jack agreed.

"I immediately texted my brother and sister and yelled at them for not forcing me to like it sooner."

Jack threw his head back and laughed. "I did tell you Berkley sounded more like my kinda girl," he said with a wink.

Jessica's cheeks heated, remembering that conversation, that night, and everything that came after.

The silence thickened, and Jack cleared his throat, realizing his misstep. "Where's bunny?"

Jessica hooked a thumb over her shoulder. "Meeting the fam. And I can't believe she lets you guys call her that."

Jack chuckled. "It started as a joke, as I'm sure you know, and we would've stopped if she made more of a fuss about it. But I really don't think she minds."

Jessica considered that and realized he was right. Kenzie wouldn't allow it to continue if she wasn't okay with it. The nickname on her was ironic, like calling Jack "tiny" would be.

Jack turned his head, zeroing in on Kenzie, Aiden, and Aiden's family, smiling knowingly. "They're good together."

"They are," she agreed. "I'm just glad Kenzie finally pulled her head out of her ass."

"Me, too," Jack said. "I was getting sick of Aiden whining."

"I'll bet," Jessica said. "Well, I'm gonna head home."

"Which way you headed?" She pointed at the west entrance, and Jack nodded. "I'll walk with you."

"Oh, no, you don't have to do that," she said.

"It's fine, Jess. My moped is out there, anyway."

And how could she argue with that?

The silence between them was oppressive as they walked toward the doors, and the moment they pushed through, Jessica gulped down the cool night air like she'd been without oxygen for days, thankful for the refresh it brought to her senses, for the way it cleared her mind.

"Jess?" someone asked, and Jessica turned to Jack, confused.

"Wasn't me," he said.

"Jess!"

She spun to her left and found Silas walking toward her, a beautiful dark-skinned girl at his side.

"Jack!" the girl squealed, then threw herself into his arms.

Wait, what?

"You guys know each other?" Jack asked Silas when he'd returned the girl to her feet.

"Who, me and Jess?" Silas asked, stepping forward to sling an arm over Jessica's shoulders. "Yeah, she's my girlfriend."

"What?" Jack asked, incredulous.

"Yeah, babe," the girl said to Jack. "I told you Silas has a girlfriend."

"Yeah, but I didn't...think it was Jessica."

Somehow, Jessica knew that wasn't what he'd been about to say, and the gears in her mind spun. But then the girl looked at her and extended her hand.

"Sofia."

"Wait, *you're* Sofia?" Jessica asked. This world was too damn small, and shrinking further by the moment. "Like...Kenzie's friend?"

The girl cocked her head to the side, her black hair cascading across a bare ebony shoulder. "You know Kenzie?"

"I'm her sister...sort of. My sister is married to her brother."

"Oh my God," Sofia said. "You're Jessica from the text messages!"

"Yes!" Jessica said. "And you're Jack's...?"

"We're just hanging out," Sofia said quickly, cutting an unreadable look at Silas.

And, okay, this was getting weirder by the second.

"Wait," Silas cut in, finally catching on to the one thing Jessica desperately hoped he wouldn't. "You two know each other?" He darted a finger between Jack and Jessica.

"Uhh, yeah, sorta," Jessica said, silently pleading Jack to play along. She didn't need another fight with Silas. Not here. And *not* about this.

"We uhh...we know each other through Kenzie and Aiden," Jack said quickly, and Jessica didn't miss the hurt that flashed across his face, so quick she was certain both Sofia and Silas missed it in the dim exterior lights of the arena. She didn't like lying any more than he did, but it was for the best—for all of them.

"This is so freaking weird," Sofia said. "We should go get a drink. Seems like we all kinda know each other anyway, so let's hang out!"

"We're down!" Silas said, tugging Jessica further into side and planting a kiss atop her head.

Jessica and Jack shared another look, so many things passing unspoken between them. There was no way out of this, not without explaining things that were better left unsaid, and they both knew it.

"Sure," Jack finally said.

Sofia squealed in excitement, and dread settled heavily in Jessica's stomach.

Jack

NOW: October 13, 2023

We should go get a drink!

Sure.

He fucking hated himself.

Getting a drink with Sofia would've been fine.

Getting a drink with Sofia *and* Silas would've been torture, but he would've endured, knowing he was the one Sofia was going home with tonight.

But getting a drink with Sofia, Silas, *and* Jessica, knowing Jessica was Silas's girlfriend? Knowing Jessica was with this tool, who obviously didn't treat her the way she deserved to be treated if Jack hadn't even thought she existed? *That* was the very definition of hell.

He needed to get drunk, and fast.

"Where do we want to go? Jessica asked.

Home, Jack thought. *Away from this nightmare.*

"How about LouHa's?" Sofia suggested, and Jack silently thanked her.

LouHa's—or Lou & Harry's as it was actually called—would be a lowkey environment that wouldn't force them into some corner booth in a crowded bar, where they'd have to get all up close and personal. They could spread out, speak normally, and relax.

They also had an incredible Greek menu, and after playing a game, Jack was ravenous.

So they set off in the direction of Grand River, and the bars beyond, Sofia and Jessica talking animatedly about some group text they're in with Kenzie, and how hilarious it was to end up meeting like this.

Internally, Jack seethed, his skin tightening uncomfortably the longer they walked and the more time he had to stew in his thoughts over tonight's turn of events.

Finally, he said, "So, Jess, how long have you and Silas been together?"

"Almost three years," Silas answered before Jessica could even open her mouth, an action that did nothing to quell Jack's rising temper.

Everything about Silas screamed "douche" to Jack. The way his dark hair was "artfully" tousled and run through with some foul-smelling pomade. How he possessively draped his arm over Jessica's shoulders, forcing her to walk in lock step with him instead of giving her space to move freely. The fact that Silas had never, at any point in the last two months since Sofia had brought him into Jack's life, mentioned Jessica's name, or even the fact that he was in a very long term relationship.

Jack hated that for Jessica, who deserved to have the world laid at her feet like the goddess she was.

And...okay. That line of thinking would get Jack in all sorts of trouble. Jessica wasn't his to worry about, to fawn over, or to want better for. She had only *just* come back into his life, and he was happy with Sofia. He thought there was something *more* between them, something that could go the distance if they played their cards right.

Jack wanted that—wanted what, even in the extremely early stages of their relationship, he knew Aiden and Kenzie were building. Sofia got along great with his teammates—when she spent time with them—and had formed a fast friendship with Kenzie. They had fun together, never ran out of things to talk or laugh about, and the sex was phenomenal.

But more than that, Jack felt like he could be himself around Sofia. He didn't have to pretend to be this big, bad, playboy, ladies' man on campus like some of his teammates or other athletes did. He could simply *be*: quiet on occasion, reserved when he wanted to be, mellow, always watching, analyzing, offering commentary or advice when the situation warranted it.

And okay, maybe he could be a bit of a shit-stirrer. After all, his dare was the reason Aiden had been suspended for eight games. But it was all in good fun, and because he took hockey so damn seriously, he had to pick and choose his moments to let loose.

Sometimes they just...backfired.

"How long have you two been together?" Jessica asked Sofia, pulling Jack from his thoughts.

"Oh not long," Sofia said, turning a sly smile on him. "We met during Welcome Weekend."

"Isn't that when Kenzie and Aiden met?" Jessica asked.

"Yep," Jack said. "At Rick's."

"Rick's? During Welcome Weekend?" Jessica asked, her forehead scrunching in confusion. "Are you sure?"

"Yes," Jack said. "I was there. I'm sort of the reason she ran away from him in the first place. I guess she saw the MSU hockey hat I was wearing and booked it."

"Okay," Jessica said slowly. "It's just…I was there that night."

To Silas and Sofia, this comment probably seemed innocent. Like, ha ha, isn't it funny that we could've met that night instead of right now?

But Jack's entire body broke into a cold sweat at the implication.

Kenzie and Aiden had met on Friday of that weekend.

Jack had met Sofia the next night.

His mind spun.

Rick's was not a big place, and it would've been so easy to find Jessica, to reconnect that night, before Sofia had ever come into the picture.

If only Jack hadn't been so drunk…

No. He shook that thought off. He couldn't go back and change anything, and there was still the matter of Silas. Even if he and Jessica had reconnected that night instead of last weekend, even if there were no Sofia, Jessica would still be in a relationship, and even if he didn't like the way it looked from the outside, she had to be happy. Otherwise she wouldn't stay…right?

Jessica didn't strike Jack as the type of girl who stuck with a guy who wasn't treating her well.

They finally arrived at LouHa's, and the moment they were

seated, Jack ordered his drink before his companions even had a chance to lift the menus from the table. He'd been here enough times to know what he wanted—he'd sampled everything—and tonight was a bourbon kind of night.

"Manhattan, please," he said to the waitress.

She simply nodded, then turned her attention to the other three. Sofia and Jessica got margaritas—mango jalapeño for Sofia, cucumber mint for Jessica—and Silas ordered a Tito's and Red Bull.

Soft, Jack couldn't help but think.

When their drinks arrived and food had been ordered, Jack dove into his Manhattan with gusto, but when he'd downed nearly half in a single gulp, he forced himself to slow and not drown himself in it.

And then his eyes rose, locking on Jessica at the exact moment her tongue darted out to scoop some salt off the rim of her glass before she sipped her drink.

As if she sensed his stare, her eyes flitted to his, their gazes holding.

They seemed to be doing a lot of that lately.

Instantly, Jack was transported back to the night they met. Tequila burning his throat, licking salt from her skin, the way her fingertips had brushed his lips when she shoved a lime wedge between his teeth.

The kiss that followed, and how tasting the liquor on her tongue had been the most addicting thing he'd ever experienced.

Tearing his eyes away, he scooted closer to Sofia, and her hand found his beneath the table—grounding him, anchoring him to this moment, with her.

Not the blonde across the table, whose boyfriend was wiping a stray drop of liquid from her top lip.

Jack was so royally fucked. He never should've agreed to this. His mind was a jumbled mess, and he wasn't sure how he was supposed to survive until the end of the meal. If his stomach wasn't screaming in protest over not being fed in hours, he'd get up and leave right now, damn the consequences. Uncomfortable, he tugged on the collar of his shirt, thankful he'd left his tie and suit jacket in his locker at the rink.

Silas and Sofia carried on a conversation revolving around some Greek thing that Jack tuned out. Neither of them seemed to notice the tension between him and Jessica.

And the thing was…he didn't want there to be any tension. He wanted nights like this, where he and his girl could go out with friends. He wanted his attention solely focused on Sofia, not split between *wanting* it to be on Sofia and trying to keep it off Jessica.

He was a fucking mess, and this night couldn't end sooner.

"So what's your plan after college?" Silas asked Jack. "Got any interest from pro teams?"

Jack was saved from answering right away by the massive swallow of his drink he'd just taken, but Sofia answered for him. "Tons!" she said brightly. "He's definitely going to play in the NHL, and I'll be there to cheer him on."

Surprised, Jack angled his head to look at her. They'd only been together a few months—and not really even *together* in the committed, defined-the-relationship sense of the word—so they'd certainly never discussed what the future held for them. But the excited glint in her eyes and the sincerity on her face made Jack *want* to have that conversation—made him want Sofia in his future.

Even if she'd just lied to Silas.

Jack had an agent, and certainly had plans to play professionally after college, but that didn't mean he'd be jumping to the pros right away. It was too early in the season, for starters, and he wasn't the kind of guy who counted his chickens before they hatched. His agent had received exploratory calls from scouts regarding Jack and his career—that much was true. But they were mainly ECHL teams, two levels below the NHL. Which wasn't a bad thing. Plenty of guys got their start on one of the farm teams before moving up, and Jack would be happy playing anywhere as long as he got to keep playing. The NHL was the dream, as it was for any high-level hockey player in the world, but Jack also knew making it to the show was hard work. His talent on collegiate ice didn't necessarily translate to that level, and he had his head on straight where the trajectory of his career was concerned.

"Yeah," Jack said finally—dumbly. "I've had some interest, but the season only just started, so I've got a long way to go before I can even talk to teams."

"Well what's your agent say? Like what are your chances?"

Silas's tone had Jack's hackles raising. He didn't like the implication in it, like his choices weren't great.

"I'll most likely start off in the EC or the A," he said, referring to the ECHL and AHL. "So I'll still be playing professionally."

"But not in the NHL," Silas said smugly. Jack didn't miss Jessica driving her elbow into his side. A little grunt was the only indication Silas gave that it pained him, and Jack didn't like the tense, close-lipped glare he turned on Jessica.

Stop it, DeLuca. She's not yours to protect.

Thankfully, Sofia unwittingly came to his rescue.

"It's so funny that you and Silas have been together so long and we've never met before," Sofia said. "Silas is like...my best guy friend."

"Really?" Jessica said, cutting her eyes to Silas before leaning forward, balancing her elbow on the table and resting her chin in her hand. "How long have you guys known each other?"

"We met freshman year!" Sofia said. "During rush week."

Jack knew this already, but Jessica's eyes widened.

"Wow," Jessica said. "You've known each other longer than we have."

"Really?"

"Yeah," Jessica said, swallowing hard and nodding. "We met at the campout that fall."

"It's really so strange we've never met before now!" Sofia said, either completely oblivious to how fucked up that was or willingly acting like it wasn't a big deal.

Anger prodded Jack's chest, threatening to climb up his throat and out his mouth. Silas, the little weasel, was playing both of them. He didn't know what he had to gain from it, since, as far as Jack knew, he'd never made a move on Sofia. But Jack did know he had to work *hard* to keep these women from meeting all these years, had to deliberately separate those parts of his life.

Jack opened his mouth to say something, to pin Silas to the table with whatever sharp words he chose to wield, but their food arrived then, saving them all. Once again, he had to remind himself that it wasn't his place to intervene on Jessica's behalf. There was obviously a lot about their relationship he didn't—and never would—understand, and it had to stay that way.

He could, however, say something to Sofia, because that *was* his place, and he made a note to do so once they left this cursed double date.

The rest of dinner passed without incident, though Jack rarely spoke, and Sofia took notice.

"What is wrong with you?" she asked when they were alone and walking in the direction of their houses.

Jack and his roommates lived a few blocks away from the bars, and beyond that were several sorority houses, Sofia's included.

That had absolutely nothing to do with why they'd signed the lease two years ago—and continued to renew it since.

"Nothing," Jack said. "Just...sore."

It was a weak lie, and Sofia called him on it.

"You're not *sore*," she said. "You were an absolute ass to Silas, and you were incredibly weird around his girlfriend!"

"I was not weird."

"You were," she protested. "You kept staring at her like she was some alien being instead of a human. What the fuck, Jack? She's a sweet girl, and you didn't make a very good first impression."

Jack nearly laughed at that. Unwittingly, Sofia had hit the nail on the head—although this wasn't the first time Jack and Jessica had met. Still, he had been weird, but he didn't know how to explain why without divulging his entire history with Jessica. And if Jessica hadn't shared it with Silas in the entire three years they'd been together, he wasn't about to unload on this girl who, in comparison, he hardly knew.

Their time together was their secret, trapped forever in that

Cancún bubble, a one perfect week in time.

"I'm sorry," he said. "I just don't like Silas, and I guess I acted weird around his girl because I don't understand how someone like her is with someone like him."

There, that seemed plausible enough, right?

Sofia blew out an exasperated sigh, but didn't fight him. "I know you don't like Silas," she said. "Which I still don't understand. But don't take it out on Jessica."

"Fair enough." And for good measure, he added, "For the record, I don't like Silas because he's obviously into you, and takes every opportunity to make me look bad in front of you. And I know we haven't been doing...this"—he gestured between them—"long, but you're with me, Sofia. Not him."

She rolled her eyes. "Your possessiveness isn't cute, Jack. Silas is not into me. We're friends. *Best* friends. And you're going to have to get used to him. He's not going anywhere."

And that right there was the problem. Silas *wasn't* going anywhere. It irritated Jack that Sofia either willfully ignored Silas's obvious feelings for her, or was truly that delusional...and he didn't think it was the latter.

Jack didn't know where that left him.

The weekend after their disastrous double date with Jessica and Silas, Jack and the Spartans were headed on a road trip.

Since that night, he hadn't heard a peep from Sofia. Normally, he wouldn't think anything of it—she was busy, he was busy, these lulls in relationships happened, right? But had it been any time but on the heels of that double date, and her calling him out for being an ass to Silas and weird with Jessica…well, the timing was a little too convenient.

So Wednesday night, before they were set to leave the next day, Jack called her.

"Hello?" she said when she answered.

"Uhh, hey, Sofia. It's Jack."

"Oh, hey," she said, and Jack couldn't put his finger on whether she was distracted or simply didn't want to talk to him.

"Look," he said. "I haven't heard from you in like a week, and me and the boys are on the road this weekend, so do you want to come over? Hang out for a bit before I leave?"

The line was silent long enough that Jack pulled the phone away from his ear to make sure she hadn't hung up on him. At last, she said, "Yeah, I'll be over in a bit."

"Great!" Jack said, mood brightening. "I'll be in my room, so just come up when you get here."

"Will do," she said, then hung up.

Fifteen minutes later, Sofia walked into his room. Normally, she'd immediately kick her shoes off, drop her purse unceremoniously on the floor, and crawl into bed with him.

Today, she did none of those things. Instead, she remained near the door—which she left open—arms crossed over her chest, looking for all the world like she'd never been here before, or like she'd rather be anywhere *but* here.

Jack was instantly on edge.

"What's wrong?" he asked, scooting to the edge of his bed and reaching for her, but she stepped away.

"We need to talk. Actually, I need to talk, and I need you to listen."

"Okay..."

"I'm sorry I've been distant this past week," she started. "It wasn't fair to you for me to go radio silent on you. For that, I apologize."

"It's okay, sweets," he said, but she held up her finger to silence him from speaking further.

"I've always known Silas has a girlfriend," she said. "I mean, I was with him the night they met—afterward. He told me all about her. This beautiful blonde girl who seemed so sweet but also didn't seem like she was all that impressed by him. 'She's fascinating,' he'd said. At that point, I...I didn't feel like I do now."

Jack's heart rose into his throat.

He'd fucking known it. All along, he'd known there was something between her and Silas. He just hadn't expected those feelings he thought were coming from Silas to really be coming from her.

"Silas and I have spent a lot of time together over the years, at various Greek functions, but also just...hanging out. Grabbing dinner on campus together. Texting anytime we weren't together. And slowly, without me ever really realizing it, I fell for him."

"Why are you telling me this now?"

"I'm getting to that," she said, then pulled out his desk chair and dropped onto it. "I've spent the last few years hanging out with her boyfriend behind her back, knowing full well he never mentioned to her just how close he and I are, still jealous of her. And that makes me a really shitty person. When I met her last weekend, and then you accused Silas of having feelings for me...I guess the blinders were lifted. Jessica is such a sweet girl, and I'll be limiting time spent with Silas from here on out. And it's not fair to either of us"—she waved her hand between them—"to stay together, to keep trying to make whatever this is work, if my heart is somewhere else."

Jack was momentarily dumbfounded. He felt vindicated that he'd been right—sort of—but also dejected over the loss of this relationship he'd really wanted to work. And his heart broke a little bit for Jessica, who was in a long-term relationship with a guy who had walked around keeping this whole other important relationship from her.

The whole thing was messy, and Jack was secretly happy to be free from the drama.

Although…if Jessica was involved, was he truly free?

It appeared, to some degree, he still had skin in the game.

Numbly, all Jack could do was nod, not trusting himself to start spewing words he couldn't take back at Sofia—words that had nothing to do with her and everything to do with Jessica.

That wasn't his problem to solve.

Later that night, after Sofia had left with an awkward hug and kiss to his cheek, Jack laid in bed, watching his ceiling fan endlessly spin while he tried and failed to sleep. Like the fan, his mind swirled with thoughts of Sofia and Silas, of him and Jessica.

An idea struck him, and he knew it was a bad idea, knew it would probably cause more harm than good, but he couldn't help himself. Rolling over, he reached for his phone and typed out four words, hitting send before he could think twice.

It was nearly two in the morning, so Jack wasn't expecting a response. Still, he felt lighter for having gotten it off his chest—light enough that he could finally drift off to sleep.

He was toeing the line, one foot in unconsciousness, one foot out, when his phone pinged.

Jack

THEN: April 7, 2020

"Well, isn't this cozy."

Jack bolted upright in bed, earning a groan from the body curled up at his side.

His half-drunk, sleep-addled brain didn't know where to look first, so his eyes darted between the guy hulking over him and the girl lying next to him.

"Jess?" Jack said, blinking rapidly, ignoring his friends altogether.

"What time is it?" she grumbled as she sat up.

"Just after three," Bethani said.

"What are you doing here?" Jack asked Jessica.

Jessica blinked slowly. "You were really drunk. I wanted to make sure you were okay."

"How did we get here?"

"I brought you back," she said, nose scrunching in the cutest way.

"*You* brought me back? By yourself?"

"Yes?" she said, forehead wrinkling with her confusion. "You don't remember anything?"

Jack closed his eyes and dropped his head into his hands, willing his brain to conjure any memory of the evening. Unfortunately, nothing came to him.

It was like that "Last Night Gus" episode of *Psych* where Shawn's memory is broken. Only flashes of light and—inexplicably—the words to "Wonderwall" floated through his mind.

"The last thing I remember was dinner," he said.

"Where you got absolutely bombed," Tyler supplied for him. "So that makes sense."

"What did we do after that?"

"Well, we tried to take you to Señor Frogs," Chad said. "But you were literally too drunk to stand. This one"—he pointed at Jessica—"took it upon herself to take care of you and get you home safe. I would've, but..."

"But you're an asshole," Jack supplied good naturedly, and everyone laughed.

"Well, there's that, yes. But also we had to make sure Tyler accomplished what he set out to do."

"Which was?" Jack said, quirking an eyebrow. And *fuck*, he wish he remembered something, *anything*, from the night.

"The waterslide, man," Tyler reminded him. "You weren't even drunk for that conversation!"

"I'm sorry!" Jack said, stumbling off the bed to stand, his legs wobbling dangerously under him. "The whole night is just...fuzzy."

"I mean, you were pounding tequila shots like it was your job," Zach said. "Even after I vomited and you won our little game."

"What game?" At the thought of tequila, bile crawled up his throat, and he held up a hand before anyone could respond. "Actually, don't tell me. I don't want to know."

"I'm surprised you're even alive, bro," Chad said, dropping a heavy hand on Jack's shoulder. "Get some sleep and rally for tomorrow. I'm going to bed."

With that, he turned on his heel and left, Zach following behind.

"We're just gonna...give you two a second," Bethani said, gesturing between Jack and Jessica before shoving Tyler onto the balcony.

Jack sat down hard on the end of the bed, the mattress jostling as Jessica scooted up next to him. The moment she reached his side, he turned and drew her onto his lap.

"I'm sorry," he said, burying his face in her hair.

"Don't be sorry," she said, scratching her fingers lightly across the nape of his neck. "You're a teenager on vacation, Jack. It could've happened to any one of us."

He pulled away to look at her, surprised by the sincerity lining her features.

"Still, you didn't have to take care of me. You hardly know me."

"That may be true," she said, tipping her head down to avoid his gaze. "But..."

He tucked his finger under her chin and forced her to meet his eyes. "But?"

"It's going to sound crazy."

"Just tell me."

"I like you," she blurted. "A lot, somehow. I know it's only been like two days, and I can't really explain it, but...there's something here, isn't there?"

Jack raised his arm and pressed a hand to her chest, right over her heart. Goosebumps pebbled her skin, whether from the air conditioning in the room or his touch, he didn't know.

"There is," he agreed. "It doesn't make any sense at all, but I'm right here with you, Jess."

Swallowing hard, she nodded, then leaned forward to capture his mouth with hers.

The kiss was slow, tentative, a soft drag of her lips against his. Right as Jack slid his hand across her collarbone and around to cup the back of her neck, intending to deepen the kiss, a pounding on the sliding door broke them apart.

He rested his forehead against hers. "I love that guy, but he's about to get his ass beat."

Jessica laughed, the sound a warm blanket on a cold day, or a cool breeze on a hot one. He wanted to wrap himself in it, and he knew he'd do anything and everything to hear it again and again.

"Bethani and I should get back to our room anyway," Jessica said, pulling herself from his arms and rising to her feet. "You know, before our moms start to worry."

She moved to the balcony door and opened it, mumbling something to Bethani. A moment later, she and Tyler came inside, and Jack stood, opening his arms.

Jessica walked over and he folded them around her, crushing her to his chest. "I'll see you in the morning?"

She tilted her head back to look at him, and he dropped one

final kiss on her mouth. "Of course."

"Good night, Jess."

"Good night, Jack."

"I'm taking you on a proper date tonight," Jack said matter-of-factly the next morning.

"Oh?" Jessica said, playfully pushing away from him in the pool, splashing him as she swam toward the bar at the other end.

He caught up with her quickly, grabbing her heel and dragging her back into his body. She turned in the water and let him wrap her in an embrace, her legs hooking around his waist. He grabbed a handful of her ass, and their mouths crashed together, Jessica's tongue sweeping against his. She smiled against him when he groaned low in his throat.

This was dangerous territory, and Jack was glad his bottom half was hidden from view.

"Yes," he said against her mouth. "I have the whole thing planned."

"Really?" she said, pulling away quickly, eyes wide in shock. "What are we doing?"

"It's a surprise," he said, grinning when she swatted at him.

"That's not very nice. How am I supposed to know what to wear?"

"Hmm, that's a good point. Okay, I'll tell you this: we'll be outside."

"And what time will it be? Is this a day date? Night? Give me details!"

He'd prepared for this. "I need you to be ready by six, and dress nice."

"I always dress nice," she said with a smirk.

"Fair enough," Jack said. "Wear a dress. And wear your hair down. I love it when you wear your hair down." He brushed his fingers through the ends where they floated on the surface around her like a golden halo, soft even when drenched with chlorine.

He meant it, too, and her cheeks blushed beneath her tan.

"If you say so." Then she unwound her legs from his waist and dropped down in the water, grabbing his hand and continuing their path toward the bar. "What do you want to do until then?"

"Whatever you want," he said.

"I want to go down to the beach. We didn't really get to enjoy it yesterday with all of the excitement around Tyler, and I want to go lay in the sand and listen to the waves."

"Then that's what we'll do," he promised her.

Drinks in hand, they waded back through the pool toward where Bethani, her and Jessica's moms, and the boys had set up. The boys, of course, were in the water, playing what appeared to be a brutal game of Marco Polo.

Don't ask Jack how Marco Polo could be brutal; with his teammates involved, someone was always liable to end up injured. Case in point: they couldn't even go boogie boarding without someone nearly drowning.

Jack waited while Jessica climbed out of the water—thoroughly enjoying the view of her ass in her tiny yellow bikini—before following.

"Jack and I are going down to the beach," she announced to

the group at large, her voice surely carrying out over the water. "Anyone want to join us?"

"We're good!" Zach yelled for him, Tyler, and Chad, then immediately went back to their game.

"I'm gonna stay here," Bethani said, holding her copy of *Beach Read* aloft. "I'm almost to the first sex scene, I can feel it."

"Bethani!" her mother scolded.

"What, Mom?" she said, grinning widely. "It's just a book."

Her mom shook her head. "I regret ever getting you a library card."

"No you don't," Bethani said, then returned to the page she'd been reading.

Her mom gave Bethani a small smile, and Jack could see the pride in it. "No, I don't."

"Just be careful in the water?" a blonde woman, who could only be Jessica's mother, said.

Though shorter in stature than Jessica, when the woman pushed her sunglasses atop her head and squinted at Jack, it was painfully obvious she'd given birth to the girl standing next to him. The same blue eyes, same nose, high cheeks, soft mouth.

"Sure, Mom," Jessica said. "By the way, this is Jack. Jack, this is my mom, Michelle."

Michelle extended her hand, and Jack stepped next to her lounge chair, clasping it in his own.

"Nice to meet you, Michelle."

"You as well," Michelle said, giving him a speculative once over before sliding her glasses back over her eyes. "Take good care of my girl."

"Yes, ma'am."

Jessica grabbed his arm, and Jack prepared to follow her, but Michelle stopped him.

"Are you boys here by yourselves?" she asked him.

"No, ma'am," Jack said, then turned and pointed across the pool and two women lounging in the shade, one clearly passed out beneath the brim of her oversized sun hat, the other with her nose buried in a hardcover book. "My and Tyler's moms."

"Oh, good!" Michelle clapped her hands excitedly. "C'mon, Lisa! Let's go introduce ourselves."

Lisa—Bethani's mom—blinked open her eyes and leveled Michelle with a glare. "Do we have to?"

"Yes," Michelle said, leaving no room for argument, and Jack laughed.

"My mom is the one on the left," he said. "Her name is Rebecca. Tyler's mom is Kristi."

"Good to know. Thank you."

Then Michelle and Lisa were on their feet and walking across the pool deck.

"Should we be worried?" Jessica asked.

"Nah," Jack said, reaching down to lace his fingers with hers. "My mom gets along with everyone."

"So does mine," Jessica said. "And she likes you. I can tell."

Jack gestured to his body, where errant droplets of water clung to the ridges of his abs and collarbones, where three straight days in the sun had turned his pasty Pennsylvanian skin to a beautiful golden shade. "What's not to like?"

Jessica shoved him. "First my sister, now my mom. Tell me, Jack, do you actually like me or are you just using me to get to the older women in my family?"

Jack tipped his head back and let out a laugh, the sound forcing Bethani to emerge from her book and scowl at them. He grabbed Jessica's hand again and, after swiping a couple towels from a nearby stand, towed her away, in the direction of the stairs to the ocean.

Once their feet hit the warm sand, Jack hauled Jessica down the beach. Chairs were sporadically placed and randomly grouped, but about fifty yards down, two chairs sat unoccupied. Jack dropped the towels onto one and pulled Jessica to him, though she had crossed her arms over her chest, bottom lip stuck out petulantly.

"Listen to me very carefully, sunshine," Jack said, brushing a lock of hair behind her ear. "The only girl I've had my eyes on the entire time I've been here is you. And that's not going to change."

Her lower lip relaxed its pout. "You promise?"

He leaned in, pressing a kiss to her mouth. "Promise."

"Good," she said brightly. "I feel the same. Now let's go cool off."

Before he could respond, she took off across the sand, kicking up streams of the tiny grains in her wake. The moment her feet touched the water, she squealed.

In a few long strides, Jack was following her in, wading out until the water was just past his knees.

Jessica took a few steps away from him and threw her arms out, spinning in a circle, the water eddying and foaming around her thighs.

"This place is beautiful," she said, tilting her face to the sky like a flower searching for sunlight. "I don't ever want to leave."

Jack stood still, watching her, the ocean breeze and sunshine on his skin distant sensations to the emotion taking root in his chest.

Life was a funny thing, and the timing of it all never ceased to amaze Jack. How he and Jessica had been born around the same time, grown up miles and states apart, yet every choice, every misstep and victory, every tear and smile led them to right here, right now. To this moment—this week—together.

Jessica paused her spinning when she caught him staring, and something on his face prompted her to ask, "What are you thinking about?"

"Do you believe in fate?"

She waded over to him and slid her arms around his waist. He mimicked her, slipping his palms down her sides, settling them low on her hips, over the ties of her bikini bottoms.

"I'm not sure," Jessica said. "I like to think there's some higher power at work, nudging us all along the paths we're meant to walk, but...I don't know. The concept of fate seems cheesy to me, like it's some cosmic force that drives why good or bad things happen to people. I think certain things happen for a reason, but I don't know that I agree that *fate* is a blanket explanation for all of it."

Jack nodded, swallowing hard.

"What about you?" she asked.

"I mean...I'm a guy, Jess. We don't get all existential like that. But..."

"But?" she prompted, rising onto her tiptoes and pressing her body against his, grabbing a fistful of his hair at the back of his head.

"But...being here? With you? If fate isn't the force that brought us together, then I don't know what is."

Her answering smile shone brighter than the sun, and Jack kissed it, kissed *her*—this girl who, in three days, had turned his life completely upside down in the best way.

Jack bent her backward slightly, sliding his hands over the humps of her ass and down the backs of her thighs, then gripped and lifted her off her feet in one smooth motion. With a squeal, and exactly as she had in the pool earlier, she wrapped her legs around his middle.

Jack lost himself in that kiss, in her lush mouth against his, in her sun-warmed skin under his fingers, in the way she wound her arms around his neck and pulled herself impossibly closer to him. He shifted so one arm was a bar beneath her thighs while the other lifted so he could angle her head and deepen the kiss. When he brushed his tongue along her bottom lip, then her tongue when she opened on a gasp, Jack groaned, and his dick swelled.

The roar of the ocean, the calls of birds and the squeals and yells and cheers from people on the beach all fell away. For those moments they were connected, all that mattered to Jack, all that penetrated his senses, was being here with her and holding her in his arms as long as possible.

Abruptly, Jessica pulled away, head turning toward the beach.

"What's wrong?" Jack asked.

"Someone is yelling at us," she said with a giggle, pointing at a man standing on the shore, waving his arms, gesturing for them to come in.

"Wanna go see what he wants?" Jessica asked.

"Not really," he said, dropping his head to her neck and pressing a kiss there.

Jessica released her legs from his waist and dropped into the water, instantly reaching for his hand.

"C'mon, big guy," she said. "Plus, we're going to have to go in before too long so I can get ready for our date."

Our date, Jack thought, a grin splitting his face. He couldn't wait to show her what he'd planned.

When they waded to shore, Jack discovered the man yelling at them had a camera slung around his neck, and he approached them eagerly.

"You two are like Ken and Barbie!" he said excitedly, brandishing his camera. "Can I take some photos of you?"

"Uhh..." Jack said, looking to Jessica for guidance.

"Do you work for the resort?" Jessica asked the man.

"Yes!" he said, holding out a little business card. "I can take pictures of you, then you can go to this website"—he pointed to a web address in small print on the bottom of the card—"and pay for the prints you want! But I also take marketing photos for the resort, and you are such a beautiful couple. Your love is obvious, and I'd love to use these photos for some promo materials."

Jack turned to Jessica, who studied the card intently. "What do you think, sunshine?"

Jessica looked up at him then, her eyes glowing in the afternoon sun.

"Let's do it."

Jessica

THEN: April 7, 2020

"Let's do it."

Jessica surprised herself when the words flew from her mouth, and she clearly surprised Jack, too, based on the way his eyes widened.

"Are you sure?"

"About basically modeling for this guy? Absolutely not. But about having pictures of us to remember our time in paradise together? Definitely."

Jack grinned, and she resisted the urge to rise onto her tiptoes and kiss him again. Truthfully, she was addicted to his kisses, got drunk on them. The rest of the world dropped away whenever he was near, and she couldn't believe she'd been lucky enough to find him. To call him hers, even for this brief moment in time.

In her periphery, she saw the man hold his camera up, and the click of the shutter filled the space between them.

"It's unbelievable how attractive a couple you two make," the man said.

"You are pretty hot," Jack whispered with a sly grin, resting his forehead against hers.

"You are, too."

"Is this okay?" Jack raised his voice to ask the photographer, though he didn't bother to turn in his direction.

"This is *perfect*," the man responded quickly. "The waves, the sun, the sand, you two. *Perfect*."

Jessica giggled at that.

It was late afternoon now, though still about two hours off from sunset. As the sun sank toward the horizon, the sky shifted from a vibrant, clear blue to something a little softer, dustier, paler. According to the photographer, it made for *the best lighting*.

"Okay," the man said. "I want you two right here." He waded into the water and positioned himself so he knelt in the foamy surf. "And I want you to kneel like this, only facing each other."

Once they were in position, Jessica sat back on her heels, and Jack reached for her arm, the one farthest from the camera, lifting it and walking his fingers up her wrist and palm until he threaded their hands together. The camera clicked away, and the photographer actually *squealed*.

"Okay, now lean in and kiss!"

Jessica rose onto her knees awkwardly, clasping Jack's forearms for support—not that she minded having that strength and soft golden hair under her fingertips—and the camera shutter continued. Jack shuffled forward and bent his head, lightly pressing his mouth to hers.

And on and on it went. For the next twenty minutes, the man moved them across the surf and sand, asking them to pose variously—her on his shoulders where he was waist deep in the water, them laying on the beach, Jessica on her back with Jack propped up over her, the muscles of his arms and abs clenching deliciously as he braced himself.

"Kiss, kiss!" the photographer shouted endlessly, and as much as she loved having Jack's tongue in her mouth, the shine had worn off several hundred pictures previously.

Or maybe her lips were just chapped.

Either way, she kissed Jack again in thank you when he pulled away from her where they were on the sand and said, "I'm sorry, man, but we've got a date tonight, and my girl has to go get ready."

Right! Jessica mentally smacked herself. *Our date!*

Despite looking a little crestfallen, the man said, "Yes, yes, I understand. Thank you both so much for helping me out." He stepped forward and shook both of their hands, placing a kiss to the back of Jessica's. Then he held up his camera. "These will be up on my website in a few days, when I've had the chance to choose and edit the best ones!"

As they walked back up the beach toward the resort, Jack started laughing.

"What's so funny?"

"That guy was just...something else." He reached out and grabbed her wrist, yanking her into his body. "But I'm very excited to see those pictures," he added, leaning down to nuzzle her neck.

Jessica scrunched her shoulders when he hit her ticklish spot, a yelp of surprise leaving her. She pushed him back and reached for his hand. "Down boy. I have a date with this really hot guy tonight," she said, then flicked her wrist to check her watch. "And he told me I need to be ready in an hour."

"Really hot guy, huh? Anyone I know?"

"Maybe?" Jessica couldn't help herself as she stepped into his space again, running her hands up his arms, lingering on his bulging biceps, before sweeping them across his chest. "He's super tall, blond, hunky as all hell."

"Hunky?"

"Yeah, *hunky*. That's what comes to mind when I see all of...this," she said, gesturing at his thick body. "And if this is what you look like at eighteen? I hope I'm around to see you in five years, or ten. Because all this? I have a feeling it's only going to get better with age."

Jack offered her a small, shy smile, his cheeks stained pink.

"If I have anything to say about it," he said, "you'll be around for a lot longer than that."

Jessica didn't know how to respond to that, and she was saved from figuring it out when Jack playfully smacked her ass and said, "Now go get ready."

"Yes, sir," she said, then sprinted up the stairs to the pool deck, Jack hot on her heels.

When getting dressed that evening, she'd really taken Jack's suggestions—wear a dress and wear her hair down—to heart. Though she was comfortable in her own skin and knew she looked amazing, the way Jack's eyes darkened and trailed over every inch of her body when he caught sight of her had her preening a little more.

Jack stood in the middle of the marble lobby, completely still as Jessica approached him. He wore a long-sleeve button down and sand-colored khaki shorts, his hair still damp from his shower, the strands standing up at odd angles, as though he'd nervously raked his hands through it.

Only when she stood inches away and rose up to give him a quick peck on the lips did he move.

One moment, Jessica was standing upright, her mouth lightly pressed against his, and the next, she was bent over backward, Jack supporting her with an arm wrapped around her waist and the other cupping the back of her head. She gasped and stiffened, but melted when he kissed her more insistently.

Then she was upright again, head spinning from more than just the sudden movement.

"Hello to you, too," she said, reaching up to wipe her lip gloss off Jack's lips.

"You are...everything," he breathed.

She stepped away and spun in a circle. "You like?"

Jack closed the distance between them again and whispered, "The only way I could like it more is if it was on my bedroom floor."

And...okay. Was it hot in here or was it just Jack?

The dress was a minty green color with spaghetti straps that tied atop her shoulders. It was fitted in the chest and tiered, flowing out wider with each layer until reaching the flouncy hem that fell mid-thigh. When Jessica spun in a circle, she risked revealing her panties to the world, but she didn't care. She'd do whatever it took to have Jack keep looking at her like that.

She paired it with a pair of canvas wedges and delicate gold jewelry, her hair falling in natural waves around her face, shoulders, and down her back.

Jack twirled a lock of her hair around his finger, then trailed his hand down her arm until he reached hers, tugging her toward the resort entrance.

"C'mon," he said. "We're gonna be late."

Outside, a cab waited for them, and after a short ride, they pulled into a marina where a massive Catamaran was docked, and people filed onto the deck. Happy chatter filled the air, layering over the smooth notes of a saxophone from somewhere aboard.

"Here?" she asked Jack dumbly.

"Here," he said with a smile. The cab parked, and Jack paid the man before getting out and extending a hand to help her.

When they reached the gangway leading onto the boat, Jack held out his phone, where the attendant scanned their tickets and waved them on, wishing them *una buena noche*.

The Catamaran consisted of two levels with both indoor and outdoor lounge and dining spaces. Several couples milled about, and waiters walked around, passing out trays of champagne and hors d'oeuvres. Jack snagged two glasses and held one out to Jessica, clinking his softly against hers.

"To us," he said.

"To us," she responded, then took a small sip. The effervescent liquid bubbled up her nose and down her throat, spreading through her chest and stomach with a warmth she didn't think was entirely from the alcohol.

"So what exactly are we doing?" she asked Jack finally. "We're here. Spill the beans."

"This is a sunset cruise," Jack told her. "There's music"—he indicated the man playing a saxophone in the corner—"and bubbly and snacks. And there's me and you and this ridiculously beautiful place."

He swept her into his arms, and she went willingly, though careful not to spill her champagne all over him. She'd hate to ruin his chambray shirt, because he looked incredible in it. His biceps stretched the sleeves to their limits, and he'd left a few buttons at the top open, showcasing the strong column of his throat, the long lines of his collarbones before they disappeared beneath the material, and the valley between the swells of his pecs.

Never, in her entire life, had she been compelled to lick a man, but Jack? She wanted to run her mouth over every single inch of his skin.

"As far as first dates go," Jessica said finally, pushing away *that* thought, "I've definitely been on worse."

Jack slid his hands down and gave her ass a squeeze, and Jessica yelped. "You can do better than that," he said, his voice low in her ear, breath warm on her neck.

She leaned back to look at him, and let a smile slowly develop, widening it until it overtook her whole face. "This is incredible, Jack," she said. "You didn't have to do all of this for me."

"I wanted to," he said. "If this is all we get, I want us to remember it forever."

If this is all we get.

Jessica didn't like the way those words settled like a weight on her chest, but she refused to acknowledge them. Tonight was about them, and about doing exactly what Jack had said: making the most of their time together.

They pulled away from the dock about ten minutes later, and Jack and Jessica found a small grouping of chairs at the bow, idly sipping their champagne and reveling in the breeze blowing through their hair. Even though it totally ruined her outfit, her mother had made her bring a sweater, and she was glad for it when the boat picked up speed and the whipping wind raised goosebumps on her skin.

Jack took that as an invitation to come closer, to haul her onto his lap and wrap his arms around her.

And Jessica wasn't complaining. In fact, she had the thought that she could stay in this spot forever.

As the boat sliced through the water, they chatted idly about their lives at home. How Jessica had won a state championship in volleyball, which embarrassed Jack to no end, knowing how much shit he'd given her for being a bad water volleyball player. How Jack's hockey season had gone, and if he was playing in college—though she didn't want to know where, and wouldn't let him tell her. What he wanted to do if he couldn't play hockey—he had no idea—and previous relationships, though there weren't any worth mentioning for either of them.

All getting to know Jack made Jessica realize was how impossible it would be to leave him. The closer they got, the more difficult it would be to disentangle herself. It was madness to consider a future for them after this vacation ended.

Still, that didn't stop her from imagining it, even if all it would ever be was a fantasy.

Sometime later, an older couple joined them, settling on two cushy chairs opposite Jack and Jessica.

"Hello," the woman said, offering Jessica a warm smile.

"Hi," Jessica replied.

"I'm Nadine," she said, "and this is my husband, Marc."

"I'm Jessica, and this is my..."

Jessica choked on the word boyfriend. As badly as she wanted to say it, to make that desperate wish a reality, she was insane to even consider it. They'd only known each other for three days.

"I'm her boyfriend," Jack said, squeezing her a little tighter, and Jessica thought, okay, maybe she wasn't so insane. "Jack."

"Nice to meet you both," Marc said. "How long have you been together?"

"Oh, you know..." Jessica trailed off, grasping at straws, searching for something to say that didn't sound crazy.

"Not long," Jack said. "Actually, we just met on Monday."

Nadine and Marc shared a look, then burst out laughing.

Jessica's eyebrows drew together, cheeks heating with embarrassment.

"Why is that funny?" Jack asked.

Nadine swept her white hair out of her face and held up her hands. "Oh, I'm sorry, dears. We didn't mean to offend. It's just...we got married two weeks after we met."

"What?" Jessica blurted.

"When we were in our early twenties, we met on vacation, like you two did," Nadine said with a wink. "And I just...knew. The moment I laid eyes on him, I knew he was it for me. And I'd do whatever I could to keep him."

"Lucky for her, I felt the same," Marc said. Nadine swatted at him, but Marc caught her hand, pressing a kiss to the back of it, and her smile softened.

"That was fifty years ago," Nadine continued. "We're back here celebrating our anniversary."

Jessica's heart swelled, and she chanced a look at Jack, only to find him already staring at her, each and every one of her thoughts and feelings echoed in his eyes.

"You two have that same look about you," Marc said. "Absolutely crazy about each other."

"Didn't your families think you'd lost your minds?" Jack asked, tearing his gaze from Jessica's.

"Oh, definitely," Nadine laughed. "My father tried to forbid me from seeing him, so I threatened to run away and never speak to him again. He came around after that."

"That's...so brave," Jessica said quietly.

"It's easy to be brave with your soulmate," Nadine said, staring affectionately at her husband. "When you know, you know, and we knew. There wasn't anything stopping us."

Jessica sniffed, surprised to find her eyes welling with tears. She turned her head away from Jack and swiped at them. Once she'd composed herself, she said, "That's the most beautiful thing I've ever heard."

"We got really lucky," Marc said. "I have a feeling y'all will, too."

Jack squeezed Jessica's hand, and as Jack and Marc steered the conversation away from love and soulmates toward fishing and whatever else men talk about, Jessica turned her attention inward.

Like every little girl, Jessica had grown up believing in fairytales, wishing for Prince Charming to come sweep her off her feet like Cinderella. But at some point along the way, life happened, and pessimism set in. Somewhere, she stopped believing in those things, and wishing they were meant for her.

Maybe it was growing up with a sister who was six years older, and watching Berkley suffer through love and heartbreak, hookups and breakups, paving the way for Jessica, that pulled the rose-colored glasses from Jessica's eyes. Maybe it was simply *growing up*.

Did she think she and Jack had something special? Of course she did. Whatever she had with him was unlike anything she'd experienced before, even if there wasn't a lot to compare it to.

But did she think this thing between them was enough to go the distance? And she didn't simply mean the longevity of their relationship. No, she meant the literal *distance*. When they went back to the States, when she returned to Michigan and he to Pennsylvania. How long would they last when they had to survive on FaceTime and phone calls, texts to check in and the occasional cross-country visit?

Jessica's mind spun, and she gave herself a little shake. She didn't want to think about this now, to let her thoughts swallow her whole and ruin this perfect evening.

"You okay?" Jack whispered when Marc finally gave him a breather from the conversation.

Jessica simply nodded, afraid that opening her mouth would send all of her thoughts spewing into the universe.

Thankfully, she was saved by the boat's crew weighing anchor in open water.

A sound system crackled to life, followed by a man speaking.

"Thank you all so much for joining us for tonight's sunset cruise," the disembodied voice said. "Sunset is about fifteen minutes off, so find a spot along the port side and get ready for the most magical night of your life. After the sun's gone, we'll dock on Isla Mujeres for dinner."

Jessica gasped and spun in Jack's arms to face him. "You didn't tell me there would be dinner...on an island!"

"I didn't want to ruin it."

"Where exactly is this Isla Mujeres?"

"There," Marc said, stepping up next to them and pointing off to the right.

And sure as shit, an island rose out of the water on the starboard side. Jessica must've been so wrapped up in her doom spiral that she'd completely ignored her surroundings.

Standing, she straightened her dress and extended a hand for Jack.

Jessica walked them to the railing on the port side, finding open space closer to the bow. Jack stepped up behind her, pulling her back against him and once again wrapping his arms around her.

And despite all of the anxious thoughts racing through her brain, when the sun was but a sliver on the horizon, the sky lit in hues of orange and pink, fading to lavender and dusty blue directly above their heads, and Jack turned her toward him and kissed her, Jessica melted.

The future was a bridge they would cross when they came to it. Right now, there was only this moment, this boy, and this kiss.

On a tiny spit of beach, the catering company had turned the white sand into a magical oasis. Under a pergola draped with gauzy white sheets that floated ethereally on the wind and strung with twinkle lights that winked like stars in the falling dusk, a long table was set for twenty. Off to the side, another was laden with steaming silver dishes, and the scent of seafood wafted on the breeze.

Once everyone was gathered under the pergola, a man stepped forward.

"Good evening, everyone! We've prepared an excellent feast for you all tonight, comprised of the freshest ingredients the Yucatan has to offer."

"Yucatan?" Jack whispered in Jessica's ear.

She giggled. "It's the name of the peninsula Cancún sits on."

"I don't know why I never knew that," Jack said sheepishly.

Jessica patted his cheek and winked. "It's okay, big guy. I'm not with you for your brain."

Jack growled and snapped his teeth at her hand, and Jessica had to cover her mouth to hold in a loud laugh.

"The buffet is self-serve, and don't worry about anything running out before you've had the chance to try it. We've got more than enough to feed everyone several times over. So, please, dig in!"

The man stepped to the side and, with a flourish, the remaining waiters lifted the lids on the silver dishes, revealing the deliciousness underneath.

Having eaten a few meals with the boy at this point, Jessica knew Jack could put it away. However, that did not prepare her for the mountain of food he piled onto his plate and took back to the table. Being allergic to shellfish didn't stop him from sampling everything—and she meant *everything*—he *could* eat.

Although...Jessica wasn't any better.

There was so much to choose from, and everything looked phenomenal. Fresh fish and seafood including tuna, cod, clams, crawfish, shrimp, and several types of crab breaded, broiled, sauteed with butter and seasonings Jessica couldn't name but absolutely melted in her mouth. There were vegetarian options like tofu and massive portobello mushrooms, plus platters of raw and steamed veggies, fruits, and another table filled with Mexican sweets and desserts.

Jack gorged himself on all the fresh fish, veggies, desserts, and even sampled some tofu and mushrooms.

By the time they finished eating, Jessica was so stuffed she could barely move.

But the saxophonist wailed out a long note, then jumped into a smooth version of "Wonderwall," and Jack turned to her with a grin.

"Dance with me."

And how could she say no?

Thankfully, other guests had the same idea, saving them from making a spectacle of themselves.

"Can you believe we're already halfway through vacation?" Jack asked as they swayed slowly to the song.

An icy finger dragged down Jessica's spine. She didn't want to think about it, mostly because she didn't want to face leaving

Jack in a few days. Somehow, inside this paradise bubble, two days had stretched into what felt like two years. At this point, she knew Jack well. Too well. There were certainly things she hadn't learned and likely wouldn't thanks to their limited time together, but she knew the important things. That he was kind, loyal, funny, and had a heart of gold, a mushy, cinnamon roll center to balance his sexy, hard-muscled body. And the chemistry that sizzled between them...she could ignore it as easily as she could ignore an elephant standing on her chest.

"No, I can't," she said, voice hoarse.

"Do you..." Jack trailed off, almost as if he sensed that she was lost somewhere in her head.

"Do I what?"

"Do you feel like we've known each other forever?"

Jessica's shoulders sagged, a sigh whooshing from her lips. That wasn't what she'd expected him to say, and this was only slightly less dangerous territory. "Yes," she said.

He wrapped his arms tighter around her. "Me, too," he said, and Jessica hoped he'd leave it at that. Of course, he didn't. "I've been thinking it's going to be so hard to leave you, and we've only known each other for three days. So we make the most of right now. And maybe after, we can..."

Jessica shook her head, fighting the urge to throw her hands over her ears and pretend she couldn't hear him. "No. We're not gonna talk about after. There is no *after*."

She hadn't meant the words to come out so harshly, but she wouldn't take them back.

When she risked a glance at him, she found his eyebrows drawn together in confusion. "Why not?"

"It's vacation," she said, finally voicing the thoughts she'd been having all evening. "It's a bubble. Nothing will be the same when it pops. And besides, you live in Pennsylvania and I live in Michigan. It's just...it'll never work."

"But—"

"No buts," she said with a raised hand. "Please? Can we just enjoy these last few days? Make the most of it, like you said."

His eyes bored a hole into hers, as though he was searching her soul for something. Something he clearly didn't find, because he only nodded and, resigned, said, "Okay."

And even though their time together hadn't yet expired, the bubble popped anyway.

Jessica

NOW: November 4, 2023

He doesn't love you.

Those four words had been a constant companion to Jessica in the three weeks since Jack's text, swirling endlessly around the forefront of her brain, never leaving her alone for long.

I know.

And her response haunted her.

She didn't know why she'd responded that way, or why she'd responded at all. Her relationship was none of Jack's concern, especially not when he was dating a great girl like Sofia. And Silas *did* love her, damnit.

What had compelled Jack to say such a thing? What right did he have to comment on her relationship? Had he noticed something on their impromptu double date? Even the people who had known Jessica for years—her roommates, her family—hadn't said anything of the sort to her, and they were the people Jessica trusted to always tell her the truth.

So what *was* the truth?

Honestly, she didn't know anymore.

The day after that double date, she'd been ill-tempered thanks to Jack butting into places he didn't belong, and when Silas had asked what her deal was, she'd lied and said Logan had pissed her off.

So now, she was lying to her boyfriend.

Not that Silas hadn't been harboring secrets of his own.

She didn't know what the fuck she was doing anymore.

What she did know was, since that double date, things between her and Silas had been surprisingly good. He'd been more attentive than ever, actually listening when she spoke about her classes, her student teaching assignment, or her tutoring clients. He'd carved out more time for her instead of constantly being with his brothers or, well...Sofia.

Jessica had to admit, the timing was suspicious. She hadn't even known Sofia existed outside of the one random text conversation they'd had with Kenzie. And then to find out that she and Silas had known each other since their first week of college, and were really good friends? She took this sudden shift in his approach to their relationship with a grain of salt, but she wasn't going to complain that they were spending more quality time together.

She'd suggested such a thing for tonight: for them to go out and get dinner and maybe see a movie, or go bowling or to Top Golf. Something fun, just the two of them.

Instead, she'd wound up at a frat party.

Honestly, she didn't mind frat parties. She knew the Greek

community got a bad rep from outsiders, but she'd always had such a good time at The Lodge house. Not because she enjoyed spending time around Silas's brothers, who were obnoxious on a good day, but because she liked their girlfriends.

Jessica was dressed comfortably in a pair of artfully distressed, wide-leg jeans and a sweater that hung off her shoulder and cropped right above the waistband of her pants. She had a green solo cup in her hand, half-full of the red wine Silas kept stashed in his room for her.

See, he could be sweet when he wanted to be.

She and a few of the girlfriends sat on one of the couches in the corner of the living room, discussing the winter-themed party the boys were hosting with the Delta Gamma girls at the beginning of December.

"Okay so what kind of winter theme are we talking about here?" one of them asked. "Like...Christmas? Winter Wonderland? I need to know these things so I can dress appropriately."

"Winter Wonderland," someone piped up, and the group collectively turned to find Sofia hovering on the edge of their circle.

"Thank you," Jessica said, giving Sofia a smile, then patting the empty space on the couch next to her. Sofia hesitated for a split second before joining them.

"How do you know that?" another one of the girls asked.

"She's in DG," Jessica supplied.

"Wait, are you Sofia?" another asked.

Sofia nodded. "I see my reputation precedes me."

The girls tittered, and Jessica sat up straighter, on high alert. From the little she knew of her, Jessica liked Sofia, and she wasn't about to let these girls bully her.

"The guys always have great things to say about you," another added. "You're DG's social chair, right?"

Sofia nodded proudly. "Yes! The girls voted me into the position last year, and I've loved every second of it."

"That's amazing!" Jessica said. "So you're responsible for planning this winter ball thing?"

"Yep! Which is how I know the theme is Winter Wonderland," she laughed. "The boys know this, so I have no idea why they haven't told you."

One of the girlfriends waved her hand dismissively. "They're men," she said. "They don't care about things like this. I'll pick out my outfit, and he'll show up in what I tell him to wear."

The rest of the group laughed indulgently, each of them knowing full well that's exactly what would happen.

"So on that note," another girl said, "what exactly is everyone wearing? White, pale blue, pale pink?" She turned to Sofia. "Does pale pink qualify?"

"I'd say so," Sofia said. "Think of like...well, think of campus when we get a really heavy snowfall. Everything is covered in white, but the green of the pine trees really pops, and the blue of the sky is pale and washed out. And at sunset, the sky turns that dusty pink. I think just Pinterest search 'winter wonderland' and you'll get some good ideas. Personally, I'm going to be wearing pale blue. I bought my dress ages ago and..." She trailed off, then leaned in conspiratorially, the girls following suit. "I'll be honest, I came up with this theme just for an excuse to wear it."

The girls burst into laughter and cheers, congratulating Sofia on a job well done. For her part, Sofia beamed.

"Guess I'm going to have to go shopping," Jessica said so only

Sofia could hear her. "Or maybe my sister has something I could borrow. Although...Berkley is like six inches shorter than me."

"What does she do?" Sofia asked.

"She's an attorney in Detroit," Jessica said proudly.

"How much older is she?" Sofia asked. "I mean, to already be a practicing attorney. At least, what, four years?"

"Six," Jessica said. "And my brother is seven years older than me."

"Damn," Sofia said, then her eyes widened. "Wait, Berkley? That's your sister's name? And you and Kenzie are really close, right?"

Jessica knew where this was headed, and only nodded while Sofia parsed out the connection in her mind.

"Holy shit," Sofia said finally, realization dawning in her eyes. "Your sister is married to Brent Jean."

"Guilty," Jessica said.

"That's...wild," Sofia said with a shake of her head. "How did they even meet?"

"Ahh..." Jessica trailed off, unsure how to even begin. "It's a long and complicated story but, about three years ago, Brent slid into Berkley's Instagram DMs, and the rest is history."

There really was so much more to it than that, including a surprise birthday party, some drama with one of Brent's teammates, and a brief breakup right before Berkley graduated from law school. But now they're together, recently married, and expecting their first child. Jessica couldn't be happier for her sister, knowing she found the love of her life, and it brought Brent and Kenzie—and their brother, Nate, she supposed, though Nate rarely left the University of Michigan hospital where he was in residency—into her life, and she would forever be thankful for Kenzie's friendship.

"That's just…crazy," Sofia said, taking a swig of her drink and scanning the crowd. Across the room, Silas looked up and caught Jessica's gaze, offering her a small smile and a dorky little finger wave.

To Jessica's discomfort, Sofia waved back at the same moment Jessica did.

"Oh my gosh," Sofia said. "I'm so sorry. I thought he was waving at me."

"It's okay," Jessica replied, offering her a thin smile. Then, desperate to change the subject, she asked, "How are things with Jack?"

"Oh…" Sofia trailed off. "Uhh…they're fine! Good, even."

Sofia didn't offer anything else, and Jessica didn't have anything worthwhile to add other than, "That's great!"

It sounded like false praise to even her own ears, but Sofia seemed to be lost in her own little bubble, looking everywhere but at Jessica.

After that, their conversation died in an awkward, fiery blaze. As if Sofia too noticed the way the air tensed between them, she drained the rest of her glass and shook it in Jessica's direction.

"I'm gonna go get a refill."

"Sounds good," Jessica said. "See you later."

"Yeah, sure." Sofia offered another smile, then she was gone.

As soon as Sofia was out of earshot, the other girls turned to Jessica.

"That was so strange," one of them said.

"What was?" Jessica asked.

"You...chatting with Sofia like you're old pals."

"I mean we're not like super close or anything," Jessica said. "But we went on a double date with her and her boyfriend a few weeks ago. That was the first time I'd met her."

"Wait wait wait," one of them said, holding up a hand. "Back up. You and Silas went on a double date with her and her boyfriend?"

"I didn't even know she had a boyfriend," another quipped.

"Yeah," Jessica said. "She's seeing Jack DeLuca."

"The hockey player?" one asked, cocking her head to the side.

"The very same."

"This world is so damn small," another added. "Isn't your, like, sister-in-law or whatever dating Aiden Fuller?"

"She is..." Jessica honestly had no idea where this conversation was going, but she didn't like it. Not one bit. And she wasn't even going to begin to attempt to explain the Daniels-Jean family dynamics. Kenzie wasn't technically her sister-in-law, but for the sake of this conversation, it was close enough.

"I've heard he's a bit of a fuckboy."

"Aiden? Absolutely not. I've only been around him a few times, but from what I can tell, he's a great guy, and he's absolutely obsessed with Kenzie."

"Well, that's good," one of them said.

"Kind of like Sofia is obsessed with Silas..." another added, so quietly that Jessica wasn't entirely sure she heard her correctly.

"I'm sorry, what?"

The girl in question—her name was Katie—sat up straighter, releasing a heavy sigh accompanied by an eyeroll. "It's just...we spend a lot of time around this house, and around the boys, and...they talk."

"About what, exactly?"

"Well, DG wasn't always their sister sorority or whatever. I know nothing about the Greek system, even after dating Trav for like, a lifetime," Katie said. "But our freshman and sophomore years, the Lodge boys always did date parties and other combined events with the Kappa Delta girls. Then Sofia became social chair and DG completely pushed KD out of the picture. The timing seems strange."

Conversations branched off from there, each of the other girls giving input on Sofia and Silas, and Jessica and Silas, offering commentary on *her* life. Jessica, meanwhile, was trapped inside her mind.

Abruptly, she stood, accidentally jostling the girl next to her and sloshing her drink all over her hand and onto the floor.

"I'm so sorry," Jessica said as she picked her way through their circle, making a beeline for Silas.

Of course, Sofia was already there.

Jessica had no qualms about barging right between them, wrapping her hand around Silas's wrist, and tugging him away.

She offered Sofia an apologetic smile and said, "Sorry. Need to borrow my boyfriend for a second."

Jessica had never been the jealous type, had never *needed* to be—or so she thought. But with Jack walking back into her life, and discovering the existence of Sofia, this woman in Silas's life who took so much of his time and attention, well...the cracks in the veneer of their relationship were starting to show.

Silas tried to pull his wrist from her grip, but she held fast, towing him through the party and upstairs, not stopping until his bedroom door was shut and locked behind them.

Then she sat down hard on his bed and dropped her face into her hands, willing herself not to cry. They wouldn't even be tears of sadness. They'd be ones of anger and frustration, and that was so much worse.

His warm palm landed on her shoulder a moment before he said, "Jess? What's wrong?"

"Do you have feelings for Sofia?" she blurted, still not looking at him, afraid his face would tell her everything she didn't want to know.

His hand slid from her shoulder to her cheek, and his feet appeared in her downcast vision. He knelt and tipped her face up to meet his eyes. "No."

Jessica squinted, searching his eyes, his mouth, eyebrows, forehead, every single line of this face she knew so well for any hint of deception.

When she found none, she breathed a sigh of relief. "Okay."

"What the hell brought this on?" he asked.

"Just...some weird conversations with the girls downstairs," she said, waving a hand, desperate to make this conversation go away now that she'd gotten what she came for.

"I wish you wouldn't listen to their nonsense," he said. "They're like those old ladies in town who go to the local bakery for coffee and scones every morning, gossiping about what everyone else is doing and ignoring their own problems."

"I like them," Jessica said defensively. Like her and Silas, a few of them had been with their boyfriends since freshman year, and it had been nice to have friends who understood what it was like dating a frat guy.

"I do, too," Silas said. "I'm just saying, they can be…shit-stir-rers."

"Well, I didn't let them stir any shit," she said. "The moment they brought it up, I came right to you."

"And I'm glad you did," he said, dropping a kiss onto her forehead.

Then he straightened to his full height and raised his arms over his head, bending side to side and backward. His back cracked and popped with each movement, and he released a satisfied yawn.

"Well, now that we're up here, I don't really feel like going back down. What do you say we get ready for bed and turn on a movie?"

Jessica perked up. "My choice?"

Silas groaned playfully, then shot her a million dollar smile. "Of course."

Jessica hopped from the bed and swiped her bag from the floor on her way to his attached bath. She made quick work of her nighttime routine: makeup remover, face wash, serums and lotions. Then she changed out of her party outfit and into a pair of sweatpants and a well-worn t-shirt. Finally, she applied her favorite lotion to her hands and arms before padding back out into the bedroom. Silas was already tucked under the covers, the opening credits of *Sweet Home Alabama* cued up on the screen.

"How did you know?" she asked as she slid in next to him.

Silas scoffed. "Please. This is your favorite movie."

The boy wasn't wrong.

She scooted over next to him, and he opened an arm so she could curl up next to him, her head resting on his chest, her hand under her head.

As the movie played, with the scent of her lotion and Silas's arms wrapping her in a warm soft cocoon, Jessica easily fell into a deep sleep, her dreams haunted by memories of spring break...and a boy named Jack.

Jack

THEN: April 8, 2020

THEIR FIRST DATE HAD absolutely not gone the way he'd planned, and Jack had been mentally kicking himself since the night before. Why had he brought up what came after they left Mexico? In the grand scheme of things, they hardly knew each other, and Jack had probably scared the shit out of Jessica by trying to talk about the future.

She'd been distant the rest of the night, but when he'd dropped her at her room and asked if she wanted to go explore the markets downtown with him tomorrow, she'd perked up, saying she'd love to and giving him a sweet, lingering kiss before disappearing behind the door.

He just hadn't expected her to bring her mom along.

Or Bethani...and Bethani's mom.

In a last ditch effort to save himself from what could've been the most awkward excursion in the history of forever, he frantically called his mom and begged her to meet them in the lobby.

"What? Why?" she asked.

"Because Jess invited her mom to go shopping with us, and I don't want to spend the whole day being interrogated. Please, Mom."

"Fine. I'll be down in a bit."

"Thank you." He hung up, then turned to the girls. "She's on her way down!"

"Oh, good!" Michelle said. "We had a lovely chat yesterday, and I'm excited to get to know her better. You know, since you two seem to be getting so close."

"Moooooom," Jessica whined, and Jack grinned.

"What, dear?" Michelle said sweetly, then turned to Lisa.

At that moment, Tyler, Chad, and Zach entered the lobby, clad in swim trunks and Hawaiian print button-up shirts that hung wide open.

"Jaaaaaack," Chad yelled, his name echoing across the marble floor and walls.

"Ugh," Jack said, then placed his hands on Jessica's shoulders and crouched behind her. "Save me."

"No can do, big guy," she said. "Hey Chad! Ty! Zach!"

The boys ran over, Tyler going so far as to scoop her up in a hug.

"Where are you guys off to?" Zach asked.

"Yeah, and why weren't we invited?" Chad quipped.

"Yeah, Jack, why weren't they invited?" Jessica asked sweetly.

Somehow, Jack just knew Jessica had invited her mom, Bethani, and Lisa to act as a buffer because things between them were getting too serious too fast. And honestly, he couldn't blame her. He'd crossed some invisible line in the sand last night, and now he had to work twice as hard to fix things before vacation ended.

There is no after.

Jack understood the motivation behind Jessica's words, but that didn't make them weigh any less on his chest.

Because if he had anything to say about it, there *would* be an after. There had to be. He already knew that, because this girl had walked into it, his life would never be the same, and he couldn't imagine carrying on after this vacation like everything about him hadn't been altered by knowing her.

"I just didn't think you guys would want to go shopping," Jack finally told his friends.

"And you do?" Tyler asked with a raised brow.

And...okay, he had him there.

With a smirk, Jessica turned her attention to a conversation with her mom about the people back home they should buy souvenirs for, and Jack jerked his head at his friends, moving them out of earshot of Jessica.

"This was supposed to be a date," he hissed. "But then she showed up with Bethani and the moms, and all my plans for the day went up in smoke."

All three of his friends stared at him with a range of expressions from stunned—Tyler—to confused—Zach—to straight up uninterested—Chad.

"I feel like I'm missing something here," Zach said. "Didn't you guys go on some hella romantic sunset cruise last night? Shouldn't you be shopping for rings and naming your children?"

Chad snorted, and Jack punched him in the arm. "It was hella romantic," Jack said wistfully, then sobered. "Until it wasn't."

Quietly, he explained to them what had happened, and was greeted by a collective groan of embarrassment.

"Dude, no."

"What is wrong with you?"

"No wonder she doesn't want to be alone with you."

"I don't get it," Jack said, pulling off his ball cap and scrubbing his hands through his hair. "Aren't girls supposed to be into all the mushy-gushy feelings talk? How is it possible that I found the one girl who ran when I basically told her I wanted to give this thing a shot when we go home?"

"DeLuca..." Tyler sighed, Jack's last name full of pity. "Did you ever stop to consider that maybe she's not looking for a relationship? And despite the fact that your chemistry is palpable and you two look disgustingly good together, that's not enough to translate into a 'real world' relationship?"

Jack pondered that. Tyler's words combined with Jessica's comments last night had him starting to think that, maybe, she was right. Vacation *was* a bubble, and everything inside of it was heightened. These emotions he experienced for her could very well be the real deal, but they could just as easily be something fleeting, lasting only for this week and disappearing the moment they were back on U.S. soil.

"You might be right," Jack said finally.

Before any of his friends could respond, his mom shouted his name from the end of the lobby, Tyler's mom in tow.

Apparently, all ten of them were heading to the market.

For the early part of the day, Jack gave Jessica her space—though he couldn't help but track her every move from the corner of his eye.

They'd wandered in and out of all the shops and stalls along Mercado 28, the moms loading themselves down with souvenirs and laughing about how they'd fit it all into their bags to take home.

"Maybe I'll leave Jack here and use his suitcase for any overflow," his mom said with a laugh.

"I mean...I'd be fine with that," Jack said, grinning at her. "This place is paradise."

"It really is," Michelle said, stepping out onto the cobblestones and spreading her arms wide, the breeze blowing her blonde hair in a twister around her head.

The rest of the group filed out of the shop a moment later, right as Michelle's gaze landed on a bar across the way.

"Let's go do a tequila tasting!"

"Are you serious?" Jessica asked her mom, stepping close to Jack for the first time in hours.

"Why not?" Michelle asked, turning a wide grin, so like her daughter's, on them all. "When in Mexico, right?"

Chad raised his hand. "I'm in!"

The rest of the group echoed Chad, and Jessica's protestation was lost to majority rule. Jack gave her a small smile and grabbed her hand, tugging her across the street after everyone.

The little bar—if it could even be called that—was a tequila lover's dream. The walls were lined with rich mahogany shelves that held endless bottles of tequila in all shapes, sizes, and colors. There was reposado and blanco, añejo and extra añejo, and cristalino. Jack wasn't overly familiar with the differences, but he quickly learned that blanco was white, reposado was darker, how the different types are aged in different types of barrels for different lengths of time, and that cristalino was the boujee tequila commonly found in the VIP club scene.

After a brief explanation of how tequila was distilled, the man working set them up at a long table in the back and brought them each a flight of five shots—one of each type.

Before downing their first, Chad raised his over the center of the table, encouraging everyone else to follow suit.

"To Mexico!" he said, then slammed his glass onto the table before tossing it down his throat.

"To Mexico!" they shouted back and followed suit.

And Jack would be damned if that wasn't the smoothest shot of tequila he'd ever had.

"Nothing like that shit we had at the club on Monday, is it?" Jessica asked.

Sitting next to him, the table small enough that they'd all squeezed together, the length of her thigh pressed against his.

Emboldened by the liquor, though he'd only downed one shot, he reached out and settled his palm on her knee.

She didn't shove his touch away, and he took that as a good sign.

Across the table, Chad was challenging the rest of the group to see who could finish their shots the fastest. Thankfully, when he pulled out his phone and pressed start on the stopwatch feature, he was too absorbed in the competition to realize Jack and Jessica weren't participating.

"Look," Jack said quietly, giving her leg a little squeeze, "I'm sorry about last night. I get where you're coming from, and if this is all we get, I don't want to spend a single second with things strained and weird between us."

"It's okay," she said quietly.

"No it's not," Jack said, knowing he needed to comfort her, to placate her, to let her know he wouldn't ask for anything she wasn't willing to give. "I crossed a line, and it won't happen again."

Before Jessica could respond, someone slammed their hand on the table, forcing the drinkware to jump and rattle. Unfortunately, that meant Jack and Jessica ended up wearing their remaining shots when they tipped and spilled.

"Chad!" Jack yelled, rising to his feet.

"What?" his friend asked. "You should've drunk them when you had the chance."

Though he was fuming, Jack grabbed Jessica's hand instead of landing his fist in the center of Chad's face.

"C'mon," he said. "Let's go get cleaned up."

"What? You don't want to smell like a raging alcoholic until we can go back to the resort and change?"

Jack chuckled at the joke. "Not particularly, no."

He towed her down the hall, where the *los baños* were located, according to a sign hanging overhead.

The restroom was much smaller than he'd anticipated, and though Jessica didn't take up all that much space, Jack certain did, and he had to contort himself awkwardly between the toilet and the sink—which were far too close together, in his opinion—while Jessica swiped a mountain of paper towels against his soaked tee and shorts.

All he could do was watch as she mopped him up, and his dick threatened to stiffen under her ministrations.

"Sunshine," he rasped.

She looked up at him, eyes wide with innocence. She really had no idea what she was doing to him.

Turning to withdraw his own stack of towels from the dispenser, he set about returning the favor. But when his eyes slid over a droplet of tequila that had landed on her collarbone and clung there, like a hiker hanging onto a cliff face for dear life, he couldn't resist.

Slowly, he leaned forward and brushed his mouth over her skin, capturing the liquor with his lips, then straightening and, eyes locked with hers, licking it away.

His name was an exhaled breath leaving her lips before she launched herself at him.

It was the most natural thing in the world to lift her off her feet, and the way she slung her legs around his waist seemed like something they'd done a thousand times. He had her backed against the wall and his mouth on hers in seconds.

Unlike their previous kisses, which were languid and unhurried, this was rushed and frantic.

Jessica bit his lip and clawed at his clothes, and she'd nearly succeeded in dropping his pants to his ankles when sense returned.

"Jess."

She froze in his arms, pulling away to look at him, her eyes wide with shock.

"Oh my gosh," she said, instantly returning her feet to the floor. "I'm so sorry."

"You never have to apologize for kissing me," he said. "But when I said we should make the most of the time we've got left together, this"—he gestured at the dingy, dirty bathroom—"isn't what I had in mind."

"Then what did you have in mind?" she asked, her fingers tiptoeing up his chest.

"A bed," he answered honestly. "Taking my time. Taking *our* time."

Jessica swallowed audibly, then said, "Is that something you want?"

"Only if you do, sunshine. We're not forcing anything or rushing anything. If it happens, it happens. If it doesn't, that'll be okay, too, right?"

"Right," she said, her small, tentative smile blooming into something that stole his breath away.

Before he could put his foot in his mouth—again—he cleared his throat and said, "We should get back out there before they come looking for us and think the worst."

"You're right," Jess said. "My mom wouldn't take too kindly to finding me in a compromising position with a boy in a Mexican bathroom."

"Please," Jack said as he ushered her out with a hand on the small of her back. "Your mother loves me."

Jessica paused, raising onto her tiptoes to give him a quick peck on the lips. "She really does."

Warmth bloomed in his chest with those words, and he followed her back to the table.

"Where did you two disappear to, hmm?" Michelle asked when they sat.

"Mom!"

"We just went to clean up," Jack said. "Nothing nefarious happened."

"I'm not worried about *nefarious*," Michelle said. "More like...*explicit*."

"MOTHER!" Jessica yelled, and the whole table devolved into laughter.

"Wow," Jack whispered to her when everyone calmed, "she really does love me."

"How can you tell?"

"She wouldn't be joking about us having sex in the bathroom if she didn't trust me with you."

"That's...true," Jessica said, and the surprise on her face had Jack chuckling.

Not long after, when the group—save Jack and Jessica—were sufficiently liquored up, they decided to continue moseying through the shops.

Somehow, Jack and Jessica ended up wandering alone, and found themselves in front of a stand where a woman had laid out rows and shelves of handmade jewelry. Jessica gasped in excitement, and immediately began sifting through.

"What exactly are you looking for?" Jack asked. "I mean, what kind of jewelry speaks to you?"

"Well it depends on the medium," she said. "See, this stuff is all handmade, so it's not what I'd consider *fine* jewelry. It is well made, and beautiful, but it's not made from expensive metals or stones, you know? For those things, I like anything, really. I'm lucky in that I look good in gold and silver, though I usually gravitate toward gold. For gems, I like opals. My birthday is in June, and I really lucked out having both pearls and moonstones as my birthstone, so I love anything with both of those as well."

As she said it, Jack's gaze snagged on a dainty bracelet, made of braided, soft yellow embroidery floss with a pearl stacked on each side of a dangling charm crafted from some stone that reminded Jack of the inside of a seashell and shaped into the letter J.

Before Jessica could see, Jack scooped it up and hid it in his palm while she continued to browse.

Ultimately, she chose a pair of pearl earrings for herself—that Jack had to admit would go great with the bracelet he was about to buy her—and a bracelet for her sister.

When they checked out and Jack paid for the bracelet, Jessica turned on him, confusion flashing in her eyes.

"Who are you buying that for?"

Jack responded by grasping her wrist and sliding the bracelet over her hand, pulling the ends to tighten it. "You. Don't say I never gave you anything," he said with a wink.

She gave him a look that said, *get real*, and aloud added, "We are not Nathan and Haley."

"The fact that you got that reference is so hot," Jack said, clasping his hand around her wrist. "Just take the bracelet and stop complaining." He tucked a finger under the charm and held it up. "See, I got one with a J so you always remember me."

Jessica raised a brow. "You do realize my first initial is also J, right?"

"Don't care," Jack said, grinning.

And truthfully, he didn't. Because as long as Jessica wore that bracelet, even if the J also represented her, she'd never be able to look at it without thinking of him.

After leaving the jewelry stand, they met back up with the rest of their group. They were planning to head back to the resort, as it was now early afternoon and the boys wanted some final quality time on the beach before the sun went down.

And that's when it hit Jack like a Mack truck: this was their last full day here.

Their flight home took off early tomorrow afternoon, which meant they'd be spending the morning packing and heading to the airport in enough time to get through security.

Which meant that, this time tomorrow, Jessica would just be...gone from his life.

Now was absolutely not the time to think about that. There weren't enough hours left in this day for him to spend a single second of them doom spiraling.

Right as they stepped onto the sidewalk of the main street to hail a cab, Lisa gasped, staring up at a shop on the corner.

Jack turned and found they stood outside a quaint little self-care shop, all six women staring longingly at it.

"You guys can go back," Kristi told the boys. "Us girls will stay here."

Jack laced his fingers through Jessica's. "I'm staying with you."

"You don't have to do that," she said. "I'll see you back at the resort. Go with your boys."

The boys in question stood curbside by a waiting van, staring expectantly at Jack.

Jack simply shook his head. "Nope," he said. "Where you go, I go."

Jessica looked like she wanted to argue further, but she seemed to quickly realize that it would be useless. He wanted to be near her, touching her, for as long as possible. He wasn't going to spend a second away from her that he didn't have to.

Jack turned to his buddies and said, "Go ahead. I'll catch you guys later."

Chad whispered something to Zach and Tyler, who sniggered in return before they loaded into the van and took off.

Jack thought it sounded suspiciously like "whipped."

"I'm about to whip something," he grumbled to Jessica. "And they're not gonna like it."

Jessica giggled and towed him into the shop after the girls.

The shelves and floor were constructed from a light bamboo that gave the place an airy feel, really leaning into the whole self-care vibe they were selling. There were lotions, body washes, shampoos, conditioners, all manner of masks for hair and skin, candles, soaps, essential oil blends, incense, and really anything else anyone could want in such a shop.

While Jessica and Bethani's moms crowded around the massive candle display, Bethani beelined for the essential oils, and Jack and Tyler's moms moved toward the bath bombs in baskets along the back wall, Jessica opted to peruse the lotions.

Jack watched as she took her time testing the samples, searching for the perfect scent. She'd groan each time she tried a new one, and Jack knew they were going to be here a while, if only because she'd take forever to make up her mind.

He decided to expedite the process by sniffing the samples she hadn't yet gotten to and discarding the ones that didn't seem like her style.

For example, she'd mentioned to him in passing that she didn't like lavender, so anything blended with that particular scent was immediately a nonstarter.

After testing a few, he was beginning to think he'd gone nose blind.

Until he picked up one labeled "summer citrus."

He barely had the cap popped open before he knew.

"Sunshine," Jack said quietly. She spun toward him, her braids swishing around her shoulders, giving him a soft smile at the nickname. He held the bottle out to her. "This is the one."

Quizzically, she stepped closer and leaned in to sniff the lotion.

It was an intoxicating blend of citrus and sunshine, like summer in a bottle, and once she squeezed some out onto her palm and rubbed her hands together, Jack knew he was right.

"How'd you know that was the perfect one?"

He shrugged. "It smells like you."

NOW: November 23, 2023

WITH THE SEMESTER WINDING down, Jessica was thankful for the break Thanksgiving provided her—even if it meant only three days off from classes and student teaching.

Still, three days was plenty when she got to spend them with her favorite people.

It was Thanksgiving morning, and Jessica woke in an unfamiliar room.

Okay, it wasn't *that* unfamiliar, but she'd spent so few nights at Brent and Berkley's house that waking up here was still a bit jarring.

Finally, after scrolling on her phone for way too long, laughing at TikToks and sharing the random ones only they would find funny with Kenzie—who was somewhere else in this house—Jessica rose, put on some sweats, and made her way downstairs to the kitchen.

Brent and Berkley's house was enormous—which wasn't surprising given the kind of money her brother-in-law made—but he and her sister had somehow managed to make it homey. Everything was bright and airy, balanced with enough earth tones throughout to make it cozy and welcoming instead of stark and inhospitable.

When she strolled into the kitchen, Logan and Berkley were already seated at the island. Berkley leaned back in her chair with her hand on her belly, her eyes closed in laughter while Logan leaned forward, his shoulders shaking with his own chuckles.

"What's so funny?" Jessica asked as she took a coffee mug down from the cupboard.

"Just this case I'm working on," Logan said.

Right, lawyer stuff that Jessica would never understand.

Before Jessica could respond, Kenzie walked into the room, followed shortly by Nate.

"Good morning!" Kenzie said brightly. "Happy Thanksgiving!"

Nate, meanwhile, only grumbled a greeting and set to chugging a cup of pure black coffee.

"Rough night?" Berkley asked him.

"Had a patient with some surgery complications," he said. "Had to go in late to monitor him."

"What kind of complications?" Logan asked.

"Low blood pressure. It seemed like an internal bleed, but it took ages to find the location. Newport eventually figured it out," he said, an edge to his tone.

"Who's he?" Logan asked.

"*She*," Berkley corrected, "is Nate's archnemesis."

"We think he's secretly in love with her," Kenzie added. "But you know Nate. He's like a robot."

"I am not," Nate mumbled. "Physical touch is just not my love language. Neither are words of affirmation for that matter."

"Or any of the other three options," Kenzie said, and everyone laughed.

Everyone except Jessica, who drew her eyebrows together in confusion. And though Logan smiled, she noticed he, too, wasn't entirely sure what was going on.

Jessica supposed there was a big piece of the story she was missing. Add it to the mystery that was Nate Jean.

"So wait, her name is Newport?" Jessica asked dumbly.

"No," Nate corrected, sliding onto a stool next to her. "It's Brooklyn. But I call her by her last name."

"He likes to conveniently forget that there's a 'doctor' in front of her name, too," Berkley piped up.

"Regardless," Nate said, shooting his pregnant sister-in-law a death glare that would've withered anyone with less steel in their spine than Berkley, "I'm not in love with her. She's a pain in my ass."

"Probably because she's a better doctor than you," Brent said as he walked into the room.

"Fuck you," Nate said, though there was no heat behind the words.

Jessica smiled into her coffee as the rest of the group continued to volley insults. She'd been blessed in the sibling department with Berkley and Logan, but the addition of Brent, Nate, and Mackenzie to their crew really had been the best thing to happen to any of them.

Later, after a day filled with board games and picture taking, the Daniels and Jean families were once again gathered around the dining room table, a full Thanksgiving feast laid out in front of them.

"This looks incredible, Michelle," Sandra Jean said to Jessica's mom as she scooped a heavy portion of mashed potatoes onto her plate.

Brent and Berkley had hosted the day's festivities, but with Berkley pregnant and Brent spending a large part of the day working out and doing administrative tasks for FLEX—even though he had a team of people to do that for him—the mothers ended up splitting the meals. Sandra had prepared breakfast, and her mom had prepared dinner.

"Thank you," Jessica's mom replied, cheeks pinkening with the compliment.

Conversation halted as everyone dug into their meals with gusto. There was enough food laid out that she knew each of them would be taking home several containers of leftovers, but Jessica didn't mind. In fact, she preferred it. She was, after all, a broke college student.

Thanks to the trust funds their parents had set up for her, Logan, and Berkley, tuition and living expenses were covered, but any "fun money," as her dad liked to call it, was up to Jessica. It's why she'd taken a job tutoring local high school kids in everything from English and Spanish, to history and geography classes.

She stayed *far* away from math and science. Neither of those was her forte, and she wouldn't subject poor, unsuspecting students to a tutor who had no idea what she was doing.

As everyone finished eating, or slowed significantly, conversation resumed.

"How are things with Aiden?" Berkley asked Kenzie, and immediately, Jessica saw Kenzie's hackles raise.

Brent's grip on his fork turned white-knuckled, and it seemed as if everyone at the table collectively held their breath, waiting for some sort of outburst from the oldest Jean sibling.

"They're good," she said. "The last few weeks have been pretty insane now that he's playing again, but yeah. We're happy."

"How's he looking on the ice?" her father, Ron Jean, asked.

"I wouldn't know," she said quickly, then slapped a hand over her mouth. "Shit."

"What do you mean, you wouldn't know?" Brent asked.

"Well, they've been on the road, so I haven't had a chance to see him play," Kenzie said quickly. Jessica knew her friend well enough to know she was lying, but judging by the deep, centering breaths she inhaled through her nose and the way she sat on her hands—presumably to hide the shaking—whatever Kenzie wasn't sharing was making her anxious.

Her brother, unfortunately, was like a dog with a bone, and had picked up on the same thing Jessica did. "There's something you're not telling me," Brent said.

"There's a lot I don't tell you," Kenzie retorted. "In case you forgot, *that*"—she pointed at Ron—"is my dad. Not you."

Brent opened his mouth to respond, but Sandra said, "Brent," in a low, warning tone, and her oldest child snapped his mouth shut.

"Enough about me and Aiden," Kenzie said suddenly, turning her gaze on Jessica. "Let's talk about you and Jack DeLuca."

"There's nothing to talk about," Jessica said, though her flaming cheeks said otherwise.

"Really?" Kenzie said, raising a brow. "Because that day at the tailgate, the whole, 'Jess, is that you?' moment really said something different."

"Jack?" her mom asked. "Like...the boy from Mexico?"

"Wait...*the* Jack?" Berkley said, mouth gaping.

Logan's eyes darted between the four women, and finally he said, "Okay, someone back up and tell the rest of us what the fuck is going on."

"Logan," their mother scolded.

"Sorry, Ma," he said.

"Last month, Jessica and I went to the hockey tailgate together. And she had a *moment* with Jack DeLuca, who is the Spartans' goalie. She told me they met in Mexico, but I haven't been able to get a word out of her about it otherwise, and Jack has been similarly tight-lipped with Aiden and the guys."

"So it's really him," her mom said, stunned.

Jessica could only nod.

"Holy shit," Berkley breathed.

"Will someone please tell me what's going on?" Logan burst out.

"Delivery could use some work," Kenzie said, pointing at Logan, "but I agree with him."

With a resigned sigh, Jessica took a deep breath and said, "I met Jack about three and a half years ago, when we were on spring break in Cancún. We had...a thing."

"Wait, is this that guy you texted us about?" Logan asked.

"Yes," Berkley confirmed.

"It was a lot more than a *thing*, Jessica," her mother scolded. "Don't cheapen it just because you don't want to talk about it."

"You're right," she said. "I don't want to talk about it, so how about we move onto something else."

"I'm just confused, honey," her mom said.

"There's nothing to be confused about. I found out Jack and I go to the same school, and have for the last three and a half years. Big deal. I have a boyfriend."

"Who's a complete tool," Logan said under his breath.

Berkley's head whipped to him. "I thought you liked Silas?"

"If by 'like' you mean I'd *like* to punch him in the face, then yeah."

The men of the table snickered, and Jessica crossed her arms over her chest.

Guess she wouldn't be telling them about the double date or the Sofia drama, then.

"He smoked you in the face with a volleyball *one time*," Jessica protested. "Let it go, big brother."

"It's not about that, and you know it."

Jessica arched a brow. "Then what's the problem?"

"The problem is that guy has never treated you well. He's the definition of a fuckboy."

"How can he be a fuckboy if we've been in a relationship for the last three and a half years?"

"He just...is."

Jessica searched the eyes of everyone at the table, silently begging for backup, for someone to pipe up and say that Silas wasn't as bad as Logan seemed to think.

No one did.

After that, the two families made quick work of clearing the table, then congregated in the den for a nightcap.

Somehow, Jessica wound up wedged on a loveseat with her mother, who wasted absolutely no time in needling Jessica about Jack once again.

"Tell me what's really bothering you," her mom said.

When she was younger, it had irritated Jessica to no end that her mother saw through her, as though she were as thin as a sheer curtain. As an adult, she'd come to appreciate this gift. It made it easier when she wanted to get something off her chest; before she could bring it up, her mother was already asking.

"Jack showing up really threw me for a loop," she said. "And it's not like he's someone I can really avoid, you know? He's Aiden's best friend, teammate, *and* roommate. And Kenzie is one of *my* best friends. There's going to be some overlap there, and I'm not sure how to navigate it."

"I guess I'm confused on why that's tripping you up," her mom said. "You have Silas. So either you're happy and secure in that relationship, and Jack's random presence in your life shouldn't be an issue, or..."

"Or I'm not happy," she whispered.

It was the first time she'd said the words aloud to anyone, and it felt a lot like taking her bra off at the end of the day: freeing because she could finally breathe.

But the thing was, she and Silas had been happy once, and she knew now, after three years of ups and downs, that things *could* be good again. And it didn't make sense to give up a sure thing for a maybe, for something that had been so fleeting.

So right in the moment, but ephemeral.

Jessica's mom threw an arm around her shoulders and drew her close, brushing her fingers through her hair exactly as she had for both her and her sister when they were kids. It was a gesture meant to comfort, to remind her that her mother was here, and would support her in whatever she decided to do.

"I think if you're this torn," her mom began, "you've already made up your mind."

"What do you mean?" Jessica asked, tilting her head to stare into those blue eyes that mirrored her own.

"I think this is the universe giving you a second chance, sweetheart. To have a love like me and your father, or"—she glanced across the room to her other daughter, who sat curled up on Brent's lap, both of their hands resting on her swollen belly—"like your sister and Brent. Ultimately, you have to decide if you want familiarity, or...something real. The kind of love that spans miles and years and other relationships, and still finds its way home."

NOW: November 28, 2023

TUESDAY AND THURSDAY OF every week—when school was in session—Jessica tutored. Her clients were spread across the city, but that particular one was, of all things, a hockey player at East Lansing High School. This was only their third session, so she hadn't learned much about him outside of the fact that he played hockey and enjoyed distance running. He had practice at four p.m. at Suburban Ice, which was a local ice rink, so Jessica opted to meet him there that day, when normally, they would've met at the school.

When she strolled inside, her winter coat bundled around her, hands stuffed into heavy mittens, it was just before three. Jessica was pleased to find Seb already waiting for her in the warming room, a thin paperback book open in front of him, his hand scrawling notes on a yellow legal pad.

That was the first thing she'd noticed about Seb when she

began tutoring him—he favored the legal pad over a notebook, and favored taking handwritten notes over typed ones like the majority of his classmates.

"It helps me retain the information better," he'd said when she'd questioned him that first time. "It's like hockey. I need to be hands on to learn."

As his tutor—and as an aspiring teacher—this information proved to be widely useful for Jessica, not just with Seb, but with her other clients and her career going forward.

Each person learned differently, and a learning plan that worked for one didn't always—in fact, rarely did—work for another.

"Hey Seb!" Jessica said brightly when she walked into the warming room.

He glanced up at her, shooting her his signature, wide, toothy grin, then dropped his gaze back to the page, hand still writing out words, presumably finishing his train of thought before he moved onto their session.

When she slid into her seat across him, he set his pen down and raised his gaze to meet hers. "Sorry about that," he said. "Just had to finish this thought before I moved on."

Jessica chuckled as he echoed her thoughts. "It's okay. What're you working on?"

"English paper," he said. "We're reading *1984* and I'm miserable."

"I hated that book," Jessica said sympathetically. "Although, I suppose the questions Orwell raised weren't too far off, were they?"

Seb laughed. "No, they weren't."

"What exactly does the paper have to be about? Do you need help?"

"It's a comparison between *1984* and a similar, more modern title. Where they differ and relate. Then comparing the overarching themes of both books, and relating them to our society. I haven't found a comparable book yet, though, and I'm running out of time so that's got me a little stressed. I don't understand why our teacher didn't just tell us what to read."

"*Little Brother* by Cory Doctorow."

"What?" Seb asked.

"We did this exact same unit when I was in high school," she explained. "And the book I used as a comparison was *Little Brother* by Cory Doctorow. I actually ended up loving that one, and I think you will, too. Lots of action. Not nearly as dreary as Orwell's work."

Seb scribbled the title and author down on his notepad, shooting Jessica a thumbs up. "Thanks, teach."

"Now, what are we actually working on today?"

"History," he groaned.

"You're gonna have to be more specific," she said.

"We're focusing on the years and months leading to the American Revolution."

"Okay," Jessica said, withdrawing her laptop from her back. "Get out your textbook."

Seb did as he was told, flipping open to a page somewhere in the middle. "This week's lesson is on the Boston Massacre and the Tea Party," Seb said when he scanned the first page of the chapter he opened.

"So what exactly is tripping you up?"

"I guess I'm not understanding the motivation behind dumping a bunch of tea in the water. What was so bad about buying British tea? And like...why are the British blamed for the Massacre when the colonists are kind of the ones who started it?"

Jessica smiled, loving when students started to realize the seedier side of U.S. history, and how it was all about perception. Historians framed it in such a way that made the British look bad, thus giving the colonists the right to rebel. And they did have a right, but it wasn't as cut and dry as the history books would have them believe.

And so, Jessica began explaining what exactly had enraged the Bostonians enough to destroy so much product, and how a wigmaker caused the deaths of five people. All the while, Seb scribbled out notes, asking insightful questions to help him better understand one of the inciting incidents for the American fight for independence.

Their hour passed in a flash—these sessions always did when Jessica was doing what she loved—and Seb checked his watch, startled by the time.

"Shit, I mean...shoot," he said, giving Jessica a sheepish grin as he rose to his feet and hastily shoved his stuff into his bag. "I gotta go suit up and get on the ice or my instructor is going to kill me."

"Instructor?" Jessica asked, confused. "I thought you had practice? Why not call him Coach?"

"He's technically a coach, but not in the sense that he oversees an entire team. This is my goalie coach."

All the blood drained from Jessica's face. "Goalie?" she asked, her words hoarse.

No, no, no. This couldn't be happening.

"Yeah!" Seb said. "That's my position. I've been starting since last season. Up until then, I played defense, but my actual coach saw something in me and decided to switch me to goalie. It's been working out pretty well, but since I'm so far behind other kids my age, I want to get some extra instruction to give myself a better shot at playing in college."

Seb was only sixteen—a sophomore—but she appreciated his work ethic. Not many kids his age had it, and while the tutoring was certainly his parents' idea—they were the ones paying her—Seb took it as seriously as if he spent his own money on it. He was always completely present, never on his phone or goofing around. She appreciated that about him, and had come to look forward to these sessions simply because she knew she could focus her energy on teaching instead of wrangling the kid to *want* to learn.

"That's great, Seb. Your dedication is admirable."

"Thanks," he said. "Hey, do you maybe want to meet my goalie coach? He's about your age, I think. He plays at Michigan State, actually."

Unease settled in her stomach, but she couldn't very well explain *why* she didn't want to meet this coach of his, so she simply nodded.

"Great!" Seb said, clearly excited about the prospect of his worlds colliding.

Not nearly as enthusiastic, and quite honestly feeling like she was walking to her death, she trudged from the room after Seb.

And there he stood, in dark green joggers, a black and white Nike windbreaker with the Spartan helmet logo embroidered firmly between his broad shoulders, a ball cap that matched his pants flipped backward on his head.

She'd never forget that hair, though it was longer now than it had been three and a half years ago. Nor would she ever fail to remember that ass, which had only grown juicier and more substantial now that he was a college athlete.

"Coach D!" Seb yelled as he made his way to his coach.

Coach D?

"Seb!" Jack yelled when he turned to face one of his students. "You better hurry up."

The two participated in some complicated bro handshake, and Seb hurried toward the locker room, leaving Jack staring wide-eyed at Jessica.

"What're you doing here?"

"I'm Seb's tutor," she said. "We had a session before practice. I...I didn't know you were his coach."

"Yeah..." Jack trailed off, nervously running his hands over the crown of his ball cap. "I've been doing this since freshman year. It's a nice way to pass my knowledge on to the next generation, and it keeps me out of trouble."

"I find that hard to believe," Jessica said. "I mean about you staying out of trouble. I've heard all about your team's little dares."

"I wouldn't consider them *little*," Jack said with a smirk. "One of them did get Fuller suspended."

"That's true."

"How long have you been tutoring?" he asked. Jessica waited to respond while another boy walked past and Jack paused to fist bump him.

"Since freshman year," she said. "I want to be a teacher, remember?"

He nodded, like he did in fact remember but hadn't wanted to assume she'd remained on that career path.

"That's great," he said. "Seb is a good kid."

"He really is. He's becoming one of my favorite clients."

"He's really coachable, isn't he?" Jack asked knowingly.

"Yeah," Jessica said with a smile. "Makes it really easy on me."

"Me, too," Jack said.

Then, Seb came out of the locker room, shooting them a shit-eating grin as he walked by. "I knew you two would hit it off."

"You have no idea," Jack said under his breath as Seb skated away.

There were six kids gathered at center ice, all clad in goalie gear in a variety of colors, staring expectantly at their coach, who had yet to set foot on the ice.

"I gotta go," Jack said, hooking his thumb over his shoulder. I have a rule that the last one on the ice does line to line sprints, and...well, I have to lead by example."

"You're going to do sprints?"

He nodded solemnly. "I can't expect these kids to do anything I wouldn't do," he said. "That would make me a bad coach."

"That makes sense and, as a future teacher, I appreciate that approach."

Jack gave her a small smile, stepping one skate onto the ice. "I'll see you around, Jess," he said, then skated off to join the group.

Jessica had always known Jack had a big heart, and that he cared deeply about others. So to see someone of his status and talent taking the time to pass the skills he'd learned onto a younger group of guys—and girls, Jessica realized as a ponytail swished along the back of one of the players—had butterflies taking flight in her stomach.

Which was the absolute last reaction she should be having to Jack DeLuca.

Still, she couldn't stop herself from sitting in the bleachers, far away from the few hockey moms and dads gathered to watch their kids, and stayed for practice.

As a semi-elite high school volleyball player—who could've played at a division two college but never wanted to—Jessica had been around plenty of coaches in her life. Good ones, bad ones, mediocre ones, great ones; she'd seen and worked with them all. And right off the bat, she knew Jack was a good one, a great one even.

He was attentive and kind, never shouting orders or getting pissed off when one of the kids messed up. Instead, he calmly explained to them, not what they'd done wrong, but a better way of doing what they already had. It was a subtle shift in mindset. Kids were infinitely malleable, but they were also fragile, their psyches not yet hardened by real world lessons. And honestly, Jessica didn't know anyone who learned best when someone yelled and screamed and raged about their flaws.

Jack understood this, and she could see why the kids so obviously loved him. The way he coached was a far cry from the first impression Jack had made on her, when he had taken a little game of water volleyball far too seriously. Instead of treating them like lesser, like children, he viewed the kids he coached as equals. Jessica was willing to bet that, if she asked him, he'd tell her he learned just as much from them as he taught them.

Halfway through practice, when one of the goalies missed several shots in a row and responded by chucking his stick at the ice and ripping his helmet off in frustration, Jack's reaction said it all.

Instead of feeding into the temper tantrum the kid was clearly having, he skated over calmly and placed his hands on the kid's shoulders. After a friendly exchange, Jack wrapped the kid in a hug, and it was obvious from the boy's shaking shoulders that he was sobbing.

Jessica had seen enough, and quickly gathered her things and rushed from the rink, not looking back once.

NOW: December 2, 2023

Jessica and Silas's anniversary happened to fall during the first week of December. They considered their anniversary not when Silas asked her out that first time, which would've been in mid-October, but when Silas officially asked her to be his girlfriend.

This year, it also happened to be the same night as the winter ball his frat was hosting with Sofia's sorority.

After her conversation with her mom, and another with Kenzie over lunch a few days previously, wherein she straight up lied through her teeth when her friend asked how things with Silas were, Jessica was trying to keep an open mind about the evening.

It helped that she got to dress up.

The sorority girls took outfit choices for these theme parties seriously, and Jessica hadn't wanted to show up looking frumpy or casually dressed in comparison. She may have gone a little over the top, but when she'd laid eyes on her dress during a random thrifting trip she'd taken to Detroit with Kenzie early last month, she couldn't resist.

The dress was actually more of a gown, with spaghetti straps and a deep V bodice that cinched at the waist before flaring out in a full, floor-length tulle skirt. Upon first glance, the dress was pale blue, but as she moved, the skirt became almost opalescent, shifting between a myriad of colors that made it look as though it was snow sparkling in the sun. The bodice was sheer across her upper stomach, and the entire top was decorated in hundreds—probably thousands—of glittering gems and sequins. She'd curled her hair into soft waves that cascaded down her back, wore a simple pair of silver diamond studs, and found a faux-fur shawl to drape across her shoulders and ward off the chill.

When she stepped foot onto the landing at the top of the stairs in her house, Silas let out a low whistle. Carefully, she descended, and he extended his arm to her.

"How did I manage to have the most beautiful girl on my arm tonight?" he asked, giving her a soft kiss on the cheek.

"Guess you're just lucky," Jessica said.

She yelled goodbye to her roommates and let Silas lead her out to the car.

When they arrived at Grewal Hall at 224 and walked inside, Jessica's breath was stolen from her lungs.

Originally built in 1926, Grewal Hall at 224 had recently been remodeled into a premiere event space like no other in the Lansing area. Jessica knew it had to be costing the fraternity and sorority a pretty penny, but it seemed they'd spared no expense when it came to this party.

The large main hall greeted them with an open-architecture ceiling and exposed steel trusses. Two floors of entertaining space included a second floor mezzanine that overlooked the open concept main floor, and the lower level, where the bar and other hospitality spaces were set up.

But the typically industrial space had been transformed into, well...into a winter wonderland. Each of the exposed steel trusses had been wrapped with icy twinkle lights, as had the railing on the mezzanine and the banister on the staircase. Fifty or so round tables had been set up across the mail floor, draped in white cloth and adorned with centerpieces of fresh white and pale blue flowers. At the back of the room was a stage where a DJ pumped bass-heavy music over the already wild crowd.

"Are we late?" she asked when she noted how many people had already gathered on the dance floor.

"Of course not," Silas said. "Everyone else was simply early."

"Did you...just quote *Princess Diaries* to me?"

"Maybe..." he said, offering her a sheepish smile, and she lightly pinched his bicep. "Okay, okay, fine. I did. Little sis made me watch it with her over Thanksgiving."

Jessica laughed, reminded that despite his outward arrogance and sometimes chilly demeanor, Silas was still the kind of guy willing to spend a night watching chick flicks with his little sister.

"Well," she said, gesturing to the dance floor. "Should we dance first? Get some food and find a table? Grab a drink?"

"What do you want to do?" he asked.

"Drinks, then dancing," she said. "If my feet aren't screaming at me by the end of the night, my shoes long gone, I don't want it."

"What the lady wants, the lady gets," he said in a horrible British accent, and Jessica giggled as he led them to the bar.

Atop the counter was a menu with signature cocktails created specifically for this evening. In addition, there were also several beer and wine options, but Jessica opted for one of the fancy ones.

"I'll have a White Witch," Jessica said. The cocktail, named obviously for the villain in the first *Chronicles of Narnia* movie, combined whipped cream vodka and soda poured over a piece of fluffy pink cotton candy and was served in a heavily frosted martini glass.

"That looks...disgusting," Silas said as he watched the bartender make her drink. Jessica was fascinated by the pink hue it turned thanks to the cotton candy, and when she sipped it, was surprised by how subtle the sweetness was.

"It's amazing," she breathed. The bartender passed Silas a beer, and Jessica shot him a wink. "I'll be back for more later."

The man behind the counter laughed. "I'll be here."

Jessica had to admit, she was starving, so before she dragged Silas out onto the dance floor, she took a moment to pass by the buffet table, where hors d'oeuvres were artfully arranged on plates, platters, and towers. Grabbing a little plate and a napkin from the end of the table, she loaded it up with finger sandwiches, chunks of cheese, mini quiche, a small, flaky roll, and a number of delectable-looking desserts like mini cheesecakes and cookies.

In a matter of minutes, she'd inhaled the entire thing, and turned to go back for seconds. Silas stopped her with a hand on her elbow, gently taking her plate from her and tossing it in a nearby trash.

"Set your stuff down and let's dance," he said, inclining his head toward the stage, where the DJ had switched from a Top 40 hit to "U Got It Bad" by Usher.

Jessica could hardly say no, so she dropped her clutch and shawl at a table, then let Silas lead her to the dance floor, where he stopped in the middle and spun her into his arms.

Automatically, her hands rose to his shoulders, and he settled his on her waist, tugging her closer until every inch of them from chest to hips was pressed together.

"I missed this," he said.

"Missed what?"

"You, us, being like this."

"Like what, exactly?"

Genuinely, Jessica had no idea what he was talking about. Things hadn't been outright bad between them lately, but they hadn't been good—and she didn't feel like one dance under a thousand twinkling lights was enough for Silas to consider this most recent rift between them magically repaired.

"Look," Silas said, his heavy sigh fanning across her neck, tickling the baby hairs along her nape. "I know we've been on shaky ground lately. And I'm sorry."

Taken aback, Jessica pulled away from him to study his face. She found nothing but sincerity there, which surprised her.

Her mother's words from Thanksgiving rang in her head.

Familiarity, or...something real.

But who was her mother to say that this—this relationship she'd been in for almost her entire college career—wasn't real?

Much later, Jessica's feet were finally screaming at her in that delicious way that only came from a night well spent on the dance floor, and she had no idea what time it was.

At some point while she was dancing with her friends, Silas had disappeared. In desperate need for water, Jessica decided to hit the bar for a glass then seek him out.

She paused for a moment to chug her water, then wandered over to the table where she had left her purse and shawl, making sure no one had stolen them and checking her phone for any messages. She responded to her sister and Kenzie, surprised to find it was after one a.m., then decided to head up the stairs in search of Silas.

At the landing for the second floor sat the bathrooms, and while the line for the women's was long, the one for the men's consisted of two guys, neither of whom were Silas. She waited for the current occupant to exit, and when that wasn't him, either, she turned and headed toward the back of the space. There was a long, dimly lit hallway that jutted into the back of the building, lined randomly with doors bearing signs like "electrical" and "employees only."

Clearly, Silas wasn't back here, and she was about to head back to the main floor when voices filtered out from an ajar door at the end of the hall.

"It's not that simple."

Silas.

Jessica was pushing the door all the way open before she fully formulated a plan to do so. Emboldened by the liquor coursing through her veins, she didn't even stop to consider what she might find.

And what she did was not what she'd expected.

After the constant rumors swirling the last few months of Sofia being in love with Silas, and Silas acting shady about his relationship with Sofia, Jessica fully expected to barge in on them in a much more compromising position.

Silas had his hand to Sofia's cheek, brushing a tear away as it tracked down her brown skin. Sofia's hands were fisted in his dress shirt. They didn't appear to be doing anything wrong. It simply looked like a friend comforting another friend.

But somehow, Jessica knew it was more than that.

"Sorry," she said quickly, shooting Sofia an apologetic smile. "Silas, I've been looking for you everywhere. Do you think we could head home now?"

Silas frowned. "You want to leave already?"

"Already?" Jessica asked. "Do you not realize it's after one?"

Silas stepped back from Sofia, who sullenly let her arms drop to her sides, and checked his watch. "Holy shit, it is. I'm sorry, Jess. We were talking and lost track of time."

"It's okay," she said, smiling. "I'll meet you downstairs."

They were out the door in five minutes, neither of them bothering to say goodbye to anyone. Jessica kept a lid on the words she wanted to spew the entire way home, bottling that shit up until she was a shaken bottle of champagne, one uncorking away from blowing her top.

She hadn't even bothered to put her shoes back on, blatantly disregarding the fact that it was winter, her feet already dirty past the point of no return. She dropped them unceremoniously on the closed porch before walking inside her house.

"Roomies?" Silas asked quietly.

"Home."

He only nodded, treading lightly up the stairs. Her house was old, and everything had a tendency to creak, but in the two years she'd lived here, they'd both gotten good at navigating around those weak spots.

Thankfully, her room was separated from either of her roommates by the fourth bedroom, which they never bothered to get a roommate for because, one, they could afford rent without it, and two, it became a sort of catchall for any overflow from their rooms.

So when Jessica stepped into her room and closed the door, she immediately whirled on Silas.

"I don't want to overreact here, Silas, but what the *fuck* was that?"

"I told you, we were just talking."

"Why was she crying?"

"Because she was upset," he said, looking at Jessica like that should've been the most obvious thing in the world.

"Why was she upset, Silas?"

Her boyfriend stared at her, the moment stretching on uncomfortably long. Jessica was almost certain he wouldn't answer her, and she opened her mouth, prepared to ask him to leave, when he finally spoke.

So quietly she barely heard him, he said, "She told me she's in love with me, and..."

"And what?" Jessica prompted, heart plummeting like an anchor. Somehow, some way, she knew exactly where this conversation was headed, knew precisely the words that would leave Silas's mouth.

She braced for impact.

"I think I'm in love with her, too. I didn't realize it until tonight, I swear. But I also think I've gotten really good at lying to myself, and you. And I'm so sorry for that, Jess. I think I've gotten comfortable with the familiarity of this relationship, and I was too afraid to risk it."

Jessica waited for the explosion, for the ground to open and swallow her whole. Waited for the breaking of her heart to echo in her chest.

Only...nothing happened. She felt surprisingly calm, almost like she'd expected this to happen and had been waiting for this proverbial shoe to drop for ages now.

All she thought was...*finally*.

And not *finally* in the sense that all of her worst fears were being made a reality, like finally getting confirmation of the bad news she'd been expecting for ages. No, it was *finally* in the way that she could finally let go of this thing that had been dragging her down for far too long.

And wasn't Silas echoing exactly what her mother had said to her on Thanksgiving?

I think if you're this torn, you've already made up your mind.

Silas was in love with someone else—and so was she.

It was useless trying to deny it. She'd been fighting it every day for the last three and a half years. Even when she'd thought with absolute certainty she'd never see him again, Jack still held her heart in his hands. It had taken him walking back into her life in the most unlikely of places to remind her that she'd never gotten it back from him, not really. The one she'd given to Silas had been a fake, a replica, never wholly his to take or hers to give.

Silas stared at her expectantly, surely waiting for the outburst of rage and indignation, for the tears to fall, for her to react exactly as any normal girlfriend would in this situation.

Instead, she surprised them both by saying, "Okay."

"Okay?"

Jessica nodded. "Okay. Look, things between us haven't been great for a while. I don't know that they ever have been, honestly. I want to be happy, Silas. Not arguing about stupid shit or going days without speaking because one of us feels slighted by the other. And I want that for you, too. I'm not that girl for you anymore."

"So we're...breaking up? That easy?"

"That easy," she said, the rightness of the decision settling over her like sunshine warming her skin after a storm.

In a rush, Silas stepped to her and wrapped her in his arms, one last time. "I want you to be happy, too, Jess," he said into her hair.

Then he was gone.

NOW: December 31, 2023

Two days after the Great Lakes Invitational championship game—which the Spartans won for the first time in fifteen years—Jack found himself staring down the possibility of spending a New Year's Eve alone.

When he'd called Jessica two days before as a favor to Aiden, he hadn't expected her to sound so excited to hear from him, or her little, "you better" in response to him telling her he'd call her later, which really had only been him attempting to save face in front of his teammates.

As he'd left, Aiden had said something about how they didn't have time to deal with whatever he had going on with Jessica, but the thing was...there wasn't anything to deal with. Jessica was still with Silas, and outside of a few random texts from her congratulating him on their recent wins, and her showing up at Suburban Ice last month, they hadn't talked.

Having had quite enough of his own little pity party, Jack rose from his bed and made his way down to the kitchen, where Asher and Luke were setting up for their New Year's Eve party.

"What's the plan for tonight?" Jack asked.

"What do you mean?" Asher responded. "We're gonna get drunk and hook up. Exactly like we do every party."

Neither Jack nor Aiden had done any hooking up—save Aiden with Kenzie—at a party in ages, and Jack found himself warming to the idea. Anything to get his mind off Jessica Daniels.

"But we could do that at the bar," Jack protested, suddenly experiencing the urge to get out of this house and lose himself in a crowd for a few hours tonight.

"*You* could do that at the bar," Asher responded. "I'm saying here, and drinking all of this." He walked to their refrigerator and pulled it open. Where the shelves had once been filled with Tupperware containers full of the boys' weekly meal preps, the wire racks were now lined with cans and cans of alcoholic beverages.

There were, of course, cans of domestic beer such as Bud Light and Miller Lite, as well as some Labatt, Corona, and Heineken. The entire bottom shelf was lined with White Claw, Truly, and High Noon in every flavor imaginable. It was a bar's worth of booze, and Jack was afraid to ask who had forked over the money for it.

"Luke and I went halfsies," Asher said when Jack reluctantly posed the question.

His shoulders sagged in relief. "Good. I was worried you guys used the can money on this mess."

"It's not a mess," Luke said, speaking for the first time since

Jack came downstairs. "It's the most beautiful thing I've ever seen. And, frankly, DeLuca, I'm offended that you think I would do such a thing. As your captain, I hope you find me more honorable than that."

Jack snorted. Luke must already have a few drinks in him, because only then did he start talking like a stuck-up prick.

"Okay fine," Jack acquiesced. "I'll stay in tonight. Who all is coming over?"

"The usual suspects," Asher said.

Jack fought back a groan. That meant his house would be teeming with their underclassmen teammates, and they would inevitably wake up in the morning and find said teammates passed out on every flat surface.

"I should warn you that Sofia will be here," Luke said. "I was out getting the mail yesterday and she walked by. I told her she and some of her sisters should come over."

This time, Jack did groan. "What made you think that was a good idea?"

Luke shrugged. "Maybe the fact that you didn't even tell us you guys broke up for ages, and you don't seem all that torn up about it."

"Bro, she dumped me. Of course I'm upset about it."

Although, perhaps not as upset as he should've been. Did it sting his pride that Sofia dumped him because she was in love with someone else? Yes. Did it hurt even worse knowing the guy in question happened to be dating the girl that got away? An even bigger yes.

How was it that Jack kept losing to Silas fucking Jeffers?

"Suck it up, buttercup," Asher said from across the room,

where he was taping a festive banner over the archway that separated the kitchen from the dining room.

"You're an asshole," Jack muttered. "What time is everyone coming over?"

"Whenever they want," Luke said. "But we told the boys no earlier than ten."

Jack checked his watch. That was four hours from now, which meant he could go upstairs and take a nap before he inevitably pulled an all-nighter celebrating in one way or another.

An hour later, his phone buzzing loudly on his nightstand pulled him from a dead sleep. Groaning, Jack rolled over and swiped it into his hand, squinting to find a text from Asher, sent to the roommate group chat.

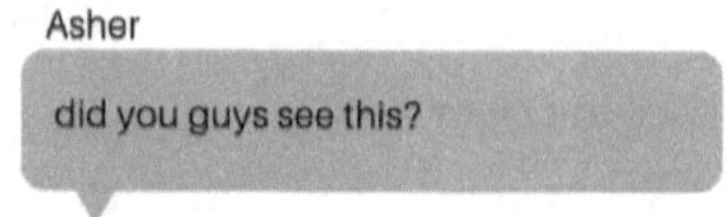

Attached was a link to an Instagram post, and Jack clicked on it, sitting up in bed.

At first, he thought his eyes were playing tricks on him, and he rubbed at them vigorously, hoping to wipe the sleep away. But when he blinked them clear and refocused on the screen, his heart plummeted.

Perfectly curated in a tiny Instagram square on Sofia's feed was a picture of her...and Silas. Kissing in front of Beaumont Tower.

Got me a new boo for the new year, the caption read.

Jack's heart dropped further, and not even for himself. No, in that moment, he realized exactly how well and truly over Sofia Kinsey he was. This pain he experienced now was all for Jessica.

Without thinking, he texted her.

Long moments passed before Jessica's response, in which Jack hopped from his bed and paced his room, prowling like a caged animal begging to be let free.

Finally, his phone buzzed.

Jack's heart beat faster in his chest. Could those two words mean what he thought they did? Ever since Jessica had walked back into his life, he knew their old spark was still there. He felt it every time he looked at her, like an ember in the ashes of a nearly-dead fire. All it needed was a little tending to ignite once again.

And now that they were both unattached…the terms of their deal that final night in Mexico rang in Jack's head.

Now was his chance. Right here. Either he took his shot, or he didn't. But he could feel it deep in his bones: it was now or never.

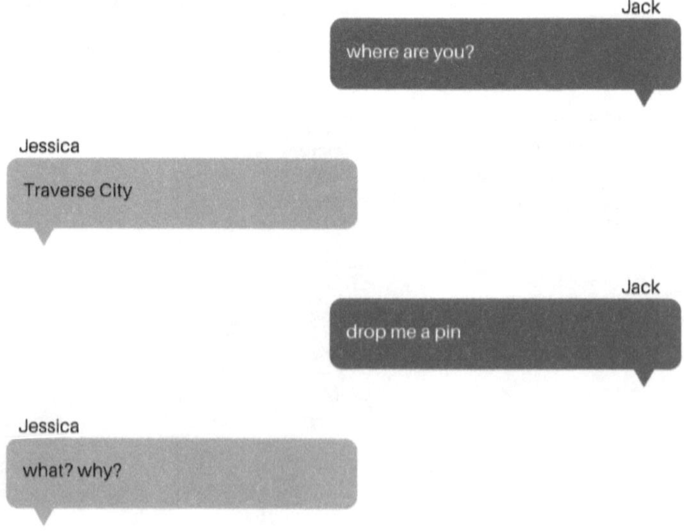

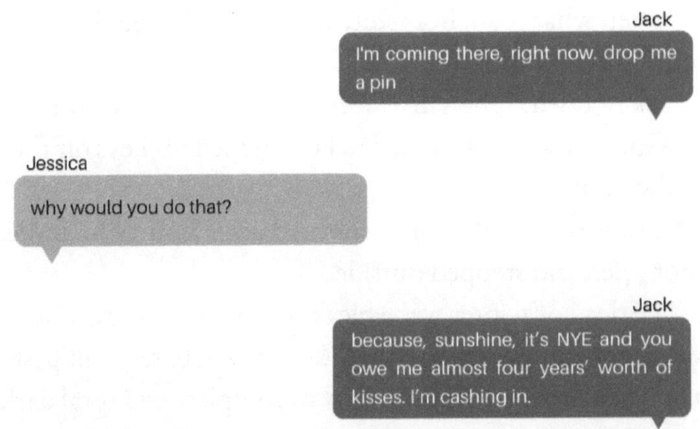

Jack didn't even wait for Jessica's response, simply dressed in dark jeans and a white button down, throwing a change of clothes, gym shorts, and any toiletries he may need for the night into his backpack. In five minutes, he was bounding down the stairs and sliding into the living room. Luke paused mid-sip of his beer and squinted at him.

"Going somewhere?" he asked.

"I'm going to get my girl back."

"Bro, Sofia is with someone else now. Get over it," Asher said.

Jack ignored him, rushing toward the door and the tiny "foyer" that consisted of a miniscule coat closet, some racks they'd hung when they moved in, and a cube organizer where they stowed their shoes to keep them out of the way. Jack grabbed his puffy MSU hockey jacket out of the closet and pulled his Timberlands out of one of his cubes, stuffing his feet and arms into both as he moved back into the living room.

"I don't think he means Sofia," Luke said in response to Asher's comment.

"Then what—oh, holy shit. You're going to get Jessica, aren't you?"

Jack nodded. "She's in Traverse City. I'll be home tomorrow."

"Good luck!" Luke yelled as Jack swiped his keys off the hook by the door.

"Use protection!" Asher shouted after him as he pulled the door open and stepped outside.

The dead of winter was a bleak time in Michigan. The sun set way too fucking early, so even though it was barely half past seven p.m., Jack drove to Traverse City in complete and total darkness, with not even the moon to guide his way. Thankfully, it wasn't snowing and hadn't in a few days, so he wasn't stressing about his little Chevy Colorado sliding all over slippery roads.

However, the farther north he traveled, the more snow covered the ground, and when he got off the interstate to travel smaller state highways into Traverse City, he was surprised by the mountains piled high along the sides of the roads.

Jessica had dropped him a pin like he'd asked before he left East Lansing, but sometime during his drive, she'd texted again with a change in plans. Jack had to stop for gas anyway, so he pulled into the nearest station, something called Holiday, which he'd never heard of before.

While his truck refueled, Jack read Jessica's messages.

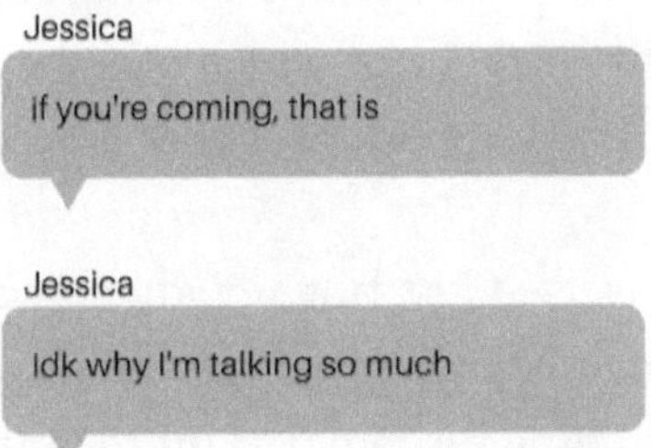

Instead of responding via text, Jack called her.

"Hey!" she shouted when she answered, the cacophony on her end of the line so loud Jack had to pull his phone away from his ear. A moment later, the sound cutoff. "Sorry about that."

"According to my phone, The Mast is about five minutes from where I'm at."

Jessica gasped. "You're actually coming here."

"I actually am. Why didn't you believe me?"

She was quiet for a moment, then said, "It was too much to hope for."

"Sunshine..."

"We can have this conversation when you get here. Drive safe, and I'll see you soon."

"Okay," he said, smiling. "See you soon."

"And Jack?" Jessica said before he could hang up.

"Yeah?"

"I'm really excited to see you."

His grin grew. "Me, too, sunshine."

Once he ended the call, the telltale *thunk* signaling a full gas tank echoed through his truck. A moment later, with the fuel nozzle hung and the gas cap firmly back in place, Jack hit the road again.

Exactly five minutes later, he pulled into a parking lot connected to The Mast, the front entrance of which was shaped to mimic the bow of a ship, a mast rising out of it with a neon sign blinking the bar's name.

Jack had never been to Traverse City, but already he was getting the vibe that it took being a coastal town very seriously.

Almost as if she'd been watching for him, the moment he slid out from behind the wheel of his truck, Jessica pushed through the door and onto the sidewalk. For a moment, they remained rooted in place, simply staring at each other.

Jack didn't know who moved first, only that one moment he'd been beside his truck, and the next he was scooping Jessica into his arms.

He inhaled deeply, the scent of her washing over him like an ocean wave, instantly transporting him back to Mexican beaches, too many shots of tequila, and endless days in the sun with her. They were a far cry from that paradise now, but having her back in his arms was exactly his idea of nirvana.

Jessica pulled away first, though her hands remained glued to his biceps. "You're here," she breathed, her words fogging in the air between them.

"I told you I would be," he reminded her.

"Yeah, but I didn't think you were serious! That's a three hour drive."

"Three hours is nothing when you're at the other end," he said.

And he meant it. There was something to be said for not having to hide his feelings anymore, and now that both of them were free to give this thing between them another chance at last, he wanted to remind her exactly what it was he felt for her.

"Jack..."

"Look," he said, gripping her hands in his. "We've waited almost four years for this. Please don't pull away from me."

"I'm not," she said. "But I just got out of a relationship. One I'd been in nearly the entire time we've been apart. How would it look if I just jumped into something new with you?"

"I think it would be perfectly acceptable considering Silas already did that exact thing...with *my* ex."

Jessica stilled a beat, then burst out laughing. "You're right! He did it first, and so did Sofia, so now we don't have to look like the bad guys when we walk in there together."

"Trust me, Jess," he said, lifting her chilled hand to his mouth and kissing the back of it, "when we walk in there and people see how I look at you, they won't even remember Silas's name."

Jack chuckled when Jessica shivered, and he was certain it had nothing to do with the cold.

For the first time, Jack and Jessica were in public together outside of the Mexico bubble, and Jack was basking in it. Simply having her near, and knowing that, while they still had some things to talk about and work through, he could hold her hand or wrap her in a hug or plant a kiss to the top of her head whenever he wanted had him absolutely giddy.

The clock ticked closer to midnight, and he and Jessica seemed to have an unspoken agreement that their first kiss—again—wouldn't happen until the clock struck twelve. They'd danced around it for the last hour and a half. He'd press his lips to her cheek, dangerously close to the corner of her mouth. She'd pull his head down when they swayed to the hip-hop pouring out of the speakers, her mouth a breath away before she spun out of his arms.

Jack was practically bursting at the seams when someone shouted, "One minute!"

"C'mon!" Jessica said, grabbing his hand and pulling him off the dance floor. She swiped their coats as they ran by their table, and she tossed him his, only letting go of his hand long enough for them to pull them on.

Every bar patron made a mad dash outside, slipping and sliding across the snowy streets down to a nearby dock, where they fanned out, eyes turned expectantly to the sky over the water.

"What's going on?" Jack asked when he and Jessica had staked their spot about halfway down the dock.

"Fireworks!" she said.

Somewhere down the line, someone began the countdown.

Ten.

Jack pulled Jessica to him, wrapping his arms around her waist. Hers went around his neck, her mittened fingers rubbing circles across his nape.

Nine.

"Jess," he whispered.

Eight.

"Jack," she said, just as quietly.

Seven.

He raised a hand and tipped her chin up, forcing her to meet his eyes.

Six.

"We don't have to do this, you know," he told her, even though the words killed him. God, he wanted to so badly.

Five.

"I know," she said, a slow smile unfurling on her face. "I want to."

Four.

Jack's arms tightened around her.

Three.

They leaned closer, heads angling in opposite directions.

Two.

A breath away now, her mouth was his for the taking.

One.

Jessica licked her lips.

Boom.

As the first firework lit up the midnight sky, Jack captured Jessica's mouth with his. And the instant the connection was made, everything else faded away. They could've been anywhere in the world, witnessing a split-second, once-in-a-lifetime phenomenon, and Jack would've only wanted to be right here.

It was exactly as he'd remembered. Soft but insistent. Slow but heart-racing.

Every minute of the last three and a half years apart had been worth it for this one perfect moment. It had all led to this, this claiming kiss beneath the stars and fireworks.

The dawn of a new year meant shaking off the old and ushering in the new. And Jack supposed that's exactly what he and Jessica were doing. Because they weren't those two spring break teenagers anymore. They'd both grown and lived and loved in their time apart.

But this kiss? It was familiar and thrilling. It was a promise, a commitment, a reminder.

This kiss was finally coming home.

NOW: January 8, 2024

On the first day of her final semester of college, Jessica found herself in her academic advisor's office. Over the years, Fran, the woman in question, had worn many hats for Jessica. Friend, confidant, mentor, a shoulder to cry on when her course load got to be a little too much the spring semester of her sophomore year.

Today, Fran was donning yet another: career advisor.

The day had come where Jessica needed to start applying for jobs after college, and she had no idea where to even begin.

"So what're you thinking, kiddo?" Fran asked, pushing her wire-framed glasses back up her nose, an action she would perform no less than twenty times over the next hour. Jessica frequently told her to get them adjusted so they actually fit, but she refused to listen.

"Well, you know it's always been my dream to teach English

as a second language," Jessica said. "The problem is, I don't even know where to start."

"What do you mean? You have a resumé and letters of recommendation and all that, right?"

"Yes. I don't mean that stuff. I mean like...finding jobs to actually apply for."

"Oh!" Fran gasped, waving a hand in the air. "That's easy."

She spun to her computer, an absolutely ancient Mac with the processor on the back, half of it that opaque white color, the other half orange, and began clacking away at the keys. Jessica had often asked her why she didn't upgrade to something sleeker, or more portable, to which Fran would reply, "If it ain't broke, don't fix it."

Hard to argue with that.

"Okay," Fran said, shoving away from her computer as her equally-ancient printer whirred to life across the room. When it spit out a piece of paper, Fran handed it to Jessica.

"Here are the ones I found with a cursory search in our database that are actively seeking applicants. I think we can eliminate a few right off the bat since you don't speak Italian or Dutch," Fran said, pointing to the job postings in question.

While teaching English as a second language meant she'd primarily be conversing with her students in her native language, Jessica had been reminded over and over by her professors—and Fran—that her life would be a lot easier if she could speak the native language in whichever country she found a position in.

As Jessica spoke Spanish and Russian, that rather limited her options. Although, Mexico, South America, and Spain were all options, and Russia itself was a giant country.

Jessica perused the list, though given her lack of experience with this sort of job search, she had no idea what she was looking at. "Do any of these stick out to you?" she asked Fran, handing the paper back.

As Fran studied the list, she chewed absently on the cap of her pen, a habit that always grossed Jessica out.

Fran set the paper down and began circling certain postings and crossing out others. Finally, she handed it back to Jessica.

"I exed out the ones in countries where you don't speak the language," she said, and Jessica noted with satisfaction that had only eliminated three of the twenty jobs on the list. "Then I circled the ones that look like the best fit for you."

Jessica scanned the sheet, her smile growing. There were quite a few postings in South America, one in Spain, one in southern Mexico, and several in Saint Petersburg and Moscow.

She'd always pictured herself as a beachy girl; growing up in the frigid north had always offended her, and on more than one occasion when she was a child, she'd begged her parents to move them somewhere warmer.

Obviously, that hadn't worked.

But she had to admit, while thoughts of Mexico conjured fond memories—namely time spent with Jack—the idea of heading to Russia and experiencing something totally new excited her.

Of course, the moment she considered moving halfway across the world, her heart clenched, and dread settled in her stomach like an anchor.

Because leaving would mean leaving Jack, and she'd only just gotten him back.

Later that evening, after a tutoring session with Seb and hours spent polishing her resume and sending job applications out to the far corners of the world, Jessica called her sister.

"I am so glad you called," Berkley said by way of greeting.

"What's up?" Jessica asked, concerned.

"Oh, nothing," Berkley said. "I'm just bored out of my fucking mind. Can you believe they've got me on bed rest for the next two months until this baby is born?"

"Actually?" Jessica said. "Yeah, I can."

"Traitor," Berkley grumbled.

"Berk, you have placenta previa," she said. "Excuse me for wanting you and my nephew to be alive and healthy."

With a sigh, Berkley said, "You're right. Now what's up with you? Why did you call?"

"You and Brent went through some really bullshit miscommunication issues," Jessica said without preamble.

"Thanks for the reminder," Berkley said dryly before Jessica could continue.

"But you worked through it, and now you're happily married with that sweet baby on the way."

"Is there a question in there somewhere?"

"How do you approach having big conversations with him?"

"Such as...?"

"Such as...I started applying for jobs today. A few in the States, but mostly, I'm still planning on teaching English as a second language, so the majority of what I applied for is out of the country. South America, Mexico, Spain, and Russia."

"Russia?" Berkley asked, surprised. "I suppose it's time you finally put all those hours on Mango Languages to good use."

"Exactly," Jessica said with a smile. "But the problem is..."

"Jack," her sister said sympathetically.

"Yes, Jack. We've only just gotten back together, or whatever it is we're doing, and the thought of losing him again scares me more than anything."

"That's a normal reaction to have," Berkley said. "You waited a long time for this. But you've also waited a long time to chase your dreams."

"I know," Jessica said, dragging a frustrated hand through her hair. "That's what makes this so hard. I want them both. I think I *need* them both."

"This had always been a sticking point for me and Brent at the beginning of our relationship," Berkley said. "My career was more important to me than anything at that point in my life. I didn't spend seven years in college and law school to throw it all away because some guy walked into my life and told me I didn't have to work if I didn't want to. I *did* want to work, and I still do. But Brent and I learned to compromise. His money is our money, and my money is our money. When I decided to go part-time at work and go back to school to open my own agency, he fully supported me. Brent is my biggest fan, and he realizes now how important it is to me to contribute to this family."

"Is there a point to this story?" Jessica asked, only partially joking. She was all too aware of the struggles her sister and brother-in-law had endured in the early days of their relationship.

"Yes, you little shit. What I'm trying to say is that Brent supports me in whatever I want to do. The right man always will. So you just need to rip off the bandage, little sis. Sit Jack down and have a candid conversation with him about your career plans, and how you want him to be in your life, but this has to come first. I have a feeling Jack will be more understanding than you'd think."

Jessica hummed noncommittally, their conversation turning to something that Jessica only paid half a mind to. Her thoughts buzzed incessantly, like a fly that simply wouldn't leave her alone.

Her sister was mid-sentence, complaining about her upcoming baby shower when the vibration under Jessica's skin grew too incessant to ignore.

"I'm sorry, Berk. I gotta go."

"Good luck," was all Berkley said before Jessica hung up.

A moment later, she was on the phone with Jack.

"Hey, sunshine," he said happily. "I'm just leaving practice."

"Perfect," she said. "Will you come over?"

Jack must've heard something in her tone, because he said, "Is everything okay?"

"Everything is fine," she promised, though it wasn't, not really. "We just...we need to talk."

"Okay..." he said slowly. "I'll be right over."

"See you soon."

In the five minutes it took for Jack to ride his little moped from Munn to her house, Jessica had worked herself into quite a state of anxiety. When she opened the door to let him in, and he wrapped his arms around her, she could barely hug him back.

Once they were safely ensconced in her room, Jack burst.

"Jess, you're scaring me. What's going on?"

"You know I've always wanted to be a teacher," she said.

"Yes?" Jack replied. "You told me so ages ago in Mexico."

"Originally, I wanted to teach English, or history, or something mundane like that, here in the States at a normal high school. But...did you know I can speak Spanish and Russian?"

Jack's eyebrows rose toward his forehead. "Spanish, yes. But Russian? Damn, sunshine, that's impressive."

"Thanks," she said, offering him a weak smile. "When I started college, and got into tutoring and student teaching, I had a professor tell me she thought I'd be great at doing something a little less cookie cutter with my career."

"Which is?"

"Teaching English as a second language."

"Like...to immigrants?" Jack asked.

Jessica wasn't surprised his mind had gone there. Hers had, too...at first.

"Initially that was the plan," she told him.

"But not anymore."

"No."

Jessica hung her head, peeking up at him through her eyelashes, not surprised when realization dawned on his face.

"You're going overseas somewhere, aren't you?"

"I don't know yet," she told him honestly. "But I did apply for several jobs today."

"Where?" His tone was flat, clinical, and Jessica's heart ached.

"Southern Mexico, Argentina, Chile, Bolivia, Ecuador, Cuba, Spain...and Russia. Moscow and Saint Petersburg, to be exact."

"Fuck," Jack said, sitting down hard at the end of her bed, the pillows at the head jumping with the force of it.

She sat down next to him and reached for his hand, lacing their fingers together, the knot in her chest easing a bit when he let her. "I don't know what this means for us."

"I think this means there isn't an us at all," he said quietly.

"Don't say that. Nothing is set in stone yet."

"I just got you back, Jess," he said, finally looking at her. "And now you expect me to let you go? Again? I don't...I don't think I can do that. At least not three or four months from now when you inevitably leave."

His words punched her in the gut, and Jessica struggled to catch her breath.

After New Year's Eve, when they returned to her parents' house, and she officially introduced him to her dad—though her parents made them sleep in separate rooms—there had been an unspoken agreement that they were together. But there'd been no formal conversation, and now, it seemed there might never be.

"What're you saying to me right now?" she asked, hands shaking as fear coursed through her veins.

"I don't know!" Jack stood abruptly, pulling his hand free from hers. "I've spent every day of the last three and a half years missing you. And I get you back only to lose you like that?" he asked, snapping his fingers. "I can't...I have dreams, too, Jess. You know? Dreams like playing in the NHL."

"I know," she said softly, rising to stand in front of him. She placed her hands on his chest, his heart thumping wildly under her touch. "I'm not saying we have to decide anything right now. I only wanted to make you aware of my plans. If I hear back from any of these jobs, or you have scouts reach out to your agent about post-graduation signing opportunities...we'll cross those bridges when we come to them. But right now..."

"Right now?"

"I spent every day of the last three and a half years missing you, too. Even though I was with Silas. When we broke up, I realized I'd never truly given him my heart." She looked up at Jack and smiled, tears pooling in her eyes as an overwhelming rush of love for this man raced through her. "See, there was this boy in Mexico. And he gave me the best week of my life. But like the stupid kids we were, we walked away. Every day since then, every moment of that time apart had just been bringing us back together. And *together* is exactly where we belong. The rest we can figure out as we go."

"We make the most of the time we do have," he said, echoing the same sentiment that had informed their last day in Mexico.

"Yes," she breathed, curling her fingers into his shirt. "I want this, Jack. Us. More than anything."

"Me, too, sunshine," he breathed, bending down to plant a quick kiss on her lips. "Me, too."

Then he kissed her again, deeper this time, more insistent. Branding himself on the very marrow of her bones. There had never been anyone like Jack, and there never would be again. She slid her hands up his chest and across his shoulders, settling them around the back of his neck to pull him closer. Within moments, she was off her feet and tossed onto the bed. Jack crawled up next to her, rolling onto his back and pulling her atop him.

Her hair fell into a curtain around them, and her world narrowed to his face, his body beneath hers, their hearts thumping to the same beat. To his hands on her hips, fingertips toying with the sliver of skin exposed where her shirt had ridden up.

To his mouth, his lips, and the words that left them next.

"I love you, you know."

In a romance novel, this was the moment where Jessica would've kicked and squealed like an excited child. The man confessing his love first was always her favorite part of the love stories she read.

But this wasn't fiction. This was real life, *her* life, and she wasted no time echoing the sentiment.

"I love you, too."

Jack

NOW: January 25, 2024

Jack had just turned his phone off airplane mode after touching down in Minneapolis when it rang with an incoming call. The readout showed his agent's name.

"What's up, Darren?" Jack asked when he answered, angling his body toward the plane window, hoping to cut down on the background noise from his teammates preparing to deplane.

"Just had an update for you on the signing front. You got a second?"

"Ahh..." Jack said, glancing over his shoulder. "Can I call you back in like an hour? We literally just landed. I haven't even unbuckled."

"Oh, sure!" Darren said. "No problem! Call me when you're settled at the hotel."

"Thanks, man. Will do."

"Who was that?" Aiden asked the moment Jack hung up.

"Darren. Apparently, he has an 'update on the signing front,'" Jack said, using air quotes around his agent's words.

"That's exciting!" Aiden said. Finally, the queue ahead of them moved up the aisle, so they both rose and slid out of their seats.

An hour later, Jack and Aiden were checked into their room and settled in for a few hours until they had evening skate. Tomorrow, they played the University of Minnesota, who was the best team in their conference and one of the top teams in the country. Jack would have to be on top of his game to hold off the Gophers' explosive offense.

"I'm gonna call Kenzie," Aiden said as he flopped down onto his bed.

"Don't!" Jack said. "Not yet. I gotta call Darren back."

"Right, sorry."

Jack lifted his phone and dialed his agent, his hands growing inexplicably clammy as it rang and rang.

Right when Jack thought it'd go to voicemail, Darren picked up.

"Sorry, man. On the line with another client," he said. "How was the flight?"

"Good," Jack said. Then, having had enough of pleasantries, added, "Cut to the chase, Darren."

Darren laughed, a full, hearty sound wherein Jack could practically see his entire body shaking with the force of it. "That's what I like about you, Jack. No bullshit."

"Well, this is my career we're talking about here," he said. "So shoot me straight."

"We've had some recent interest," Darren said. "Nothing concrete yet, but you've got options, both here in the States and overseas."

Jack sat up straighter at the word *overseas*. "Where exactly overseas?"

"Ahh, lemme see…" Darren said, trailing off as papers shuffled in the background. The man was a hell of an agent, representing quite a few of the NHL's top guys in addition to signing high-caliber college players like Jack, but his organizational skills left something to be desired.

"Oh! Here it is," Darren finally said. "Looks like SKA and CSKA."

"In English, please," Jack said, and Aiden shot him a look that said, *be patient.*

"SKA is in Saint Petersburg, and CSKA is in Moscow."

"Russia," Jack breathed, his heart pumping harder in his chest.

Oblivious to his freak out, Darren plowed ahead. "There's also been interest from Toledo, WBS, Kalamazoo, San Diego, Manitoba, and Ontario," he said, listing out a combination of ECHL and AHL teams.

Any one of them would be an incredible opportunity for him, and put him one step closer to his dream of playing in the NHL. But…*Russia.* The name lodged in his mind like a popcorn kernel stuck between his teeth.

The end of the season was still a long way off, and Jack wasn't going to make any decisions about his future at the moment. Plus, there weren't any decisions to make. He couldn't officially sign anything until after he'd played his final minute of college hockey, and if he had anything to say about it, that wouldn't be until April, after the Spartans lifted that national championship trophy.

"That's all great to hear," Jack said to Darren, and the silence from both his agent and his roommate told him he'd missed some crucial part of the conversation.

"You didn't hear a single word I just said, did you?" Darren asked with a laugh.

Jack chuckled sheepishly. "No, sorry."

"I know you can't sign anything yet, but you could give any one of these teams a verbal commitment whenever you want."

"I'm not ready to do that," Jack said quickly. "I..."

He scrambled for a reasonable explanation that wasn't "I don't know where my girlfriend will be in four months, and I don't want to make any decisions without talking to her first."

Ultimately, he settled on, "I want to talk to my dad and brother first."

Jack was kind of a hockey legacy. His father had a short stint in the pros before an injury sidelined him for good, and he'd been an NHL scout ever since. Jack's older brother, Josh, was a defenseman for the Pittsburgh Quakers. Basically, Jack would've wound up playing whether he wanted to or not. It just so happened that he loved the game, and was a highly-skilled goalie.

"Perfectly understandable," Darren said. "Send Joe and Josh my best."

"Will do," Jack said, ready to hang up.

"Oh, and Jack?"

"Yeah?"

"Good luck this weekend!"

Jack smiled. "Thanks, man. Talk soon."

"Do you really want to talk to your dad and brother?" Aiden asked. "Or do you actually want to talk to Jessica first?"

"Both," Jack answered honestly. "But I really am about to call Dad and Josh."

"Hell yeah!" Aiden said, hopping up from his bed to jump on Jack's. "I haven't seen Papa D in way too long."

"Me, either," Jack grumbled. Between his dad's scouting schedule, and Jack and Josh's game schedules, the DeLuca men connected sporadically, usually via five minute phone calls and "good game tonight, kid!" texts.

Jack navigated to his dad's contact info and pressed the button to FaceTime him. When his dad answered, before Jack could even say a word, Aiden shouted, "Hey, Papa D!"

"Hey, Fuller!" his dad said back, then turned his attention to Jack. "Hey, son."

"Hey, Dad. Hold on a sec, I'm gonna get Josh on."

A moment later, Jack's older brother's face filled half the screen.

"Sup, pops. Sup, little bro. Sup, Fuller."

"Hey, Josh," they parroted.

Honestly, the whole thing felt a little Charlie's Angels.

"So what's up, Jack?" his dad asked. "Obviously, there's a reason you called."

"I just got off the phone with Darren," he said.

"And?" Josh prompted. "Lemme guess: WBS is on the list of teams that want you when your season is over."

"How could you possibly know that?" Jack asked. "I just got that news myself."

Josh shrugged. "You're a DeLuca."

Right, as if that explained everything.

"You guys didn't say anything, did you?" Jack asked his father and brother suspiciously.

"Of course not," his dad said. "I'm a scout for the Mustangs. You do remember that, right?"

Jack laughed. How could he forget? None of the teams Darren had mentioned were affiliates of Philly, which meant his father didn't have his hand in any part of this.

WBS, or Wilkes-Barre/Scranton, however, was an affiliate of…the Pittsburgh Quakers.

"What did you do, Josh?" Jack asked, glaring daggers at his brother through the phone.

"I simply reminded the powers that be that I have a little brother getting ready to graduate, and that he's a hell of a goalie."

"I didn't ask you to do that!"

"You didn't have to," Josh said with a shrug. "This sport is all about nepotism. I'm just doing my part."

"You're an asshole."

"You won't be saying that in four months when you're playing in the AHL."

"I'm good enough to make it without your help, Josh," Jack said through clenched teeth.

"Well, Jacky boy," Josh said, using that infernal nickname Jack had hated for his entire life, "I'm your big brother, and I want you to have the best shot at the NHL. Playing in the A is it."

"You think I don't know that?"

Of course, he knew that. Everyone knew that. A lot of the time, players who remained in college all four years weren't quite good enough to jump straight to an NHL roster. Time in the minors was exactly what players like Jack—and Aiden, and even Brent Jean—needed after college to get used to playing a bigger and faster game. Jack had no delusions about his talent level. He was good, but not jump-straight-from-college-to-the-NHL good. He was more than willing to put in his time in the AHL—or even the ECHL—pay his dues, and hopefully get a shot in the show. And if he never made it to the NHL? That would be fine, too. At least he'd be playing professionally, doing what he loved for a living.

But there were also those Russian offers to consider...

"What do you guys know about the KHL?" Jack asked, referring to the Russian Kontinental Hockey League.

"Not much other than it produces some insanely talented Russian guys," his dad said. And he would know firsthand, having taken multiple trips overseas to watch said guys play.

"Did Darren say something?" Josh asked.

"Yeah, he said the SKA in Saint Petersburg and the CSKA in Moscow inquired about me, too."

"Hey, that's great, kid!" his dad said.

"Are you seriously considering going over there instead of staying in the States?" his brother asked, incredulous.

"I don't know," Jack said.

Next to him, Aiden coughed something into his fist, something that sounded suspiciously like "liar."

"What was that, Fuller?" Josh asked. "C'mon, don't be shy. Share with the class."

"He's considering it," was Aiden's reply.

"You asshole," Jack said, shoving his teammate so hard that Aiden fell off the bed, hitting the floor with a *thud* and string of impressively filthy expletives. Instead of rejoining Jack, he crawled onto his own bed and stuffed his AirPods in his ears. The faint, heavy drums of rock music filtered to Jack's side of the room.

"What is he talking about?" Josh asked.

Jack sighed, knowing he wasn't getting out of this one. Jack's mom was an amazing woman to have tolerated the three of them this long, because they were nothing if not annoyingly persistent when they were on the scent of something fishy.

And this was definitely fishy to his dad and brother.

"Okay so, you know how Jessica and I are together now, right?" They nodded in response. "So, Jessica wants to be a teacher."

"She can teach anywhere," Josh said.

"You would say that," Jack said with an eye roll. His brother's sole focus was his career, and he'd be damned if he let a woman derail that. But to Jack, Jessica wasn't just any woman. She was *the* woman. The only one he wanted forever. "She could be a teacher anywhere, yes, if she wanted to be your run of the mill school teacher. But she doesn't. Jessica wants to teach English as a second language, and she's applied to jobs all over the world. Well...not all over. In Spanish speaking countries, and in Russia."

"Ahhhhh," his dad said, dragging out that single syllable.

"So you're going to give away your shot at the show for a girl?"

"We haven't made any decisions yet," Jack said. "But I'd be lying if I said those Russian offers didn't sound like a gift right about now."

"This is the dumbest shit I've ever heard," Josh said, and a moment later, his face disappeared from the screen.

His father sighed. "I don't know how you two can be so alike, yet so different at the same time."

"You mean how he's a hot head and I'm the most laid back guy on the planet, but we're both incredibly smart, loyal, and love hockey?"

"Pretty much," his dad said with a laugh. "Look, Josh was out of line. You're an adult, and you can do what you want. But..."

"Ahh, there it is," Jack said.

"You're only twenty-one. Maybe...take a beat before you go making big life decisions with your girlfriend in mind. This is the time of your life when I encourage you to be selfish."

"I don't know if I can, Dad," he said. "Not because I don't *want* to be, but because I don't know *how*."

"I know, son," his dad said. "That's one of our favorite things about you. You've got some time. All I'm asking is that you make sure you and your career are your number one priority."

Jack hummed noncommittally and ended the call with his father not long after.

Jack didn't have a selfish bone in his body. When it came time to disburse personality traits to the DeLuca sons, Josh took the lion's share of that one. But in that moment, Jack tried, he really did, to envision what he wanted his future to look like, and what decisions he would make to get there.

The only problem was, there wasn't a single version of his future Jack could imagine that didn't have Jessica in it.

 Jessica

NOW: February 14, 2024

Valentine's Day also happened to be Jack's birthday, and while he had been vehement in his insistence that the day be about *them* instead of *him*, Jessica couldn't help planning something a little extra special.

This was, after all, *Jack*. The man who made her feel like the most precious thing he'd ever laid eyes on. And for once, he deserved to be spoiled.

The original plan had been a quiet night at his place, ordering takeout and curling up together with a movie, then seeing where the night took them. But Jessica had other ideas.

"We're going out tonight," she said when he called her that morning.

It was a Wednesday, so he was just walking out of morning skate, and the locker room was boisterous in the background.

"I don't want to go out," Jack whined, and Jessica giggled.

"Why not? It's your birthday."

"That's exactly why," he protested. "It's my birthday, and I don't want to share you with anyone else."

Jessica's toes curled in her boots at the promise in those words. They hadn't yet broached the subject of adding sex to their relationship—though it wouldn't be their first time. Somehow, unspoken, they'd decided to wait for the right time. And Jessica knew without a doubt that tonight was that time.

"I don't want to share you, either," she said quietly. "But I made reservations, so we're going out, and that's the end of it."

"Fine," Jack said. "But don't be surprised when I up the ante."

"What's that supposed to mean?" she asked. "Don't go doing anything crazy!"

"Me? Crazy? Never," Jack said sarcastically. "Bye, sunshine."

Before Jessica could protest or prod him further about whatever scheme he was cooking up, he ended the call, and she was left thinking that, even though she wanted to celebrate him tonight, her plans would pale in comparison to Jack's.

That evening, they walked into Troppo, a local Lansing restaurant not too far from campus. In deference to the holiday, the restaurant had decorated tastefully, with red cloth napkins where they usually favored black, and vases with red, pink, and white roses on each of the tables. The board at the hostess stand boasted signature cocktails for the evening, as well as a steak special.

"That's what I'm getting," Jack said, pointing at the special.

"You can get whatever you want, big guy," she said, patting

him on the chest.

Before she could pull away, he captured her hand and held it to his body.

"I already have everything I want," he said.

As her insides melted, Jessica said, "When did you become such a romantic?"

"I've always been a romantic, sunshine," he said. "At least, with you I have. Don't you remember our first date?"

How could she forget? A Mexican sunset cruise followed by a delicious fresh seafood dinner and dancing on the beach under the stars? It had been magical—if she forgot about the part where she'd ruined it all.

In her defense, she'd been a dumb kid, so afraid of the emotions this boy she barely knew had stirred in her. There was so much she would've done differently.

But they'd still somehow ended up here, and that alone was worth celebrating.

Once the hostess seated them at a cozy little booth tucked into a corner and their waiter appeared, Jack took it upon himself to order a bottle of red wine—the most expensive they had on the menu.

"Jack..." Jessica protested, but he waved her off.

"It may be my birthday, Jess, but it's still Valentine's Day. And if I want to spoil my girl with a bottle of wine, I'm going to."

"I didn't even know you liked wine," she said.

"We're a long way from Mexico," he reminded her. "There's a lot you don't know about me. At least, this version of me."

Jessica reached across the table and slid her hand into his. "I want to know it all."

"And you will," he promised with a smile.

The thought of leaving this man—of losing him again—sat in the back of Jessica's mind like a low level hum she couldn't ignore no matter how hard she tried. But tonight was about them, and she would do everything in her power to remind him how much she cherished him, and this relationship, and that they would figure the rest out together.

Dinner was delicious, and as Jack drained the final drops of the bottle of wine into her glass, Jessica stood abruptly.

"I'm sorry," she said when his face crumpled with concern. "I just really need to go to the bathroom."

She hurried off without waiting for a response from him, quickly taking care of business. As she stood at the sink washing her hands, she took a moment to study her reflection and was surprised by what she found—what Jack must see when he looked at her now.

Four years ago, she'd been cute, with her button nose, freckles, and long, blonde hair. Since then, almost without her realizing, she'd grown into a woman. Her freckles—though still present—had faded. There were faint laugh lines around her eyes, nothing to be concerned about but enough to make her realize that she'd lived in that time. Her cheekbones and jaw were sharper, those last vestiges of baby fat melting away to reveal the delicate bone structure beneath. And her eyes, though bright from the alcohol and the promise of what the night might bring, were wearier, though still the vibrant blue that every member of the Daniels family shared.

She loved this face and was proud of the story it told.

Finally, she dried her hands and stepped out of the bathroom...right into Jack's waiting arms.

"What're you doing?" she asked as he snaked his hands around her waist and pulled her close.

"Kissing my girlfriend," he said, and did just that.

Jessica would never tire of the reality that she got to kiss Jack again. Every time, kissing him was like coming home, and Jessica could do nothing but melt into him completely, the world outside where their bodies fused blurring to a distant memory.

The best thing about Jack was how he had the innate ability to make Jessica feel as though she were the only person on the planet, even if they were standing in the middle of a crowded room—or in the bathroom hallway of a very crowded restaurant.

As the youngest in her family, she craved that kind of attention. For someone to look her in the eyes and really hear what she was saying as she spoke, to truly understand her deepest desires.

Her family was amazing, but compared to Logan and Berkley, Jessica was rather...plain and unimpressive. At least, that's how she saw herself. No matter how frequently her family told her otherwise, Jessica's deepest shame, her darkest secret, was that she was letting her family down.

But Jack? Jack made her feel like a diamond in a handful of rocks, like she outshined anyone and everything around her.

Jack made her feel special, treasured.

With his strong arms wrapped around her, she lost herself, and made a noise of protest when he pulled free from their kiss and rested his forehead against hers, breathing heavily.

"Do you..." Jack started.

"Do I what?"

"Do you want to get out of here?"

"Yes," she breathed against his mouth, and a moment later, they were walking back to their table. They paused only long enough to grab their coats, and for Jack to throw down enough money to cover their meal, before they were speed walking for the door.

"So, I did a thing," Jack said once they were strapped into his truck.

"What kind of thing?" Jessica asked, confused.

"The thing where I got us a hotel room for tonight so we didn't have to worry about roommates."

"That's a bit presumptuous of you."

"Fuck," Jack breathed. "I'm so sorry. I should've asked first. It's just...it's been so long, and I wanted our first time—again—to be special."

Jessica burst out laughing, and Jack tore his eyes off the road to shoot her a confused, my-girlfriend-is-crazy look.

"I was just kidding," she said. "I will *happily* spend the night at a hotel with you."

"Oh, thank God," he said.

"It *is* your birthday," Jessica reminded him. "I think I can put out for that."

Jack tipped his head back and laughed. "How gracious of you."

"The pleasure is all mine," she said.

"It will be," Jack told her, his wide grin dimming a bit from amusement to mischievousness.

All Jessica could say in response was, "Hurry up."

Jack had booked a room at the Marriott that sat smack dab in the middle of downtown East Lansing. When they pulled up, he ran inside the check in and when he came back out, he handed her the key.

"Why are you giving that to me?" she asked. "Aren't you coming with?"

"Of course," he said. "But I'm going to bring my truck home so I don't have to pay to park it here. Plus I have a present for you that I forgot to grab."

"Jack..." Jessica started to protest, but he cut her off.

"I don't care if it's my birthday," he said, taking the words right out of her mouth. "Tonight, I want to spoil you."

And she couldn't very well argue with that, could she?

Though she had no luggage with her, no overnight bag or really anything else save the clothes on her back and her teeny-tiny clutch, she strode into the hotel lobby with her head held high.

Their room was on the very top floor, and when Jessica pushed inside, she was greeted by an incredible bird's-eye view campus. From here, she could see the top of the football stadium, Munn, and the basketball arena, as well as the well-lit paths traveled by students as small as ants. Below, the city was sparkling.

After turning on one of the bedside lamps and pulling the curtains closed, she kicked off her heels and stretched her feet. Right as she was about to drop onto the bed and lounge until Jack showed up, he knocked.

When she opened the door for him, he walked in and held out a bottle of champagne, a potted lily, and a small, black velvet jewelry box. Jessica didn't know which to grab first, but Jack decided for her when he set the plant and champagne on the nearby table, extending the box out to her.

"Before you open this and freak out, I want you to know something."

Jessica swallowed hard, afraid of where this was headed. "Okay," she croaked.

"I have spent every day since Mexico subconsciously wishing for this. For you to be here, in my arms again. And I know the road ahead is going to be difficult, but I need you to know that I cannot go through the pain of losing you again. Not when the universe has brought us back together like this. So this," he said, popping open the ring box to reveal to Jessica a simple rose gold ring with a flower engraved on it, "is nothing more than a promise. It's not a promise ring in the sense that I want you to wear it on your finger and promise to marry me one day. It's...a symbol of our promise to each other. To love each other. To give ourselves a real chance at this. Is it soon? Yes. Are we probably too young to make these kinds of promises to each other? Also yes. But I lost you once, and I'll be damned if I let it happen again. There is no version of my future that doesn't include you, Jess. If that's something you want, too, then I want you to wear this. I don't care which finger. But if you're not ready, I understand that, too. I just want you to know where my head is."

She knew he would've continued to babble if she let him, so she put them both out of their misery by whispering, "Yes."

"Yes?"

"Of course," she said. Instead of sliding it on a finger, though, she unhooked her necklace—the one her grandma had given her when she graduated high school with a miniscule diamond resting in the hollow between her clavicles—and added the ring to the chain. "I want all of those same things. I want them with you."

In the next moment, Jack had her backed against the wall, maintaining only a foot of space between them.

Far enough away that she could still breathe, could still maybe keep her wits about her if she wanted. Because that gleam in his eye—that was new. Wicked. Possessive. The kind of look that told her, wherever it was this night was about to take them, she would be irrevocably altered because of it.

"Jess," he said, that single syllable a sigh as it left his lips.

"Jack," she replied, voice shaking.

It was unfair, really, how good their names sounded together. And how badly Jessica wanted to always see and hear them side by side.

Jessica and Jack. Jack and Jessica.

Jack stepped forward, and the tips of her breasts brushed against his hard chest, causing her to suck in a sharp breath. They'd been close like this in the month since getting back together, but never with this same intention. Knowing what came next lit up every nerve ending in her body, set her blood on fire.

He laughed, reaching up to twirl a lock of her hair around his finger. "You feel it, too, don't you? Everything is about to change, sunshine. I bet your skin tingles when I look at you. I bet you've spent these last few months wondering what new tricks I've learned." He paused, brushing another finger along the line of her jaw. When he spoke again, his tone had gotten impossibly deeper, voice barely above a whisper. "And I bet when you're in bed at night, feeling lonely, you think about me while you get yourself off. Picturing my fingers replacing your own. Imagining what it would be like if you finally got naked with me again."

Jessica's heart rate rose to dangerous levels, her skin prickling with a flood of adrenaline.

The thing was, he wasn't wrong.

In the days and weeks—and okay, months—after Mexico, Jessica had done exactly that. Had touched herself at night thinking of him, wondering what he would do to her if he was there, what she'd do to him, and what they'd do together. Imagining all the things they would try if they'd been given the opportunity to explore their sexual appetites together.

And since Jack had reappeared in her life, she'd had more than one filthy dream about him, her unconscious mind conjuring up all sorts of pleasurable positions she and Jack could find themselves in.

It was finally time to unleash all of those fantasies.

Jack braced a hand on the wall by her head, leaning in, outwardly calm. But Jessica was close enough to see his pulse jumping erratically along the vein in his throat. All she'd have to do is raise onto her tiptoes, shift forward a bit, and her mouth would settle against his.

In her last relationship, the sex had been almost clinical, and rarely—if ever—had Silas scratched that desperate itch inside of her. But Jack had been her first, and she hoped he'd be her last. He hadn't spent their time apart like a monk, and she could admit the prospect of handing over control of her pleasure to him thrilled her. To let him help her figure out what she liked and didn't like, in a way that none of her previous partners—all two of them—ever had.

"Jess," he whispered, "if it makes a difference, I want you so bad I can't think straight. You are on my mind every second of every day. I'm going crazy. This has always been inevitable. I always knew we'd end up here again. Please put me out of my misery."

With his admission, that invisible string between them pulled taut and tugged. Almost against her will, Jessica crashed into him, fusing her mouth with his.

THEN: April 8, 2020

IT SMELLS LIKE YOU.

The words rattled around Jessica's head as she checked out, not one, but two, bottles of the lotion Jack had found for her tucked into an adorable, reusable canvas bag with the shop's logo on the side. Jessica had been pleased to find the shop also had a website, and after a brief conversation with the owner, learned she could order online when she ran out. She had a feeling she'd be using this lotion until she died...or the store stopped making it.

They piled into a van to head back to the resort, each of the women armed with bags exactly like Jessica's, plus others filled with the day's spoils.

As they rode, the windows down and whipping Jessica's hair into a cyclone around her head, Jack slid his arm across the seat back behind her, rubbing gentle circles on her neck.

Grounding her.

She knew he didn't even realize he was doing it, but she was more thankful for his touch in that moment than she could say. The closer they got to the resort, the more her mind spun out of control. The clock on their time together ticked closer to zero, reverberating in Jessica's thoughts.

"I'm not ready to say goodbye," she blurted, looking up at him.

He gave her a sad smile in return and leaned forward to press a kiss to her temple. "Me neither."

When they pulled up to the resort, before Jessica could head inside, Jack pulled her to a stop just outside the entrance.

"What're we doing tonight?" he asked.

"I don't know yet," she said. "What do you want to do?"

"Whatever it is you want to do."

"Gosh, you guys are cute," someone said from behind them, and Jessica glanced over her shoulder at her mom. "And I really hate to steal her away from you, Jack, but we're having a girls' dinner tonight. I promise I'll give her back after."

Jessica groaned. She didn't want to be apart from Jack too long when their time together was so limited, but she'd hardly spent any of this vacation with her mom, so she couldn't talk her way out of this one.

"See you upstairs, Jessica," her mother said as she walked off.

"It'll be fine," Jack said, leveraging her head up to meet his gaze with his thumb pressed under her jaw. "We just...don't sleep tonight."

"No sleeping, huh?" Jessica said with a raised brow and a smirk.

"That's not what I meant," Jack said quickly, his panicked expression softening when Jessica laughed. "But I mean, I'm not opposed..."

Jessica shoved him away. "We'll just have to wait and see what the night brings."

The truth was, she wasn't opposed to the idea of spending the night with Jack, either. Not one bit.

For dinner that evening, they chose the fanciest restaurant at their resort. Jessica's mom kicked off the evening by ordering a bottle of red wine for the table, and though Jessica didn't typically drink wine, she did so tonight.

Jessica raised her glass to her three companions and said, "Thank you, Mom and Lisa, for this amazing trip. I couldn't have asked for a better graduation present, and I love you both so much."

"Ditto!" Bethani quipped.

"We're very proud of both of you," Jessica's mom said.

"To our graduates," Lisa added, and they clinked glasses.

After taking a large swallow of her wine, Jessica's mom said, "So, Jack seems like a really—"

"Hot guy?" Bethani asked. "Because we know."

"I was going to say he seems like a really nice boy," Jessica's mom said, "but sure, that works, too."

"Mom," Jessica sighed. "Can we please not do this?"

They'd only just sat down, and Jessica wasn't in the mood for an interrogation, though her mother had likely been working up to this very thing for days

And, God, had it really only been three days since this boy had walked into her life and turned the whole thing upside down?

"Do what? I'm simply making an observation."

"You have an agenda, and I know exactly what it is."

"And what's that?"

"You're trying to feel me out," Jessica said. "You want to see how serious I am about this boy, and whether or not you should tell Dad about him when we get home."

"Well...should I?"

"No," Jessica said firmly. "There's no need."

"And why not?"

"I'm going to tell you the same thing I told Jack last night. This"—she swung her arms around her—"is vacation. This isn't the real world. We're trapped inside this giant bubble right now, and the minute we step foot on that plane to go home tomorrow, the bubble pops. Where does that leave me?"

"Honey," her mom said gently. "There's nothing that says you can't stay in touch with him when we leave here."

"Personally, I think you should keep talking to him," Bethani piped in, and Jessica shot her a death glare that had her friend raising her hands in surrender.

"I don't understand where this is coming from, anyway," Jessica's mom said. "What's wrong with staying friends with this boy?"

"What's wrong is I can't!"

"Jess..."

"I can't, Mom," she said, fighting back tears. "I care about him too much to be only friends. We can't go from this, how we are here, to texting and phone calls and FaceTime. It's just easier to rip off the bandage."

"You're too young to be so jaded," her mother said, frowning.

"I'm also too young to think this guy I met on vacation is going to be the one I spend the rest of my life with. I have plans, you know? Things I want to accomplish with my life. And I'm afraid if Jack and I stay in touch, if we try to stay friends or even try to maintain some sort of long distance relationship, I'll lose sight of all of that. And I can't let that happen, not when I've worked so hard for it all. I may not be doing something noble like Logan and Berkley, but that doesn't make my dreams any less valid than theirs."

"Is that really what you think?" her mom asked. "That we don't appreciate you and what you want to do with your life the way we do your brother and sister?"

Jessica slumped in her chair, embarrassment heating her cheeks. This wasn't how she'd planned to have this conversation with her family—in fact, she'd never planned on having it at all. And while having Bethani and Lisa here, staring between them like they were tracking the volley of a tennis match, wasn't ideal, it was too late to back down.

Jessica had always wanted to be a teacher. For as long as she could remember, that was what she'd felt called to do. Maybe it wasn't living up to the standards her elder siblings had unfairly and unwittingly set, but Jessica still considered it to be a worthwhile endeavor.

"Sweetheart," her mom said, reaching for her hand. "Your father and I are immensely proud of you, exactly as much as we are of Logan and Berkley. Those two...they live in their own little world. It's been like that since they were kids. But you are just as smart and talented as they are, and your father and I support you in whatever it is you want to do. No matter what. Do you understand me?"

Jessica could only nod.

"As for the Jack situation…" her mom started.

"Please, no," Jessica said.

"Actually, I think you need to hear whatever she has to say," Bethani said. "Go ahead, Mrs. Daniels."

"Thank you, Bethani," her mom said. "What I was going to say is that, if you have feelings for this boy, the big, scary kind that make you want to run in the opposite direction, those are usually the relationships worth holding onto. I'm not trying to tell you what to do here, Jess, but you have to stop making choices with your head so much and let your heart have a say in the conversation. Otherwise you're just letting yourself down, and possibly missing out on something really amazing in the process."

Grudgingly, Jessica admitted, "You make some great points, Mom."

"Yeah, Mrs. Daniels! Almost like an attorney."

"Well, I may not be a lawyer myself, but I did raise two, so I picked up a few things along the way." Then she added, "And speaking of, have you talked to your sister about this?"

Jessica shook her head. "Berk is busy with school. She doesn't want to hear about my lame ass teenage drama."

Her mother shrugged. "You may feel that way, but Berkley certainly doesn't. In fact, I think you should message both of your siblings and see what they have to say."

Jessica scoffed. "You already know what Logan will say. If it were up to him and Dad, I wouldn't date until I was thirty."

Her brother wasn't as overprotective or overbearing as some older siblings were prone to be, but he still had a tendency to treat Jessica like a baby. Secretly, she thought the motivation behind not wanting her to date was because he'd lived like a monk since he and his long-time college girlfriend had broken up. When he'd decided to move back to Traverse City in a few months once he finished law school, she hadn't wanted to "live in the middle of nowhere." And poof. Four years down the drain. The whole family had thought they would be getting married after graduation, not splitting up. It came as quite the shock to all of them.

"I'm just saying, maybe they'll have some insight that might make you feel better about your decision, one way or another."

Truth be told, Berkley *was* Jessica's favorite person to go to for advice, and she supposed getting a second opinion on the Jack situation couldn't hurt matters.

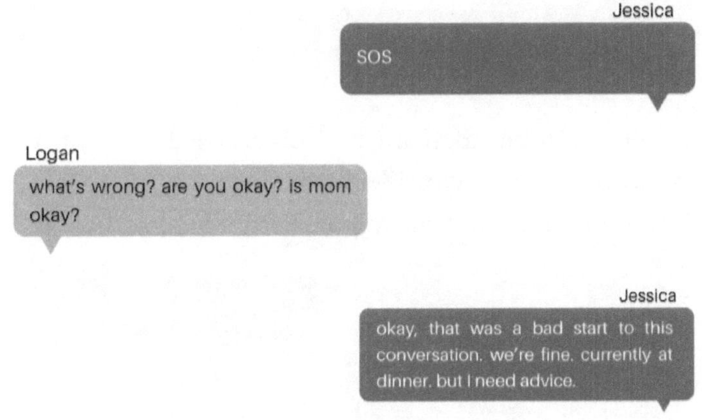

Logan

then you've come to the right place

Berkley

Jess, if you needed advice, you could've just texted me without including your dopey big brother

Logan

need I remind you, little one, that I'm YOUR dopey big brother, too

Berkley

trust me, I've spent nearly 25 years trying to forget

Jessica

guys, please

Berkley

right, Jess needs advice. what's up?

While her mom, Bethani, and Lisa carried on a conversation around her, Jessica considered the best way to go about this without inciting a riotous response from her brother.

Jessica

do you guys believe in soulmates?

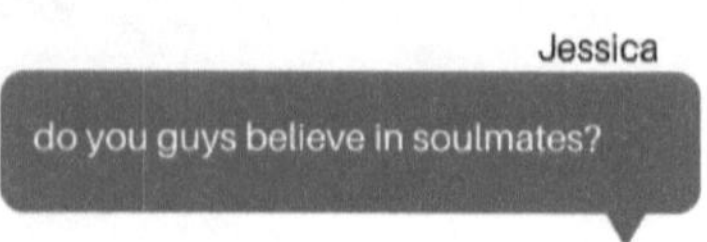

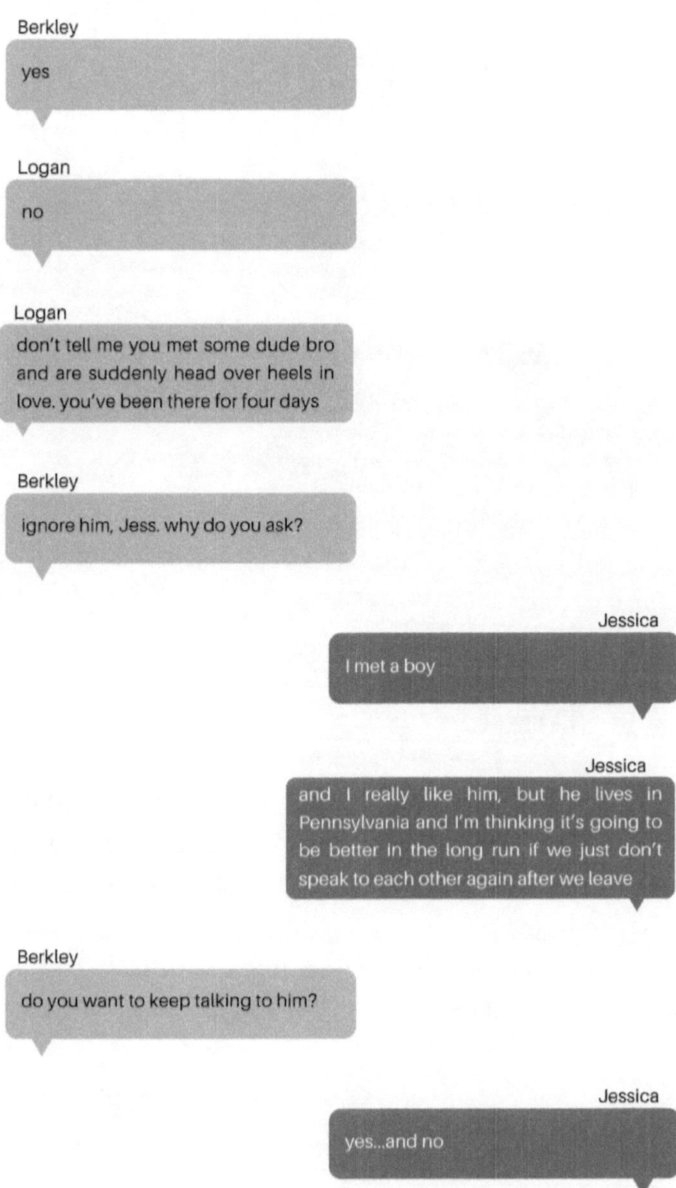
Berkley
yes
Logan
no
Logan
don't tell me you met some dude bro and are suddenly head over heels in love. you've been there for four days
Berkley
ignore him, Jess. why do you ask?
Jessica
I met a boy
Jessica
and I really like him, but he lives in Pennsylvania and I'm thinking it's going to be better in the long run if we just don't speak to each other again after we leave
Berkley
do you want to keep talking to him?
Jessica
yes...and no

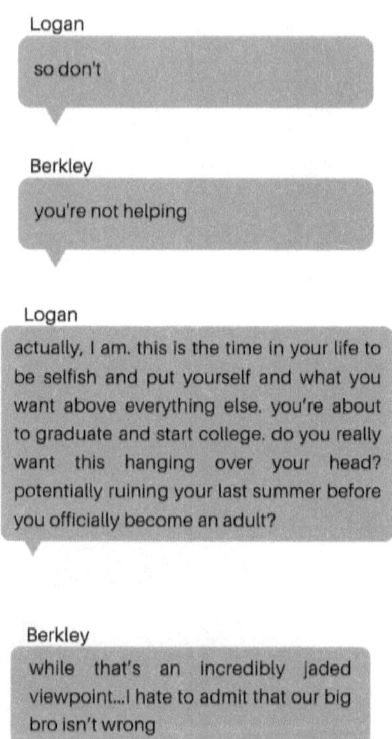

Jessica sighed, resigned. Her siblings had only voiced her exact thoughts, yet their words settled on her chest like a stone. It wasn't what she'd *wanted* to hear, but she knew it was what she *needed* to hear.

She would enjoy this one final night with Jack, and then tomorrow, it would be over.

Jack

THEN: April 8, 2020

"YOU GONNA GIVE IT up to blondie tonight?" Chad asked Jack as they made their way to dinner that evening.

Before Jack could, Tyler reached out and smacked Chad on the back of the head. "Shut up," Tyler said.

Jack fist-bumped him.

"But honestly," Zach piped up from the back of the group, "I want to know the answer. Is this going to be the night our boy finally loses his v-card? Honestly, DeLuca, I could think of worse places and people than Mexico with a little hottie like Jessica."

"Wait..." Jack said, stopping to level his friend with a glare. "You...know? That I'm..."

Chad burst out laughing, and Zach's grin grew. Tyler even bit his lips, fighting a smile of his own.

"Of course we know," Chad said. "It's pretty obvious. The real question is whether or not you're finally going to do something about it."

"That's privileged information," Jack said noncommittally, and his friends groaned. He was surprised, yet not, that his friends knew he was still a virgin, and was honestly relieved that they weren't making a huge deal out of it.

The truth was, Jack had no idea how tonight was going to go. Did he want Jessica? Of course he did. He was a guy after all, and Jessica was beautiful. More than that, their connection was something that Jack didn't think even fully grown adults ever found.

And...was it so wrong of him to want to keep some piece of her for himself? And to give her this part of him that no one else would ever have? He didn't think so, and Jack felt like they'd spent the entire week dancing around this, leading up to this. Tonight would be the culmination of that.

I'm not ready to say goodbye.

Jessica's earlier words ping-ponged around his brain. She could've been talking about the vacation, and not wanting to leave this paradise they'd discovered. But somehow, he knew that wasn't what she'd meant.

No, Jessica wasn't ready to say goodbye to *him*, to *them*. And neither was he. He wanted to milk every last second of magic and, dare he say, pleasure from this vacation before it was over.

Once he and the boys were settled at dinner, and the waitresses came by with their drinks, Tyler, staring at Jack expectantly, said, "So..."

Jack groaned. "I don't know if Jessica and I are going to hook up tonight, boys. I really don't."

"But you want to," Zach said, and it wasn't a question.

"Of course I do. Have you seen her?"

"We have," Chad said with a shit-eating grin, "and we approve."

"I just don't know if she'll want to," Jack said.

Tyler shifted in his seat so his body was turned toward Jack's. "Have you guys talked about this? Like...do you know if she's a virgin?"

Jack swallowed hard, reluctant to confirm or deny that statement. It wasn't his secret to share, but he also, grudgingly, wanted his friends' opinions. "She is."

"Oh my," Zach said. "This is like some fairytale, romance novel type shit."

Chad turned to him with a raised brow. "What do *you* know about romance novels?"

"Older sisters, remember?" Zach reminded him. "I know all about that shit, and this is basically the plot of a book."

"I don't know what I'm supposed to do with that information," Jack said.

"Look, I'm not saying you have to do this either way," Tyler cut in. "Go with what you feel. But you should know that the first time...it's going to be awkward as hell. Especially since you're both inexperienced."

"And it's probably not going to be great for her," Zach added. "Like...it's probably going to hurt."

"Fuck," Jack said. "I don't want to hurt her."

"It's kind of unavoidable, my dude," Chad said, clapping a hand on Jack's shoulder from across the table. "Though, you've got a small dick so maybe it won't be that big of a deal."

The table erupted into laughter, and Jack threw a piece of

steak at his friend, where it smacked Chad right in the forehead.

"Fuck you," Jack said, grinning widely as Tyler and Zach doubled over, gasping for air around their laughter.

When they quieted, Tyler looked at Jack and said, "Honestly, I'm sure it'll be fine."

"I hope you're right."

The last thing he wanted to do was make Jessica uncomfortable, but now that the idea was lodged in his brain, Jack couldn't shake the thought of sharing this experience with her. If tonight really was their last night—if they never spoke again after this—sex, to him, seemed like the perfect way to wrap up the perfect week. But he also wasn't going to force her into anything. The worst thing she could do is say no, and he'd never know if he didn't ask.

It was fitting to Jack that they'd be spending this last night of vacation the same way they spent the first—at a nightclub. Though, it was comical to Jack how different tonight felt from that one. For one, instead of being jealous that Jessica was spending her night with another guy, he had his arm wrapped around her. She was his, and he planned on keeping her for as long as she or the universe allowed.

Tonight, the resort-sponsored club was Dady'O. Jack was awestruck when their group stepped into the dimly lit interior. Where The City was all flashing lights, exposed steel trusses, and wide open spaces, Dady'O was the exact opposite. The inside had been modeled after a sort of cavern, with rough-hewn walls, dim lights that glowed like a flickering campfire, and a modestly-sized raised platform in the center that served as the dance floor. One side was flanked by an even higher stage, and booths and tables were spread around the other three.

Their group picked a table, and before they could even consider sitting down, a waitress approached with several bottles of vodka, as well as pitchers of orange and cranberry juice.

"We didn't order this!" Jack shouted at her over the pulsing of the music.

"It's on the house!" She nodded at his wristband. "That's your ticket to whatever you want tonight," she added, throwing him a flirtatious wink before she walked away.

"I think she likes you," Jessica teased as Jack stared, dumbfounded, after the waitress.

Snapping out of it, Jack grinned down at her. Under the glow of the black lights lining the ceiling, Jessica's teeth shone bright blue when she smiled at him. "Unfortunately for her, there's nothing this place could offer me that I don't already have."

"Good save," she said, rising onto her tiptoes to plant a kiss on his lips.

When she moved to pull away, Jack cupped the back of her head, holding her in place. Jack felt more than heard her hum of appreciation as he ran his tongue along the seam of her mouth and licked his way inside. They hadn't had a single drink yet, and Jack was already drunk on Jessica's *everything*. The way she anchored herself to him by gripping his shirt in her fists, how the silky strands of her hair fanned out across his hands and arms as he hauled her in impossibly closer. He kissed her like this was the last time, like this was goodbye.

And Jessica returned his kiss with fervor, responding so enthusiastically that she basically crawled up his body and wrapped herself around him.

Jack wasn't mad at it.

But before things could get too heated—in a very public place, no less—a tap on his shoulder had Jack pulling away, gasping for air, Jessica's own breath rasping in his ear.

"Hate to break up what was sure to be an impressive show," Zach said with a grin, "but we're taking shots."

Reluctantly, Jessica released her legs from his waist and returned to her own two feet, though she remained tethered to Jack by threading her fingers through his. They turned to the table, where the entire group watched them expectantly. Bethani held out a shot for Jessica, and Tyler had one ready for Jack.

Together, the six of them raised their glasses over the center of the table.

"To spring break," Jack said, smiling down at Jessica. "It's been one hell of a ride."

"To spring break!" they echoed, then lowered their shots to tap them on the table before tipping them back.

Unlike the tequila they'd been shooting all week, vodka went down a lot smoother, though it burned the inside of his nostrils like that sterile scent of medical grade antiseptic. He poured himself a shot of cranberry juice into the same glass to chase it down.

"I'm gonna go get a beer!" he yelled to Jessica over the music. "I can't drink this shit all night."

"I'll come with you!" she said.

As Jack turned toward the bar, the waitress once again appeared at his side.

"Can I get you guys anything?" she asked.

"I would love a beer," he said, then turned to Jessica. "What do you want, sunshine?"

"I'll have what he's having!"

"I'll be right back with those," the waitress said, then vanished into the crush of bodies.

After she'd returned, and Jack washed away the lingering burn of vodka with a few swigs of his beer, Jessica tugged on his arm.

"Let's go dance!"

Before he could protest—not that he would have—Jessica towed him onto the dance floor, pushing her way through the throng until they were deep in the middle of the crowd. Overhead, warm-toned lights flashed in time with the bass, and on stage, a woman in a feathered and sequined outfit performed aerial tricks on a long swath of fabric hanging from the ceiling.

Jessica spun and pressed her ass into his lap, leading them in rocking side to side to the beat. He still had no idea what the words accompanying the music were, but with Jessica in his arms, it didn't matter.

Finally, a song Jack did recognize blasted over the crowd, and a cheer went up as the whole club began shouting the chorus of "Gasolina" by Daddy Yankee.

On the heels of that came "Despacito," and Jack turned Jessica to face him, settling his hands low on her hips and tucking her hand between them against his chest.

The frantic pulse of the crowd from moments before settled into a slower sort of sway, and Jack allowed himself to bask in the moment. For the duration of the song, he wasn't worried about potentially losing his virginity tonight, or losing Jessica tomorrow. He was fully present, his world containing only him, Jessica, and this song. The places their bodies connected. Her inhalations and exhalations coincided with his, the thump of her heart against his chest timed perfectly to his own.

Jessica rose onto her tiptoes for a kiss, and Jack gave it to her, lingering on her lips for as long as he could.

"Let's get out of here," he said against her mouth.

She pulled away enough to study him. "And do what?"

"What do you think?" Jack said, smirking, though he felt it wobble at the edges. "But only if you want to."

"Of course I want to," she said. "More than anything."

Those words took root in his chest and bloomed, spreading warmth along his limbs that had nothing to do with the press of bodies around him.

"Just...give me a second to track down the boys. I have to tell Tyler he needs to stay with Zach and Chad."

Jessica nodded, her throat bobbing as she swallowed. "I need to talk to Bethani anyway."

They weaved their way off the dance floor and found their friends at their table, right where they'd left them.

"We're heading back," Jack said to the guys.

Chad, of course, responded by yelling, "Get it, boy!" at Jack.

To their credit, Tyler and Zach had more subdued reactions. They each offered him a fist-bump and a "good luck, bro."

"Sorry, Ty," Jack said. "You're gonna have to stay with Dumb and Dumber tonight."

"Rude," Chad said.

"As long as I'm not Dumber," Zach said with a laugh.

Ignoring them, Tyler said, "That's fine man. We'll see you in the morning."

"Sounds good!" Jack shouted, then turned to find Jessica waiting at Bethani's side, staring expectantly at him. He could practically see her limbs vibrating in anticipation, much like his own were.

The cab ride back to the resort passed too quickly and seemed to drag all at once. Soon, they reached the door to his room, and Jack keyed it open, leading Jessica inside.

He didn't remember the last time they'd been here alone, and tonight, he was grateful he'd had very little to drink. He was going to savor this, remember every word, etch every sound she made on the walls of his mind so he'd never forget them.

Jack had planned to take his time, but Jessica had no such compunction. Before the door had fully closed behind him, she was on him.

Her hands were everywhere at once: in his hair, smoothing over the slopes of his shoulders and biceps, scratching down his back. Finally, they settled on the buttons of his shirt, slowly working each loose until it flapped open and she could push it off his shoulders.

Jack responded in kind by skating his fingers along the exposed skin of her stomach until he gripped the hem of her flowy crop top and lifted it over her head.

The rest of their clothes joined their tops on the floor, and they fell onto the bed, pressed skin to skin.

Nervous as he was, Jack couldn't stop himself from blurting, "This is the first time I've been completely naked with a girl."

Jessica giggled, lifting her hands to his shoulders, drawing circles with her fingertips on his skin. "This is the first time I've been completely naked with a boy."

"I still..."

"What?"

"I don't understand how we found each other. Here, of all places."

Jessica shook her head. "Neither do I. But we're here now, and that's all that matters."

Jack grinned, and leaned down to kiss her. He ran his hand down the warm, smooth skin along her ribs, settling it on her hip, digging his fingers into the side of her ass.

He pulled away. "Tell me what you like."

"I don't know," she whispered, and Jack's gaze locked on her face in time to see her cheeks turn pink. "I...I haven't done much. I mean, I've done *some*, but mostly giving, and always rushed."

"So we'll figure it out together."

THEN: April 8, 2020

Jessica didn't think anyone actually knew what they were doing the first time they had sex, and she and Jack were no different.

It was awkward, clumsy, slightly painful—for her, not him, though he winced sympathetically every time he moved and she gasped at the discomfort.

But it was also beautiful and wonderful, an experience Jessica will always be grateful for despite the soreness between her thighs, because she got to share it with him.

Naked and sticky with sweat, she and Jack curled on their sides, facing each other. Absentmindedly, he trailed his fingers along her arm, side, back, thigh—basically anywhere he could reach.

"Tell me about your family," she said, breaking their comfortable silence. "I feel like you know so much about mine, and I know so little about yours."

"What do you want to know?"

"What are your parents like? Do you have any siblings?"

Before he answered, Jack rolled onto his back and pulled Jessica closer. She rested her head and a palm on his chest, his heartbeat beneath her hand steady and reassuring.

She would miss this, the easy way their bodies fit together, and their easy conversation.

"My parents are the best," he said. "My dad actually played five seasons in the NHL before a compound fracture to his tibia that was poorly set healed wrong and forced him into early retirement. After that, he became a scout, met and married my mom, and they had my brother, Josh, then me. When Josh was born, they made the decision that my mom would be a stay-at-home mom, since my dad was on the road so often. Josh is five years older than me, and when he was ten and I was five, my dad got a job scouting with Philadelphia, so we moved."

"Where did you live before that?"

"Massachusetts," Jack said. "Peabody, to be exact. My dad was coaching Josh's team and doing some college scouting for Boston University. But his dream had always been to get back into the NHL however he could, so he couldn't pass up the opportunity when it arose."

"Did you like growing up in...Peabody?" The pronunciation felt funny in her mouth.

"It was great," he said. "It's a suburb of Boston, and really close to Salem and all that jazz. Our last Halloween there is the only one I remember before the move. Dad happened to be home for a long weekend, and he and Mom took us to Salem to do all the witchy shit. That place was madness. There's absolutely nothing like it at that time of the year. Essex Street was so crowded we could hardly move through it, and there were nighttime cemetery walks and bus tours to all the haunted, witchy, and ghostly hot spots. It was one of the best days of my life."

Jessica tried to imagine a teeny-tiny Jack, a fraction of the size he was now, dressed up for Halloween and participating in such a production. Unfortunately, she had a difficult time reconciling the sexy hockey player before her with that little boy.

"Are you and your brother close?" she asked. Five years was no small thing, and she knew from experience that it could be difficult to relate to older siblings with that sort of age gap between them.

"In the way that highly competitive brothers can be," Jack said with a smile. "He's always wanted better for me than I sometimes want for myself. He's a crazy talented defenseman. He played college at Penn State, and he actually just got signed by one of Pittsburgh's farm teams."

"That's amazing!" Jessica said. "I know nothing about hockey, but I'm assuming that's a dream come true for him and your family."

"It is," Jack said. "But it'll never be enough for Josh. He wants to play in the NHL, to follow in Dad's footsteps, and he'll work his ass off until he gets there. I wouldn't be surprised if he makes it happen within the next couple of years."

"It must be difficult to live up to those expectations."

"It can be," he said quietly. "But it's different for me. I'm a goalie, and goalie jobs in the NHL are so much harder to come by since teams only keep three on their active roster at any given time. So I'll give it everything I've got. But I know my family is proud of me regardless."

Jessica thought back to the conversation she'd had with her mom earlier, and wished she felt that secure within her own family. While she knew her parents, Berkley, and Logan, were proud of her, she couldn't always quiet the insecurities of that little girl inside her who felt embarrassed to tell people she wanted to be a teacher when both of her siblings were on their way to becoming attorneys.

"Hey," Jack said, sliding a hand up to cup her jaw and angle her face toward his. "Where'd you go?"

She must've been silent longer than she realized.

"Just thinking about my own family."

"Well, if anyone understands the pressure of being the youngest child by a wide margin, and having successful older siblings, it's me."

Jessica smiled at him, the knot of tension in her chest easing slightly. She'd never had someone she could speak to so openly about her feelings of inadequacy.

"I love Logan and Berkley," she said. "So much. But compared to them, I feel…" She paused, searching for the right word, though she wasn't sure there was a single word that could encapsulate all of the ways she felt inferior to her siblings. "Inconsequential isn't the right word, because it's so much more complicated than that, but it's the best I can do."

"Being a teacher is just as admirable as being a lawyer," Jack said softly, his words a balm on her slightly jagged edges.

Jessica only nodded, swallowing hard, the tips of her hair swishing around her shoulders, caressing her bare breasts, and

Jack's attention strayed long enough for him to drop a hand to her chest and brush a thumb along the soft underside.

"I sort of started my own tutoring business in high school, when I realized I had a knack for helping others learn. But even before that, when I was in elementary and middle school, I was fascinated by my teachers. I loved how teaching styles varied from person to person, and how fine the line was between a good teacher and a bad teacher, between passiveness and assertiveness. Between genuinely caring about whether or not your students were fully grasping the material, or letting them fend for themselves. I took an active interest in how my classmates were faring in their studies the older we got, and by eighth grade, I was hosting study sessions at my house so often that I had other parents reaching out to *my* parents, asking if they could schedule one-on-one sessions with me for their kids."

"That's incredible," Jack said. "To be so young and yet know so confidently what you want to do. The world always needs more teachers."

"They need more professional hockey players, too," she said, shooting him a cheeky grin, suggestively trailing her fingers over the ridges of his abs.

He responded by rolling on top of her, and they didn't speak for a long time after that.

"Are you sure I can't talk you into keeping in touch after this?" Jack asked from beside her, a little breathless from their recent joining. Thankfully, the second time was much more pleasurable than the first.

"I'm sure," she said, giving him a sad smile. "You know it's better this way."

"It's not," he said. "There are these things called cell phones, you know. They have this really cool feature where you can talk to people from thousands of miles away. You can even see them!"

She swatted playfully at him, her hand remaining resting on his bicep. He flexed a little, and she giggled. It would be so easy to give in to him, and while every fiber of her being begged her to reconsider, she knew snipping those threads connecting them was the best option—the *only* option.

"You know what I mean," she said. "We're about to start college, and we have the whole rest of our lives ahead of us. I just...it scares me how much I care about you already, and we've known each other for four days. I can't risk bringing this home with us and it blowing up in our faces down the line. Not when I have so many things I want to accomplish. And I can't be the thing that holds you back from giving everything to your own dreams."

The look on his face told her he didn't like it, but he understood where she was coming from. Instead of answering, Jack settled his hand on Jessica's lower back and pulled her closer, his body already stirring once again with her nearness.

"How about we make a pact?" she said as he set to nibbling on her earlobe.

"What kind of pact?" he asked against her skin, and she tilted her head to give him better access.

"A pact where if, at some future date, the universe decides to bring us back together, and we're both unattached, we give this a real shot."

Jack pulled away to truly study her, and she lost herself in his crystal blue gaze.

"Seriously?" he asked, surprised. Jessica nodded. "So you're saying, if we go home and in two months, I randomly run into you on the streets in Philly, you'll agree to date me? Or at the very least give me your number?"

"That won't happen," she said quickly. "But yes, that's the gist of it."

He answered before she'd even finished talking. "Yes."

Jessica tipped her head back and laughed, shaking both of their bodies with the force of it. He pressed a kiss to the underside of her jaw.

"You didn't even think about it!" she said, sliding her hands into the hair at the base of his skull and pulling. He responded in kind, wrapping the length of her hair around his fist and tugging, and Jessica would be damned if the sting didn't make her eyes roll back in her head, falling just on the good side of the pleasure versus pain line.

"I don't have to think about it," he said, giving her a one shoulder shrug. "If it was up to me, we wouldn't even be having this conversation because you'd stay in my life after we left. So if this is what you want, then this is what I'll give you."

Jessica sighed. "This is what I want."

"Then you've got it. Should we shake on it?"

"Wait!" she said as he extended his hand, then rolled them so he was once again on his back, and she straddled his lap. It was a dangerous position, one that could easily pull Jack's attention away from her face and down, down, down. But he surprised her when his gaze remained locked on her eyes.

"What?" he asked, his thumbs pressing into her hip bones.

"There has to be rules."

"What kind of rules?"

"Let's see…" she said, momentarily distracted by the slow circles he drew on her skin, each pass arching closer and closer to her center. She had to get this out before all hope was lost—and they lost themselves in each other once again.

"No social media stalking," she said quickly. "Don't even try to find me."

"I don't know your last name, and 'Jessica' is fairly common, so that shouldn't be a problem."

They hadn't exchanged last names; she'd never even heard the guys utter his in her presence in that typical way boys do, refusing to call their buddies by their first names.

"Yeah, but my sister's name isn't all that common. Just…don't go looking for me. If we're doing this, leaving whether or not we come back together up to the universe, we need to let it happen naturally."

"Got it," Jack said, moving to sit up so they were face to face, his abdominals clenching deliciously as he pulled himself up. "Let the universe work its magic. It already did once, right?"

Jessica nodded, reminded of the conversation they'd had on the beach a few days before.

"Remember how you asked me if I believe in fate? And I told you I thought it was just some cheesy platitude people used to explain why they ended up where they had?"

"Yes…" he said slowly, leaning forward to press a kiss to the center of her chest, right over her heart.

"I think...I might feel differently now."

"How so?" he asked against her skin.

"I think that maybe you, and me, and us, this vacation, this week...maybe because of all of that, I believe in the magic of fate now."

"I'm glad you're finally on board," he said, brushing his mouth over her collarbone, sweeping a slow path up. In a moment, he'd reach her mouth.

"If the universe wants us together," she said as his lips paused a breath away from hers, "it'll bring us back together. And Jack?"

"Yeah?"

"I *really* hope it brings us back together."

THEN: April 9, 2020

WHEN JACK WOKE THE next morning, before he even opened his eyes to confirm it, he knew Jessica was gone.

While he wanted to rage and scream, this was part of the agreement. They'd made a deal, and he'd honor it, though the thought of never seeing her again was like a bullet wound in his chest.

At last, he cracked his eyes open and rolled over, running his hand over the spot where she'd slept, surprised to find the sheets cool to the touch.

But then his fingers brushed over a piece of paper, and he rose fully to consciousness, shooting up straight, his eyes darting over the message.

Jack—

I'm sorry for leaving like this, but I couldn't do the whole tearful goodbye. Walking away from you was hard enough as it was. I just wanted to thank you for this week. I'll cherish it always, and you will forever be special to me.

Remember our deal.

Love,
Jess

By the time he got the end of the note, tears blurred his vision, a few escaping his eyes to drop heavily onto the paper, smearing Jessica's words. And for the first time in as long as he could remember, Jack DeLuca cried.

Jack

NOW: February 14, 2024

THE MOMENT JESSICA LAUNCHED herself at him, Jack scooped her off her feet and pressed her into the wall. When his aching dick made contact with her warm center—even through their layers of clothing—they both groaned.

"Jess," he rasped against her mouth. "I can't...we can't go slow this first time. I need you too bad."

"Then have me," she said.

In one smooth move, he spun them from the wall and dropped her on the bed. Her hair fanned around her in a blonde halo like the corona of the sun.

Before he could reach for her, she sat up and rose onto her knees, her fingers flying to the delicate faux-pearl buttons on her silky, blush-pink blouse. As she began unfastening them, her eyes never left his, and Jack watched in rapt attention as she revealed inch after inch of creamy skin, the tan he knew she picked up in the summertime faded under the gray clouds of winter.

"You, too," she said, nodding toward his own clothing.

So Jack mirrored her, sliding the buttons on his own shirt free. When he finished, he left the shirt on, letting it hang open, offering her tantalizing glimpses of the body he'd honed over years and years of hard work.

"You want this off?" he asked, tugging at the shirt. She nodded. "Then come take it off."

Jessica crawled across the bed to the edge and reached for him. But she didn't go for the shirt right away. She started at his waistband, undoing his belt and pulling it free, then popping the button and lowering the zipper. A moment later, his pants pooled at his ankles, and he stepped out of them.

Jessica scraped her fingers along his boxers before pressing her palms flat against his stomach and dragging them up, up, up. His muscles jumped beneath her touch as she went, and he gasped when she lightly scraped her thumbnails over his nipples. A moment later, she brushed her hands over his shoulders and pushed his shirt off. A shrug and shift of his arms had it joining his pants on the floor.

Before she could pull away fully, he gripped her wrist, the beads and thread of a worn bracelet she wore digging into his palm. Slowly, he relaxed his grip, deftly spinning the bracelet around, searching for...*there.*

"You kept it," he said, tone filled with the same wonder and awe bubbling in his chest.

Jessica withdrew her hand from his touch and fingered the bracelet. The ends were frayed, the yellow embroidery floss muted and drab. The pearls had scuffed and faded, the tiny J charm that had once shined like the soft inside of a seashell now dull. It was, impossibly, the one he'd bought her in Mexico. "I never took it off…"

In a heartbeat, Jack scooped her into his arms and tossed her back on the bed, moving to hover over her. "You mean to tell me you've had this on for *four* years?" he asked, incredulous.

Jessica smiled then, the expression lighting her entire face, igniting a warmth in his chest that only she could provide. "I missed you," she said simply. "Every day, every hour, every minute. The missing you never stopped, and this was all I had left of you."

Jack bent to nip at her collarbone, her throat, her jaw, pausing a breath away from her lips. "Fuck, I love you," he growled.

"I love you, too," she said softly, stretching up to peck his lips quickly. And then, "Now take my clothes off."

With a wicked grin, Jack wasted no time doing as she asked. He ignored her open shirt and the lacy cups of her bra. Instead, he stood and began at her feet, slowly peeling off her socks and tossing them over his shoulder. He pressed a kiss to the sole of each foot, then crawled between her legs, the end of the bed bowing under his weight, and tugged her closer. Leaning over her, he placed a palm flat against her pubic bone, and she wriggled beneath him. He dipped his fingers below the waist band, his other hand joining as he hooked them around the fabric and tugged. Jessica lifted her ass off the bed, freeing the material, and Jack slid the leggings off and dropped them.

Backing away from her, he knelt on the floor at the foot of the bed and dragged her once more to the edge, until he was face-to-face with her pussy.

She rose onto her elbows to watch what he'd do next, and Jack's gaze remained locked with hers as he lowered his mouth and pressed a kiss to her clit through her panties. Even that simple brush told him how wet she already was, and it took every ounce of self-control he possessed to back away instead of slipping that scrap of lace to the side and burying his face in her flesh.

He did, however, slide his thumbs under the leg holes and pull them off, baring her to him.

They made quick work of their remaining clothing, and after a brief detour to the doorway, where he'd dropped a bag containing a box of condoms, he once again loomed above her.

Neither of them spoke as he rolled the condom on and gripped his dick at its base, dragging in through her arousal.

"Jack," Jessica gasped, and he smiled. He would never tire of that, of his name like a prayer on her lips.

"I know, sunshine," he said, and sheathed himself inside her.

The memory of her, the fact that they'd done this before, hadn't prepared him for how exquisitely her pussy gripped him, how perfectly she wrapped around him, and how easily he fully seated himself inside her.

He'd always known Jessica had been made for him, and this simply confirmed it.

With a heavy groan, and an experimental roll of Jessica's hips, he braced one hand next to her head, the other on her hip, and began to move.

It thrilled him how soaked she was, to know that she'd wanted him as badly as he wanted her—so badly that he hadn't even needed to warm her up first, to prepare her for this main attraction.

Once again, he had every intention to go slow, to savor this reconnection, but his body and mind had other ideas, had him picking up speed within a few pumps, desperate to claim her once again after all these years.

And Jessica met him thrust for thrust, her moans and broken pleas urging him on.

"I'm sorry, sunshine," he said through gritted teeth, even as he drove into her harder and faster.

"Why?" she gasped, shifting, gripping the backs of her knees and opening her legs wider, bringing him impossibly closer.

"Because...I'm...really...not...going...to...last...long," he said, each word punctuated by a slam of his hips against her.

"I don't care," she breathed, and moved her fingers out of his hair to scrape them down the bunching muscles of his back.

For a moment, Jack's eyes rolled back into his head, blacking out the world around him. And when things righted, he came apart, the force of it so surprising that he released an unattractive groan. He quaked in Jessica's embrace, his arms shaking as he struggled to remain upright, his arms straining as he propped himself over her.

A moment later when Jessica lifted her hips and, catching him unawares, flipped him onto his back so she straddled him.

And while he was still hard inside her despite his release, his girl took the reins on her own pleasure, smoothly gyrating her hips, rubbing her clit against his pelvis. All Jack could do was hold her in place as she sought her climax, as she writhed against him. At last, she threw her head back, her body going rigid before it broke and shook, muttering expletives at the ceiling as she rode out her orgasm.

When she collapsed on top of him, his dick finally pulling free from her wet warmth, Jack could do nothing but say, "Wow."

Jessica only nodded against him, the top of her head scratching at the underside of his chin.

It amazed Jack, how much had changed in the last four years, but ultimately, how little actually had.

At their cores, they were still the same Jack and Jessica, only in a different place at a different time. While he'd been pressed inside her, things hadn't felt any different at all. It was almost as if that time apart had simply vanished. They'd both certainly learned some things in the intervening years, but that thing that settled on his chest and spread like honey through his entire body was exactly the same today as it had been four years ago.

"I love you, you know," he said to her, again, as he had every day since they'd gotten back together. "Yesterday, today, tomorrow, four years ago and four years from now. Hell, forty years from now. It's always been you."

Jessica lifted her head and rested it on her hands to stare at him.

"Yesterday, today, tomorrow, always, and forever," she agreed.

He kissed her then, the sweet press of his lips so at odds with their frantic joining, but imbued with every bit of love for and devotion to her that he could possibly convey.

Already, blood once again flowed to his cock, prepared to go again and again and again with this woman. But Jessica crawled off him and rose to her feet.

"Where are you going?" he asked, not that he minded the sight of her naked body one bit.

First, she disappeared from view, returning a moment later

with a couple of the plastic-wrapped cups from the bathroom. Then, she grabbed the bottle of champagne off the table and carried the lot back to the bed.

Jack could think of worse ways to spend his time than having a naked Jessica Daniels bring him champagne in bed after a mind-blowing sexual reunion.

"We're celebrating, remember?" she said, holding the bottle out to him while she freed the cups from their plastic wrap.

"Right," he said as he removed the foil and cage from the bottle, then gently freed the cork so they didn't wind up soaking themselves and the bed in champagne.

Although...he wouldn't mind licking the sticky sweetness off Jessica's body.

A cup in each hand, she extended them, and he filled them halfway before setting the bottle on the nearest nightstand and taking a glass from her.

"What exactly are we celebrating?" he asked.

"You."

"*Us*," he corrected.

"And maybe...the universe."

If the universe wants us together, it'll bring us back together.

I really *hope it brings us back together.*

The hope he'd held onto all these years, echoing through his mind in the form of the words she'd spoken their last night together.

A hope, it seemed, Jessica had held onto as well.

Careful not to spill, he scooped her up and sat her on his lap, pressing a kiss to her temple. Then he clinked his shitty plastic cup against hers and said, "To the universe."

"And to us."

After they'd finished those first glasses, Jessica got it into her brain that she couldn't have champagne without some sort of dessert, so she called down to room service and ordered an assortment, including chocolate covered strawberries and crème brûlée.

"Don't forget the whipped cream," she told the hotel worker, shooting him a mischievous grin.

Fuck, Jack thought. *This girl is going to ruin me.*

And then he reminded himself, *she already has.*

By the time their room service arrived, over half the bottle of bubbly was gone.

When Jack filled her cup yet again, Jessica waved him off, setting the full glass on the nightstand.

"Oh, I don't care about that," she said, dropping the fluffy robe she'd donned to answer the door to the floor and lifting the can of whipped cream from the dessert tray. "I just wanted an excuse to order this so you could lick it off me."

"Jessica..." he growled, his voice full of the heat that had blood rushing right to his cock as he rose from the bed to meet her.

"I never got to experiment," she said suddenly, and Jack moved to her, slipping his hands around her waist and pulling her close. "I never felt fully comfortable enough to ask for it. With...in my last relationship, sex wasn't about pleasure. At least, not mine."

That caveman part of his DNA had him internally balking at the thought of her being with anyone but him, and he wanted to murder Silas Jeffers with his bare hands for not cherishing her the way she'd deserved. For not worshipping her body every day. He opened his month to offer her those reassurances, to remind her that she'd been wasting her time with boys who didn't know how to take care of her, but he stopped himself. She was bringing this up for a reason, and the fact that she was meant she felt safe with him in a way she never had with anyone else.

Silently, Jack vowed to give her whatever she wanted, whenever she asked for it, every day for the rest of their lives.

"I want to try new things," she said, twirling the can of whipped cream around in her hand. "New positions and toys and...food play. Test my boundaries." She looked up at him then, her face determined, eyes sure. "And I want to do all of that with you."

"I want that with you, too," he said. "Whatever you want, sunshine. But there's no rush. You know that, right?"

"Of course I do," she said, pushing out of his arms and once again climbing onto the bed, kneeling in the middle. "But when are we going to have the chance to have an entire, uninterrupted night to ourselves, without roommates or practice or games or classes or whatever else in the way? We've got all night, Jack, and this"—she gestured to him with the can of whipped cream, and he took it from her—"is something I want to do *right now*."

Jack didn't need to be told twice and joined her on the bed. This—food play, as she called it—was new to him, too, and he was painfully turned on at the prospect of consuming this sugary substance off the most sensitive parts of her body. One stroke of his cock, even a breath of air pointed in its direction, would have him exploding.

"Where would you like me to start?" he asked, pressing the nozzle to the side and squeezing some of the sweet foam into his mouth.

"How about...here?" Jessica said, her fingertips brushing over her nipples as she reclined.

Jack nodded and swallowed hard, then reached a shaky hand toward her. Two presses of the nozzle had Jessica's nipples decorated. Discarding the can next to him on the bed, he lowered his head and took one in his mouth.

Determined to get every last morsel of whipped cream—and heighten Jessica's pleasure while he was at it—he swirled his tongue lazily around the tip of her breast, lightly scraped at her flesh with his teeth, and sucked hard before he pulled away, then blew a breath of air over the wetness.

When he caught Jessica's eyes, they were squeezed shut, her fingers white-knuckled gripping the sheets at her sides.

"That good, hey?" he asked with a smirk.

Her eyes flew open, and she said, "I didn't realize my nipples were that sensitive."

Jack grinned, loving that he was the one helping her discover these things.

He gave her other breast the same attention, and before she could direct him further, he took over.

First, he sprayed a long trail from between her breasts to her belly button, and licked her skin navel to chest, groaning against her as her lungs hollowed out and she dug her fingernails into his scalp.

Then, he drew a long line from hip bone to hip bone and ran his tongue along the smooth skin across her waist.

Finally, he paused with the tip of the nozzle a breath away from her clit and flicked his gaze to hers, silently asking—no, *begging*—for permission.

This was one thing they hadn't done in Mexico: given and received oral pleasure. And Jack had been dying to taste her. That teasing lick as he'd undressed her earlier hadn't been enough. *Nothing* would ever be enough.

"Please," she breathed.

He pressed the nozzle, spraying a line from her clit to her entrance. She gasped at the coolness of the cream against her heated skin, a sound that quickly turned to a drawn out moan when he dove in and consumed every bit of that cream up in one long lick.

The sweetness of the cream mixed with her natural flavor had Jack immediately diving back in, not allowing her any moment of reprieve from his mouth on her sensitive, swollen pussy.

He ran his tongue around her clit, traces of the cream clinging to his taste buds as he settled his lips around her and sucked. Her back arched from the bed, and Jack watched through heavily lidded eyes as she drew her knees up higher, giving him better access.

"You like that, don't you?" he asked, voice husky, darting his tongue out and tracing a path with only the tip. Using the fingers of one hand, he opened her wider, then said, "What about this?" before inserting two fingers.

"Fuck," she breathed, her hips already thrusting against his fingers.

As it turned out, Jessica already knew what she liked in bed, and that appeared to be whatever Jack was willing to give her.

His tongue and his fingers moved in tandem, working her closer and closer to the edge. Jack knew she was ready to throw herself off the cliff when her thighs clamped around his head, and he curled his fingers inside her, grazing his teeth a little against her clit before suctioning his mouth around it.

She detonated, harder than she had earlier with his dick inside her, coating his fingers even more so with her release. When she climaxed, she tried to turn her body away from him, but he held her firmly with his free hand on her stomach, forcing her to feel every second of it. And he continued to work her through it, letting her fuck his hand until the tiny aftershock spasms ceased and her breathing slowed considerably.

Making this girl come undone was a high all its own.

Jack crawled up her body and placed a soft kiss against her temple. "I don't know about you," he said, "but that was the hottest thing I've ever done."

Jessica turned her head toward him, a blissed-out, completely sated smile plastered on her face. "I came so hard I saw stars," she said, and he burst out laughing.

Tucking her closer into his side, he shifted and began pulling the sheets and comforter out from underneath them.

"Shouldn't we clean up first?" she asked, dipping her hand between her legs. When she withdrew, her fingers glistened with the evidence of her orgasm.

"You're probably right. I'll get a washcloth."

"Or..." Jessica trailed off but slid out of bed after him. "We could take a shower."

He pulled her into his arms and dropped a kiss on her mouth, one that went from tender to a tangle of tongues and teeth in a millisecond.

"You're insatiable," he said when they broke apart.

"We have a lot of time to make up for."

That they did, he thought as he led her into the bathroom.

NOW: March 5, 2024

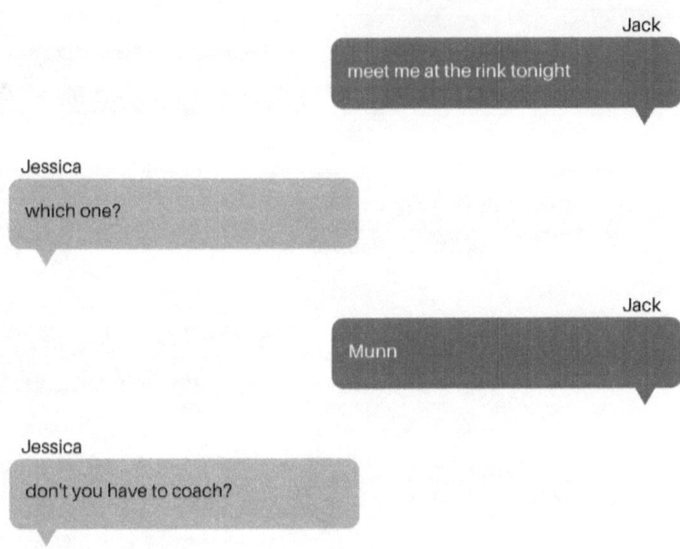

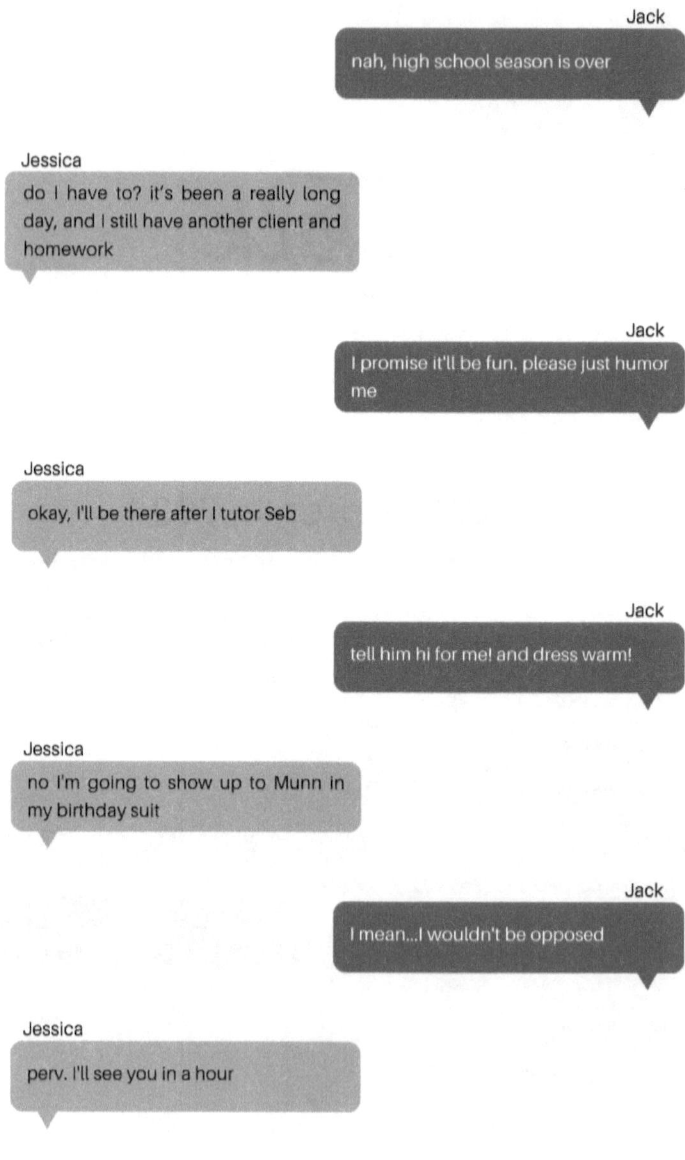
Jack
nah, high school season is over

Jessica
do I have to? it's been a really long day, and I still have another client and homework

Jack
I promise it'll be fun. please just humor me

Jessica
okay, I'll be there after I tutor Seb

Jack
tell him hi for me! and dress warm!

Jessica
no I'm going to show up to Munn in my birthday suit

Jack
I mean...I wouldn't be opposed

Jessica
perv. I'll see you in an hour

One of the upsides of being a collegiate athlete—and there were many—was having free reign of the ice arena and the facilities whenever he wanted or needed them. It was a Tuesday night, and Jack couldn't stop thinking about Jessica and Valentine's Day. Though they'd gotten naked together several times since then, he and Jessica had always been good at the physical side of a relationship. But lately, Jack had been feeling the urge to talk to her more, to dive deeper into their time apart and truly learn what made her tick.

So he'd planned this impromptu date.

Once he'd showered and changed after practice, and his teammates, coaches, and other staff had cleared out of the arena, he got to work setting everything up. He guessed at Jessica's shoe size and borrowed a pair of skates from the pro shop, then pushed a net out onto the ice and set it up at one end.

After that, he walked back into the locker room and headed straight for the lounge, where he'd laid out a feast of pastries from Jessica's favorite bakery in Old Town, hot chocolate that he made himself in a CrockPot—thanks to his mother's help—and other snacks he knew Jessica loved.

Jack had always known Jessica wasn't a big hockey fan; she'd told him so that first night in Mexico. But over the last few months, she'd come to enjoy it, if only because she loved him. He wanted to share this part of him with her, as hockey was a huge piece of who he was.

Plus, he planned to marry Jessica Daniels one day, which would make her a WAG. She was going to have to get used to being around the game regardless.

Promptly at six p.m., Jessica texted saying she'd arrived. Before heading up to the concourse to meet her, Jack spun in a circle, surveying the lounge and making sure everything was perfect. He would've liked to add some candles—he had compromised with battery-operated ones—and rose petals and other cheesy shit, but this was an ice arena, not a hotel room, so he refrained.

"Hey, sunshine!" he yelled up to her when he reached ice level.

"What are you doing?" she shouted back.

Jack lazily pushed off the bench and skated in a slow circle at center ice. "Skating."

"No shit," Jessica said. "But why? Didn't you just have practice?"

"Quit asking questions and get your ass down here."

"Do I have to?"

"We've been over this, Jess. I promise you'll have fun. Do you trust me?"

"Of course I do."

"Then come here."

Jessica's exasperated sigh was audible in the deserted arena, but she made her way down the stairs, then walked along the glass to meet him at the Zamboni entrance where he waited for her, borrowed skates in hand.

When she reached him, Jessica dropped her bag and crossed her arms over her chest. "You can't seriously expect me to put those on."

"I do, and you will."

Jessica raised an eyebrow. "You don't tell me what to do."

"Sunshine," Jack groaned. "Please?"

He supposed if she fought him on this and outright refused to get on the ice, he could just take her down to the lounge and let the rest of the evening play out earlier than he'd planned, but he knew he'd be disappointed if she wouldn't do this one thing for him. Somehow, getting Jessica onto the ice seemed vital to him—and their relationship.

"Fine," she said at last, and Jack grinned, then led her onto the ice.

In her street shoes, she slipped and slid all the way to the bench, but Jack kept a firm grip on her hands, towing her along as he skated backward. He'd offered to carry her, but she shot him a death glare that had him raising his hands in surrender.

They reached the bench, and Jessica sat and kicked her shoes off.

"I have no idea how to put those on," she said, "so you'll have to do it for me."

Jack had planned on doing just that anyway, but still, he nodded solemnly as he knelt in front of her. Her skinny jeans were already tucked into her socks, which was good, as it would prevent her socks from slipping off and giving her major chafing blisters from the skates. The other upside to borrowed skates was that they were already broken in, so Jessica wouldn't have to deal with the stiffness that came with skating in a brand new pair.

The backs of Jack's ankles and his heels were permanently calloused from the time it took to soften a new pair up, and he wouldn't wish that hell on anyone.

Jack undid the knot where the laces of the skates were tied

together, then loosened the left one. Gently, he lifted Jessica's leg and slid the skate over her delicate foot. They were the perfect fit, like Prince Charming finding his Cinderella.

"I like it when you're on your knees for me," Jessica said quietly.

Okay, maybe not a fairytale, then. With the way his cock swelled and his thoughts strayed to all of the things he could do to his girl from this position, Jack knew he was no prince. But he'd still worship Jessica like a princess if she let him.

Once he tightened the laces and wrapped them around the boot of the skate, stabilizing her ankle, he brushed his fingers over her calf and up her thigh, then trailed them down the other side, chuckling when Jessica shivered.

"Why aren't we at home right now?" she asked. "Preferably naked."

"Because," Jack said, making quick work of the other skate, past teasing her now that the situation in his pants had grown dire. He envied women and the fact that their desire didn't physically manifest in the way a man's did. "We can't spend all of our time in bed."

Jessica pouted, and Jack laughed. Who knew his girl was such a freak?

"But I like being in bed with you."

"Later," he promised her, pulling her to her feet. "Right now, I want to take my girl ice skating."

"You do know I've never done this before, right?" she asked as he led her to the boards, inches away from putting her natural athleticism to good use but clearly apprehensive to take that first step.

"Yes," Jack said, gripping her hands tighter. "I promise I won't let you fall."

Jessica took a fortifying breath, and Jack watched as the apprehension in her eyes turned to determination, as her spine straightened and her chin lifted.

Then, she stepped off the bench.

As he'd promised, he held her hands as he glided backward, easing them in a slow lap around the rink. Jessica's movements were stiff and awkward at first, but by the time they made one full loop, she'd loosened up, taking Jack's murmured instructions under advisement.

"I think you can try on your own now, don't you?" he said.

"No!" she protested, but Jack had already pulled away.

"You've got this, sunshine!" he yelled as he blazed a path across the ice. Rarely did Jack get to skate without all of his gear on, and he took the opportunity to bask in the freedom of unrestricted movements, of not being bogged down by his pads and glove and oversized stick.

Jessica simply watched him, and Jack relished in the way her eyes clung to his body as he skated backward. He didn't miss the way her chest rose and fell rapidly despite the fact that she stood still.

Jack grinned wickedly at her, skating to her side and coming to a stop, showering her skates and shins with ice shavings.

"Where'd your mind just go?" he asked roughly, reaching up to tuck a strand of hair behind her ear.

"I'm still wishing we were home in bed," she said. "But that"—she gestured to his body, and presumably to the way he'd moved across the ice—"explains the stamina."

She reached out for him, and he skated closer, pulling her into his arms.

"Those pads are heavy," he said against her mouth, his lips brushing across hers in a tantalizing caress that had her surging forward—but Jack skated out of reach.

"Jack!" she whined.

"Nope," he said, grinning at her, though he'd surprised himself with his self-control. Every molecule of his body screamed at him to take her, even if they were standing on a sheet of frozen water. But there would be time for that later.

"Then what are we doing here? Because I'm not gonna lie, I'm not having a good time."

Jack balked at that, his skates instantly coming to a stop. "Really?"

"Really," she said, crossing her arms once again. "I'm not good at this. And I'm fucking freezing!" she yelled, her words echoing from the rafters.

Without hesitation, Jack was at her side, scooping her into his arms and rushing back to the bench. Jessica squealed, but didn't protest. When they reached the bench, he wordlessly placed her on it and untied her skates, then slipped her boots back on.

"I'm sorry," she said quietly when she was once again in street shoes, feet planted firmly on the ground.

"It's okay, Jess," he said, giving her a small, reassuring smile. Then he extended a hand for her. "Come on."

"Now where are we going?" she asked as he led her down the tunnel and through the bowels of the building. Thanks to the addition and upgrades to the facility, this path was a lot less dark and dank than it used to be. It was well lit, warm, and decorated in Spartan green and white.

"You'll see," he said as he led her down the hall, past the physical therapy pools and tables, the equipment rooms and showers, the storage lockers and media rooms. Finally, they rounded a corner into the lounge, and Jessica gasped.

"Is this all for me?" she asked, meeting his gaze.

"Yes," he said somewhat shyly.

"It's...beautiful."

"Come, let's sit."

He led her to the couch in the corner, the table in front of it laden with the spoils of his earlier shopping trip. Jessica's hand flew to her mouth when she spied the label on the pastry boxes.

When they were seated, Jack reclined against the couch back, Jessica's back to his front, relaxed against him, and Jessica had been sated by pastries, she asked, "Why here?"

"What do you mean?"

"Why are we here, Jack? Why couldn't we have had this date at the bakery, or at home?"

"Home is too tempting," he said. "And at a bakery, I'd have to share you. I just...wanted to talk for once."

"About what?" she asked, tilting her head back to look up at him.

"Everything."

Jessica laughed. "You're going to have to be more specific than that. We've got almost four years' worth of life to catch up on."

"Okay, fair enough," he said. "I've been dying to ask this since Valentine's Day, and you totally don't have to answer because I know it's not important, but...how many people have you been with besides me?"

"Two."

"That...explains a lot," he said. "You and Silas never...?"

He wasn't sure how he'd been about to finish that question. Never experimented? Never brought whipped cream into the bedroom? Never had marathon sex that lasted for hours?

"For all his outward charm and frat boyishness, Silas is pretty straight-laced in the bedroom. We...we only ever had sex in missionary, and he never seemed to care about getting me off. There was more than one occasion where he'd pass out and I'd get myself off with my hand."

"I hate that guy," Jack said through gritted teeth. How someone could've looked at Jessica, had her in his arms, ready and willing to let that wild part of her heart free, and had never taken the time to give her what she wanted was unforgivable in his eyes.

"He's not all bad," she said. "He just wasn't the guy for me."

Jack pressed a kiss to the top of her head. "It's really lucky for you that you found the right guy, then."

"It's weird," she said. "How safe I feel with you. But it's also not? I don't know if that makes any sense at all, but with you, wrapped in your arms? It's the safest place in the world to me. I gave you my virginity because I knew you'd take care of me. Losing it was never as big a deal to me as other people make it out to be, but I couldn't have dreamed up a better scenario than getting to experience that with you. I think..."

"What?" he prompted when she trailed off.

"I think I've been holding every relationship since then to those same standards. And that *really* doesn't make sense, given we had less than a week together, but...everything in Mexico was heightened, you know? It's like I completely let go of all of my inhibitions and reservations and just let myself *feel*. Even if we hadn't found our way back here, I'd forever cherish what you gave me that week."

"That makes perfect sense," he said quietly. And he meant it. He'd had these exact same thoughts, had spent their years apart yearning for that connection with someone. All that time, he'd been willing to settle for something even a fraction as magical because he knew he'd never find the real thing again. Not without Jessica.

"Even though he was the one to say he was in love with someone else first, I still feel bad for how everything went down with Silas. We had broken up and gotten back together a lot over the years, and I think subconsciously, that was just me pushing him away when he didn't measure up to you. I tried to move on and forget you, but I don't think I ever would've been truly happy if we didn't end up right here, together again."

"I looked for you in every girl I gave myself to," Jack said. "Your smile, your laugh, the way your hands felt on my body, how it felt to have you wrapped in my arms. It was torture, knowing you were out there somewhere and I couldn't even look for you. And you'd been here the whole time. It's...fucking insane to me, some cruel twist of the universe's sense of humor, that we didn't cross paths until October. We could've spent a few months apart instead of several years. Think of how happy we would've been all this time."

"I can't let myself focus on that," she said, twisting in his arms to straddle his lap, capturing his face between her palms. "And I don't want you to, either. We can't change it, Jack. And I think that we were brought back together when we were because we weren't ready before now. I firmly believe it was good for us to go out and experience other relationships and life outside of this. We might not have ended up here otherwise."

Jack studied her face, the shape of her brows, the fringe of lashes outlining her crystal blue gaze, the smattering of freckles across her cheeks and the fullness of her lips. Everything about her was infinitely precious to him, and he realized she was right. He had been crazy about her in Mexico, and that feeling would have remained the same had they found each other again that fall. But the years apart had taught him a lot about himself and relationships, had allowed him to grow as a man—had let him become the perfect man for her. And the same could certainly be said of Jessica, who was still that same girl from Mexico, but not. The boy he'd been four years ago cared deeply for Jessica, sure, but the man he was now?

That man knew how to care for her, to be the man she deserved. That man loved her with everything he had.

"It's all about timing," Jessica said, pulling him from his reverie. "You've always been the right person for me, but Mexico wasn't the right time, and neither was any day across those years before we reunited. Remember how you asked me in Mexico if I believe in fate?"

"Yes."

"I didn't then," she reminded him. "And my opinion of that hadn't really changed until that day I walked out onto the patio upstairs and heard you say my name. That was the day you tipped my world upside down—again. That was the day the stars finally aligned for us."

NOW: March 23, 2024

THE CONNECTION JESSICA AND Jack had formed in Mexico only strengthened now that they were older and wiser and in the "real world." The last few months together had been pure bliss. She couldn't imagine how she'd gone so long without him, but it also felt as if no time had passed at all.

It made sense, then, that the universe threw a wrench into the whole thing on a Saturday in late March.

The day started like any other. Jessica woke up that morning, planning on applying for more jobs and pulling together some lesson plans for student teaching, as well as for her tutoring clients.

And she had accomplished quite a bit of that. By early evening, right as the sun disappeared from view for the night, she closed her laptop, intent on getting some housework done. Jack had late practice before playoffs started next weekend, so she thought she'd pick up her room while she waited for him to be done.

With her attention completely elsewhere, she didn't think anything of it when her phone pinged with an incoming email. She navigated to the app and opened it.

FROM: ADMIN@ELS.RU
TO: JDANIELS@MSU.EDU
SUBJECT: JOB APPLICATION

DEAR MISS DANIELS:

I AM WRITING TO YOU TODAY ON BEHALF OF THE ENGLISH LANGUAGE SCHOOL LOCATED IN SAINT PETERSBURG, RUSSIA. WE HAVE REVIEWED YOUR APPLICATION AND, PENDING A PHONE INTERVIEW, WOULD LIKE TO OFFER YOU A POSITION TEACHING AT OUR SCHOOL AFTER GRADUATION.

PLEASE RESPOND TO US AT YOUR EARLIEST CONVENIENCE TO SET UP THE INTERVIEW.

WE LOOK FORWARD TO HEARING FROM YOU.

SINCERELY,
POLINA MOROZOV
SECRETARY, ELS

Jessica's hands shook so bad she nearly dropped her phone. Before she had fully processed what she read, she typed out her response.

FROM: JDANIELS@MSU.EDU
TO: ADMIN@ELS.RU
SUBJECT: RE: JOB APPLICATION
DEAR POLINA,

IT'S WONDERFUL TO HEAR FROM YOU! I KNOW WITH THE TIME DIFFERENCE, IT MAY BE DIFFICULT TO SET SOMETHING UP, SO HOW ABOUT YOU TELL ME WHAT WORKS FOR YOU, AND I CAN MAKE IT HAPPEN ON MY END?

SINCERELY,
JESSICA DANIELS

Excitement bubbled in her chest at the thought of telling everyone she knew, everyone who had helped her get here—her family, her professors, her friends, colleagues, classmates.

Jack.

The thought of her boyfriend had that bubble deflating. She had to tell him, immediately, before anyone else. She owed him that much.

As if he knew she'd been thinking about him, her phone rang, showing his name on the screen.

"Hey, you," she said when she answered, willing her voice to remain steady.

"Hey, sunshine. What're you doing?"

"I was about to clean the house, but I'm distracted."

Jack didn't ask why; he simply said, "You wanna come over? We can talk about it...or I can distract you further."

Despite the racing of her heart and the anxious sweat prickling at her underarms, she smiled. "I'll be over in a bit."

"See you soon!"

It took Jessica all of five minutes to throw some overnight stuff into a bag—because she knew she wouldn't be coming home tonight—and head out the door.

When she walked into Jack's house, she was unsurprised to find Kenzie and Aiden in the kitchen cooking dinner. The boys took turns making meals, and whenever it was Aiden's turn, Kenzie had a habit of helping out.

Probably because of that one time Aiden nearly burned the house down while trying to make chicken marsala.

"Hey, sis!" she yelled at Kenzie as she rushed up the stairs. Kenzie's response was lost as Jessica unceremoniously pushed her way into Jack's bedroom, dropped her bag on the floor, and threw herself at him.

Jack caught her easily, chuckling as he settled them comfortably on the bed. "Hello to you, too," he said, and she offered her mouth to him.

"I missed you," she said against his lips.

"You just saw me yesterday."

"Yes, well, even two minutes is too long to be parted, let alone fifteen hours."

"So needy," he said, digging his fingers into her sides. She squirmed and squealed on his lap, gasping for air as she begged him to stop.

Thankfully, Jessica's phone rang, and Jack was forced to let her go so she could answer. Both the Daniels and Jean families were on high alert these days thanks to Berkley's advanced pregnancy.

Jessica's heart crawled into her throat when she saw her mom's name on the screen.

"Hello?"

"Hi, honey," her mom said. "Just calling to let you know your sister is in labor!"

"Oh my God, oh my God, oh my God!" Jessica squealed. "I'm at Jack's right now, but Kenzie is here, too. We're on our way."

"Drive safe!" her mom yelled before Jessica could hang up the phone.

"What's going on?" Jack asked.

"My sister is in labor. Kenzie and I need to leave, like, right now."

Jessica bent to pick up her bag, thankful she hadn't even gotten settled, and turned to rush downstairs.

But Jack stopped her with a hand on her elbow. "I'm coming with you," he said when she looked up at him.

"Are you sure? Don't you have practice tomorrow?"

Jessica asked because she honestly didn't know. Maybe that made her a bad girlfriend, not paying closer attention to his practice schedule, but practices weren't important. She knew exactly when his next game was. In fact, she hadn't missed a home one since they'd gotten together, and planned to go to South Dakota next weekend, where the Spartans were playing their quarterfinal games.

"We have late practice again," Jack said. "And it's just a weight lifting session. I'm coming with you."

"Okay," she said, smiling. "Pack a bag. We can stay at Brent and Berk's tonight."

"Are you sure they'll be okay with that?"

"Considering they won't even be there? Yes, I'm sure. Worse comes to worst, we can stay with Kenzie's parents. They live like three miles away from B and B, and Sandra and Ron's house is actually closer to the hospital."

Before Jack could respond, Kenzie shouted Jessica's name up the stairs.

"Her mom or brother must've called her," Jessica said. "Hurry up!"

Jack did as he was told, quickly shoving anything he'd need overnight—mainly an extra pair of socks, underwear, sweatpants, and his phone charger—into his backpack.

When he was finally ready to go, Jessica made their way downstairs, finding both Kenzie and Aiden waiting.

"Fuller's coming, too?" Jack asked, reaching out to fist-bump his buddy.

"You think I'm letting bunny go alone?" Aiden said, and Jessica laughed.

Aiden Fuller, it turned out, was about as territorial over Kenzie as Jack was over Jessica.

At first, Jessica wasn't sure about Aiden, especially not after she realized that the "bunny" nickname he and his teammates had given Kenzie was short for "puck bunny." But, as Jack had said all those months ago when she'd asked him about it at Munn, Kenzie—who was the furthest thing from a puck bunny—didn't mind it, and Jessica had to admit it was kind of sweet. Like the way Jack called her "sunshine."

"Are we ready?" Kenzie asked, bouncing on the balls of her feet.

"Yes," Jessica said quickly. "Let's go!"

"We can take my Jeep," Aiden said. "It has the most room."

The only problem was, Aiden's Jeep was buried in the driveway, both Jack's truck and either Asher or Luke's car parked behind it.

"Fuck," Aiden said. Then, quieter, "I'm sorry, bunny. Hold on."

Aiden rushed back up the front steps, opened the door, and hollered, "ASH! Get your ass down here and move your car!"

Asher shouted a reply, something muffled that Jessica couldn't quite make out.

"Because I fucking said so!" Aiden yelled. "Berkley is in labor, and we need to get Jessica and Kenzie to Detroit like right now!"

Then Aiden turned and said, "Jack, catch!" before whipping his keys across the distance between them. Jack caught them easily and slid behind the wheel of his truck.

A moment later, Asher exited the house, grumbling the entire time about how he'd been taking a nap, and it was rude to interrupt someone's sleep.

Aiden simply said, "My girl's sister-in-law having a baby is a little more important than your nap."

Asher shut up after that, and after some shifting that ended with Asher's car where Aiden's had been and Jack's pulled up behind it, they were on their way to Detroit.

Late March and early April weather was always hit or miss in Michigan. It could be sunny and seventy-five one day, then below freezing and snowing the next.

Unfortunately for them, today was one of the shitty days. While Aiden was a good driver and took it nice and easy the entire ninety miles to Detroit, Jessica's knuckles still ached from gripping the oh shit handle, and her shoulders and jaw were sore from tension.

At last, they safely pulled up to the hospital, and Jessica and Kenzie left the boys in favor of running inside and up to the OB wing.

Both of their families were crowded in the waiting room, and Jessica threw herself into the seat next to her mom while Kenzie hugged her own parents.

"Has there been any news?" she asked.

"Nothing except the baby is breech," her mom said, and Jessica took a moment to study her, noticing the fine lines of tension around her mouth.

"What does that mean?"

"It means they're going to try and flip him, but if that doesn't work, your sister is going to have to have a c-section. Which we were prepared for, given her pregnancy complications. But…"

"But what, Mom?"

"A c-section could kill her," Logan croaked from behind her, and Jessica turned to her brother, surprised.

"How did you beat me here?" she asked.

"I was already in town. Work thing."

"Can I see her?" Jessica asked her mom.

"Sure," she said, then looked at Kenzie. "Kenz? You wanna go, too?"

"Yes, please."

And so, Jessica's mom led her, Kenzie, and Sandra down the hall to a birthing suite, and before they even opened the door, a string of expletives shouted by a very aggravated female greeted them in the hall.

"Sounds like it's going well," Kenzie said, and she and Jessica snickered.

The four of them pushed inside, and Jessica's gaze immediately fell to her sister. Berkley was propped up in her hospital bed, a sheet pulled high around her waist, her gown pulled up to reveal her swollen belly. A nurse stood at her bedside, pressing on Berkley's stomach, presumably to encourage the baby to flip around.

It didn't seem to be going well.

"That's clearly not fucking helping!" Berkley said through gritted teeth.

For his part, Brent stood at Berkley's other side, the picture of calm as his wife clearly attempted to crush every bone in his right hand.

"Cut her some slack, Berk," Brent said softly. "She's just trying to help."

"I don't need her help. Just cut him out of me and be done with it."

"You don't mean that," Brent said.

"I do. Just put me out of my misery."

Jessica's mom walked further into the room until Berkley's eyes landed on their little group.

"Jess," her sister said, tears forming instantly in her blue eyes.

Jessica rushed to her sister, careful of the belly as she pulled her sister in for a hug.

"You guys didn't have to come!" Berkley cried as she hauled Kenzie in on the other side, Brent stepping out of the way for his sister.

"We wanted to be here," Jessica said. "Jack and Aiden are here, too."

"Jack?" Berkley said, perking up. The nurse had ended her torture of Berkley's abdomen and left the room, leaving space open for both her mom and Sandra to approach the bed.

The Daniels and Jean women. What a crew they made.

"Yes, Jack," Jessica said, then looked around, shocked not to find him in the room with them. Then again, she and Kenzie had left him and Aiden in the dust on their way up here.

Kenzie's eyes widened at the same time Jessica's did. "Fuck," Kenzie said. "You left him out there with your dad and Logan?"

"I wasn't thinking clearly!" Jessica protested, then moved around her mom, shouting, "I'll be back!" at them over her shoulder.

When she reached the little waiting room, Jack was indeed surrounded by not only her dad and Logan, but also Ron and Nate as well. With a wince, Jessica approached their group, forcing her way to Jack's side and sliding her hand into his.

"Hi Dad!" she said brightly. "Hi Ron, hi Nate."

Then men parroted greetings, then Logan said, "We were just getting to know your boyfriend here."

"Yeah, sorry," she said sheepishly. "I was so excited to see Berk that I forgot to introduce him to everyone. Jack, this is my brother, Logan, Kenzie's dad, Ron, and her other brother, Nate." She pointed at each of them in turn, and they responded by nodding their heads in Jack's direction.

Had Jessica mentioned before how much she loved this blended family of theirs? Because right now, she'd like to withdraw that statement.

Glaring at each of the men in turn, including Aiden, who had done nothing to come to his friend's aide, she turned to Jack. "Do you want to come meet my sister? And I'm sure my mom would love to say hi."

"Tell Kenzie to come get her boy," Nate said.

Aiden, the *boy* in question, slung his arm around Nate's shoulders. "This is a good time for us to bond, bro," he said with a cheeky grin.

Nate shrugged his arm off and growled, "Don't call me *bro.*"

Aiden's grin only grew. "How about...bro-in-law?"

Jessica pulled Jack away before Aiden and Nate started arguing and Jack was forced to back up his friend.

"She's not like, naked in there, is she?"

"I mean, no. She's got a sheet and hospital gown covering the important parts," she told him as she tugged him along.

Jack swallowed hard, pulling Jessica to a stop in the middle of the hall. "Maybe this isn't the best time to meet her," he said. "She probably doesn't want all kinds of random people waltzing in and out of there."

"You're hardly random. You're my boyfriend, and I love you. Berkley will, too. Now come on, big guy," she said. "Quit stalling."

"I'm not stalling," he said under his breath.

When they pushed into Berkley's room, Jessica's mom was the first to react.

"Jack!" she squealed, rushing up to throw her arms around him, then pulling away and taking stock of him. "Oh, it's good to see you."

Jack grinned, and Jessica watched some of the tension melt from his shoulders. Her mom had always loved him, and Jessica was confident the rest of her family would, too. "Hi, Michelle. It's good to see you, too."

"Was Fuller behaving himself out there?" Kenzie asked

"He was about to get his ass reamed by Nate for touching him and calling him 'bro,'" Jessica said with a laugh.

"Ouch," Kenzie winced. "Nate will get over the 'bro' thing, but he hates being touched without giving permission. I should've warned him."

"Oh, whatever," Berkley said from behind Kenzie. "Nate will get over it. Now, little sister, bring that boy over here."

With a smile and a reassuring squeeze of his hand, Jessica led Jack to Berkley's bedside.

"Berk, this is Jack. Jack, this is my big sister, Berkley."

Jack extended his hand, but Brent stepped in. "I wouldn't do that," he said. "She's awfully strong for someone so tiny. I'm not sure I'll ever be able to shoot accurately again."

"Please," Berkley said with an eye roll, but the rest of whatever she'd been about to say was cut off as she screwed her face up in pain. With a world-weary sigh, Brent held out his hand, and Berkley latched on, her knuckles going white while his fingers turned a terrifying shade of beet red as the circulation was cut off.

"See?" Brent said to Jack through clenched teeth. "This could've been you."

When the contraction passed, Brent withdrew from his wife's grasp and shook his hand out. "I'm Brent, by the way," he said, awkwardly extending his left hand.

Jack, still clearly starstruck, stuck out his as well, and the men shared an awkward handshake.

Then Brent turned to Jessica. "Is he okay?"

"I think so?" But she wasn't entirely sure. Jack appeared to be broken, struck dumb and silent by the presence of Brent Jean. "Jack?" she asked, snapping her fingers in front of his face.

Slowly, he turned to her, blinking several times as if to clear the fog from his brain. "Sorry," he said. "It's just...not every day you walk into a hospital room and meet Brent Jean."

"You say that like you didn't know exactly who my brother-in-law is."

"It's one thing to be *told* your brother-in-law is Brent Jean," Jack said. "It's entirely different to *see* it."

Jessica laughed, and even Berkley, as in pain as she was, chuckled.

"I know the feeling," Berkley said through labored breaths. She hooked a thumb at her husband and said, "It took this guy throwing me a surprise birthday party to even get me to talk to him."

Jack looked at Jessica quizzically, and before she could open her mouth to tell him it was a long story she'd tell later, a voice behind them said, "And you fucking hated him for it."

"I did not!" Berkley protested, but her petulance quickly turned to a misty-eyed smile when she laid eyes on her best friend.

Lexie Monroe breezed into the room, dressed like she was attending a New York City Fashion show and not coming to see her friend in the hospital.

As the women embraced, Mitch Frambough strolled in behind his girlfriend, walked up to Brent, and tugged him into a hug. When he let go, he asked, "How's my girl?"

"Dying," Berkley said dramatically.

"You are not. Don't say shit like that." Jessica didn't miss the way her brother-in-law's face had gone white as a sheet. He turned to the newcomers. "The baby is breech, so they're trying to get him to flip. If he doesn't, she'll have to have a c-section."

"And a c-section is the last thing we want," Lexie said.

Another contraction overtook Berkley, and as she reached out for someone's hand, Brent said, "You're up, Mitch. You don't need that hand to play anymore."

"No, but he needs it for other things," Lexie said with a smirk, instantly diffusing the tension in the room.

"Alexandra!" Jessica's mom scolded, and for the first time since she walked in, Lexie spun in a circle, taking in the crowd gathered around Berkley.

"Sorry, Michelle." Though Lexie's grin said she wasn't sorry at all. Over her shoulder, she added to Berkley, "Only you would have four thousand people at the hospital when you give birth."

"We have big families," Berkley said through clenched teeth, as if that explained everything.

Lexie waved her away, then worked her way around the room, giving everyone one of those signature Lexie smiles, the kind that said she could eat any one of them alive if she wanted, but chose not to.

"Jess!" Lexie said when she laid eyes on Jessica, and stepped toward her to pull her into a hug. "I haven't seen you in ages! How's school going? Still planning on doing that whole overseas teaching thing?"

Jessica smiled, her cheeks blushing, flattered that Lexie had remembered. Then again, with no siblings of her own, and as

Berkley's best friend, Lexie had taken it upon herself to adopt all of the Daniels and Jean siblings—except Nate, because that would be weird—as her own.

"Yep," she said, and almost continued by telling Lexie she'd just gotten a job offer today, but held her tongue. She hadn't told Jack yet, and now was not the time.

As if noticing Jack for the first time, though it was hard to miss him, Lexie looked him up and down. "And who is this?"

"Jack DeLuca," Jack said, thrusting his hand out to Lexie.

With a quirked brow at Jessica, Lexie shook his hand and said, "He belongs to you, I take it?"

"Babe, why are you always scaring the young men?" Mitch asked, walking over to them and sliding a hand around Lexie's waist.

"Because it's so fun." She studied Jack for a beat longer, and Jessica choked on a laugh when he laced their fingers together and she discovered that his were shaking. "How is it that these kids keep getting better looking?" Lexie asked. "I mean, first you've got Kenzie with...*that*"—she waved a hand at Aiden, who had appeared a moment ago—"and now the littlest Daniels shows up with this guy?" She looked up at Mitch. "Did you look like this at his age?"

"I looked like I do now," Mitch said. "But with fewer wrinkles and grey hair because I wasn't dating you."

"You love me," she said with a smirk.

Mitch gave her a soft smile and said, "I do."

Before they kissed, she and Jack turned away, sharing a small smile of their own.

That's where I want us to be in ten years, she thought. *I want us to be that happy.*

Jessica

NOW: March 24, 2024

"Jess."

Jessica hadn't realized she'd fallen asleep until someone gently shook her awake and whispered her name. She blinked her eyes open to find Brent standing over her. Across the room, Kenzie and Aiden were rousing from the small loveseat, and Jack was doing the same in the chair next to hers.

"What time is it?" she asked, sitting up and stretching out her aching neck.

"After midnight," he said. "The doctor was just in. He said we're in a holding pattern right now, and it's unlikely anything will happen before morning." He dangled his keys in front of her face. "Why don't you guys go get some sleep at the house?"

"Are you sure?" Jessica asked. "What about the parents?"

"Jay and Michelle went home with my parents," he said. "But you four"—he jerked his head at Jack, Kenzie, and Aiden—"can crash at our place and come back in the morning."

"Okay," Jessica said, grabbing the keys from him and rising to her feet.

Unexpectedly, Brent pulled her in for a hug. "I'll call you guys if anything happens."

"Please do," Jessica said, then she and her friends left the room.

The drive to Brent and Berkley's house was quiet, each of them still barely awake. Thankfully, the roads were empty, and it had stopped snowing.

"Which room do you want?" Kenzie asked as she punched in the code on their security system and let the group inside.

"The usual one," she said.

"Perfect. We'll take the one at the opposite end of the house," Kenzie said with a wink. "You know...just in case."

Jack barked out a laugh, and Aiden playfully swatted Kenzie on the ass as they strode from the room and up the stairs. Playful squeals from Kenzie and low growls of words Jessica couldn't make out floated down behind them. It seemed those two had found their second wind.

Jessica led Jack up the stairs as well, turning left where Kenzie and Aiden had gone right, padding all the way to the end of the long hall.

The moment she opened the door and flipped on the light, she threw herself backward onto the bed.

"What a day," she said.

Jack crawled up next to her. "I agree," he said. "But I can't help thinking about what Kenzie was suggesting downstairs. About what those two are clearly getting up to right now."

"And what do you think she was suggesting, exactly?" Jessica asked as she slipped her hands under his shirt, smirking when his abdominals twitched beneath her touch.

"I think she was suggesting," he said as he lowered his head until their lips were a breath apart, "that I get you naked and make you come a few times before we pass out."

Jessica was already sitting up and shucking her shirt, eager to feel her man's body against hers, around hers, and inside of hers.

Before he took care of his own clothing, Jack helped Jessica remove hers. He reached behind her and flicked open the clasp on her bra, and Jessica wasted no time in tossing it across the room. Then she flopped onto her back and let him rid her of her leggings and panties.

Finally, she was fully naked, the cool sheets beneath her caressing her back, Jack's heated gaze dragging up and down the front of her body.

"Fuck, you're beautiful," he said.

"Thank you," she said with a smile. She reached up and ran her pointer finger along his brow, down the slope of his nose, over his full lips. "You are, too. Now get naked."

Jack didn't need to be told twice, and a few tugs had him dropping his shirts—all three layers—pants, and boxers on the ground.

In Mexico, Jessica had never been able to simply drink in the sight of him in this way. Their joining had been a frantic rush of two kids fumbling through their first time together, and with that came the awkwardness of not being entirely comfortable being naked in front of each other.

But now, there was no rush, nor were there any barriers between them, no walls or looming departures. They could slow down, savor, and drink in every delicious sight and sound.

Four years ago, Jack had been muscular in the way all teen boys who spent a little more time in the gym than their peers did were. But four years playing hockey at the collegiate level had turned Jack from an attractive teenager to a chiseled man. The contours, the rises and hollows of his muscles then were nothing compared to the man before her. She'd told him in Mexico that she couldn't wait to see what he looked like in five years if that was how he looked then, and...she'd been beautifully rewarded. He *had* gotten better with age, exactly as she predicted. Having seen him in all states of dress and undress—in his goalie pads, in a suit and tie for game day, in street clothes, comfy clothes, and no clothes—Jessica would forever marvel at the fact that this man somehow looked bigger off the ice than he did on.

Each muscle—his traps, shoulders, biceps, along the thick cords of his forearms; over his heavy pecs and his carved abdominals; down the massive ridges of his thighs that tapered into his knees, then flared out again at his calves—had been carefully developed and maintained. There wasn't an ounce of fat on him, and Jessica wanted to spend forever learning every nook and cranny, until she knew it as well as her own.

She rose onto her knees and reached for him, tugging him closer with her hands on the sharp indents at his hips, which led her eye straight to his cock, already hard and fully at attention for her.

Swiping her thumb over his head, where a bead of moisture had collected simply from her staring at him, she looked up at him and said, "I want to try something."

Jack grinned wickedly. "Those are becoming my favorite

words."

"I want to...sixty-nine," she said.

"Fuck yes."

Add this to the list of reasons she loved this man: he didn't balk when her more adventurous side made an appearance in bed. He was right there with her, throwing himself wholly into whatever she wanted to try next.

Jack moved her hand from his dick and crawled up next to her. He situated himself so he was laying on his back, then gripped her by the hips and turned her away from him. "You're going to sit that perfect pussy on my face," he said, "and you're going to take me in your mouth at the same time. Whoever comes first loses."

"Or wins," Jessica said, shooting him a saucy grin over her shoulder.

Then she did what he'd said, raising one leg and placing it on the other side of his head, backing her ass and pussy right into his face. And Jack dragged his tongue from front to back, giving her a little smack on her right cheek as he said, "Good girl."

Jessica found it incredibly hard to concentrate when he once again brought his mouth to her, his tongue flicking against her clit, but this had been her idea, so she lowered her head to his cock.

With the combined efforts of her hand and mouth, Jessica worked him slowly. She stroked him a few times first, getting him warmed up, though he was already hard as steel against her palm. Then, she ran her tongue along his length, pausing to swirl her tongue around his tip.

"Jessica," he growled, and the words vibrated against her clit, causing her to gasp.

"Fuck," she whispered, and he chuckled but went back to work.

Right as Jessica closed her lips around him and sucked hard enough that he bucked into her mouth, Jack stopped teasing her as well. It was almost impossible to think straight when he sucked her clit into his mouth at the same time he inserted the tip of one finger into her entrance, then another, pumping them in and out in time to the sucks and licks he delivered to her little bundle of nerves, but she gave it her best shot.

Curling her hand around his base, she squeezed hard and dove in, taking him so deep that she gagged a little, and he stopped what he was doing to growl, "Fuck, sunshine. Do that again."

His voice was wrecked, tone hoarse, and Jessica's only response was to pull off with a little pop and say, "Don't you fucking stop again."

"Yes ma'am," he responded, punctuating his words with another smack to her ass.

After that, it was all whispered pleas and satisfied moans and pleasure coiling tightly in her core. It wasn't only that Jack was so damn good with his mouth, constantly delivering the exact amount of pressure she craved with his tongue and fingers, knowing when to edge her along and when to let her fly. It was also that she was so damn turned on by *turning Jack on*, by pushing him closer and closer to his own release. And when Jack lost all control and started fucking her mouth, his hips thrusting, his dick branding the back of her throat in time with his licks and fingers inside her, Jessica came undone.

One more rough squeeze of his cock in her fist had him groaning against her clit and spilling into her mouth at the same time he grazed his teeth along her sensitive flesh and curled his fingers against some hidden inner wall she wasn't sure even she could reach herself, and she shattered right alongside him.

She moaned against his dick, but pulled off, Jack spilling all over her hand and his stomach as her orgasm tore a scream free from her throat.

Then she collapsed and rolled off him, landing at his side on the bed.

"I think we both won that round," he said after several long moments in which the only sounds were their heavy breathing.

"I'd say so," Jessica replied, still breathless, her clit still tingling with the aftershocks of her orgasm.

"Now what?" Jack asked, raising onto his elbows to look down at her.

"First, we get you cleaned up," she said, gesturing to the cum all over his stomach. "And then...dealer's choice."

"You mean I get to pick?" he asked, placing a hand on his chest as if to say, *moi*?

"Yes."

She rose from the bed and padded into the attached bathroom—grateful her sister and brother-in-law were rich enough that they bought a house where nearly every bedroom had an en suite—wet a washcloth, and rejoined Jack.

She sat at his side, her knees pressed against his thigh as she mopped him up, and he drew lazy circles on her hip while she worked. The moment all the cum was cleaned from his skin, he sat up, tossed the washcloth across the room, and lifted Jessica until her back was pressed to his front.

He brushed her hair off her shoulder to whisper in her ear. "I want you to hold onto that headboard while I fuck you from behind."

Jessica shivered and eagerly turned away from him, scrambling toward the head of the bed. The headboard was really a frame, metal and matte black, and the perfect height for Jessica to hang onto while backing onto Jack's dick.

"Like this?" she asked, wiggling herself into position.

"God, yes," Jack said. "Just like that. Don't move."

She wouldn't dare. She'd never had sex in this position, which seemed insane to her given that doggy was one of the most common ones. But neither of her previous dalliances—the short-lived fling the summer before she left for college, or Silas over the last three years—had been all that adventurous, and like she'd told Jack on Valentine's Day, she'd been afraid to ask.

But not with him. With Jack, Jessica wasn't afraid of anything. With Jack, Jessica was as safe as she could possibly be.

A zipper hissing filled the room, followed by what sounded like a box being ripped open, and Jessica looked over her shoulder in time to watch Jack tear into a condom wrapper, withdraw the rubber, and roll it down his length. Her heart rate kicked up. She didn't know why, but there was something so fucking sexy about seeing his massive hand wrapped around his dick, giving it a few experimental tugs before he rejoined her on the bed.

"You do realize we're living out a scene from one of my favorite fantasy novels right now, right?"

"Really?" Jack asked. "And how do I compare to that guy?"

Jessica craned her neck to study him. Truth be told, Jack was built like she imagined Cassian to be, though shorter and without the wings, blond where Cassian was dark-haired.

And there was the fact that Jack wasn't an immortal being in a fictional faerie land, but he loved her like Cassian loved Nesta, and that was worth its weight in gold.

"You're better," she said at last.

"And why is that?"

"Because you're real."

Jack's gaze softened, but he said, "Eyes forward," and Jessica whipped her head away from him. A heartbeat later, the tip of his cock nudged her slick pussy. "Hold on, sunshine."

He gave her no warning as he slammed into her, and Jessica's grip on the bed frame tightened as he withdrew and pushed in again.

Jack set a punishing rhythm, giving her no time to adjust or prepare. All she could do was react, to press her ass back into him with every one of his forward thrusts, to clench around him like a vise.

Surprisingly, another orgasm stirred in her core. She'd never gotten off simply from penetration before. Of course Jack would find a way.

Only, he wasn't done, and when he paused deep inside her, Jessica risked a glance over her shoulder, only for him to band an arm across her chest, his large hand cupping one of her breasts as he pulled her back against him. If she thought he'd gone deep before, she'd been mistaken. Seated on him like this was a whole new ball game, the angle and gravity allowing him to hit some impossible spot inside of her. And when he began to move, tweaking her nipple at the same time his other hand found her clit, well...Jessica could do nothing but hang on for dear life.

His breath was hot against her neck, his murmured, "you're so fucking tight," and "that's my girl," and "holy fuck, Jess, I'm close," in her ear only serving to coil that tension tighter and tighter inside her.

It was a whispered, "Come for me. Come all over this cock," that broke the dam at last, and she threw her head back onto his shoulder, unable to do anything but claw at his arms as she came apart, begging him to stop but also never wanting it to end.

And Jack came a moment later, punching his hips up into her in fast, deep strokes, biting down on her shoulder, she knew, to keep himself from yelling loud enough to wake the dead.

Jessica went limp in his arms, and Jack tipped until he was flat on his back, Jessica spread eagle on top of him.

"I think we both won that round, too," she said.

NOW: March 24, 2024

IT WAS NEARLY TWO a.m. by the time they rolled off each other, finally fully sated. They both rose to clean up and throw on some pajamas, but the moment they were curled around each other in bed once again, Jessica said, "Jack, I have to tell you something."

"Why did you wait until after nearly two hours of mind-blowing sex to drop this on me?" he whined. "Why didn't you do it before?"

"Because I wanted you too bad to ruin it."

"And whatever you have to tell me is going to ruin it?"

"I don't know," she said. "And that's what scares me."

Jack tugged her closer to his side, anchoring her next to him in case whatever she said next had the potential to break him. His heart was a fragile little thing, and she had no idea she held it entirely in her hands.

"Whatever you tell me changes nothing, sunshine. You know

that."

"I got a job offer today," she said. "Or, well, yesterday. Right before I came over."

Fuck.

"I'm assuming you were afraid to tell me because it's not in the continental United States."

She shook her head, and he brushed back a lock of hair that had fallen over her eyes. "No. It's in Saint Petersburg."

Double fuck.

"And look," she continued. "I know we've been avoiding this conversation, saying we'll cross that bridge when we come to it, but...the bridge is here, Jack. And the water is rising."

"What do you want me to say?" he asked. "That I'm happy for you? I *am* happy for you, but...I'm not happy for us."

"I knew this was a bad idea," she muttered.

"What? Telling me you're leaving? Being with me?"

"All of it!" she exploded, rising from the bed to pace at its foot.

"You don't mean that," he said

"Don't I?" she said. "Tell me you don't think that every day, Jack. Tell me you don't think of how much easier this whole graduating and moving on and pursuing our dreams thing would be if we hadn't gotten back together."

"Nothing would be easier without you, Jessica. *Nothing.* Don't think for one second I want to give this up simply because you're moving clear across the planet."

Jessica stilled, gaping at him, and he experienced a spark of satisfaction that he'd managed to surprise and shock her silent.

"Do you mean that?" she asked, taking a tentative step toward him.

"Of course I do," he said, closing the distance between them and crushing her to his chest. "We're going to figure whatever comes next out together. I won't have it any other way."

"I love you," she said into his shirt, and he smiled. He would never tire of hearing those words.

"I love you, too," he said into her hair.

"But I can't..."

"You can't do what, Jess?"

"I can't ask you to give up on your dream for me. And I can't give up on mine for you."

As he reached between them to cup her hands in his, he relaxed. The truth was he didn't want to give up on his dreams any more than she did. That wasn't to say there wasn't a lot that Jack wouldn't do where Jessica Daniels was concerned, but asking that of each other? That was too much.

Hockey was the very air in his lungs, and he'd worked too damn hard every day for the past four years—hell, every day for the past four*teen*—to give up now.

She pulled one of her hands free of his and reached up to press her palm to his cheek. Jack closed his eyes and leaned in to her touch, inhaling deeply.

His eyes sprung open, and he held her at arm's length.

"Why do you smell like..." He'd been about to say *Mexico*, but it was more than that. Something about the blend of her lotion, or maybe it was perfume, triggered something in his brain. It was like smelling apple pie and being reminded of when his grandmother would bake one for every Thanksgiving and Christmas when he was growing up. This scent was attached to a core memory, wrapped so tightly around it that he'd never be able to separate the two.

"Sunshine and citrus?" she finished for him.

"You smell like...you."

Her face softened, as if she knew the deeper meaning behind his words. "You're just now realizing this?" she asked. "We've been back together for almost three months."

"Why do you smell like that, Jessica?" he asked, turning them and gently pushing her down on the bed, then crawling up between her thighs.

They'd just come back to Earth after marathon sex and still, Jack instantly thickened, reading for round...whatever it was.

"I have that lotion," she whispered.

"*Still?*"

"That little shop has a website," she said with a shrug. "I've been ordering from them for years."

"Why?"

He already knew the answer. At least, he thought he did. But he wanted—no, *needed*—to hear her say it.

"It reminds me of you," she said. "And that week. And what we had. I...I didn't ever want to forget."

"Fuck," he breathed, grinding himself against her. "I love you."

Around a moan, she beamed, and that smile lit his entire world. "I love you, too."

"We'll figure this all out, okay? We'll do long distance, or—"

She cut him off with a hand over his mouth.

"Just kiss me," she said, her voice hoarse with desire. "Please."

He did what she asked. He could never deny her. Never.

By the time they finally drifted off to sleep, they were awoken what felt like seconds later by Jessica's phone blaring from the nightstand.

"Oh, fuck off," she grumbled, but rolled over to answer it anyway. "What?"

"Jess."

In the dark quiet of the room, Jack heard that single syllable loud and clear.

"Mom? What's wrong? Is it Berk?"

"Yeah, honey," Michelle said, her voice thick. "She's okay, but the baby isn't. His umbilical cord is wrapped around his neck, and if they don't get him out soon, he…" Michelle trailed off as a choked sob echoed through the phone. "He might not make it if they don't deliver right away. They're prepping her for surgery right now."

"And what about Berk?" Jessica cried, sitting up and flipping on the bedside lamp. Her eyes shone brightly with unshed tears, and Jack moved over, wrapping his arms tightly around her shoulders and tugging her back against his chest. "What about her placenta previa? Isn't her risk of hemorrhaging like…really high?"

"It is," Michelle confirmed. "But she made the call. This is your sister's decision."

"Well didn't someone try to talk her out of it? Didn't Brent knock some sense into her?"

"She's a mom, Jess," Michelle said quietly. "There's no talking her out of it when her baby's life is on the line."

"Fuck," Jessica said on an exhale, and turned her face into Jack's chest, her back rising and falling with her heaving, deep breaths.

"I know," Michelle said. "I think you should come back to the hospital."

"Yeah, Mom, of course. We'll be right there."

"See you soon, honey. Drive safe."

Jessica was out of bed and across the room within seconds of ending the call, and while her footsteps faded down the hall, Jack rose and dressed, then dug through her bag and laid out clothes for her as well.

A few minutes later, Jessica returned, gave Jack a small smile, and wordlessly dressed. Teeth were brushed, bags were repacked, and then they headed downstairs, meeting Kenzie and Aiden at the car.

The drive back to the hospital passed in tense silence. Jack couldn't offer Jessica much in this moment. He only had a brother, and he was a guy, so he'd never understand that bond only sisters shared. But he loved Jessica with his whole entire being, and he felt like he was experiencing her dismay and anxiety and pure terror right alongside her. So he held her hand, doing his best to quell the shaking in her fingers with his presence.

When they arrived, the four of them made their way to the doors, but before they could step into the lobby, Jessica stopped dead outside.

"I can't do this," she said.

Before Jack could move, Kenzie was at Jessica's side, pulling her into a fierce hug. The two girls stood the same height, one light-haired, one dark. Sisters not by blood, but by choice. And Jack was more thankful than ever for Mackenzie Jean in this moment, that she could fill in the gaps when Jack's knowledge of how to comfort Jessica lacked or failed.

"It's going to be okay," Kenzie whispered. "She's going to be okay. The baby is going to be okay."

"You can't know that."

Kenzie pulled away and cupped Jessica's face between her palms. "Listen to me, Jess. Your sister is the strongest person I know. She'll be okay because she won't accept anything else. For her, or for that baby."

As Kenzie's thumbs swiped at Jessica's cheeks, Jessica gave her a watery smile and nodded.

"Okay, you're right."

"I know," Kenzie said with a smirk, then she let Jessica go.

Immediately, Jessica extended her arm, and Jack took her hand.

"Together, sunshine."

She nodded again. "Together."

So the four of them walked inside, a solemn procession to the obstetrics wing, bracing themselves for what they might find when they got there.

"What took you so long?" Michelle asked as she rushed toward them, tugging her daughter into her arms.

"It's a fifteen minute drive, Mom," Jessica said, shooting Jack an eye roll over the top of Michelle's head, and he bit back a snort.

"Why do you look so tired?" Michelle asked when she pulled away, sweeping her thumbs across the shadows below Jessica's eyes.

"I was too worried about Berk to sleep," Jessica said quickly, shooting Jack a wink the moment her mom averted her gaze.

"How is Berk?" Kenzie asked.

"No news yet," Michelle said, then turned and gestured to the waiting area. "Come sit with us."

Jack's ass had barely greeted the seat of his chair before he was on his feet again as Brent pushed into the room.

All at once, the members of the Daniels and Jean families spoke, asking questions, all of which were lost in the cacophony.

"She made it through surgery beautifully," Brent said over them all, and though Jack barely knew him, he understood the lines bracketing Brent's mouth meant he'd been through hell and back tonight. "And the baby is okay, too. The nurses are running tests on him to make sure his restricted oxygen didn't cause any brain damage, and Berk is getting stitched up. Hopefully, we'll be able to introduce you all to our son very soon."

Jack pulled Jessica into his side and whispered, "Congrats, auntie."

She looked up at him, every line of her face slack with relief, her smile tired but still the most beautiful thing he'd ever laid eyes on. "I like the sound of that."

They were so far off from any sort of conversation involving children, but still, Jack couldn't help but wonder if that was in the cards for them—or if Jessica even wanted a family. More than anything, Jack did, and he wanted it with her.

It was in that moment that he realized he'd do whatever it took to keep this girl and make her his forever, and he needed her to know that.

Right now.

With a tug of her hand, he jerked his head toward the door and said, "Walk with me."

She shot him a quizzical look but followed anyway.

Jack didn't take them far. He wanted to remain close enough that they'd know if and when Brent came back with news, but go far enough that they couldn't be overheard.

"What's going on?" she asked when he stopped them halfway down a hallway. At this hour, the hospital was quiet, only the barebones, nighttime staff manning this particular floor. "You're kind of freaking me out."

"You're moving to Russia," he blurted. It wasn't a question, and Jessica didn't treat it as such.

"Yes..." she said slowly. "I mean, pending a phone interview with the school that wants to hire me, yeah."

"I want that for you, Jess."

"I...okay? Thank you?"

He wasn't making any sense, he knew, and he needed to get to the point before he lost his nerve.

"I don't want that to be the moment I lose you again," he said. "I don't want you moving to a foreign country to be the moment our relationship ends again."

"Well, I don't want that either," she started. "But I don't see how—"

He pressed a finger to her lips, silencing her. "We do long distance," he said. "Just...agree to that much, please. We'll take it day by day. But please say yes."

"Yes." The word flew from her mouth, and Jack grinned, the weight easing off his chest.

"Remember how, when we were in Mexico, we made the most of every moment? And we didn't worry about the future so much as we simply enjoyed what time we did have?"

"Yes…"

"Let's do that now."

"Do what?"

"Make the most of whatever time we have left until you leave. I get what you've been saying. We both have dreams, things we want to do with our lives. I can't ask you to stay in the States with me any more than you can ask me to move to Russia with you. It's not fair to either of us. We're too young to compromise, and I don't want either of us to wake up one day and regret our decisions, or resent each other."

Her lips quivered as she said, "That would never happen."

"I'd like to think you're right, but you can't know that." He gave her a sad smile, slightly amused by the way the tables of this particular argument had turned.

On the surface, it would seem there were no winners here, no matter what they did. Either way, it was going to hurt like hell, death by a thousand cuts, so much worse than parting ways in Mexico had been.

But he'd meant what he said, both when he'd told her that he wasn't going to lose her again, and that he wanted to soak up every single second together before they had to find out how to be together from over four thousand miles apart.

"I have an idea," he said.

Jessica stepped toe to toe with him, her hands snaking around his waist and settling at his lower back. "I'm listening," she said, tipping her head to meet his gaze, chin resting on his chest.

"A bucket list," he blurted.

"What kind of bucket list?"

"I don't know," he said with a laugh. "A bucket list of things we want to do—*you* want to do—before you leave."

"Like...watch my super hot hockey player boyfriend play in a national championship game?"

Jack's smile grew, loving her more in that moment than he thought possible for the simple fact that she said *play* and not *win*. "Exactly," he said with a nod.

"And what about you?" she asked. "What do you want to do?"

"I want..."

Jack trailed off, considering his answer. What could he ask this girl for that she hadn't already given him?

"I want us to spend a weekend in Traverse City with your family," he said at last.

"I want to *meet* your family," Jessica retorted.

"You've met my mom," he reminded her.

"So I want to meet your dad and brother."

He pressed a kiss to the tip of her nose. "I think that can be arranged."

And he knew that would be simple, coordinating a meeting between her and his family, but he also knew right then he'd move Heaven and Earth to give Jessica whatever she asked for, forever.

Because he hoped that, one day, his family would be her family, too.

NOW: April 5, 2024

ON THE FIRST FRIDAY of April, Coach had blessedly given the team the day off from practice. They'd won both of their games the previous weekend in South Dakota, which meant the Spartans were heading to the Final Four in St. Paul. They didn't play again for another week, so Coach gave them one day to rest, relax, and recover before they were back at it tomorrow.

It also happened to be four years to the day since he'd first laid eyes on Jessica Daniels.

To celebrate, they were holed up in the living room at his house, her final project before receiving her teaching degree spread out on the floor around her while Jack mindlessly scrolled through his phone on the couch behind her.

It had all the makings of a perfectly normal, quiet day.

Until Aiden and Kenzie walked into the room, his teammate wearing a shit-eating grin, Kenzie apprehensively trailing behind him.

Jack's hackles immediately rose.

"I don't like that look," he said to Aiden.

"I have an...idea," his teammate blurted. Next to him, Kenzie scoffed, and Aiden shot her a glare. "Okay, fine. It's less an idea and more...a dare."

"No," Jack said instantly. That devilish gleam in Aiden's eye couldn't mean anything good, and if he'd learned anything in the fall when Aiden got suspended, it was that no dare was worth risking playing time. Especially not when they were one win away from playing in a title game.

"You haven't even let me say what it is!"

"The answer is still no."

"Just hear him out," Kenzie said, looking resigned. "It won't affect hockey."

"Just spit it out, Aiden," Jessica said, rising from the floor to stand, crossing her arms over her chest.

To Jack, Aiden said, "I dare you and Jess to get matching tattoos."

"Wait what? Why are we dragging Jess into this?"

"In case you forgot," Kenzie said, "I wasn't exempt from dares, so why should she be?"

"Thanks a lot, Kenz," Jessica said sarcastically, though Jack noted there was no actual anger in her tone.

He turned to her and curled his hands around her upper arms. "You don't have to do this."

"I think she does," Kenzie said.

"Butt out, bunny," Jack said without looking at her.

"I'm just saying. You guys made me make out with Aiden in

front of like fifty people. A video of which ended up online. A tattoo is small potatoes compared to that."

"A tattoo is *not* 'small potatoes,'" Jack said, throwing quotation marks around the words. "Tattoos are really permanent. Like...the most permanent."

"You already have one," Aiden reminded him. "What's one more?"

"Jess doesn't have any, though," Jack said, still not taking his eyes off her.

"I'm not opposed to the idea," she said quietly.

Jack blinked slowly, unsure he'd heard her correctly. "Are you sure?" he asked. "A tattoo is one thing, but a matching tattoo? With me?"

"What's so bad about that?"

"I mean, nothing really," Jack said. "Only, what if..."

He trailed off, unwilling to voice the words aloud. What if they didn't stay together? He wanted Jessica by his side for the rest of his life, but sometimes, things didn't always work out the way one planned.

Jessica, though, knew what he was thinking, and she rose onto her tiptoes, pausing with her lips a breath away from his.

"I guess we'll just have to stay together forever."

Before he'd even approached Jack and Jessica, Aiden had called the tattoo parlor to be sure they'd have time to take walk-ins that day. Apparently, he and Kenzie were also getting matching tattoos, which turned this dare into some sort of painful double date.

Although, it would never be as painful as that time he and

Jessica had gotten drinks with Sofia and Silas. He would take physical discomfort over the emotional trauma that particular evening had dealt out.

Aiden was antsy, practically rushing them out the door, and Jack and Jessica still hadn't settled on what to get.

"I have another idea," Aiden said, and even Kenzie groaned alongside Jack and Jessica.

"We're already getting tattoos, Fuller," Jack said. "What more do you want?"

"You know this parlor has one of those mystery tattoo vending machine things, right? Like the kind that you used to stick a quarter into as kids and a gum ball would pop out? What if you let that decide?"

Jack opened his mouth to protest, but found he didn't completely hate the idea. After all, he and Jessica had a lot to thank fate or chance or whatever for, so this was kind of perfect.

"I love that idea," Jessica said, reading the words in Jack's eyes before he spoke them.

"Me, too," he said with a grin, then grabbed her hand and pulled her out the door.

When they walked through the doors, the tattoo parlor still smelled the same as it had four years ago, when, as a freshman, Jack got his Spartan helmet tattoo. The walls were still painted the same shade of creamy white, and the same oversized maroon leather couch sat in the corner of the waiting area. The air was filled with the buzz of tattoo guns, alternative rock music played softly over the speakers, and quiet conversation hummed from each of the partitioned tattoo spaces.

"Welcome to the Inkwell!" a man said as he rushed up front to greet them. His eyes swept over their group, landing on Aiden and crinkling at the corners as he smiled. "Fuller! How's my favorite client?"

"I'm good, Drew," Aiden said as the two of them performed a bro hug.

Every inch of Drew's exposed skin was covered in ink, and Jack's first thought was how much money had gone into that many tattoos. The man was about six feet tall, a ball cap flipped backward atop his thick brown hair, the bottom half of his face covered by a wiry, red-brown beard.

"So what are we doing today?" Drew asked.

"Me and my girl are getting those tattoos I sent you the other day," Aiden said, then turned his attention to Jack and Jessica. "These two are getting matching ones."

"Do either of you have any ink?" Drew asked, gaze apprising Jack and Jessica.

"I do," Jack said. "You actually did it. Spartan helmet on my right shoulder blade."

Drew snapped his fingers at the jogged memory. "That's right! You and Fuller got those the same day," he said, tapping Aiden's exposed shoulder, where his deltoid was permanently marked with the same tattoo Jack had on his back. Aiden's entire sleeve had been built around that piece. Then he looked at Jessica. "What about you?"

"Nope," Jessica said. "This will be my first."

"Virgin skin!" Drew said with a grin. "Right on. What will you guys be getting?"

Jack glanced at the dispenser near the door, which was indeed filled with little plastic balls with multicolored caps, each holding a square of white paper with some unknown design printed on it.

"We're gonna let that thing decide," Jack said, realizing how ludicrous the idea was now that he was confronted with it.

"Fuck yeah!" Drew shouted, pumping a fist into the air. "All of those in there are my designs. Some are cute, some funny, some a little rebellious." He moved behind the counter and started tapping away on the iPad set up there.

Once they'd paid—each of the gum ball machine designs were a set price—Drew handed them a token. Jessica took it and turned toward their prize.

"Good luck," Aiden said with a smirk as he pushed Jack and Jessica along.

Jessica marched over confidently, but Jack dragged his feet, afraid of what that thing was going to spit out at them. He'd be damned if he walked around with something lame or offensive on his body for the rest of his life. Although, if that ended up being the case, maybe he'd finally do as Aiden asked four years ago and get it tattooed on his ass.

Before inserting the token into the machine, Jessica held it up in front of his face.

"Blow on it for good luck," she said.

Jack indulged her, though he secretly thought it wouldn't do any good.

With a flourish, Jessica dropped the token into the slot and turned the knob. The machine rattled to life, the balls within jostling as they shifted around, until one dropped down the shoot with a *plunk*.

Jessica withdrew it and held it up. "Blue cap," she said. "That seems lucky, right?"

Jack quirked his eyebrow dubiously. "Whatever you say, sunshine. Now open it up, please."

Simply because she knew he was on edge, she took her time popping the cap off the ball and removing the folded slip of paper inside. She held out the empty ball to Jack, her attention never leaving the paper as she revealed what they'd be getting.

When she gasped, Jack reached for her, taking the paper from her hands.

The moment his eyes settled on the design, his jaw slackened in surprise.

"Well?" Aiden asked, his eyes darting back and forth between Jessica and Jack. "What'd you get?"

Jack flipped the paper toward them, showing the small sunshine bobbing on the horizon of a body of water, rays branching off the small orb.

His eyes met Jessica's, and she gave him a watery smile.

Sunshine.

Because why the fuck wouldn't the universe do this for them, too?

"Love that one," Drew said. "A little girlie for you, though," he added, smacking Jack on the chest.

"No," Jack said, still holding Jessica's gaze. "It's perfect."

"Great!" Drew said, clapping his hands together. "Then let's get you guys inked!"

Jack grabbed Jessica's hand and followed Drew, Kenzie, and Aiden to the back, into a larger room with a small loveseat along one side.

"Who wants to go first?" Aiden asked.

"I will!" Jessica said excitedly, and Jack was surprised by how calm she was being about this. Most people, when presented with participating in something they *knew* would hurt, would balk, but not his girl. Jessica's fearlessness was one of the things Jack loved most about her.

"Where do you want it?" Drew asked as he set about printing the stencil to give him a guide on Jessica's skin.

Without hesitation, Jessica extended her left arm and pointed to the spot right above the crease of her elbow, where her biceps tapered down. "Right here."

"Alright, little lady," Drew said, patting the chair. "Climb on up."

Jessica settled on the cushy black leather, and Drew wheeled a stool and a tray over, getting himself situated before laying Jessica's arm across his lap. As he fired up the gun, Jessica said, "Jack?"

"Yeah, sunshine?"

"Hold my hand?"

Jack moved around to the other side of the chair and gathered her right hand in his. "Always," he said, giving her a smile.

Across the room, someone gagged, and Jack looked up in time to see Kenzie smacking Aiden upside the head. "Be nice," she scolded him.

"They're just so cute it's disgusting," Aiden said.

"You say that like you two aren't the same way," Jessica said with an eye roll, and Jack barked out a laugh.

"She's got a point, Fuller," Kenzie said with a grin, and Aiden pouted.

"We're not that bad," Aiden said.

"Yes you are," Jack and Jessica said in unison.

"Alright, love birds," Drew said. "Here we go."

Jack knew the moment the needle touched down on Jessica's flesh, because her hand gripped his a little tighter.

"You okay?" he asked quietly.

"Yes," she said, though her teeth were gritted. "It just stings a bit."

"You're doing great," Drew said encouragingly. "We're actually almost done. I love these little guys because they're so quick."

Jack glanced down to where Jessica's arm was splayed over Drew's knee, surprised to find he was indeed nearly finished with the tattoo. He watched as Drew scratched out the little sun rays, then wiped the ink away to make sure it was all filled in properly. After a few more swipes of the needle across Jessica's skin, Drew straightened and said, "Ta da!"

Jessica tilted her head to study her fresh ink, then turned her face up to Jack, grinning.

"It's perfect," she said. "Don't you think?"

Jack bent until his mouth hovered over hers, then pressed a kiss to her lips. "Yes."

"Good," she said. "I do, too. And now it's your turn."

Jack couldn't hold back a groan, and Jessica pinched his side.

"I can't believe I let you talk me into this, Fuller," Jack grumbled to his teammate as he stretched out on the chair Jessica had just vacated. It was warm from her body, and Jack couldn't help thinking how he wanted that warmth to surround him all the time.

And then he decided he couldn't entertain that line of

thought, otherwise Drew and his friends were about to get an eyeful of his fully erect dick. Instead, he focused on the pain he was about to endure, forcing his thoughts away from getting Jessica naked.

"Where do you want yours at?" Drew asked him.

"Same spot," Jack said.

"We dared you to get matching tattoos," Aiden said. "That doesn't mean you have to get it in the same spot. Drew was right, bro, it is kind of girly."

"It's not girly," Jack said. "I call Jessica 'sunshine.' We met in Mexico. Feels pretty appropriate if you ask me."

"I'm just saying you could hide it if you wanted."

"I don't," Jack responded, and Aiden clamped his jaw shut, clearly understanding from Jack's tone that they were done arguing.

Exactly as he had done for her, Jessica stood on Jack's right and held his hand in hers.

"Ready?" Drew asked.

"As I'll ever be."

As an athlete, and a hockey player at that, Jack had a reasonably high pain tolerance, and getting his first tattoo four years ago hadn't bothered him much, despite the fact that he'd gotten right over his scapula. This one, which was situated in an admittedly sensitive part of his arm, was relatively painless in comparison.

Although, not entirely painless. There were a few spots where Jack clutched Jessica's hand a little tighter, though mindful of her delicate fingers. But for her, if these few moments of pain meant he got a permanent reminder of their love story, a me-

mento of their time together that no one could ever take away from them? Well, he'd endure far worse than this.

For Jessica, he'd do anything.

Jessica

NOW: April 11, 2024

"Man, I wish I could come with you guys," Berkley said with a pout. "I never got to go to a Frozen Four."

"Babe, I took you to Vegas for All-Star Weekend three years ago. What more do you want?" Brent said from across the kitchen, where his head was buried in the refrigerator.

"Yeah, against my will."

Brent snorted and backed away from the fridge, bottles of beer in his hands. He walked over to the island and passed them out, setting one in front of his wife, his sister, and his sister-in-law in turn. Berkley, though only two weeks postpartum, had opted to bottle feed Brooks.

"It was hardly against your will, Berk," Brent said, sliding onto the stool next to her.

"You basically guilted me into it by buying tickets for all of us. How was I supposed to say no to that?"

"It was three years ago! You gotta let it go at some point."

"Never," Berkley whispered to Jessica, who giggled in return.

Secretly, Jessica lived for nights like this, when the family was gathered in one place and they simply relaxed, playing games or watching movies, sharing a few drinks and talking about nothing and everything. Her final semester of college was winding down, and school had become a whirlwind of endless deadlines, all-nighters in the library, and hardly any sleep. And that was just her. She didn't know how Jack was doing all of that on top of practices and preparing to play for—hopefully—a national championship.

It was a Wednesday night, and even though both Jessica and Kenzie had a ridiculous amount of work to do before school was over, they were taking a long weekend to go to the Twin Cities to watch the boys play in the Frozen Four. Tomorrow, the Spartans would take on Harvard in the first semi-final game. If they won, they'd play the winner of the University of North Dakota and Princeton game on Saturday in the title game.

"Why are you even whining about missing this?" Jessica asked her sister. "You're going to be living and breathing hockey when Brooks gets older."

"If I let him play," Berkley said, shooting her husband a devilish smirk, one that told Jessica they'd had this same argument before.

"He *will* be playing, whether you like it or not," Brent said.

"What if he doesn't want to?"

Brent scoffed. "Please. His dad is *Brent Jean*," he said, gesturing to himself. "He'll want to."

As if he knew they were talking about him, Brooks, who had

been fast asleep upstairs, let out a squawk through his monitor, and Berkley rose to her feet.

Brent stopped her before she could move too far. "Don't," he said. "Hang out here. I got him."

Without argument, Berkley dropped back into her seat and brought her bottle of beer to her mouth.

"Let me tell you what, girls," she said after downing a long swig. "Don't ever marry or have babies with a man who doesn't worship the ground you walk on."

Jessica and Kenzie shared a look before they both burst into belly-aching laughter.

When they finally composed themselves, Jessica said, "That's a good joke coming from you, the girl who tried to throw her entire relationship away because her boyfriend was doing just that."

Berkley frowned, and tears gathered along her lower lash line.

"Shit, Berk," Kenzie said, reaching out to rub Berkley's back. "We didn't mean to make you cry."

"It's not your fault," Berkley said with a sniff. "I cry all the time now. But you know, when it comes to your relationships, do as I say, not as I do. Because you're right, Jess. I almost threw away the best thing that's ever happened to me, and the chance at living this life"—she waved her arm around the house to demonstrate—"because I was too damn stubborn to let someone help me. Hell, I was too stubborn to even *ask* for help. I'm just thankful Brent fought for us when I couldn't. Who knows where we'd be otherwise. But in order to make a relationship work, both sides have to be willing to compromise. Brent and I learned that the hard way."

Jessica nodded solemnly, reaching out to grab her sister's hand and give it a squeeze.

Stubbornness was a trait both Daniels sisters shared, as was the need for complete independence. And Jessica had been thinking more and more lately about her future.

What she had with Jack was more than she ever could've imagined for herself. Their story was the kind normally found in romance novels or movies, and its rarity made it all the more magical.

But Berkley's words stuck in her mind. Compromise. Fighting for each other. So far, Jessica hadn't done either of those things. When it came to her career, she'd been laser focused, unwavering in her desire to move to a foreign country and start her life there. Was she making a mistake by not being willing to bend even a little bit? Jack was arguably the most important thing in her life, but she also hadn't busted her ass the last four years to throw it all away for a guy—even if he was the best man she'd ever known. Even if their relationship was everything to her.

A phone buzzed on the marble counter, pulling her from her reverie, and Jessica looked down to see it was hers.

Confused as to who would be calling her at nine p.m., she picked up.

"Hello?"

"Hello, is this Jessica?" a woman asked in heavily-accented English.

"Yes?"

"Hi, Jessica," the woman said. "This is Polina from the English Language School in Saint Petersburg. Is this a good time to talk?"

"Oh, hi, Polina!" Jessica said, rising from her seat and mouthing to Berkley and Kenzie that she'd be right back. "This is a great time. Well, it's nine at night, but that's no big deal."

"Oh goodness," Polina said. "I am so sorry. I must have calculated the time change wrong."

Jessica laughed as she settled herself on an oversized armchair in Brent and Berkley's den. "It's not a big deal at all," she said.

"Well, good. So I am calling because, after our phone interview last week, we are officially offering you the position to join our staff after your graduation."

A massive grin bloomed on Jessica's face. All thoughts from a moment ago vanished at her dream being presented to her on a silver platter. "That's amazing news," she said. "And I happily accept."

"Good, good," Polina said. "I will email you over the contract and everything for your signature. All that is left is to set your start date and get you set up with somewhere to live in the city. Is your passport current?"

"Yes.".

"Good, good," Polina said again. "That will make getting you here easier. So my next question is...how soon do you graduate?"

"Graduation day is April twenty-seventh."

"Excellent," Polina said. "In that case, we are hoping you can start as soon as possible thereafter. How does May the thirteenth sound?"

A pang of fear spread through Jessica's chest.

That was only a month away.

For only a moment did she consider asking for more time to enjoy graduating college and prepare for the move, but she figured if she was doing this, there was really nothing holding her back from starting immediately.

"That will work perfectly," Jessica said, though her words wobbled at the edges.

"Good, good," Polina said once more, and Jessica was beginning to think it was her catchphrase. "I'll email everything over as soon as we end this call, and we'll be in contact with further information about getting here and living arrangements."

"Great!" Jessica said. "Thank you so much for this opportunity."

"Of course," Polina said. "Welcome to the team."

Jessica hung up and walked back into the kitchen in a daze.

"Who was that?" Berkley asked.

"The Russians," she said. "They've officially offered me the job, and I have a start date."

"Oh my gosh!" Kenzie said, jumping up to throw her arms around Jessica. "That's amazing! Congratulations, sis."

"When do you start?" Berkley, ever the pragmatist, asked.

"May thirteenth."

"Holy fuck," her sister breathed. "That's...soon."

"What's soon?" Brent asked as he returned to the room.

"Jessica got the job. And she starts in a month."

"Holy shit," Brent said. "That *is* soon. But congrats, little sis!" He walked up and tucked her into his side, giving her a squeeze.

Jessica knew she should be happy. She should be ecstatic, over the moon, jumping for joy and popping bottles of champagne in celebration. But a little ball of dread had formed in her chest, and it grew with each passing second.

"Brent," Jessica said suddenly, desperately, and three pairs of eyes swiveled to her, each of them scrunching at the corners in confusion.

"Yeah?"

"Do you..." Her voice went hoarse, cutting off the rest of what she'd been about to say. She took a deep breath and tried again. "Do you think Jack has a shot at an NHL career?"

Berkley and Kenzie's frowns deepened, but realization flashed through Brent's eyes, his expression relaxing a bit.

"I haven't seen him play much," Brent said. "Mostly just at the GLI. But he's good. Really good. Quick for his size, has a great read on the puck, and his reflexes are ridiculous. And I've played against his brother a few times. Josh works hard, keeps his head down from what I've seen, and is a hell of a defenseman. So...if Jack is anything like that? I'd say yes. He's got a bright future ahead of him."

The words settled like a stone in Jessica's stomach. She didn't know enough about hockey to judge Jack's talent, but hearing that he was good enough to make it at the highest level from someone who currently lived that exact dream didn't surprise her. She knew how seriously he took his game, and the Spartans were having a phenomenal season thanks in large part to his stellar play.

With a sudden clarity, Jessica realized that, up to this point, she'd been holding onto the hope that this would all work out. That, when she left for Russia, she wouldn't be ripping her heart out of her chest and leaving it here in Jack's hands. But with Brent's words, that hope shriveled up and died in her chest.

Maybe if things were different, if Jack wasn't as talented as he was, or if Jessica hadn't worked so hard for everything that was now firmly in her grasp, there would be some way to compromise here. But they weren't, and Jessica could see no way where they both got everything they wanted, where she got to chase her dreams and hold onto her dream man. She'd agreed to long distance, yes, but she couldn't stop from asking herself...what was the point?

A good night's sleep and a quick flight to Minneapolis had done nothing to soothe the jagged edges of Jessica's anxiety. When the idea of leaving Jack to move halfway across the world had been the seed of an idea, Jessica had been okay. It was one of those out of sight, out of mind things. But now that it was an inevitability? It had her second guessing everything.

And she still had to tell Jack.

But not this weekend. She refused to ruin this trip.

Kenzie, for her part, understood Jessica was internally struggling and was doing everything in her power to take her mind off of it. It paid, Jessica supposed, to have a friend with severe anxiety, because Kenzie was a master at distracting herself from the negative thoughts that constantly swirled in her brain. And, of course, Jessica had a new appreciation for her now. She was drowning here because of this one—albeit not inconsequential—thing, whereas Kenzie dealt with these kinds of intrusive thoughts, often with no rhyme or reason, daily.

When they touched down and left the airport, their first stop was the hotel to drop their stuff off. Then they went in search of food, because Jessica's stomach had been growling for hours.

That morning, she'd been too stressed to eat anything, but her appetite returned with a vengeance.

They wandered around downtown, surprised by the number of people in hockey jerseys or gear representing their college of choice, a lot of them repping Michigan State.

When it was finally time to head to the arena, Kenzie looped her arm through Jessica's and pulled her through the mass of people bottlenecking through the doors.

The game passed in a blur of skates slicing the ice, cheers and jeers from the crowd, the rocking of boards when two opponents clashed, and, of course, goals.

Though none for Harvard. Even to her barely knowledgeable hockey mind, Jessica could tell Jack had played the game of his life, and the Spartans were on to the championship game on Saturday.

That night, once the boys had gone through post-game press conferences and dined as a team, Jack and Aiden invited Jessica and Kenzie to hang out at the pool with them. All Jessica needed was to hear the words "hot tub" and she was in. She could think of nothing better right now than a few hours spent soaking in warm water, and she hoped it alleviated at least a little bit of her stress.

The boys were on cloud nine and spent most of their time acting like little kids, having chicken fights, playing Marco Polo, and generally causing a ruckus. Jessica would've liked to spend some more time alone with Jack, but she couldn't deny him this time with his teammates.

Eventually, though, he heaved himself out of the pool, and

Jessica had to wipe her face to make sure she wasn't drooling as all six-foot three-inches of him sauntered her way. His swim trunks hung indecently low on his hips, and water pearled and dripped across the toned, taut skin of his pecs and abs, clinging to the peaks and valleys of his muscles.

Jessica experienced a keen sense of dejá vu in that moment, and it only got worse when Jack held out his hand and said, "Come play volleyball with us."

Those were the first words he'd ever spoken to her, and the wide grin on his face told her he remembered, too.

That draw she'd felt to him even in that first moment was still there, pulling her out of the hot tub and into the frigid water of the pool. Only now, Jack was sweet and thoughtful, setting her up for perfect shots, high-fiving her and cheering her on, using every spare opportunity he could find to put his hands on her body below the water. To nip at her exposed shoulder, or press a kiss to her chlorine-drenched hair.

Jessica held tight to that, to the reminder of how far they'd come, and if they could survive three and a half years apart and still come back together, better and stronger, then surely a little thing like long distance couldn't tear them apart. Right?

As if their time in the pool had been foreplay, the moment Jack and Jessica stepped foot into their room—which was actually Jack and Aiden's; she and Aiden switched so they could spend the night with their significant others—Jack wasted no time in getting Jessica naked. With four quick tugs on the strings of her bikini top and bottoms, Jessica was completely bare, and Jack was lifting her into his arms to carry her to the bed.

When he dropped her onto the mattress, she immediately rose to her knees and dug her fingers into the waistband of his shorts, pulling them down his legs. Then he stepped out of them and joined her on the bed.

He crawled up her body and placed his hands on either side of her head, hovering over her, peppering her forehead, chin, cheeks, eyelids, and nose with kisses.

"Promise me something, Jess," he said, his lips a breath away from hers.

"Anything."

"Promise me you won't say goodbye."

Jessica blinked rapidly, that ball of anxiety once again rooting and spreading across her chest, like kudzu in the South. Somehow, he'd found out her news, and he was as scared as she was.

But she breathed a sigh of relief—albeit a small one—when he continued. "Whatever happens. This week, this month, after graduation, five years from now. Ten. Just...promise me you'll always be right here." He patted his chest to show he didn't mean physically, and Jessica softened.

"I promise," she said, voice barely above a whisper.

Jack grinned, then pressed his lips to hers.

His kiss was all-consuming, the kind that quickly turned her thoughts away from everything she wasn't saying so she could only focus on here and now, on every point where his warm, hard body pressed against her soft curves. She lost herself in the feel of his wet, silky hair sifting through her fingers, of his hands caressing every inch of her skin, of the kiss he imbued with so much love that Jessica couldn't help but respond in kind.

Jack pulled away, his joyful grin replaced with something more mischievous, and he said, "Now I'll make you a promise of my own."

"What's that?"

"I promise I'll make you come several times tonight."

"I like that idea," she said, wiggling beneath him, the hard length of his cock rubbing against her slick center.

"Where should I begin?" he asked, sitting back on his haunches to stare down at her. "With my hands? Maybe my mouth? Or..." he trailed off, dropping his gaze to his lap and bringing a hand to his dick, giving it a few strokes as Jessica watched.

"I vote cock," she said.

"I don't think you get to decide, sunshine," he said, once again moving so they were face to face. "You'll take what I give you, and you'll love every second of it."

Jessica's toes curled. She loved when he talked like this, like he knew he was right.

And that's because he *was* right. There wasn't anything Jack could do to her in bed that wouldn't have her breaking apart at the seams faster than she ever dreamed possible.

All Jessica could say was, "Yes please."

Jack chuckled, pressed another kiss to her mouth as his hand cupped her pussy, then said, "I think I'll start with my mouth. I want to devour this pussy. Would you like that?"

"God, yes," she moaned. He'd barely gotten started, and already she was panting and ready to beg for it.

"Good," he said, then lowered his head to her.

He nipped and sucked a path along her jaw and down the

column of her neck, pausing to swipe his tongue along the length of each collarbone. He nudged her breasts with the tip of his nose, inhaling her skin, before giving each of her pebbled nipples a few slow, savoring licks. He pressed a kiss to the soft underside of her breast, the dip of her belly button, the smooth skin at her hip bone. Each press of his lips had Jessica's breath hitching, wondering if this was the time he'd connect with her clit, if he'd finally move to her pussy and deliver the pressure she so desperately craved.

When he finally did reach her aching pussy, Jessica was only moments away from coming apart. She would forever marvel at how this man managed to make every single inch of her body an erogenous zone. And under normal circumstances, Jessica would offer to give while she received, but every muscle in her body was coiled tight in anticipation of the moment his mouth would suction around her clit, every nerve ending primed for the release she knew was coming.

Jessica's hips bucked in surprise, then pleasure, when Jack ran a finger through her arousal and held it in front of his face.

"Look how wet you are for me, sunshine," he said, then sucked his finger into his mouth. "I'm going to lick every inch of this pussy clean. How does that sound?"

"Jack," Jessica gasped.

"Yes?"

"Stop talking and put your mouth on me."

With one last devilish grin, Jack did as he was told.

And Jessica wasn't even remotely surprised when she came not five minutes later.

Jack, of course, crawled up her body and settled his hips between her thighs, a smug smile on his face. "I think that's a new record for me," he said. "I'm going to have to tease you more often."

She wanted to argue, but she was boneless beneath him, her clit still tingling as her body worked through the last vestiges of her orgasm. All she could do was attempt to sit up and reach for him.

"But not tonight," he said, knowing exactly what she wanted. He gripped his cock at its base and lined it up with her entrance. "Right now, I just want to be buried in you."

"Then do it," she said, her words breathless as anticipation once again built in her core.

"Since you asked so nicely," he said, then pushed home.

And as their bodies joined, as Jack slowly rocked his hips in and out, as Jessica enthusiastically met every one of his thrusts, from that first push inside to the moment they detonated together, every anxious and worried thought floated from her mind until there was only this. Until there was only Jack.

NOW: April 16, 2024

THE SPARTANS LOST THE national championship game and returned to East Lansing with heavy hearts.

Despite the loss, the city and their classmates welcomed them home with open arms, proud of the incredible season though it hadn't ended the way they'd hoped.

The absolute last thing Jack wanted to do after costing his team a title was go to the bar and pretend to be happy and enjoying himself while people offered him useless platitudes and words of encouragement—not to mention the fact that it was a Tuesday night—but the boys refused to take no for an answer.

It was supposed to be a team bonding thing, a way for them to send the seniors off in the only way they knew how—with lots of alcohol. Aiden had already left, gone to Toledo to play for the Warriors' farm team there, and it didn't feel the same without him. His best friend's absence only added to Jack's somber mood.

So, he made it clear he would only be going if Jessica went, hoping she would say she had too much work to do and couldn't, which would then give Jack an excuse to beg off. Unfortunately, Jessica surprised him by saying a night out was exactly what she needed.

Jack tried to enjoy himself, he really did. But his mind had other ideas, and despite the endless string of shots and bottles of beer and glasses of mixed drinks that passed in and out of his hands, he simply wasn't in the mood for celebrating. After all, they'd *lost*. What was there to celebrate?

When the clock struck midnight, Jack had had enough, and he rose from the bench he'd tossed himself on the moment they walked into Rick's. The crowd was thin, so he hadn't suffered too much under the weight of pitying stares and people making comments about their "hell of a run." Honestly, he'd feel better if people were mad at him. After all, he was the reason they'd lost. He was the *goalie*; it was his fucking job to stop pucks, and he hadn't been good enough to do that against North Dakota.

"I'm going home," he told his teammates, who, after only a few hours, had descended into complete and utter alcohol-fueled chaos.

"No!" Luke shouted, tugging on Jack's arm. "Stay. Please. This is our last chance to celebrate."

Jack shook his arm free. "Nah, man. I just...I can't be here right now." He looked at Jessica. "Are you coming with me?"

"Of course," she said, following Jack out of their dimly lit corner and up the stairs to street level without another word to anyone.

The few blocks they had to walk between Rick's and his house passed in silence fraught with all the things Jack could tell Jessica wanted to say, but was holding onto until they were safely inside.

And of course, the moment the front door closed behind them, she wasted no time in leveling him with a concerned stare and saying, "What's wrong?"

Jack heaved a sigh, wishing he could ignore the question but knowing there was no way out of this. "I just don't feel like celebrating," he said. Not a lie, but not the full truth, either.

"There's more to it than that," she said.

Most of the time, Jack loved how well his girl understood him, how easy he was for her to read. But right now, he wished he was less transparent.

"Maybe I don't want to talk about it," he said.

"Maybe you don't *want* to," she said, "but you should."

Ignoring her, he trudged up the stairs, every footstep heavy with the weight on his shoulders, a weight that should've vanished at the conclusion of the season. There was nothing to carry any longer. No next win, no survive and advance, no title within their grasp.

There was only loss.

And he'd been so busy mourning that shattered dream that he hadn't properly mourned the end of his collegiate career. He would never again suit up with Aiden and Luke and Asher, would never again don the green and white and play a game as a Michigan State University Spartan. The realization hit him like a freight train, and he stumbled when he reached the landing.

Jessica's hands were on him in an instant, steadying and grounding. "Let's get you into bed," she said.

Jack only nodded, knowing that her dropping the subject of his melancholic mood was too much to hope for.

They didn't speak as they shuffled into his room, as Jessica stripped him out of his jeans and t-shirt, leaving him only in his boxers. As she drew back the covers on his bed and gave him a gentle nudge, urging him to crawl in. Wordlessly, he turned the TV on, navigating to an episode of *Psych*—one of his favorite comfort shows—in hopes that it would lift his spirits. Jessica left the room, and a moment later, he heard the water running in the bathroom, where she was presumably preparing for bed.

When she returned, she was fresh-faced, though more beautiful than ever, wearing one of his t-shirts and a pair of well-worn cotton sleep shorts. She slid into bed next to him, and he automatically opened his arm and dragged her into his side.

"I love you, you know," she said quietly.

Jack nodded, swallowing hard, then said, "It's my fault we lost. That's what my problem is."

"Honey..." Jessica started, but Jack shook his head, brushing off her protestations.

"No, Jess. I'm the *goalie*. It's literally my job to prevent goals. And I didn't do that against North Dakota. It's all my fault."

Jessica rose from his side and slung her leg over his waist, moving so she straddled his thighs, then shifting so her face was inches from his. She cupped his cheeks between her palms, forcing him to meet her gaze.

"Listen to me, Jack DeLuca. You are only one man on a team of them. It was no more your fault that you let in a few goals than it was Aiden or Asher's for not scoring more. North Dakota got a few lucky bounces. And don't even get me started on the absolute piss poor excuse for officiating." She gripped his face harder. "You guys win as a team, and you lose as a team. Don't beat yourself up over something out of your control."

"But that's the thing, Jess," he said, his words coming out flat thanks to Jessica squishing his cheeks. "It was well within my control. Stopping pucks is literally my job!"

"You can't stop them if you can't see them," she said. "And I hate to say it, honey, but those North Dakota assholes did nothing all night but sit someone in the crease in front of you. There was nothing you could've done."

With a deep inhale, Jack realized—albeit somewhat distantly—that she was right. North Dakota had done one thing without fail on Saturday, and that was to station one of their forwards, the biggest one on the ice at the time, right in his face. Luke—or whatever other defenseman on the ice at the time—did their best to shove them out of the way, but Jack had spent all night essentially blind.

And the officiating had been, to use Jessica's words, piss poor. And that was a polite way of saying it.

There was nothing he could've done.

His teammates had told him the same thing repeatedly, reminding him over and over that the loss hadn't been his fault. Figured it took the words coming out of Jessica's mouth for him to actually believe them.

"Okay," he said.

"Okay?" she asked, that little crease forming between her brows.

He reached up and smoothed it with the pad of his thumb, then said, "You're right."

Jessica blinked in surprise, but a slow smile bloomed on her lips. "Of course I am."

Jack grinned back, then in one fluid motion, flipped them so Jessica was flat on her back beneath him. "I think that deserves a reward."

Right before Jack's lips met hers, Jessica said, "Lucky me."

Nah, Jack thought. *I'm the lucky one.*

The next morning, with no practice to drag him out of bed at an ungodly hour, and no class until noon, Jack fully intended to sleep in.

Unfortunately, his dad had other ideas.

"Yo," Jack said when he picked up the phone, his eyelids still heavy with sleep.

"Good morning, Jacky boy!" his dad said, his voice booming through Jack's quiet bedroom. Next to him, Jessica stirred, grumbling something unintelligible.

"Dad," Jack said, exasperated. "It's barely seven."

"I know," his dad said brightly. "Early bird gets the worm and all that. Don't tell me you're still in bed."

"Of course I'm still in bed!" Jack said. "This is the first time in four years I don't have to be up for practice at a ridiculous hour."

"Well, get up," his dad said. "Get to the rink and lift or skate or something. You've gotta stay sharp for when those professional offers start rolling in."

Jack groaned. "Is that why you called, or is there some other reason you're torturing me right now?"

"Oh, right!" his dad said. "We'll be in Detroit tonight."

That got Jack's attention, and he shot upright, the sheets pooling around his naked waist. He glanced sideways at Jessica, who was sprawled out on her stomach next to him, the bare expanse of her lean back tempting him where the covers bunched around her hips.

Jack bit his lip, resisting the urge to reach out and run a hand over her skin, to cup her ass, to flip her toward him and bury himself in her.

"Jack?" his dad asked, returning him to the conversation at hand.

Right. His dad. Detroit.

The blood rushing to his cock slowed.

"Why are you coming to Detroit?" Jack asked.

"Playoffs?" his dad said with a tone that indicated Jack had asked a particularly stupid question. "Josh and the Quakers are playing the Warriors tonight."

"Right!" Jack said, snapping his fingers as the lightbulb in his brain turned on. At the sound, Jessica lifted her head and glared at him.

"You know it's like...barely seven, right?" she asked, her voice hoarse from sleep.

"I know, sunshine," Jack said. "I'll be done in a minute."

"Who is that?" his dad asked.

"Jessica," Jack said. "You know, my girlfriend?"

"Right!" his dad said, his voice so like Jack's own that Jessica's eyes narrowed. "Well, bring her with you! We booked a box."

"How did you manage that?" Jack asked.

"Please," his dad said, but what he really meant was, *get to know me already.* "I'm Joe DeLuca."

Jack supposed he had a point, and that attitude was exactly where Jack and Josh had gotten their cockiness from, though Josh had taken it a step further and become kind of a dick. Not that Jack would ever tell him that. He loved his brother, thorny personality and all.

"Fair enough," Jack said with a snort. "What time should we be there? Of course, I'll have to check with Jess first."

"I'm in," she said with a smile. "You've met my family. It's about time I met yours."

"Great!" his dad boomed. "Puck drop is seven, so get there at six-thirty or so."

"Sounds good, Dad," Jack said. "We'll see you later."

"Looking forward to it. Love you, son."

"Love you, too," he replied, then hung up, turning to Jessica. "Are you sure you want to do this?"

"Of course," she said, sitting up. The sheet fell from her body, and Jack found it difficult to focus on anything coming out of her mouth when her breasts were staring him in the eye. Still, he made a valiant effort, especially when she fingered the chain around her neck where the ring he'd given her on Valentine's Day hung. "I made you a promise. Meeting the fam is part of that."

Jack leaned forward and kissed her, the gentle press of his lips against hers quickly turning heated in the way they always did with them. Before he could lay her out and make her scream his name loud enough the neighbors heard, she pushed on his shoulder.

"Jack," she breathed.

"Yeah, sunshine?" he asked, tracking his lips over her jaw and throat.

"I have to tell you something."

Jack's heart plummeted. "Okay..."

"I...I was officially offered a job."

"Let me guess," he said. "It's not anywhere on this continent, is it?"

Jessica shook her head, and Jack watched her throat bob with a swallow in the dim, early morning light. "No. It's the one in Saint Petersburg."

Fucking Russia, Jack thought. What he said was, "Okay. We knew this would happen. Is that all of it?"

"No," she said. "I got my start date, too."

Though Jack was terrified of the answer, he asked, "When?"

"May thirteenth," she said quietly.

"Fuck," Jack breathed, unable to hold the expletive back. That was less than a month away. "When are you leaving then?"

"We decided on May fifth."

"Fuuuuuuuck."

"I'm sorry," she said.

"It's...okay," he said. "Actually, no it's not. How long have you known?"

"Since last week. They called late Wednesday."

An entire week she'd known, and she was dropping this bomb on him now? When he was already more than a little fragile mentally?

"You should've told me then."

"And ruin your final weekend of college hockey?" she said, raising a dubious brow. "No thanks."

"So why are you telling me now?"

"Because I've been trying to find a way for a week, and because I'm about to meet your family, which is a big deal. In fact, if you no longer want me to, I understand."

Anger and irritation warred in his chest with the desire to drag her to him and never let her go. He had half a mind to tell her that no, he didn't want her to meet his family if she was just going to leave him in a few weeks. But...she still wore that ring around her neck, and she seemed to still be willing to honor that promise they'd made to each other those months ago. It wouldn't be easy, but he had all the faith in the world that they'd figure this out—together.

"I still want you to meet them," he said. "Of course I do. I'm just...processing."

He met her mouth with his again, and against her lips, said, "We'll figure this out, right?"

The words were more a plea than a question, and Jessica nodded against him.

"Yes," she said. "We'll figure this out together."

They didn't speak for a long time after that.

NOW: April 17, 2024

IN THOSE DAYS AFTER Mexico, when Jack had done nothing but mope around, missing Jessica, Josh had mercilessly made fun of him for being so spun out over a girl he'd only known for five days.

But Josh didn't understand, and Jack didn't think anyone ever would. That pull he'd felt to Jessica, like they were two halves of a whole begging to be rejoined—it was inexplicable, and probably would only ever make sense to them.

All that to say, Jack was a little nervous for Josh and Jessica to meet. Josh wasn't the type to believe in fate, or soulmates, or any of the other mushy stuff where love was concerned, and Jack was afraid of what would come out of his brother's mouth when confronted with the love of Jack's life. Honestly, he'd be fine with Josh teasing him if it meant he left Jessica alone.

Thankfully, Jessica had already met his mom, but they hadn't seen each other in four years. She wasn't sure how his mom would react to this real world version of the relationship that had taken root and bloomed under the Mexican sun.

The only member of his family he wasn't worried about was his dad. His dad loved everyone, and Jack knew he'd welcome Jessica into the family with open arms.

Naturally, he was right. They arrived at the arena promptly at six-thirty, and Jack was greeted by his mother with a hug around his middle—as that was as high as she could reach—that forced the air from his lungs. His dad, more stoic, gave Jack a fist bump and said, "Sorry about your season."

Jack gave him a tight smile, but before he could respond, his mother smacked her husband. "Be nice, Joseph," she said. Then, without warning, she turned to Jessica and also enveloped her in a hug.

Holding her at arm's length after pulling away, Jack's mother said, "It's so good to see you again."

"You, too, Mrs. DeLuca," Jessica said with a shy smile.

"Oh, please," his mother said with a wave of her hand. "Call me Becca."

Jack smiled. Rarely was anyone ever allowed to call his mother, Rebecca DeLuca, by anything other than...Rebecca—save their father, who called her Becky, and Jack and Josh, who, of course, called her Mom.

While they'd been in Mexico, his mother had taken an instant liking to Jessica. Not that Jack was surprised. Jessica—like her nickname—was pure sunshine. Her personality was magnetic, and Jack would be hard pressed to find anyone with a bad word to say about her. In the nearly four years they'd been apart, that light she emanated hadn't dimmed a bit. In fact, it had grown, encapsulating everything and everyone around her in a safe, warm glow.

Jack was all too happy to bask in that warmth.

"Well, you sure got yourself a looker," his dad said, and once again, his mom smacked her husband.

"Joseph!"

Jack's dad shrugged, then to Jessica, he said, "It's a pleasure to finally meet you, Jessica. We've heard a lot about you."

Jack willed his cheeks to remain free of a blush but was unsuccessful. Jessica dipped her head, a small smile playing in her lips, before meeting his father's gaze and saying, "Thank you. It's great to meet you as well."

Then Jack's mom hooked her arm through Jessica's and pulled her away from the men, chattering as she led Jessica toward the bar.

"You did good, kid," his dad said to Jack once Jessica was out of earshot.

"You have no idea," Jack replied, watching Jessica laugh with his mom.

He must've had stars or hearts or something else equally cheesy in his eyes, some indication that he was wildly in love with this girl, because his dad said, "Don't let Josh see you look at her like that. You'll never hear the end of it."

"Fuck Josh," Jack said lightly.

"I'm just saying," his dad said. "You know he doesn't feel things the way you do."

"I'm aware," Jack said. His brother's entire life revolved around hockey, and once, Jack had been the same. But ever since

Jessica Daniels had walked into his life four years ago, the scope of the things that were most important to him had shifted. Since then, he'd been chasing the feelings from that week when he'd been with her, desperately searching for that again. When she'd come back to him, everything had once again clicked into place.

"I'm not going to let Josh make me feel bad about finding the love of my life," Jack added to his dad. "He's just going to have to get used to it."

"It's that serious, then." It wasn't a question.

"The most serious I've ever been about anything in my life, Dad. She's the one. She's it for me."

Jack swallowed hard around the thick emotion clogging his throat, then risked meeting his dad's gaze.

Only, his father wasn't looking at him.

No. Joe DeLuca was staring at his wife.

"I know the feeling," he said quietly.

Halfway through the third period, Jessica whispered to Jack, "It feels weird to be here without Kenzie."

"I mean, she's still here, isn't she? Doesn't her family have a box?"

"Yes," Jessica said. "I'm just saying it's weird to not be watching a game with her. I've never done that, and her brother is playing."

"Well, so is *my* brother," Jack reminded her.

"That's the other problem," she said. "I have no idea who to cheer for."

Jack chuckled. "I'm only rooting for Pittsburgh because Josh will be in a far better mood after a win."

"Okay," Jessica said. "Me, too."

Thankfully, the Quakers were only about two minutes away from said win, as long as they held onto their two goal lead.

Naturally, as soon as Jack had the thought, Brent Jean decided he had other ideas and cut the lead to one with an absolutely filthy backhand that sailed over the left shoulder of the Quakers' goalie. To the rest of the arena, it probably looked like a lucky shot, but Jack, with his goalie eyes, knew better. The Quakers' goalie had been a fraction of a second too slow in stopping the shot, a flaw in his game that Jack had noticed earlier and had been waiting to see if anyone else would, too.

Leave it to Brent Jean.

The fans were feral as the final seconds ticked off the clock, as the Warriors pulled their goalie in favor of an extra skater, as they peppered the Quakers' goalie with shot after shot, as though sheer will would get one past him.

Unfortunately for the home team, they were unsuccessful, and the Quakers took a one to nothing series lead. Game two would be played here in Detroit on Friday before they headed to Pittsburgh to continue the series early next week.

"Well, that was fun," Jack's dad said when Jack and Jessica made their way back into the box. "Josh will be in a good mood."

Thank God for that, Jack thought.

And when his brother pushed his way into the suite later, Josh greeted his family with a wide smile. Despite the five years between them, Josh and Jack could easily pass for twins, and though she'd seen pictures of Josh in the months since they'd reunited, Jessica still gasped and gaped at Jack.

"I mean…you told me," she said with zero explanation, though she didn't need to give one. "But it's totally different to see it for myself."

Her words must have floated over to Josh, because he bypassed offering any hellos to his family in favor of beelining for Jessica and extending his hand.

"Josh DeLuca," he said. "The better looking DeLuca brother. You must be Jessica."

Jessica accepted Josh's proffered hand, and Jack watched as her gaze trailed up and down his suit-clad body.

Finally, Jessica said, "I don't know about better looking. You're a bit leaner than Jack, aren't you?"

Behind them, Jack's dad snorted, and Jack bit back a smile.

This girl. Sunshine with a little burn. Instinctively, Jack drew her into his side, though he knew she didn't need protecting. It was simply a reminder to his brother to be on his best behavior.

With Jessica's words, Josh blinked slowly once, twice, then tossed his head back and laughed, his still wet hair dripping onto the collar of his suit jacket.

"I like her," he said once he composed himself. "You did good, kid," he added, hauling his little brother into a hug with an arm hooked around his neck.

Once Josh hugged their parents and everyone congratulated him, their dad clapped his hands in that dad's way of his and said, "Let's eat!"

Half an hour later, they were seated in a fancy restaurant on one of the many levels of the Renaissance Center, and Josh was entertaining them with stories of the game.

"After Brent Jean scored that goal late in the third, I almost punched him in the face," Josh said. "But taking a late-game penalty, especially a dumb one like that, just wasn't worth it."

"I'd watch what you say about him," Jack said.

"Why, because he's some god around here and at MSU? I don't care."

"No," Jessica said. "Because he's my brother-in-law."

Three sets of eyes swiveled to Jessica, and Jack smiled smugly at his brother.

"I'm sorry...what?" Josh said.

"Brent's wife, Berkley? She's my big sister."

Josh's mouth dropped open, and he gave his head a little shake, blinking rapidly. Then he turned to Jack. "What a small fucking world," Josh said.

"You want it to get even smaller?"

Jack's dad leaned forward, clearly fully invested in the tea Jack was about to spill. "Let's hear it."

"You know Fuller's girlfriend Mackenzie?"

"Yes..." Josh and his dad said in unison, causing Jessica to giggle next to him.

"*She* is *Brent's* little sister."

Josh sat back in his chair so hard it rocked up onto two legs before crashing back to the floor. "And you're all at MSU together," Josh said.

"Yep," Jessica said proudly.

"This is...wild."

It really was, Jack thought. The threads of fate wove together in mysterious ways, but he'd never question it, because it had all brought him here, to this moment. To this life with Jessica.

"Well, speaking of siblings..." Josh trailed off, shooting Jack a devilish grin.

"Oh, fuck off," Jack said, knowing instantly what story Josh was about to tell.

"Mine is kind of a dumbass," Josh finished. "And incredibly gullible."

Their parents chuckled good-naturedly, and Jessica leaned forward in her seat, intently waiting for Josh to share this mortifying piece of Jack's past.

"Once, we went camping at this lake in the middle of nowhere Pennsylvania," Josh started. "It was us, our cousins, Mom, Dad, grandparents, aunts and uncles. The whole gang. At the time, Jack was maybe five or six. It wasn't until after we moved. And...we had a habit of picking on him."

"More like endlessly harassing me," Jack muttered.

"It was all in good fun," Josh protested. "This particular trip, we were walking through the woods, playing some dumb game as kids do, when Jack stopped suddenly and bent to examine something on the ground. We all crowded around him to see what it was."

"And?"

"It was deer shit," Josh said, and his grin grew.

"Oh no," Jessica said, slapping a hand over her mouth, as though she already knew where this was going.

"Oh, yes," Josh said. "We convinced little Jacky here that the deer shit was pieces of chocolate left in the woods by magical fairies, and if he ate some, he'd grown big and strong, and all of his wildest dreams would come true."

Jessica turned to him, pure horror written on her face. "You didn't."

Jack grimaced. "I'm afraid I did, sunshine." Then he paused and gestured to his body, and his girl sitting next to him. "In my defense...it worked."

"Jack!" Jessica yelped, then burst out laughing. "You let me kiss you knowing you've eaten deer poop before!"

"To be fair, it was almost twenty years ago," he said. "I think it's worked its way out of my system by now. And why are you worried about that when you should be concerned about the fact that *he*"—Jack pointed an accusatory finger at Josh—"convinced poor, innocent me to do something so vile."

"That's a good point," Jessica said, whirling that crystal blue gaze on Josh. "Explain yourself."

Josh shrugged. "He's my little brother. It's my job to toughen him up."

Jack laughed and shook his head. In the grand scheme of things, Josh had been a great big brother, and the whole deer shit incident really was something they could look back on now and laugh about.

As his parents and brother continued to regale Jessica with embarrassing stories about Jack from childhood, though Jack tried to join the merriment, he couldn't. There was an undercurrent of sadness to the whole affair. Jack could easily picture endless nights like this, where he and Jessica spent hours with his family—or hers—telling stories and making memories, and he wished so badly that he could have them.

But she was leaving, and days of just the two of them were numbered and dwindling quickly. It was like watching sand pass through an hourglass. Now that it had been tipped on its end, there was nothing Jack could do to stop it.

Jessica

NOW: April 20, 2024

"ARE YOU NERVOUS?" JESSICA asked Jack.

"Why would I be?" he asked, shooting her a sidelong glance from the driver's seat before returning his attention to the road. "I've already met all these people. The hard part is over."

"Okay, that's fair," Jessica said slowly. "But, you know...this is my hometown. People are inevitably going to ask me what my plans for after graduation are. I guess what I'm asking is if you're sure you'll be okay hearing people talk about it all weekend."

Truth be told, *Jessica* wasn't going to be okay talking about it all weekend, but there was no getting around it. In fact, Jessica didn't even want to *think* about the fact that she'd be leaving Jack—and the only place she'd ever known—in two short weeks. Time was moving too fast, and Jessica felt herself spinning out of control along with it. The harder she tried to hold on, the quicker the days slipped through her fingers. She planned to come home for a few days after graduation, but that would mainly be to move anything she wasn't taking to Russia into storage in her parents' basement.

This weekend, this trip to Traverse City with Jack to spend time with her family, was her last chance to say goodbye.

She wasn't ready, but she didn't think she'd ever be.

"I don't want to talk or even think about it," Jack said, echoing Jessica's exact thoughts. "But we can't avoid it, and it's going to happen whether I want it to or not."

Jessica knew he didn't want this, but as much as she loved him, she couldn't give up on this dream for him. But she was going to do everything in her power to make long distance work for however long they had to. One day down the road, they'd be living together, happily ever after. She had to believe that.

"I know this isn't going to be easy," she said to him finally. "But...I love you. I hope you always remember that."

Jack reached across the console and gripped her hand, bringing it to his mouth and pressing a kiss to the back. "I know, sunshine."

"I never knew anything like this existed in Michigan," Jack said, clearly awestruck, and Jessica grinned.

"It's pretty amazing, right? Unless you're from Michigan, most people don't realize this place is tucked away up here."

Admittedly, people from all across the globe traveled to the Traverse City area—and the Old Mission and Leelanau Peninsulas—to visit Michigan's version of wine country. Jessica knew the Great Lakes State wasn't exactly synonymous with wine when places like Napa existed, but Michigan wineries had routinely produced award-winning wines. The climate in the area was similar to that of Washington and Oregon, making it ideal for whites such as Riesling and Pinot Grigio, but the wineries in the area offered a wide array for every wine drinker.

When they'd cobbled together their little bucket list, this was the only thing Jack had asked for, and Jessica loved her hometown with her whole heart, so she was more than happy to make it happen.

Upon arrival, Jessica immediately took Jack out to the balcony at Chateau Delatou—which was located in Suttons Bay on the Leelanau Peninsula—overlooking the verdant vineyard sloping up and down the soft rolling hills far into the distance.

"It's beautiful up here," Jack said.

And it truly was. Chateau Delatou was one of the oldest wineries on the Leelanau Peninsula and was owned by close family friends. It was also Jessica's favorite winery in the whole state.

"Well, well," a soft female voice said from behind them. "Look what the cat dragged in. We haven't seen you guys up here in a while!"

"Chloe!" Jessica's mom said excitedly, standing from the cushy patio chair she'd dropped onto the moment they arrived to draw the woman into a hug.

Chloe Delatou was average height and curvy, with a heavy curtain of near-black hair that fell halfway down her back in soft waves and flawless olive skin that indicated her Greek heritage. She was the oldest of the five Delatou sisters, and was Logan's age. In fact, Jessica's older brother and the eldest Delatou sibling had spent enough time together from childhood until they graduated high school that Jessica had started to consider Chloe another older sister. Chateau Delatou was owned by her parents, and as the oldest, it would one day pass to her.

Chloe made her way around the group, starting first with Jessica's dad, then Logan, who gave her a healthy squeeze and said, "It's good to see you, Clo."

There was nothing romantic about the hug, but still...Jessica had read too many romance novels not to let her mind wander. She would be *thrilled* if Logan ended up with someone like Chloe, and she knew the rest of the family would be, too.

Chloe paused for a moment to give Berkley a congratulatory hug and coo over Brooks, who, in Jessica's humble opinion, was the cutest baby alive.

Finally, Chloe set her sights on Jessica.

"How's my favorite little sister?" Chloe asked when she pulled Jessica into an embrace.

Jessica laughed and said, "Don't let your actual sisters hear you say that."

Chloe pulled away and waved a dismissive hand. "They'll survive. But that's beside the point. Tell me everything! What's new with you? You're getting ready to graduate, aren't you?"

With the mention of graduation—and thus Jessica's impending move across the globe—Jack stiffened beside her, and Jessica reached down to squeeze his hand.

"Things are good! I graduate next week, and then I'm moving the week after."

"Moving where?" Chloe asked, fully invested. "You're going

to be teaching right?"

Jessica nodded, swallowing hard before she answered. "I got a job teaching English as a second language in Saint Petersburg."

Jack tensed further, and Chloe, whose golden eyes missed nothing, easily latched onto his change in body language. "I take it you don't mean Florida."

"No," Jessica said. "Russia."

"And we're so proud of her," Logan said, walking up to sling an arm around his little sister.

"Thanks, Logan," Jessica said, giving her brother a tight but grateful smile.

"Although, I'm sure Jack was wishing Jessica wasn't so talented right about now."

Jessica turned her face up to Jack, who offered her brother his own tight smile that was really more of a grimace. "I'm proud of her, too," Jack said quietly.

"Alright, alright," Berkley said. "Enough catching up. I haven't been able to drink in nearly a year. It's time I made up for it.

And just like that, the tension evaporated, the group devolving into laughter as they followed Berkley's lead and headed back inside.

Along the back wall of the cavernous tasting room, a long table lined with wine glasses had been set up for their group. Once everyone had settled in their seats, Chloe stood at the head of the table and said, "Amara will be right out!"

"Why don't you join us?" Jessica's mom asked. "It's not that busy."

Chloe glanced around the room, gnawing on her bottom lip,

and when another woman who looked remarkably similar to her pushed out of the back, Chloe seemed to make up her mind.

"Delia," Chloe said, "I'm joining the Daniels fam for this tasting."

Delia, who was a year younger than Berkley but wasn't as close with her as Chloe was with Logan, simply shrugged. "Fine by me."

After some slight shuffling of seats, Chloe dropped into a chair between Logan and Jessica. As though she'd done this a thousand times—and Jessica supposed she had—Chloe opened her mouth and said, "Today, we have—" before she was cut off by her sister.

"This is my show, Coco," Delia said with a tense smile at her sister. "I got it."

Chloe gestured with her hands. "By all means."

"Alright, today we have a full array of all the best Chateau Delatou has to offer. I know it's been a while since you've made the trip up here, and when we booked your party, Dad asked that we roll out the good stuff."

Berkley clapped excitedly. "I love being a VIP," she said.

"So you guys can try the vintage Rieslings, Pinot Grigio, Moscato, two types of bubbly, a Rosé, some fruit wines, and, of course, our world-famous ice wine. How does that sound to everybody?"

"That sounds amazing," Jessica's mom gushed, already looking at the little piece of cardstock in front of her, circling tasting options like crazy.

Jessica was more selective with her choices than her mother had been, taking time to carefully read the tasting notes that accompanied each selection and circling a Riesling, Pinot Grigio, both bubbly options, the Rosé, and the ice wine.

"What exactly is ice wine?" Jack murmured into her ear.

"It's made from grapes that aren't harvested until they're frozen. It makes the juice more concentrated, so they're only produced in the half-size bottles," she said, nodding at Delia, who approached the table with a vibrant blue glass bottle in hand, the Chateau Delatou label prominently displayed. "It's typically sweeter, and always served chilled."

"That sounds...interesting," Jack said, his forehead creasing as he stared down at his tasting card.

"I appreciate you doing this with me," she said, reaching under the table to squeeze his hand. "I know this isn't really your scene, but we've been coming here for years, and...this is home."

Jack gave her a small, secret smile, the kind he only reserved for her, then bent down and gave her a light kiss. "Where you go, I go," he said.

Jessica grinned back, a sense of relief falling over her shoulders and trickling through her entire body. She didn't know what it was about being here of all places, not when she and Jack had been spending every possible minute together that they could, that made her forget all of her worries for the moment. Maybe it was the simple fact that she was home, surrounded by the people who knew her and loved her best. Maybe it was Jack's solid and steady presence next to her, reminding her that he was fully committed to making long distance work, reminding her that he wasn't going anywhere.

To be loved by him in such a way was a gift, and she knew as long as that remained true, there was nothing they couldn't handle. As long as they remained together, everything would be okay.

That night, after a wine tasting that went on for much longer than it should have, after the alcohol loosened limbs and tongues, the Daniels family retreated to their home in Traverse City. Although, Jessica supposed, it wasn't *her* or her sibling's home anymore. That thought made her a bit melancholic, and she was heavy-hearted as she and Jack trudged up to bed.

The somber mood didn't last long, however. The moment Jessica's childhood bedroom door shut behind them, Jack walked her backward until the bed pressed into the backs of her knees and she buckled, sprawling out across its surface.

"I've been waiting to get you alone all day," Jack said, whipping his shirt over his head and tossing it to the floor. "I have to have you right now."

"You had me this morning," she reminded him, propping herself up onto her elbows. "And, no offense Jack, but I think we're pressing our luck here with sharing a bedroom. I'm not really sure I want to take it a step further and have sex under my parents' roof."

"Haven't you already done that?"

"Well, yeah..." she said, mind traveling back to that summer after Mexico, when she'd brought her situationship home a few times. It had been a nice change of pace from fucking in the back seat of their cars. "But not while they were here."

Jack frowned. "Are you sure I can't talk you into this?" he

asked.

"I'm sure," she said, grabbing his hand and pulling him down next to her. "But we can make out for a while if you want."

"I like the way you think, Daniels."

He bent and pressed his mouth to hers, then his entire body, pushing her into the mattress. His weight was a comfort on top of her, and though his hands roamed across her sides and thighs, cupping her breasts and burying themselves in her hair, he never took it any further than that. Though, by the time they finally broke away, Jessica was beginning to question why she hadn't already welcomed him inside her body. Her pulse throbbed heavily in her clit, and when Jack shifted so his thigh was between her legs, she ground against him, desperate to relieve that pressure.

Jack chuckled. "You sure you don't want me to take care of that for you?"

"Just...hold still," she gasped, and Jack shifted so the hard muscle of his quad pressed right where she needed it. With reckless abandon, Jessica writhed against him, swirling her hips, each circle around coiling that pleasure tighter and tighter inside her until, finally, she shattered, and Jack clamped a hand over her mouth as she loudly gasped his name over and over again.

"Fuck," Jack said when she came back to herself. "That might be the hottest thing I've ever seen."

"You say that every time we do something new."

"I mean it every time, too."

Sated, though her chest still rose and fell a little faster than normal, she sat up and reached for Jack's pants. "Let me take care of you."

Jack grabbed her wrists and held her hands away from him.

"No chance," he said.

Jessica frowned. "Why not?"

"Because if I let you touch me right now, I will come unhinged, and nothing will stop me from fucking you into this mattress until the entire house hears you screaming my name as you come."

Jessica's toes curled in response, and she let out a heavy breath. "I already can't wait to be back in EL," she said.

Jack shucked his pants and laid down beside her, drawing her into the circle of his arms. "Don't wish this away yet, Jess," he said quietly into her hair. Jessica was surprised to find herself already teetering on the edge of consciousness, and dazedly allowed Jack to peel her out of her jeans and take her bra off. "We don't have too many days like this one left. Savor them."

"I will," she promised right before falling into a deep, dreamless sleep.

Jack

NOW: May 4, 2024

Unbeknownst to Jessica, for the past several weeks, Jack had been colluding with her family to throw her a surprise going away party, and today was the big day.

The best part was, the entire thing wasn't costing them a penny. Jack supposed it paid to be surrounded by professional hockey players, because Mitch Frambough, who happened to be Brent Jean's best friend and was dating Berkley's best friend, Lexie, owned a loft in Greektown, Detroit, and offered it and the bar he always had fully stocked up to the Daniels family for free.

Brent, for his part, offered to pay for the caterer—though Berkley put up a fight and ultimately lost.

"She's my little sister, too," Brent had said. Berkley, in her postpartum hormonal state, had softened and acquiesced.

So on Saturday afternoon, the day before Jessica was set to fly out, Jack found himself at the loft with Berkley, Brent, Logan,

Nate, Mitch, Lexie, both sets of Daniels and Jean parents, plus Aiden, Asher, Luke, and a whole slew of other various Warriors and Michigan State hockey players, setting up for the evening. The loft really was stunning in its own right without any added frills or decoration, so the boys were really just there to stock the beer cooler, lug boxes of liquor upstairs from the street, and move furniture around until it was arranged to Berkley's liking.

Jack hadn't noticed before how bossy she was, and he choked back a laugh when Lexie called her out on it.

"Berk, we've hosted hundreds of parties in this place over the years," Lexie said with an exasperated sigh. "There's never been a problem with the setup of the furniture before."

"I want everything to be perfect," Berkley pouted, brushing a hand over the top of Brooks' fuzzy head where he was wrapped against her chest.

"It will be," Lexie said. "You know Jess would be happy with dinner at Five Guys as long as she got to spend her last night with you guys."

"She's right, you know," Jack said to Berkley.

He couldn't believe Jessica was leaving so soon, that this time tomorrow, Jack would be adjusting to life with her halfway across the world. He didn't know what he would do when he could no longer drive five minutes up the road, wrap her in his arms, and bury himself in her body. He couldn't wrap his head around the fact that in less than twelve hours, she'd be physically out of reach.

Jack shook off those thoughts. They still had a whole night of celebrating ahead of them, and he refused to bring the mood down with thoughts of how he was going to live without her.

"When is she getting here?" Brent asked as he and Mitch once again hefted up a couch and moved it a few feet to the left until Berkley deemed it perfect.

Jack flicked his wrist to check his watch.

"Fuck," he breathed. "They should be here in a half hour."

He spun on his heel, surveying the room, surprised to find that the loft had begun to fill while his attention had been elsewhere. College and family friends—the bulk of them people Jack didn't know—milled around, conversing in small groups or lingering by the bar, where Mitch's bartender worked overtime to fill drink orders.

As if on cue, Aiden pulled his phone out of his pocket and said, "They're on their way. Kenzie texted that they just left Brent and Berkley's house."

"Fuck," Jack said again.

Aiden, who had always been in tune with Jack's moods about as well as Jessica was, walked over and tossed an arm around his shoulders. "C'mon, buddy. Let's get you a drink."

A drink. Alcohol. Yes, that would definitely help.

Asher and Luke trailed after them, and when they reached the bar, Jack said, "Four shots of tequila, please."

His roommates groaned but didn't argue.

When the bartender set the shots in front of them, along with a salt shaker and four lime slices, they performed the ritual of licking their skin and sprinkling salt on the wetness, then grasping the glass in one hand and the lime wedge in the other.

"To Jess," Jack said.

"Shouldn't we toast something else? Since she's not even here?" Asher said, and Luke elbowed him in the ribs.

"Shut up, Ash."

"Just saying..." Asher mumbled, and Jack couldn't help but laugh.

Some things never changed.

"To Jess," the boys echoed, and they downed the shots as one.

The closer Jessica and Kenzie got to the loft—Aiden was tracking them; he and Kenzie shared their locations with each other, because of course they did—the higher Jack's anxiety rose. This was Jessica's last night in the States for God knew how long, and it was her final opportunity to say goodbye to her friends and family. He wanted it to be special for her, even if that meant he'd have to spend the majority of the party sharing her with other people.

"They just pulled up!" Aiden yelled over the crowd, and Jack's heart shot into his throat. There was no way Jessica didn't have some idea of what was happening. Kenzie wouldn't just randomly bring her to the loft for fun. They'd told her they were having a small catered dinner here since they had such big families and so many people to take into account, but it was a weak cover story.

He simply hoped she'd be surprised by the sheer number of people that had showed up to celebrate her.

Abruptly, the music cut off, and the guests gathered in front of the large sliding door at the entrance to the loft.

"They just got off the elevator," Aiden said.

"Any second now!" Jack yelled.

And not even ten seconds later, someone—Jack presumed it was Kenzie—banged on the metal door hard enough to make everyone jump. A moment after, it slid open, revealing the two girls, one blonde, one brunette, one with her mouth gaping in shock, the other wearing a shit-eating grin.

"Surprise!" everyone yelled at once, followed by the eruption of several confetti cannons and Jessica's family rushing to her side, everyone's words lost when they all spoke at once.

Jack stood on the outskirts, watching Jessica wade through the crowd, her shocked expression turning to one of awe then excitement. She hugged everyone she spoke to, from her little old grandmother to her youngest, smallest cousins, from random family friends to Aiden, Asher, and Luke.

Finally, it was Jack's turn.

"Hey, sunshine," he said with a grin.

Jessica said nothing, only threw herself at him. Jack caught her easily as she snaked her arms around his neck, and he crushed her to his body.

"You didn't have to do this," she whispered against his neck.

"I wanted to," he replied. "You're about to realize your dream, Jess. That's worth celebrating."

She pulled back to look at him. "I thought we were going to celebrate...as a family."

Jack spun her around so she could get a good look at the entire room, though her eyes never left his. "All of these people *are* your family," he reminded her.

"I suppose you're right," she relented. "But still, I would've been happy with you, and me, and a bottle of wine."

He pressed a kiss to the tip of her nose. "The night is still young."

She grinned at him before kissing his lips, soft and slow in deference to the crowd of people surrounding them, but it still held the promise of all the ways she wanted to thank him later.

"Thank you," she whispered.

Jack set her back on her feet, but not before giving her butt a little squeeze and a playful smack. "You're welcome," he said. "Now go mingle. I'll be right here."

"I love you," she said as she trotted off, making a beeline for her parents.

"I love you, too," he said, but she was already gone.

"You two are disgusting," Asher said from behind him, and Jack turned with a sigh.

"You're just jealous," Jack said.

Asher didn't say anything, only turned and headed back to the bar. Jack followed.

Though they spent the bulk of the evening apart, Jack knew exactly where Jessica was at any given moment. Every cell in his body begged him to go to her, to glue himself to her side and not let her out of his sight until she left tomorrow morning. But he couldn't. He wasn't the only one she was saying goodbye to tonight, and Jack needed to give her the space to do that.

Even if his heart was breaking in his chest.

He couldn't even imagine how she was feeling. She'd put on a brave face the entire night, but he could tell from looking at her that her smiles were often forced, their edges wobbling, her eyes shined over with an emotion most mistook for excitement but Jack knew was sadness.

The later it got, the more the loft emptied out of the elderly people and those families with young kids who needed to get home for bedtime. Soon, all that remained were the Daniels and Jean families, a handful of Warriors and Spartans, her roommates and a few college friends, Jack, Asher, Luke, and Aiden.

Jack sat with his teammates in one of the small conversational groupings of furniture Berkley had asked them to set up earlier, each with a beer in hand, Jack and Aiden on a loveseat while Luke and Asher sat across from them in matching oversized leather armchairs.

"How did you manage to get tonight off?" Asher asked Aiden.

Aiden shrugged. "We had practice earlier, and we don't play again until Wednesday."

After he put up crazy good numbers in April with Toledo, the Assassins, the Warriors' AHL team in Grand Rapids, called Aiden up, and that's where he'd been playing for the last few weeks.

"Plus," Aiden added, "you know I wouldn't miss saying bye to Jess."

Jack smiled when Asher rolled his eyes. Aiden treated Jessica like Jack treated Kenzie—like she was his sister. As the love of Jack's life, Aiden treated her as if she was family, and Jack was forever grateful for this group of guys—even Asher.

A moment later, Asher, who anyone who'd met him would agree didn't have a romantic bone in his body, said to Jack, "So, what're you going to do about Jess?"

"What do you mean?" Jack asked. "She's leaving tomorrow."

"Right..." Asher started. "And you're just going to *let* her leave? Without putting up a fight?"

"I put up a fight months ago, Ash," Jack said, his jaw

clenching. He didn't want to be having this conversation right now—or ever—and Asher knew how sore of a subject this was for him. "She's not going to change her mind. She's leaving, and I'm staying here."

"But...you don't *have* to stay here."

Three sets of eyes swiveled to Asher, and it was Luke who spoke first. "What are you talking about, Ash?"

"I'm just saying...if Jack loves Jess as much as he claims he does—"

"Of course I do, you asshole."

"—then why isn't he going with her?"

"Because hockey is here," Jack said.

"You say that like there isn't hockey in Russia, dipshit," Asher said, his mouth quirking into a smirk. "You say that like your agent couldn't get on the phone right now and get you a deal in Moscow or wherever the fuck Jess is going."

"I—what?" Jack said dumbly, his mind whirring with the possibilities.

"Go with her," Asher. "I honestly can't believe you didn't think of this yourself."

"I did...but it's complicated."

"I don't think it is," Asher said. "You love her; she loves you. She's moving, and you haven't signed a contract to play anywhere in the States yet. I think you've been waiting for someone to tell you it's okay to do this. That it doesn't *have* to be complicated. It can really be as simple as following her and playing hockey in Russia. I'm sure no one has bothered to tell you this, and I can't believe it's me that finally is, but...you can have both, DeLuca."

And…could it really be *that* simple? Jessica had never asked him to come with her, exactly as Jack had never tried to convince her to stay. As much as they loved each other, neither of them had been ready to give up on their dreams to chase this relationship. A relationship that was exactly what Jack had wanted and dreamed about every day since Mexico, but one that was, by all standards, very new and untested. Jack didn't like it, but he'd agreed.

Hockey was his life.

But so was Jessica, perhaps a more important part of it now than the game ever had been.

As Jack's mind spun with the possibilities, Asher spoke again.

"I don't think I believe in fate or soulmates, Jack, but if I did…you and Jessica would be why."

Luke, Aiden, and Jack froze, slack-jawed, gaping at Asher.

"That is…the nicest thing you've ever said to me," Jack said as he leapt to his feet and crossed the space to pull Asher out of his chair and into a hug. Once he released him, Jack withdrew his phone from his pocket and said, "Excuse me, boys. I have to call Darren."

Despite the fact that it was after ten p.m., Darren picked up on the first ring.

"You ready to sign that contract with WBS?" Darren asked without preamble.

Like Aiden, Jack could've easily signed a deal the minute his collegiate career ended. But…he'd selfishly wanted to enjoy what time he had left with Jessica. Luckily, WBS had been willing to wait. Only, now, he'd have to turn them down…hopefully. Either way, he'd be signing a contract sometime within the next twelve hours. He'd make sure of it. With Jessica leaving, he had no more excuses to delay.

"Actually..." Jack said, taking a deep breath before he dropped this bomb on Darren—and himself. "I was curious if those Russian offers were still on the table. Particularly the Saint Petersburg one."

Darren was quiet for an excruciating amount of time, so long that Jack mentally braced himself for Darren to tell him that wasn't an option anymore. Instead, Darren said, "Let me make some calls."

"I'll be waiting," Jack said and hung up.

Then he went to find his girl.

She was across the room, chatting with her two roommates and a few other college friends, and Jack smiled at them apologetically as he gripped Jessica's arm and tugged her away from the group.

"What're you doing?" she hissed.

"I haven't seen you all night," he said, shooting her a look over his shoulder.

"That doesn't mean you can just—"

The moment the lock on the bathroom door clicked into place behind them, Jessica's protestations were cut off as Jack pressed her against the wall.

"I need you," he said.

"Now?" she asked, eyes wide with shock. "In the loft bathroom?"

"Now," he growled.

Roughly, Jack ran his hand over her body, blazing a scorching trail from her throat to the apex of her thighs, slipping his hand underneath the flouncy material of her skirt and cupping her pussy. He shifted the thin lace of her panties aside and slid one of his fingers through her desire, groaning as Jessica arched into him.

"This pussy is mine," he said against the skin of her neck, following his words with a nip of his teeth.

Jessica looked him dead in the eye, unafraid of the ferocity and possessiveness he knew she found there. "Always."

Jack deftly undid his belt and fly and freed himself—already impossibly hard—from the confines of his boxers. Then he lifted Jessica off her feet and hooked those long, silky legs around his waist. Within moments he was buried within her.

Before he started moving, he kissed her, long and hard, both of them gasping for air when they pulled apart. He shifted, withdrawing until only his head was left inside her, then driving home with a swift pulse of his hips.

He slammed into her relentlessly, and Jessica met every thrust, grinding down onto him so her clit rubbed against the coarse hair that trailed down the lower plane of his stomach.

"I love you," he said.

"I love you," she replied, her breaths coming harder and harder, matching his as they both raced toward that finish line.

"What if I—" he started.

Jessica's hand covered his mouth, cutting him off. "No," she said on a gasp. "We're not ruining this with what-ifs."

He wanted to tell her what he'd planned, but he didn't want to get either of their hopes up if Darren couldn't come through—if Russia no longer wanted him.

Plus, she was right. For right now, this was the last moment they had like this, their last chance to come together, for him to lose himself in the feel of her clenched so tightly around him he could burst at any second.

On his next thrust, Jessica tightened further, every muscle in her body pulling taught around him before she broke apart, stifling her moans by burying her face in the soft spot where his neck met his shoulder, quivering and panting as she rode out the waves of pleasure, her heels digging into the small of his back, her thighs quaking under his palms.

With two more pumps of his hips, Jack was following her down, biting down softly on her shoulder to keep himself from yelling himself hoarse—and letting everyone else know what they were up to.

When the aftershocks ceased for both of them, Jessica released her legs, and Jack dropped her to her feet. She grabbed a handful of paper towels and cleaned them both up, then righted her clothes and made sure Jack was presentable, too.

Before they left the bathroom, he pulled her close and kissed her again.

"I love you, you know," he said against her mouth. "We'll be okay."

"I know, honey. I love you, too."

Finally, they rejoined the party.

NOW: May 5, 2024

"Let me stay with you tonight," Jack begged.

"I can't," she said, not bothering to look at him. Instead, she buried her face in his chest, stamping his warmth and his scent on her memory.

They were on the street outside the loft, stretching out their farewell, neither of them willing to be the first to let go and walk away.

"Why not?"

"It's too hard," she said, finally meeting his eyes, if only because he tucked a finger under her chin and gently forced her head back.

"So you'd rather do this here?"

"I..." Jessica trailed off. "I can't do the whole tearful farewell in the morning. It's going to be hard enough saying goodbye to my family at the airport without adding you to the mix. Please,

Jack," she said. "Don't make this harder than it has to be."

"It's already too hard," he said quietly. "But okay, if that's what you want."

She nodded. "It is."

"Just...don't say goodbye to me right now, okay? This isn't the end for us."

"You can't know that."

"I do know that. Mexico wasn't, right? This won't be either. Plus, you promised."

He was right; she *had* promised. In the hallway at the hospital. In that hotel room in Minnesota, moments before they'd lost themselves in each other.

Promise me you won't say goodbye.

Now he was reminding her—and begging. And the truth was, she didn't *want* to say goodbye. The time zones and miles between them would be difficult to navigate, and more than anything, she wanted to share in his belief that everything would be okay.

Even if that logical part of her brain whispered that this wasn't the end of some vacation romance, where they'd go back to their real lives and move on. This *was* real life, and Jessica was moving clear across the world.

All she knew was right now, she would give Jack whatever he wanted...except stay.

That was the one thing she couldn't do, no matter how much she loved him.

And she knew it was the one thing he'd never ask for.

Through her tears, Jessica nodded, and let him press kisses to her forehead, cheeks, eyelids, the tip of her nose, before he finally settled his mouth over hers.

When he pulled away, Jessica was surprised to find his own eyes and cheeks glistening with tears. "This is the first time I've cried since I woke up in Mexico to find you gone," he said quietly. "Promise me this won't be like that."

"I promise," she said, reaching for the chain around her neck and withdrawing the ring dangling at the end from beneath her shirt. The metal was warm to her touch, and Jack wrapped his fist around hers. "We have a deal, remember?"

"Yesterday, today, tomorrow, always, and forever."

"Exactly," she said, giving him a watery smile. "I love you."

"I love you, too, sunshine. Call me when you get to the airport in the morning."

"I will," she promised.

Reluctantly, she withdrew from Jack's embrace, and wrapped her arms tight around herself as he walked away to join Aiden, Kenzie, Luke, and Asher. The five of them were staying at Kenzie's parents' house tonight, and Jack didn't look back as he climbed into Aiden's Jeep and sped away.

Jessica's alarm went off at an ungodly hour the next morning, but the fact that the sun hadn't yet risen wasn't the only thing keeping her safely cocooned under the covers of her sister's guest bed.

She was moving to Russia today.

A cold finger of fear snaked down her spine.

It wasn't so much the move that was freaking her out as was

the thought of leaving the only place she'd ever known in favor of something that could not be more different.

Down the hall, even through her favorite rain sounds playlist coming from her phone, Jessica heard Brooks squawk.

Wide awake now—thanks to the weight of anxiety that had settled on her chest—she rose and padded across the carpet to the door.

Once in the hall, instead of turning toward the kitchen for some coffee before she got ready and finished packing, she moved to the nursery.

Brooks had quieted some, but still squealed excitedly when Jessica's face appeared over his crib. She understood he was too young yet to have memorized her face, but she took it as a good sign that he didn't scream and cry every time she held him.

"Oh, yes," she said as she lifted him out of his crib. "You love your auntie Jessica, don't you?"

"He does," a deep voice said from behind her, and she turned to find Brent silhouetted in the doorway.

"God, you scared the shit out of me!" she hissed. "You can't sneak up on women in the dark like that, especially not ones that are holding your fresh baby."

Brent chuckled. "Sorry," he said. "Your sister is still passed out, but I heard him on the monitor so I got up to check on him."

Jessica sat in the nearby rocking chair—which was really an overstuffed armchair that rocked—and rubbed a thumb over Brooks' smooth cheek.

"He's perfect, you know," she said.

Brent moved so he stood over them. "He really is," Brent said. "Berk did good."

"You both did," he said, brushing a hand over Brooks' healthy head of downy-soft, deep-brown hair. "He didn't get this from my blonde sister."

Brent chuckled. "No, I suppose not."

"How's it been?" Jessica asked.

"Really good," Brent said, then when Brooks let out another squawk, said, "C'mon, I think he's hungry."

Jessica trailed after her brother-in-law all the way to the kitchen, keeping Brooks tucked tight to her body like a football.

"He's the best thing to ever happen to us," Brent said, finishing his thought from upstairs. "I can't believe we lived so long without him."

"I mean, you sure didn't waste any time after the wedding," she said, throwing him a wink.

Brent burst out laughing. "To be fair, we never planned on getting pregnant that fast. She went off birth control before the wedding because every doctor and friend of ours said it takes some time for that hormone to work its way out of her system. Of course, for us, it took no time at all, so I think that myth has been debunked."

Jessica simply nodded and returned her attention to her nephew.

It was mind-blowing, to her, how quickly things had changed for all of them. Berkley met Brent in 2020, and here they were, less than four years later, happily married, with a beautiful home and a beautiful son. Jessica had also met Jack in 2020, and now she was preparing to enter into a long-distance relationship with him.

She wanted what Brent and Berkley had, and she wanted it

with Jack.

Moving across the world was a scary thing, but moving across the world when the love of her life was staying here? That was the kind of thing that kept Jessica awake at night.

"How did you know?" she blurted.

The dark slashes of Brent's eyebrows drew together over his blue eyes. "Know what?"

"That Berkley was it for you."

Brent's expression softened. "You remember when we broke up right before she graduated law school?"

"Vividly," Jessica said with a laugh. Her sister had been a train-wreck those two weeks they'd spent apart.

"A few days before that, Mitch took pity on me and forced me to go to lunch with him. I was just as much of a mess as I'm sure your sister was, and Mitch had enough. He basically told me to pull my head out of my ass or I was going to lose her. And it got me thinking about our relationship as a whole, and how I ignored her every time she asked me to stop doing something. I just...I thought that's what she needed from me. But it wasn't. What she needed was for me to simply be there for her, and support her in whatever it was she wanted to do. If that girl came to me and told me she wanted to go sky diving, or base jumping, or fucking anything...I'd be the first one in line behind her."

"That's sweet and all," Jessica said, "and I'm eternally grateful you found each other, but that doesn't really answer my question."

Brent finished the bottle he was preparing for Brooks and walked over to the island, passing it over the surface to her, then leaning heavily on his elbows.

"The moment I knew Berkley was it for me was the moment I realized her happiness was more important to me than mine."

Jessica gritted her teeth, fighting to hold the tears that threatened to spill at bay. Ultimately, she was unsuccessful, and her brother-in-law gave her a sad smile when one slipped free and rolled down her cheek.

As hard as it was going to be, Brent's words made Jessica realize how right she was in her decision to make sure Jack chased his dreams. Because isn't that exactly what she'd been thinking when she told him not to make decisions on his future with her in mind? Yes, she wanted him in her life forever, but not at the expense of them giving up the things they'd worked so hard for in the process.

"I take it you know what I'm talking about," Brent said quietly.

"I do." She really, really did.

Jessica was finishing her first cup of coffee when her sister came downstairs, followed shortly by their parents and Logan.

Jessica could barely look at any of them, knowing that, in a few short hours, she'd be walking through security at the airport, not knowing when she'd see them next.

His own mug of coffee in hand, her dad walked up behind her and pressed a kiss to the top of her head. She didn't miss the way he sniffed as he backed away.

"You all packed, sweetheart?" her mom asked.

"Almost," Jessica said, then rose from her stool. "I need to shower, too."

Logan flicked his wrist to check his watch and said, "Better get going. We've gotta leave in an hour."

"Don't remind me," she grumbled as she trudged up the stairs.

She'd expected the shower to loosen some of the tension in her body, but the warm air and spray of the water did nothing but suffocate her, and she wound up curled into a ball on the smooth tile floor, tears streaming down her face.

More than anything, she wished Jack was here. She wished she hadn't turned him away last night when he begged to stay with her. At least she'd have an anchor in this sea of uncertainty, even if saying goodbye to him at those airport gates would rip her heart from her chest. But she'd endure that, happily, to have the safe cocoon of his arms around her right now. Would gladly leave her heart a bloody mess in his hands as long as he held hers until he could no longer.

Finally, she dragged herself out of the bathroom, dressed and, on autopilot, piled anything she hadn't been able to pack last night into her bags. She was traveling with two hard-sided suitcases, one full sized, the other a carry on, plus her backpack. The seams of all three strained against everything she'd stuffed inside them. She knew she'd blown well past the fifty pound limit for her checked bag, but she needed to bring enough with her to survive for the time it took for her parents to ship the rest of her things overseas.

And *that* was a whole other added stress. What if everything got lost along the way? What if, in addition to starting a new life in a new country, she also had to replace her entire wardrobe and book collection?

No, she couldn't think like that. Today was going to be hard enough without worrying over things she couldn't control.

"Knock knock," Berkley said from the doorway to Jessica's guest room. "Are you about ready?"

"Almost," Jessica said, drawing one last zipper closed on her backpack, then surveying the items laid out on her bed that she'd stuff into her belt bag. Phone, portable phone charger, wallet with ID, credit cards, and cash—though that last one wouldn't do her much good once she left the States—passport, AirPods, lip balm, hand sanitizer, and a tiny bottle filled with any meds she could possibly need on an intercontinental flight. After carefully placing everything inside and strapping the bag over her chest, she turned to her sister.

"Ready," she said, offering Berkley a strained smile.

"Oh, Jess," Berkley said, then rushed to her. Jessica threw her arms around Berkley and pulled her close, not bothering to hold back the sobs racking her body.

"I'm scared," she admitted to her sister through her sobs, saying those words out loud for the first time.

"I would be, too," Berkley said, pulling away to hold Jessica at arm's length. "This is a huge life change."

"Not as big as having a child," Jessica said. "You handled that like a pro."

Berkley barked out a laugh, then pushed Jessica backward until she collapsed onto the end of the bed.

"Jessica, I cried for like a week straight after we brought Brooks home."

"What?" Jessica shouted, incredulous.

One thing Jessica had always admired about her sister was that nothing scared her, and nothing phased her. She was stubborn, to her detriment more often than not, but she was also the most fearless person Jessica knew. So hearing this, that she not only cried, but cried for *days* after bringing her son home, was a shock.

"Are you trying to tell me *you* wouldn't be terrified to bring a whole ass life into the world, and then bring him home and not be even more freaked out by the fact that you now have to keep him alive?"

"No, I would absolutely shit my pants," Jessica assured her. "But I never expected you..."

"I'm not a robot, Jess, and being a first-time mother is no fucking joke. The point I'm trying to make here is that the changes that scare us the most are usually the most worthwhile."

Jessica's mind whirred back to four years ago, when her mother said something similar to her about her relationship with Jack. Then, Jessica had ignored the advice because she knew it would've been the wrong move for her at the time. But now? Now, she knew Berkley was right.

"You're right," she said, speaking her thoughts out loud.

Her sister tapped Jessica's nose with her pointer finger and said, "I usually am."

"Whatever," Jessica replied with a laugh and a shove.

Then she stood and hefted her backpack onto her shoulders.

"Let's do this."

"That's the spirit."

The last thing Jessica wanted was a whole crowd of people at the departure terminal, doing the whole tearful goodbye thing that was better left to the movies or the ends of sappy romance novels. Unfortunately, her family couldn't be dissuaded from bringing her to the airport. And doubly unfortunate was the fact that, with the addition of Brooks to the family, they couldn't take one vehicle. So Jessica would be riding with Brent, Berkley, and Brooks, while her mom, dad, and Logan took a separate car.

"I'm gonna load this in the truck," Brent said, lifting Jessica's large suitcase off the ground like it weighed nothing.

And she supposed, to him, it probably did.

"Show off!" Berkley yelled after him. "You know it's got wheels, right?"

"Don't care!" Brent shouted back, and Berkley rolled her eyes as she continued to strap Brooks into his car seat.

A moment later, the squeaking and hum of the garage door opening echoed into the house, followed by Brent yelling, "Hey, Jess? Can you come out here for a sec?"

"Sure!" she shouted back, shooting Berkley a confused look. Her sister simply raised her hands in the air as if to say, *I have no idea*.

When Jessica reached the garage, the interior was lit only by the faint glow from the light affixed to the garage door motor.

"Brent?" Jessica said, searching for her brother-in-law.

"Jess," a male voice said from behind her, but it didn't belong to Brent.

Slowly, Jessica turned toward, going utterly still when she took in the man before her.

"Surprise," Jack said, giving her little jazz hands.

"What are you doing here?" she hissed. "Not that I'm not happy to see you, but...I really can't do this right now, Jack. Saying bye to my family is going to be hard enough. I thought we did this last night. I thought we agreed—"

Her ramblings were cut off when Jack wrapped his arms around her shoulders and crushed her to his chest. "You're cute when you ramble," he said.

"What are you doing here?" she repeated, pulling away and putting a few feet of space between them.

"I'm coming with you."

"Like hell you are."

Jack hooked his thumb over his shoulder, where Brent was hauling an overstuffed hockey bag up the driveway. With a wink at Jessica, he tossed it into the bed and disappeared inside, pointedly closing the door behind him.

"It's already done," Jack said with a shrug.

"I don't know how many times I have to tell you this, Jack, but I can't let you do this. I can't be the reason you give up on your dreams."

Jack closed some of the space between them, only enough so he could reach out and cup her chin in his hand, lifting it so her eyes met his.

"Listen to me very carefully, Jessica Daniels," he said. "I know you can't and never would ask me to do this. You think you're doing the noble thing by giving me this out. But let me tell you something—my dream is *you*. It's always been you. Every day of that week in Mexico, every mile and memory and moment until the day we reunited, and every single second since. *It's always been you*. And I'd be the dumbest fucking man in the universe if I let you walk away again."

"When did you decide all of this?" she asked, unwilling to acknowledge everything he was saying. Not yet.

"Last night at the party," he said. "Which, by the way, you really should text Asher and tell him thank you."

"Asher?" Jessica asked, confused.

"It's a long story," Jack said. "I'll tell you on the plane."

Those words cracked something inside of her, and she reached for him, settling her hands on his chest. "This is real," she said. "I'm not dreaming. You're really coming."

In response, Jack raised his hand and placed his palm over Jessica's heart.

"This?" he said, pausing to let it beat against his touch. "This was a heart worth finding, a heart worth waiting for, and a heart I would go to the ends of the world to keep. To make sure it's always beating in time with mine."

"What about Scranton?" she asked, though her eyes welled with tears at the truth she already knew, already saw in every single line and slope of his face. She couldn't help it; this—him being here—was too good to be true.

"Fuck Scranton," Jack said, smiling and raising his hand to cup her cheek when Jessica choked on a laugh. "I can play hockey anywhere. But *you* aren't anywhere. *You* are going to Russia, so I'm going to Russia."

"You can't give up hockey."

"I'm not," he said, and Jessica cocked her head, confused. "Late last night, I accepted an offer to play with a team in Saint Petersburg."

The tears flowed freely now, and Jessica wrapped her arms around him, burying her face in his chest. She inhaled deeply, exactly as she had last night, when she had thought she was saying goodbye. Now, instead of branding the smell and feel of him on her memory as a way to get her through the long days and nights without him, she was comforted by the fact that she would always be surrounded by it. That this man—this ridiculous hunk of a man—was giving up a straight shot to the NHL to follow her across the world.

Tilting her head, she looked into the face that had become more precious to her than anything else. "What did I do to deserve you?"

"You took a spring break trip to Mexico and got really lucky," he said with a wink and a kiss pressed to the tip of her nose.

She playfully shoved him away, but he caught her wrist and pulled her back in, capturing her mouth in a slow, searing kiss. Last night, she'd savored every press of their lips, every touch, every smile, and every word he spoke, knowing each one might very well be the last. Now, she savored this simply because she knew with certainty that she'd get to do it whenever she wanted, that she wouldn't have to go days or weeks or months missing him. She'd never have to know what it was like to be in a long distance relationship, to survive on FaceTime sex and birthdays and anniversaries celebrated through the mail. Digging her fingers deeper into the material of his shirt, she held on for dear life, knowing now that she'd never have to let go.

They broke apart only when someone cleared their throat nearby. Sheepish, Jessica turned in Jack's arms and faced her sister and brother-in-law.

"Hate to break up this little love fest," Brent said, gesturing between them, "but we really have to go if you guys don't want to miss your flight."

Jessica tilted her head and looked up at Jack again. "What do you say, DeLuca? Wanna move to Russia with me?"

Jack grinned, the corners of those cornflower blue eyes crinkling. "I thought you'd never ask, Daniels."

LATER: New Year's Eve, 2025

TWO YEARS TO THE day since he and Jessica had reunited, Jack rose like it was any other morning. He woke Jessica with his head between her thighs, as he'd been known to do when they didn't have much time in the morning but he wanted to make her feel good before she left for work. Plus, two years with this woman would never satiate him. He would forever crave her.

They eventually dragged themselves out of bed, and he made breakfast while she showered and got ready. They ate, Jack gathered his things for practice, and they walked out the door of their flat together, pausing at the threshold to share a kiss before they went their separate ways.

During practice, Jack tried to give it his full attention, but his mind was elsewhere.

Namely, the fact that he was going to ask Jessica to marry him tonight.

Honestly, he should've done it years ago, but they were young and still figuring out what they wanted out of life and each other.

But it was time. At least, Jack thought so. Jessica had given no indication she knew what was coming, nor had she ever even brought up the prospect of getting married. Although, Jack assumed that was because he'd moved halfway across the world to be with her, and she felt selfish asking for more than what she thought he wanted to give, not because she didn't actually want to marry him.

What she still didn't seem to realize was that he'd give her anything and everything.

He was confident she'd say yes, if a little unnerved by the prospect of asking.

After practice, he rushed home to shower and change. There was no need for it; Jessica wouldn't be back from teaching for hours yet. But he had errands to run, an entire flat to decorate, and a meal to cook.

As he twisted the knob on their apartment door, arms laden with reusable grocery bags, his phone rang. He quickly and unceremoniously dropped everything in the middle of their living room and pulled the phone out of his pocket.

"Did you do it yet?" Kenzie asked by way of greeting.

"No!" Jack said, heaving a sigh. "You do realize it's only like three p.m. here, right?"

"Fuck," Aiden said in the background. "I told you we called way too early."

"Isn't it like...eight in the morning there?"

"Yes," Kenzie said, somewhat defensively, and Jack laughed.

"What are you two doing awake so early?"

"Fuller has a game tonight, so he's gotta go in for skate."

"Ahh, that's right," Jack said, remembering that the Warriors played a home New Year's Eve game every year.

Jack smiled and relaxed onto his and Jessica's ancient thrifted couch while Kenzie and Aiden prattled on about what was new with them.

He was thankful that, over the course of the last year and a half—and the over four thousand miles and an ocean that separated them—he, Aiden, and Kenzie had remained close.

Then again, Kenzie and Jessica were family. They'd been the first ones he'd gone to when he'd decided he wanted to propose. Kenzie helped him pick out the ring over endless FaceTime calls at odd hours of the morning and night.

"So what've you got planned for your big night?" Aiden asked.

"Fancy dinner, champagne, pop the question, hope like hell she says yes."

"She will," Kenzie said confidently, and some of the tension in Jack's chest eased.

It wasn't that Jack didn't think Jessica loved him enough to want to be together forever, but there was always that chance that maybe he'd read her silence on the subject wrong, and she simply wasn't interested in changing the status of their relationship.

"I hope you're right," he said.

"She *will*," Kenzie stressed. "That girl loves you more than anything."

Jack grinned, then checked his watch. "Fuck," he said. "I gotta go."

"Oh, boo!" Kenzie shouted at him.

"Bunny, we've been on the phone for over an hour. I have to cook before Jess gets home."

"Oh, fuck," Kenzie said. "Bye! Good luck!"

"Good luck, bro!" Aiden yelled before Jack hung up.

The next hour after getting off the phone with his friends was a blur of cooking dinner, littering their two room flat with rose petals from three bouquets and a disgusting number of candles, and setting the table with the fanciest plates and silverware they had, complete with a single rose in a small mason jar and a bottle of champagne chilling in bucket.

He was just plating the food when Jessica walked through the door.

Right on time.

When Jessica walked into the room, Jack stood by their small, circular dining table, the bottle of champagne in his hands, waiting to be popped open.

Jessica stopped in her tracks. "What is all of this?"

"It's our anniversary!"

"Technically, our anniversary is tomorrow," she said. "Since that kiss didn't happen until after midnight."

Jack waved a hand. "Semantics. If I say today is our anniversary, then today is our anniversary."

"Okay..." Jessica said. "Is that why you're dressed like that?"

She gestured at his person, where he'd switched out his usual lounge attire for a starched—heavily, he should add; the dry cleaner down the street always used too much of the stuff—white button down and khaki slacks, foregoing his standard bare feet for black socks.

He refused to propose with bare feet. He didn't know why,

but something about that grossed him out. He wanted every single aspect of this evening to be perfect, for him and for Jessica especially, and his knobby old athlete's feet just ruined the picture.

"What?" he asked, looking down at his outfit. "Can't a guy dress up for his girl every now and then?"

"Honey, you wear a suit like every other day."

That was true, he supposed. Being a semi-professional hockey player meant he had to look the part when he arrived at the arena on game days.

"Just...don't worry about my outfit," he said, moving to pull one of the chairs away from the table. Jessica sat, but not before shooting him an incredulous look.

"Oh, now what?" he asked. "Am I not allowed to pull chairs out for my girl either? Next you're going to tell me I can't hold your hand or kiss you goodnight."

"I'm not saying any of those things," she said. "You're just acting...strange. Fidgety."

Well, shit. Apparently, he wasn't doing a great job at quashing his nerves. Then again, it was hard to hide anything from the one person in the world who knew him better than all the rest.

"I'm just happy to be celebrating another anniversary with you, sunshine."

Her face softened, those blue eyes crinkling at the corners as her lips turned up into a small smile. "Can you believe that April will be six years since Mexico?"

Jack shook his head. He couldn't believe that, had a hard time wrapping his mind around the fact that he'd been only a kid when he'd met the love of his life—and had lost her for three and a half years before finally getting to keep her for good.

At least...he hoped it was for good.

Everything changed tonight, either for better or worse.

The ring box practically burned a hole in his pocket, and he was thankful these pants of his were a looser fit so she wouldn't see the outline and ruin the whole thing.

"How was work today?" he asked as he took his seat across from her.

"Wonderful," she said, getting that faraway, dreamy look in her eyes she always did when she spoke about her job. She'd been teaching English as a second language to the citizens of Saint Petersburg for nineteen months, and had, somehow, grown to love it more every day.

As she spoke about how two of her students were near fluent and had moved onto softening their words and brushing their accents away when they talked, Jack popped the top on the champagne and poured them each a flute—which were actually just more mason jars.

Then he rose and moved to the kitchen counter, carrying back the platter with the steaks, fingerling potatoes he'd roasted in garlic, olive oil, and a fragrant herb seasoning they'd found at a local market last summer, and the bowl of salad.

"Show off," Jessica said when she took in the spread.

"Hardly," Jack said with a snort. "This stuff is all ridiculously easy to make."

"I disagree," she said with a pout, and Jack remembered the time she tried to make instant mac and cheese, and it exploded all over the inside of the microwave. He still hadn't figured out how she'd managed that.

"We'll just leave the cooking to me," he said, dropping a kiss atop her head before returning to his seat.

"Forever," she said as she moaned around a bite of steak. He hadn't cut it open before serving to check and see how close he'd gotten to the preparation he wanted, but he was greeted by a healthy slash of pink in the middle of Jessica's sliced steak. "You can cook for me forever."

"Forever," he agreed, his throat suddenly clogged with emotion.

And he realized right then that he couldn't wait another second to ask this woman to marry him.

"Jess?" he said quietly, and her head shot up, gaze immediately locked on his.

"What's wrong?" she asked.

"Nothing is wrong," he said. "It's just...you know how much I love you, right?"

Jessica swallowed hard, her fork and knife clattering to her plate. "Yes."

"Well, as much as I love you, I can't keep doing this."

"Doing what?"

"This whole being your boyfriend thing."

Jack rose from his seat at the same time Jessica did. "I'm sorry...what?" she asked. "You...don't want to be my boyfriend anymore?"

The pure terror on her face was almost enough for him to abandon his plans and drag her into his arms, but he didn't. Not yet.

"No," he said, and it broke his heart as tears welled in her eyes. "No, Jessica Rose Daniels." He withdrew the ring box from his pocket and dropped to one knee. "I was thinking we might try 'fiancé' on for size. And then, maybe later, 'husband'?"

Her hand flew to her mouth, which had dropped open on a sob.

"Jack..."

"Will you marry me?"

"Are you sure?" Jessica asked.

Jack threw his head back in exasperation. "Sunshine..." he warned.

A smile bloomed on her face, and Jack's heart rate slowed in response. This girl. Even in the most terrifying moment of his life, she *had* to needle him. Then again, he supposed it was payback for making her think he was ending their relationship, when he only wanted to make it official forever.

"I'm just saying," she said. "Maybe you've finally grown sick of me."

"Never," he said quickly. "I moved halfway across the world for you because you *are* my world."

"Aww, that's sweet."

"Jessica! Please put me out of my misery and answer the question."

She held her left hand out to him, and his breath left him in a sigh of relief.

"Yes, honey. A thousand times, yes."

First and foremost, to Mom, Dad, and Sissy: thank you. It's been a crazy year on this ride, but I couldn't have done any of it without you. Especially Sissy for being the one who catches all my mistakes, and being the first person to shout about my books on social media. I love you guys so much.

To Granny J and Grandpa Vic: thank you both for your constant love and support. Granny, I love that you love my books as much as I do, and it means the world to me.

To Grammy and Grumpy, my angels: keep watching over me. I know you're always here, and I know you're proud of me. I miss you both so much.

Alright, enough with the sappy shit.

To Mer: I guess I could get sappy here, too, but I won't. This book would not have happened without you. From cheering me on when I busted my ass to write the entirety of this thing in less than four weeks, to being the first person to read these words.

For the endless streams of TikToks that made me laugh when I wanted to cry. For putting up with my long winded rants, talking over plot points, approving interior designs (mostly by shooting me straight when I asked if something looked dumb), and just being my favorite person. I have been infinitely blessed by your friendship. I love you like Joey B loves thirst traps.

To Jen: thank you for alpha reading, for your invaluable insight, and for being a champion of me and my work since day one. I appreciate your support, and your friendship, more than I could ever say.

To Tricia, Kenna, Hannah, and Meaghan: thank you for being the BEST beta team. Your feedback made this story more polished than I could've made it on my own.

To my freaking INCREDIBLE street team, Aaron, Alyssa, Ashley, Meg, Jordan, Hannah, Mel, Mer, Victoria, Cort, Tricia, and Abigail: THANK YOU. I was so apprehensive to start a street team simply because I know how overwhelming group chats can be, and I was worried there wouldn't be enough interest to make it worthwhile for me. But I really lucked out with y'all. Thank you for EVERYTHING.

To Samantha: there's not much I can say here that I haven't already said or told you. Working with you is a dream—even though I'm positive I'm a pain in your ass. Thank you for giving me the covers of my dreams every damn time we do this, and for capturing Jack, Jess, and campus in the winter so perfectly. Here's to a few hundred more of these ;)

To Meg Jones, the creator of the "dicktionary," for letting me include one in the back of this book, and to Hailey Dickert for the "spread your" pages wording. Appreciate you both so much!

Last but certainly not least, thank you to my readers. I couldn't and wouldn't want to keep going without y'all. Every time one of you pops up in my DMs raving about one of my books, or when someone stops me on the street at home, I swear an angel gets its wings. Four books—and more to come—would not have been possible without you!

about the author

AMANDA CHAPERON REALIZED HER passion for books, and for writing, at a young age. Growing up, she was rarely found without a book in her hands, a hobby she carried into adulthood. After joining bookstagram in 2020, she felt the pull to try her hand at novel writing. She writes what she loves to read: messy, relatable characters, lots of steam, and always a happily ever after.

She currently lives in Michigan's Upper Peninsula with Gryffin, her Golden Retriever. She loves all things romance, fantasy, young adult, and thrillers that keep her up at night. You can follow her on Instagram, Threads, and TikTok at @achaperonwrites.

Dicktionary

My dear sweet reader, please use this guide to avoid (or seek out) the spicy scenes, which can be found in the following chapters:

Chapter 25
Chapter 28
Chapter 31
Chapter 34
Chapter 35

Spread those pages, my friend.